Jack Vance

Golden Girl and Other Stories

Jack Vance

Golden Girl
AND OTHER STORIES

Jack Vance

Spatterlight Press Signature Series, Volume 25

Published by Spatterlight Press

Cover art by Howard Kistler

ISBN 978-1-61947-151-1

Spatterlight Press LLC

340 S. Lemon Ave #1916
Walnut, CA 91789

www.jackvance.com

Contents

Golden Girl

The Des Moines Post scooped the world on the greatest story in history, and Bill Baxter became a hero.

An hour after the edition hit the streets, every road leading to Kelly's Hill was choked by caravans of the curious — the amateur public and the professionals: reporters, photographers and correspondents to the news-services, domestic and foreign. The FBI and Army Intelligence had arrived first. Road-blocks turned back a thousand cars, cordons through the fields intercepted walkers, fighter planes chased off the airplanes which wafted toward Kelly's Hill like moths to a light.

The survivor of the crash lay through the night at Dr. Blackney's small hospital where Bill Baxter had taken her. She awakened early in the morning, lay staring at Dr. Blackney, clenching the sheets with golden fingers. A pair of federal agents stood by the door to her room; two hundred others guarded the hospital and turned back the crowds of those who came to stare and marvel and murmur among themselves. An Army doctor and a spare aseptic individual reputedly connected with the Secret Service checked Blackney's diagnosis of a cracked collarbone and attendant shock, approved his treatment. The woman submitted with an air of helpless distaste.

The secrecy stimulated rather than deterred the press. Imagination was encouraged to run wild. The crash was a wind from exotic islands, an intimation of tremendous new fields of truth. The rest of the world dwindled to a locality; the lustiest news seemed stale and trivial. Thousands of columns were filled with speculation, tons of newsprint lavished on rumor, acres of photographs, charts, star-maps, imaginative drawings were published. Someone had even located a picture of Bill Baxter—the reporter who thinking to investigate a spectacular meteorite had found a wrecked spaceship and pulled out the limp young woman with the golden skin. To add the final gloss to this magnificent bubble of sensation—the final compelling overtones—it was rumored that the golden woman was beautiful. Young and fantastically beautiful.

From the first, Bill Baxter refused to be separated from the woman. Every minute possible he spent in the armchair across the room, covertly studying her face. The golden woman was something intimate and intricate, a wonderful jewel he had found in the night. She fascinated him; she aroused his fiercest protective instincts, as if by lifting her from the burning hull he had taken her for his property.

His assumption of sponsorship met grudging acceptance, as if even the government recognized some primitive law of the treasure trove—or at least admitted that Baxter had as much right to act as her agent as anyone else. Dr. Blackney took his presence as natural and desirable; the federal agents watched him with quiet sarcastic remarks to each other, but made no attempts to limit his contact with the woman.

She ate little, mostly broth and fruit-juice, occasionally a piece of toast, rejecting eggs, milk, meat with faint repugnance. For the most part, during the first two days, she lay limp and passive, as if stunned by the catastrophe which had beset her.

The third day she raised to her elbow, stared around the room, looked through the window a minute or two, then slowly lay back. She gave no heed to Baxter and Dr. Blackney, who were watching her from across the room.

Blackney, a grizzled country doctor with no pretensions to omniscience, clicked his tongue thoughtfully. "It's not right for her to be so limp... she's perfectly healthy, perfectly sound. Her temperature's a degree up, but that might be normal to her race. After all, we know little about her."

"Normal." Baxter seized on the word. "Is she a—*normal* human woman, Doctor?"

Blackney smiled faintly. "The X-rays show a—humanoid skeleton, and apparently human organs. Her features, conformation—well, you can see for yourself. The only distinguishing feature is her metallic skin."

"She seems only half-conscious," muttered Baxter. "She takes no interest in anything..."

"Shock," said Blackney. "Her brain is letting itself go slow...That's why she's not being moved."

"Moved?" cried Baxter. "Why moved? Where? By whose orders?"

"Orders from Washington," said Blackney. "But there's no hurry. She's weak, confused. She should have time to pick up the pieces. She's just as well off here as anywhere else."

Baxter agreed emphatically. In Washington, among so many official people, he might be shouldered aside. He rubbed his chin, compressed his lips. "Doctor, what would you estimate her age to be?"

"Oh—if she's aged according to our rates, perhaps nineteen or twenty."

"If so, she's a minor in the eyes of the law...Do you think I could get appointed her legal guardian?"

Blackney shook his head. "Not a chance in a thousand years, Bill. Don't forget this girl is not an ordinary waif who needs a guardian."

"Somebody's got to look after her," said Baxter stubbornly.

Blackney smiled faintly. "I imagine she'll be made a ward of the government."

Baxter frowned, clenched his hands in his pockets. "That remains to be seen."

On the afternoon of the fourth day, Baxter was astonished to see her throw off the coverlets and leave the bed with no evidence of weakness. She went to the window, where she looked several minutes out across Blackney's garden. Baxter fidgeted behind her like a nervous hen, worried lest she weaken herself, yet reluctant to thwart her in any way. At last she turned, and in the long white nightgown she seemed absurdly young and inoffensive. For the first time she appeared to notice Baxter—surveying him from shoes to hair with a scrutiny most casual and cool.

Baxter employed the technique recommended by a thousand precedents. He took a step forward, touched his chest, and said, "Bill."

She raised her eyebrows as if surprised that he commanded an intelligible thought, and repeated "Bill" in a soft voice.

Baxter nodded eagerly, pointed to her. "You?"

She touched herself and spoke a word full of slurred consonants and throaty vowels. The closest Baxter could make was a sound like *Lurr'lu*, or *Lurulu*.

Earnestly he began to teach her the language, and though unenthusiastic, she grasped ideas instantly and never forgot a word once it passed her lips.

Her story, as Baxter gathered it bit by bit, was simple enough. Her home was a world "very far past the stream of blue stars"—so she expressed it, and she called it *Ghh'lekthwa*. Baxter, unable to master the beginning guttural, pronounced it merely *Lekthwa*, which appeared to amuse the girl.

The spaceship was a pleasure-craft, she told him, on the order of an Earthly yacht; they had chanced on Earth with no particular end in view. A careless repair had weakened one of the control motors, which—failing at a critical time—had plunged the ship to destruction against Kelly's Hill.

On the seventh day Blackney pronounced the girl in good health, and Baxter sent a nurse out for clothes. When he returned to the room—although she exhibited no trace of personal modesty—he found her examining herself in a mirror, with an expression of satisfaction.

"Were any of my personal garments found in the wreck? These—" she pulled at the cashmere skirt "—they are picturesque, but they chafe, they feel strange against my skin."

Baxter, who thought her magnificent, stammered a reply. "Everything was destroyed in the heat… But if you'd tell me what you want, I could have something made for you. Of course, you'd be rather conspicuous."

She shrugged. "I will wear these."

Baxter asked a question which had long been burning inside him. "Do you—expect to return to your home? Can you communicate with your people? Do you know how to build a space-ship?"

She stared off across the garden. "No, just the barest principles… Lekthwa is many stars distant. I would hardly know how to go."

Baxter looked at her sharply. Her voice had been cool, very soft, like a dark pool in the forest. With an anxious tightness in his throat, and watching her sidelong, he reached for one of the books he had brought. Joining her at the window, he showed her a map.

"This is where we are," and he indicated. She bent her head, and Baxter studied her profile. This was the closest he had been to her since the night he had carried her from the wreck, and a strange fluttering pulse awoke in his neck.

She glanced up, and Baxter stared deep into the amber eyes. He saw the pupils change, and she moved slightly away. She turned her eyes back to the map. "Tell me more about your world."

Baxter gave her a thumbnail history of civilization, indicating the Nile, Mesopotamia, the Indus Valley. He showed her Greece, described Hellenic thought and its effect upon European culture, sketched the Industrial Revolution and brought her to date.

"So today there are still sections of the world independent and hostile to each other?"

"That is unfortunately true," Baxter admitted.

"Several hundred thousand years ago," mused Lurulu, "we had a period called 'The Era of Insanity'; this was when the white-haired people of the south and the golden-haired people of the north purposely killed each other." She paused, then said vaguely, "They had a culture roughly equivalent to yours."

Baxter examined her. "Your hair is a very light golden."

"The white-haired and the golden-haired peoples are well-mingled now. In the barbarous ages, there was great prejudice against the golden-haired people, who were somehow considered less admirable. It seems so peculiar and cruel now."

She put down the book, went to the window. "I would like to be in the sunlight. Yours is a sun much like ours." An airplane passed across the sky. "And there is air flight on Earth?" she asked in mild surprise.

Baxter assured her that air travel was commonplace, and had been so for the last twenty years. She nodded abstractedly.

"I see. Well — let us go for a walk then."

"As you wish," said Baxter.

The federal agents in the hall followed slightly to the rear.

Lurulu motioned to the guards. "What is their function, and what is yours? Am I a prisoner?"

Baxter hurriedly assured her that she was as free as the air. "They are merely to guard you from annoyance by eccentrics. As for me — I am your friend." And he added stiffly, "I will not intrude upon you, should you so desire!"

Lurulu did not answer, but walked out on the sidewalk, looked up and down the street. The police had thrown up barriers across the ends of the block, and at either end stood a small crowd, hoping for a glimpse of the out-world woman. The guards ran out ahead, waved them back.

Lurulu ignored the onlookers, completely indifferent to the staring eyes and excited babble. Baxter, uncomfortable and somehow resentful, followed at her elbow as she turned up the street. She seemed to enjoy the sunlight, and held her hand outstretched, as if feeling the texture of the light. Her skin glowed like rich satin. She breathed deeply, glanced in at the houses which lined the street. Blackney's little hospital was in a pleasant suburb, shaded with great elms, and the houses sat well back among gardens.

Suddenly she turned to Baxter. "Your people all live on the ground, then?"

"Well — we have apartment houses," replied Baxter. "They go hundreds of feet up into the air... How do you live on Lekthwa?"

"We have pleasant places floating in the sky — sometimes out in the clear sunny air, sometimes among the clouds. There is no sound but the wind. We enjoy the aloneness and the splendid vistas."

Baxter stared, half in disbelief. "No one lives on the ground? Are there no houses?"

"Oh —" she made a vague gesture "— occasionally by some beautiful lake or forest there is a cottage or a camp. The face of Lekthwa is for the most part wild — except for the Industrial Segment and the photosynthetic basins."

"And who works in the industries?"

"Young people mostly — children. The work is part of their education. Sometimes they improve the machinery or develop new biologotypes — is that a word? No? — No matter. After a period of machine tending, those who wish become designers or engineers or advanced technicians."

"And those who prefer not?"

"Oh — some are idle, some become explorers, some artists, musicians, some do a little of everything."

For a few seconds Baxter marched in glum silence. "Sounds stagnant to me... Sounds as if you'd be bored."

Lurulu laughed aloud, but made no answer or argument which, perversely, annoyed Baxter even further.

"And are there any criminals?" he asked presently.

She glanced at him, still smiling slightly. "On Lekthwa everyone likes living, likes his own personality. Only rarely do offenses exist, and these are treated by a form of brain-arrangement."

Baxter grunted.

"Crime occurs when the society is unpopular," she added offhandedly, "when the culture provides no out-alleys for human drive."

Baxter asked with a slight edge of sarcasm in his voice: "How can you discuss social problems so authoritatively when you don't have any on Lekthwa?"

She shrugged. "We know of several worlds where social problems exist. We have installed missions on these worlds, and are gradually bringing about reform."

Baxter asked in perplexity, "Do men—human beings—live on these other worlds too? I consider it very strange that even our two worlds have produced identical species..."

She smiled wryly at the word. "I suppose our physical structure is more or less the same. But we are hardly 'identical'."

She stopped to examine a bed of flowering red geraniums. Baxter wondered what her reaction would be if he put his arm around her waist. His arm twitched—but the guards sauntered close behind and eyes stared from all sides.

They reached the corner and halted. Lurulu looked into the corner grocery store, observed the meat market. She turned to Baxter wide-eyed. "Are those carcasses?"

"Well—yes," admitted Baxter.

"You eat dead animals?"

It began to irritate Baxter to be constantly on the defensive. "They're not poison," he growled, "and they're a healthful source of proteins."

"You haven't fed me any of that—that animal flesh?"

"So far, very little. You seem to prefer fruits or greens."

Lurulu turned, walked quickly past the store.

"After all," said Baxter, "it's only carbon, oxygen, hydrogen... You show a rather peculiar obsession, rather narrow-minded prejudice."

Her voice had become cool and vague once more. "There are psychological reasons for not putting death in our mouths..."

The next morning a black car of unmistakably official nature pulled up in front of the hospital; a man in an Army uniform and two others in civilian clothing alighted. The FBI guards stiffened slightly. There was a muttered interchange and the three swung up the steps. In the front office they were met by Dr. Blackney.

"I am Major-General Devering," said he who wore the uniform. "From the OSS. This is Dr. Rheim, of the Institute of Advanced Research, and this is Professor Anderson of Ledyard University."

Dr. Blackney shook hands with all three — Major-General Devering, a thick-set man with a pink lumpy nose and shining, slightly protruding eyes; Dr. Rheim, long, thin, solemn; Professor Anderson, short, fat, equally solemn.

"I suppose," suggested Dr. Blackney, "that you've come in connection with my guest?"

"That's right," said Devering. "I suppose she's well enough to be questioned? My men tell me she took a walk yesterday and appeared to be conversing with Mr. Baxter."

Blackney squinted thoughtfully, pursed his lips. "Yes, she's sound enough physically. Perfectly well, as far as I can see."

"Perhaps then," suggested Dr. Rheim, "it would be possible to move her to a place more readily accessible to us?" He raised his eyebrows questioningly.

Blackney frowningly rubbed his chin. "Accessible for what purpose?"

"Why — for study, various types of examination..."

"She's physically able to go anywhere," said Blackney. "But so far her legal position has not been established. I really see no need to move her — unless she herself wants to go."

Major-General Devering narrowed his eyes. "Aside from that aspect, Doctor, this young woman may have information of great value to the country. Don't you think it's important that we check into it? In any event, you have no authority in the matter."

Blackney drew his chin back, twice opened his mouth to speak, twice snapped it shut. Then he said: "I have authority over who enters this office. However, you may speak to the young woman."

Devering stepped forward. "Please show us to her room."

"Down this hall, please."

Bill Baxter sat beside Lurulu at a card table, teaching her to read. He looked up, in surprise and annoyance.

Blackney introduced the visitors. "These men," he said to Lurulu, "wish to ask you about your life on Lekthwa. Do you object?"

She glanced at the three with little interest. "No."

Major-General Devering moved forward a trifle. "We have a rather extensive program, and would like you to accompany us to new quarters — which will be more convenient for everyone concerned."

Baxter jumped up. "No such thing!" he shouted. "God, you've got your nerve! One thing that's not going to happen is an 'extensive program', third degree, whatever you want to call it!"

Devering eyed him stonily. "I'd like to remind you, Mr. Baxter, that you have no official standing in regard to the young lady; and that she is the ward of the government, and subject to security laws."

"Have you got a warrant?" inquired Baxter. "If not, you're in a worse position officially than I am. As far as questioning goes, I appreciate that there's much that you want to know, and I'd like to help you — but you can do your questioning here, an hour or so a day. You can fit your questioning to the young lady's convenience, rather than she to yours."

Devering's mouth opened slightly, showing white teeth, and his chin protruded. "We'll damn well do what we see fit, with no interference from some whippersnapper of a reporter."

Dr. Blackney interposed. "May I suggest, gentlemen, that you leave the decision to the lady? After all, she is the one person most directly involved."

Lurulu had been watching with a slightly wrinkled forehead. "I do not care to go with these men. But I will answer their questions."

A nurse entered, whispered into Blackney's ear. Blackney raised his eyebrows, quickly arose. "Excuse me, it's the President calling."

"Let me talk to him," said Baxter wildly. "I'll tell him a thing or two."

Blackney ignored him, left the room. A sullen silence fell, Devering and Baxter glowering at each other, the scientists eyeing the Lekthwan woman, and she, oblivious, watching a hummingbird outside the window.

Blackney returned, breathing rather hard. "The President," he told Lurulu, "has invited you to spend a week at the White House."

Lurulu looked involuntarily at Bill Baxter. Grudgingly he said, "I suppose it would be the best thing for her, in the circumstances. When does the visit start?"

Blackney reflected. "I suppose right away. I didn't think to ask."

Baxter turned. "We might as well leave at once."

Devering wheeled toward the door, departed without a word, and the two scientists, after bows to the Lekthwan woman, followed.

Washington reacted to the Lekthwan woman with unprecedented fervor. In the first place, she was no celebrity of the usual sort. She had built no empires, destroyed none, had been elected to no office, performed no antics on stage or screen, was not associated with any vice or depravity. She was a visitor from another star. Further it was reported that she possessed a wonderful beauty. The total effect was dramatic.

Lurulu seemed indifferent to the tumult. She went to several parties, attended the opera, and received numerous gifts from publicity-hungry manufacturers — four new automobiles, clothes of every description, perfumes, baskets of fruit. One contractor offered to build her a house to any specifications she cared to submit. She was taken on a lavish sight-seeing tour to New York. Mrs. Bliss, hostess of the expedition, inquired if such monumental edifices existed on her own planet. No, replied Lurulu, she doubted if on all Lekthwa there was a structure even three stories in height, or a bridge longer than a few feet of tree trunk spanning a brook.

"We have no need for these great masses," she told Mrs. Bliss. "People are never assembled in groups large enough to need large buildings, and as for rivers and seas, they are merely part of the planet's surface above which we spend much of our lives."

Baxter was her constant companion, an association which she now encouraged. Baxter was aware of her likes and dislikes, and protected her from most of the hostesses and agents. And as she came to find him useful, so did he come to feel necessary to her, and nothing in his life had meaning other than Lurulu.

A lewd rumor reached his ear, and in a troubled spirit he confided it to Lurulu. She looked up in surprise. "Really?" Then she took no further interest in the subject. Baxter departed in anger.

He arranged two hours daily interviews with scientists — biologists, physicists, linguists, historians, anthropologists, astronomers, engineers, military tacticians, chemists, bacteriologists, psychologists and others. These found her general knowledge vast and exciting, but vague in detail — helpful mainly in that she was able to indicate boundaries of regions yet to be explored. After one of these sessions, Baxter found her in the apartment he had rented for her, alone on a settee. The time was about twilight and she sat looking across the park, into the luminous blue-gray sky.

He sat down beside her. "Are you tired?"

"Yes — very tired. Of curious people... Ponderous questions... Talk... Nonsense..."

He said nothing, sat staring out into the twilight. She sensed the quality of his silence.

"Excuse me, Bill. I never mind talking to you."

His mood instantly changed; he felt closer, more intimate with her than at any time of their association.

"You've never mentioned your personal life," he began diffidently. "Were you... married?"

She answered quietly. "No."

Baxter waited.

"I was an artist — of a sort unknown to you here on Earth." She spoke softly, her eyes still out on the darkening sky. "We conceive in the brain — color, motion, sound, space, sensation, mood, all moving, shifting, evolving. When the conceiver is prepared, he imagines the whole sequence of his creation, as vividly as possible — and this is picked up by a psychic recorder and preserved. To enjoy or experience the creation, a person inserts a record into an apparatus, and this plants the same images into his mind. Thus he sees the motion, the color pattern, the flows and fluxes of space, the fantasies in the artist's mind, together with the sights, the sounds, and most important, the varying moods of the piece... It is a difficult medium to master, for it requires tremendous concentration. I am merely a novice, but certain of my imageries have won praise."

"That's very interesting," said Baxter heavily. Then after an interval: "Lurulu."

"Yes?"

"Do you have any plans for the future?"

She sighed. "No. Nothing. My life is blank." She stared into the sky where now the stars were showing. "Up there is my home and everything I love."

Baxter leaned forward. "Lurulu — will you marry me?"

She turned, looked at him. "Marry you? No, Bill."

"I love you very much," he said, looking out into the sky. "You've become everything in the world to me. I worship you — anything you do — or say — or touch... I don't know whether you care ten cents for me — I suspect not — but you need me, and I'd do anything in the world to make you happy."

She smiled faintly, abstractedly. "On Lekthwa we mate when we find someone in rapport with us psychically. To you we may seem cold-blooded."

"Perhaps you and I are psychically right," suggested Bill Baxter.

She shuddered almost imperceptibly. "No, Bill. It's — unthinkable."

He arose. "Good-night." At the door he paused, looked back to where she sat in the dark, still staring up at the night sky, the far white stars.

Returning to his own apartment, he found Dr. Blackney awaiting him, sitting comfortably in an armchair with a newspaper. Bill greeted him with subdued warmth. Blackney watched intently while Bill mixed a couple of stiff highballs.

"I thought I'd see how my ex-patient was adjusting herself to life on Earth."

Bill said nothing.

"What's your opinion?" Blackney asked.

Bill shrugged. "She's getting along all right. Pretty tired of so many people... I just now asked her to marry me."

Blackney leaned back with his highball. "And she said no —"

"That's about it."

Blackney put down his glass, picked up a book beside him on the couch. "I just happened to chance on this, rummaging through some old stuff… It's rather a long chapter. I won't read it. But the gist of it—" he opened the book to a page covered with fine print, looked quickly up at Bill. "The title, incidentally, is *Strange Tales of the Seven Seas.* Published in 1839, and this chapter is called 'Shipwrecked Off Guinea, a Personal Diary'.

"It's about a wreck—in 1835, when a British ship went down in a gale off Equatorial Africa. In the confusion Miss Nancy Marron, a girl of gentle upbringing, found herself alone in one of the ship's boats. The boat weathered the storm, presently drifted near a small island, then uncharted, but now known as Matemba. The continent of Africa lay about thirty miles past the horizon, but this naturally was unknown to Nancy Marron. In any event, she was able to drag herself ashore and up on the beach, where a native found her and took her to his village." He turned the page. "She was received with great reverence. The natives had never seen a white man or woman, and thought her a divinity. They built her a grand new thatched hut; they brought her food, much of which, so she noted in her diary, she found inedible—slugs, entrails, and the like. In addition, they were cannibals, eating the bodies of any of their tribe who died."

Blackney looked up. "Her diary tells all this rather objectively. She was a good reporter and, in the main, keeps her homesickness out of the text. She learned the native tongue, found that she was the first white person ever seen on Matemba, and that vessels never approached the island. This discovery ended her last trace of hope. The last entry reads: 'I can stand it no longer here among these savages, friendly as they may be. I am sick at heart, I long for England, the faces of my family, the sound of my own blessed tongue, the smells and sounds of the pleasant old countryside. I know I shall never see or hear them again in this world. I cannot bear this hideous loneliness any longer. I have a knife, and it will be very easy for me to use it. May God understand and forgive.' "

Blackney looked up. "There the diary ends."

Baxter sat like a statue.

"Odd, isn't it?" said Blackney.

"Very," said Baxter.

After a moment he jumped to his feet. "Just a minute, Blackney..." He ran up the stairs, two at a time, turned down the hall, stopped by a white door. He rang the bell, waited... waited.

He threw himself against the panel; the lock splintered and Baxter staggered into the dark room. He switched on the lights, stood staring at the figure on the floor, the golden figure with the chest welling red blood...

Masquerade on Dicantropus

Two puzzles dominated the life of Jim Root. The first, the pyramid out in the desert, tickled and prodded his curiosity, while the second, the problem of getting along with his wife, kept him keyed to a high pitch of anxiety and apprehension. At the moment the problem had crowded the mystery of the pyramid into a lost alley of his brain.

Eyeing his wife uneasily, Root decided that she was in for another of her fits. The symptoms were familiar — a jerking over of the pages of an old magazine, her tense back and bolt-upright posture, her pointed silence, the compression at the corners of her mouth.

With no preliminary motion she threw the magazine across the room, jumped to her feet. She walked to the doorway, stood looking out across the plain, fingers tapping on the sill. Root heard her voice, low, as if not meant for him to hear.

"Another day of this and I'll lose what little's left of my mind."

Root approached warily. If he could be compared to a Labrador retriever, then his wife was a black panther — a woman tall and well-covered with sumptuous flesh. She had black flowing hair and black flashing eyes. She lacquered her fingernails and wore black lounge pajamas even on desiccated deserted inhospitable Dicantropus.

"Now, dear," said Root, "take it easy. Certainly it's not as bad as all that."

She whirled and Root was surprised by the intensity in her eyes. "It's not bad, you say? Very well for you to talk — *you* don't care for anything human to begin with. I'm sick of it. Do you hear? I want to go back to Earth! I never want to see another planet in my whole life. I never want to hear the word archaeology, I never want to see a rock or a bone or a microscope —"

She flung a wild gesture around the room that included a number of rocks, bones, microscopes, as well as books, specimens in bottles, photographic equipment, a number of native artifacts.

Root tried to soothe her with logic. "Very few people are privileged to live on an outside planet, dear."

"They're not in their right minds. If I'd known what it was like, I'd never have come out here." Her voice dropped once more. "Same old dirt every day, same stinking natives, same vile canned food, nobody to talk to —"

Root uncertainly picked up and laid down his pipe. "Lie down, dear," he said with unconvincing confidence. "Take a nap! Things will look different when you wake up."

Stabbing him with a look, she turned and strode out into the blue-white glare of the sun. Root followed more slowly, bringing Barbara's sun-helmet and adjusting his own. Automatically he cocked an eye up the antenna, the reason for the station and his own presence, Dicantropus being a relay point for ULR messages between Clave II and Polaris. The antenna stood as usual, polished metal tubing four hundred feet high.

Barbara halted by the shore of the lake, a brackish pond in the neck of an old volcano, one of the few natural bodies of water on the planet. Root silently joined her, handed her her sun-helmet. She jammed it on her head, walked away.

Root shrugged, watched her as she circled the pond to a clump of feather-fronded cycads. She flung herself down, relaxed into a sulky lassitude, her back to a big gray-green trunk, and seemed intent on the antics of the natives — owlish leather-gray little creatures popping back and forth into holes in their mound.

This was a hillock a quarter-mile long, covered with spine-scrub and a rusty black creeper. With one exception it was the only eminence as far as the eye could reach, horizon to horizon, across the baked helpless expanse of the desert.

The exception was the stepped pyramid, the mystery of which irked Root. It was built of massive granite blocks, set without mortar but cut so carefully that hardly a crack could be seen. Early on his arrival Root had climbed all over the pyramid, unsuccessfully seeking entrance.

When finally he brought out his atomite torch to melt a hole in the granite a sudden swarm of natives pushed him back and in the pidgin of Dicantropus gave him to understand that entrance was forbidden. Root desisted with reluctance, and had been consumed by curiosity ever since...

Who had built the pyramid? In style it resembled the *ziggurats* of ancient Assyria. The granite had been set with a skill unknown, so far as Root could see, to the natives. But if not the natives — who? A thousand times Root had chased the question through his brain. Were the natives debased relics of a once-civilized race? If so, why were there no other ruins? And what was the purpose of the pyramid? A temple? A mausoleum? A treasure-house? Perhaps it was entered from below by a tunnel.

As Root stood on the shore of the lake, looking across the desert, the questions flicked automatically through his mind though without their usual pungency. At the moment the problem of soothing his wife lay heavy on his mind. He debated a few moments whether or not to join her; perhaps she had cooled off and might like some company. He circled the pond and stood looking down at her glossy black hair.

"I came over here to be alone," she said without accent and the indifference chilled him more than an insult.

"I thought — that maybe you might like to talk," said Root. "I'm very sorry, Barbara, that you're unhappy."

Still she said nothing, sitting with her head pressed back against the tree trunk.

"We'll go home on the next supply ship," Root said. "Let's see, there should be one —"

"Three months and three days," said Barbara flatly.

Root shifted his weight, watched her from the corner of his eye. This was a new manifestation. Tears, recriminations, anger — there had been plenty of these before.

"We'll try to keep amused till then," he said desperately. "Let's think up some games to play. Maybe badminton — or we could do more swimming."

Barbara snorted in sharp sarcastic laughter. "With things like that popping up around you?" She gestured to one of the Dicantrops who had lazily paddled close. She narrowed her eyes, leaned forward. "What's that he's got around his neck?"

Root peered. "Looks like a diamond necklace more than anything else."

"My Lord!" whispered Barbara.

Root walked down to the water's edge. "Hey, boy!" The Dicantrop turned his great velvety eyes in their sockets. "Come here!"

Barbara joined him as the native paddled close.

"Let's see what you've got there," said Root, leaning close to the necklace.

"Why, those are beautiful!" breathed his wife.

Root chewed his lip thoughtfully. "They certainly look like diamonds. The setting might be platinum or iridium. Hey, boy, where did you get these?"

The Dicantrop paddled backward. "We find."

"Where?"

The Dicantrop blew froth from his breath-holes but it seemed to Root as if his eyes had glanced momentarily toward the pyramid.

"You find in big pile of rock?"

"No," said the native and sank below the surface.

Barbara returned to her seat by the tree, frowned at the water. Root joined her. For a moment there was silence. Then Barbara said, "That pyramid must be full of things like that!"

Root made a deprecatory noise in his throat. "Oh—I suppose it's possible."

"Why don't you go out and see?"

"I'd like to—but you know it would make trouble."

"You could go out at night."

"No," said Root uncomfortably. "It's really not right. If they want to keep the thing closed up and secret it's their business. After all it belongs to them."

"How do you know it does?" his wife insisted, with a hard and sharp directness. "They didn't build it and probably never put those diamonds there." Scorn crept into her voice. "Are you afraid?"

"Yes," said Root. "I'm afraid. There's an awful lot of them and only two of us. That's one objection. But the other, most important—"

Barbara let herself slump back against the trunk. "I don't want to hear it."

Root, now angry himself, said nothing for a minute. Then, thinking of the three months and three days till the arrival of the supply ship, he said, "It's no use our being disagreeable. It just makes it harder on both of us. I made a mistake bringing you out here and I'm sorry. I thought you'd enjoy the experience, just the two of us alone on a strange planet—"

Barbara was not listening to him. Her mind was elsewhere.

"Barbara!"

"*Shh!*" she snapped. "Be still! Listen!"

He jerked his head up. The air vibrated with a far *thrum-m-m-m*. Root sprang out into the sunlight, scanned the sky. The sound grew louder. There was no question about it, a ship was dropping down from space.

Root ran into the station, flipped open the communicator—but there were no signals coming in. He returned to the door and watched as the ship sank down to a bumpy rough landing two hundred yards from the station.

It was a small ship, the type rich men sometimes used as private yachts, but old and battered. It sat in a quiver of hot air, its tubes creaking and hissing as they cooled. Root approached.

The dogs on the port began to turn, the port swung open. A man stood in the opening. For a moment he teetered on loose legs, then fell headlong.

Root, springing forward, caught him before he struck ground. "Barbara!" Root called. His wife approached. "Take his feet. We'll carry him inside. He's sick."

They laid him on the couch and his eyes opened halfway.

"What's the trouble?" asked Root. "Where do you feel sick?"

"My legs are like ice," husked the man. "My shoulders ache. I can't breathe."

"Wait till I look in the book," muttered Root. He pulled out the *Official Spaceman's Self-Help Guide*, traced down the symptoms. He looked across to the sick man. "You been anywhere near Alphard?"

"Just came from there," panted the man.

"Looks like you got a dose of Lyma's Virus. A shot of mycosetin should fix you up, according to the book."

He inserted an ampoule into the hypospray, pressed the tip to his patient's arm, pushed the plunger home. "That should do it — according to the Guide."

"Thanks," said his patient. "I feel better already." He closed his eyes. Root stood up, glanced at Barbara. She was scrutinizing the man with a peculiar calculation. Root looked down again, seeing the man for the first time. He was young, perhaps thirty, thin but strong with a tight nervous muscularity. His face was lean, almost gaunt, his skin very bronzed. He had short black hair, heavy black eyebrows, a long jaw, a thin high nose.

Root turned away. Glancing at his wife he foresaw the future with a sick certainty.

He washed out the hypospray, returned the Guide to the rack, all with a sudden self-conscious awkwardness. When he turned around, Barbara was staring at him with wide thoughtful eyes. Root slowly left the room.

A day later Marville Landry was on his feet and when he had shaved and changed his clothes there was no sign of the illness. He was by profession a mining engineer, so he revealed to Root, en route to a contract on Thuban XIV.

The virus had struck swiftly and only by luck had he noticed the proximity of Dicantropus on his charts. Rapidly weakening, he had been forced to decelerate so swiftly and land so uncertainly that he feared his fuel was low. And indeed, when they went out to check, they found only enough fuel to throw the ship a hundred feet into the air.

Landry shook his head ruefully. "And there's a ten-million-munit contract waiting for me on Thuban Fourteen."

Said Root dismally, "The supply packet's due in three months."

Landry winced. "Three months — in this hell-hole? That's murder." They returned to the station. "How do you stand it here?"

Barbara heard him. "We don't. I've been on the verge of hysterics every minute the last six months. Jim —" she made a wry grimace toward her husband "— he's got his bones and rocks and the antenna. He's not too much company."

"Maybe I can help out," Landry offered airily.

"Maybe," she said with a cool blank glance at Root. Presently she left the room, walking more gracefully now, with an air of mysterious gaiety.

Dinner that evening was a gala event. As soon as the sun took its blue glare past the horizon Barbara and Landry carried a table down to the lake and there they set it with all the splendor the station could afford. With no word to Root she pulled the cork on the gallon of brandy he had been nursing for a year and served generous highballs with canned lime-juice, Maraschino cherries and ice.

For a space, with the candles glowing and evoking lambent ghosts in the highballs, even Root was gay. The air was wonderfully cool and the sands of the desert spread white and clean as damask out into the dimness. So they feasted on canned fowl and mushrooms and frozen fruit and drank deep of Root's brandy, and across the pond the natives watched from the dark.

And presently, while Root grew sleepy and dull, Landry became gay, and Barbara sparkled — the complete hostess, charming, witty and the Dicantropus night tinkled and throbbed with her laughter. She and Landry toasted each other and exchanged laughing comments at Root's expense — who now sat slumping, stupid, half-asleep. Finally he lurched to his feet and stumbled off to the station.

On the table by the lake the candles burnt low. Barbara poured more brandy. Their voices became murmurs and at last the candles guttered.

In spite of any human will to hold time in blessed darkness, morning came and brought a day of silence and averted eyes. Then other days and nights succeeded each other and time proceeded as usual. And there was now little pretense at the station.

Barbara frankly avoided Root and when she had occasion to speak her voice was one of covert amusement. Landry, secure, confident, aquiline, had a trick of sitting back and looking from one to the other as if inwardly chuckling over the whole episode. Root preserved a studied calm and spoke in a subdued tone which conveyed no meaning other than the sense of his words.

There were a few minor clashes. Entering the bathroom one morning Root found Landry shaving with his razor. Without heat Root took the shaver out of Landry's hand.

For an instant Landry stared blankly, then wrenched his mouth into the beginnings of a snarl.

Root smiled almost sadly. "Don't get me wrong, Landry. There's a difference between a razor and a woman. The razor is mine. A human being can't be owned. Leave my personal property alone."

Landry's eyebrows rose. "Man, you're crazy." He turned away. "Heat's got you."

The days went past and now they were unchanging as before but unchanging with a new leaden tension. Words became even fewer and dislike hung like tattered tinsel. Every motion, every line of the body, became a detestable sight, an evil which the other flaunted deliberately.

Root burrowed almost desperately into his rocks and bones, peered through his microscope, made a thousand measurements, a thousand notes. Landry and Barbara fell into the habit of taking long walks in the evening, usually out to the pyramid, then slowly back across the quiet cool sand.

The mystery of the pyramid suddenly fascinated Landry and he even questioned Root.

"I've no idea," said Root. "Your guess is as good as mine. All I know is that the natives don't want anyone trying to get into it."

"Mph," said Landry, gazing across the desert. "No telling what's inside. Barbara said one of the natives was wearing a diamond necklace worth thousands."

"I suppose anything's possible," said Root. He had noticed the acquisitive twitch to Landry's mouth, the hook of the fingers. "You'd better not get any ideas. I don't want any trouble with the natives. Remember that, Landry."

Landry asked with seeming mildness, "Do you have any authority over that pyramid?"

"No," said Root shortly. "None whatever."

"It's not — yours?" Landry sardonically accented the word and Root remembered the incident of the shaver.

"No."

"Then," said Landry, rising, "mind your own business."

He left the room.

During the day Root noticed Landry and Barbara deep in conversation and he saw Landry rummaging through his ship. At dinner no single word was spoken.

As usual, when the afterglow had died to a cool blue glimmer, Barbara and Landry strolled off into the desert. But tonight Root watched after them and he noticed a pack on Landry's shoulders and Barbara seemed to be carrying a handbag.

He paced back and forth, puffing furiously at his pipe. Landry was right — it was none of his business. If there were profit, he wanted none of it. And if there were danger, it would strike only those who provoked it. Or would it? Would he, Root, be automatically involved because of his association with Landry and Barbara? To the Dicantrops, a man was a man, and if one man needed punishment, all men did likewise.

Would there be — killing? Root puffed at his pipe, chewed the stem, blew smoke out in gusts between his teeth. In a way he was responsible for Barbara's safety. He had taken her from a sheltered life on Earth. He shook his head, put down his pipe, went to the drawer where he kept his gun. It was gone.

Root looked vacantly across the room. Landry had it. No telling how long since he'd taken it. Root went to the kitchen, found a meat-axe, tucked it inside his jumper, set out across the desert.

He made a wide circle in order to approach the pyramid from behind. The air was quiet and dark and cool as water in an old well. The crisp sand sounded faintly under his feet. Above him spread the sky and the sprinkle of the thousand stars. Somewhere up there was the Sun and old Earth.

The pyramid loomed suddenly large and now he saw a glow, heard the muffled clinking of tools. He approached quietly, halted several hundred feet out in the darkness, stood watching, alert to all sounds.

Landry's atomite torch ate at the granite. As he cut, Barbara hooked the detached chunks out into the sand. From time to time Landry stood back, sweating and gasping from radiated heat.

A foot he cut into the granite, two feet, three feet, and Root heard the excited murmur of voices. They were through, into empty space. Careless of watching behind them they sidled through the hole they had cut. Root, more wary, listened, strove to pierce the darkness … Nothing.

He sprang forward, hastened to the hole, peered within. The yellow gleam of Landry's torch swept past his eyes. He crept into the hole, pushed his head out into emptiness. The air was cold, smelled of dust and damp rock.

Landry and Barbara stood fifty feet away. In the desultory flash of the lamp Root saw stone walls and a stone floor. The pyramid appeared to be an empty shell. Why then were the natives so particular? He heard Landry's voice, edged with bitterness.

"Not a damn thing, not even a mummy for your husband to gloat over."

Root could sense Barbara shuddering. "Let's go. It gives me the shivers. It's like a dungeon."

"Just a minute, we might as well make sure… Hm." He was playing the light on the walls. "That's peculiar."

"What's peculiar?"

"It looks like the stone was sliced with a torch. Notice how it's fused here on the inside…"

Root squinted, trying to see. "Strange," he heard Landry mutter. "Outside it's chipped, inside it's cut by a torch. It doesn't look so very old here inside, either."

"The air would preserve it," suggested Barbara dubiously.

"I suppose so — still, old places look old. There's dust and a kind of dullness. This looks raw."

"I don't understand how that could be."

"I don't either. There's something funny somewhere."

Root stiffened. Sound from without? Shuffle of splay feet in the sand — he started to back out. Something pushed him, he sprawled forward, fell. The bright eye of Landry's torch stared in his direction. "What's that?" came a hard voice. "Who's there?"

Root looked over his shoulder. The light passed over him, struck a dozen gray bony forms. They stood quietly just inside the hole, their eyes like balls of black plush.

Root gained his feet. "Hah!" cried Landry. "So *you're* here too."

"Not because I want to be," returned Root grimly.

Landry edged slowly forward, keeping his light on the Dicantrops. He asked Root sharply, "Are these lads dangerous?"

Root appraised the natives. "I don't know."

"Stay still," said one of these in the front rank. "Stay still." His voice was a deep croak.

"Stay still, hell!" exclaimed Landry. "We're leaving. There's nothing here I want. Get out of the way." He stepped forward.

"Stay still ... We kill ..."

Landry paused.

"What's the trouble now?" interposed Root anxiously. "Surely there's no harm in looking. There's nothing here."

"That is why we kill. Nothing here, now you know. Now you look other place. When you think this place important, then you not look other place. We kill, new man come, he think this place important."

Landry muttered, "Do you get what he's driving at?"

Root said slowly, "I don't know for sure." He addressed the Dicantrop. "We don't care about your secrets. You've no reason to hide things from us."

The native jerked his head. "Then why do you come here? You look for secrets."

Barbara's voice came from behind. "What *is* your secret? Diamonds?"

The native jerked his head again. Amusement? Anger? His emotions, unearthly, could be matched by no earthly words. "Diamonds are nothing — rocks."

"I'd like a carload," Landry muttered under his breath.

"Now look here," said Root persuasively. "You let us out and we won't pry into any of your secrets. It was wrong of us to break in and I'm sorry it happened. We'll repair the damage —"

The Dicantrop made a faint sputtering sound. "You do not understand. You tell other men — pyramid is nothing. Then other men look all around for other thing. They bother, look, look, look. All this no good. You die, everything go like before."

"There's too much talk," said Landry viciously, "and I don't like the sound of it. Let's get out of here." He pulled out Root's gun. "Come on," he snapped at Root, "let's move."

To the natives, "Get out of the way or I'll do some killing myself!"

A rustle of movement from the natives, a thin excited whimper.

"We've got to rush 'em," shouted Landry. "If they get outside they can knock us over as we leave. Let's go!"

He sprang forward and Root was close behind. Landry used the gun as a club and Root used his fists and the Dicantrops rattled like cornstalks against the walls. Landry erupted through the hole. Root pushed Barbara through and, kicking back at the natives behind him, struggled out into the air.

Landry's momentum had carried him away from the pyramid, out into a seething mob of Dicantrops. Root, following more slowly, pressed his back to the granite. He sensed the convulsive movement in the wide darkness. "The whole colony must be down here," he shouted into Barbara's ear. For a minute he was occupied with the swarming natives, keeping Barbara behind him as much as possible. The first ledge of granite was about shoulder height.

"Step on my hands," he panted. "I'll shove you up."

"But — Landry!" came Barbara's choked wail.

"Look at that crowd!" bit Root furiously. "We can't do anything." A sudden rush of small bony forms almost overwhelmed him. "Hurry up!"

Whimpering she stepped into his clasped hands. He thrust her up on the first ledge. Shaking off the clawing natives who had leapt on him, he jumped, scrambled up beside her. "Now run!" he shouted in her ear and she fled down the ledge.

From the darkness came a violent cry. "Root! *Root!* For God's sake — they've got me down —" Another hoarse yell, rising to a scream of agony. Then silence.

"Hurry!" said Root. They came to the far corner of the pyramid. "Jump down," panted Root. "Down to the ground."

"Landry!" moaned Barbara, teetering at the edge.

"Get down!" snarled Root. He thrust her down to the white sand and, seizing her hand, ran across the desert, back toward the station. A minute or so later, with pursuit left behind, he slowed to a trot.

"We should go back," cried Barbara. "Are you going to leave him to those devils?"

Root was silent a moment. Then, choosing his words, he said, "I told him to stay away from the place. Anything that happens to him is his own fault. And whatever it is, it's already happened. There's nothing we can do now."

A dark hulk shouldered against the sky — Landry's ship.

"Let's get in here," said Root. "We'll be safer than in the station."

He helped her into the ship, clamped tight the port. *"Phew!"* He shook his head. "Never thought it would come to this."

He climbed into the pilot's seat, looked out across the desert. Barbara huddled somewhere behind him, sobbing softly.

An hour passed, during which they said no word. Then, without warning, a fiery orange ball rose from the hill across the pond, drifted toward the station. Root blinked, jerked upright in his seat. He scrambled for the ship's machine gun, yanked at the trigger — without result.

When at last he found and threw off the safety the orange ball hung over the station and Root held his fire. The ball brushed against the antenna — a tremendous explosion spattered to every corner of vision. It seared Root's eyes, threw him to the deck, rocked the ship, left him dazed and half-conscious.

Barbara lay moaning. Root hauled himself to his feet. A seared pit, a tangle of metal, showed where the station had stood. Root dazedly slumped into the seat, started the fuel pump, plunged home the catalyzers. The boat quivered, bumped a few feet along the ground. The tubes sputtered, wheezed.

Root looked at the fuel gauge, looked again. The needle pointed to zero, a fact which Root had known but forgotten. He cursed his own stupidity. Their presence in the ship might have gone ignored if he had not called attention to it.

Up from the hill floated another orange ball. Root jumped for the machine gun, sent out a burst of explosive pellets. Again the roar and the blast and the whole top of the hill was blown off, revealing what appeared to be a smooth strata of black rock.

Root looked over his shoulder to Barbara. "This is it."

"Wha — what do you mean?"

"We can't get away. Sooner or later —" His voice trailed off. He reached up, twisted a dial labeled EMERGENCY. The ship's ULR unit hummed. Root said into the mesh, "Dicantropus station — we're being attacked by natives. Send help at once."

Root sank back into the seat. A tape would repeat his message endlessly until cut off.

Barbara staggered to the seat beside Root. "What were those orange balls?"

"That's what *I've* been wondering — some sort of bomb."

But there were no more of them. And presently the horizon began to glare, the hill became a silhouette on the electric sky. And over their heads the transmitter pulsed an endless message into space.

"How long before we get help?" whispered Barbara.

"Too long," said Root, staring off toward the hill. "They must be afraid of the machine gun — I can't understand what else they're waiting for. Maybe good light."

"They can —" Her voice stopped. She stared. Root stared, held by unbelief — amazement. The hill across the pond was breaking open, crumbling...

Root sat drinking brandy with the captain of the supply ship *Method*, which had come to their assistance, and the captain was shaking his head.

"I've seen lots of strange things around this cluster but this masquerade beats everything."

Root said, "It's strange in one way, in another it's as cold and straightforward as ABC. They played it as well as they could and it was pretty darned good. If it hadn't been for that scoundrel Landry they'd have fooled us forever."

The captain banged his glass on the desk, stared at Root. "But *why*?"

Root said slowly, "They liked Dicantropus. It's a hell-hole, a desert to us, but it was heaven to them. They liked the heat, the dryness. But they didn't want a lot of off-world creatures prying into their business — as we surely would have if we'd seen through the masquerade. It must have been an awful shock when the first Earth ship set down here."

"And that pyramid..."

"Now that's a strange thing. They were good psychologists, these Dicantrops, as good as you could expect an off-world race to be. If you'll read a report of the first landing, you'll find no mention of the pyramid. Why? Because it wasn't here. Landry thought it looked new. He was right. It *was* new. It was a fraud, a decoy — just strange enough to distract our attention.

"As long as that pyramid sat out there, with me focusing all my mental energy on it, they were safe — and how they must have laughed. As soon as Landry broke in and discovered the fraud, then it was all over…

"That might have been their miscalculation," mused Root. "Assume that they knew nothing of crime, of anti-social action. If everybody did what he was told to do their privacy was safe forever." Root laughed. "Maybe they didn't know human beings so well after all."

The captain refilled the glasses and they drank in silence. "Wonder where they came from," he said at last.

Root shrugged. "I suppose we'll never know. Some other hot dry planet, that's sure. Maybe they were refugees or some peculiar religious sect or maybe they were a colony."

"Hard to say," agreed the captain sagely. "Different race, different psychology. That's what we run into all the time."

"Thank God they weren't vindictive," said Root, half to himself. "No doubt they could have killed us any one of a dozen ways after I'd sent out that emergency call and they had to leave."

"It all ties in," admitted the captain.

Root sipped the brandy, nodded. "Once that ULR signal went out, their isolation was done for. No matter whether we were dead or not, there'd be Earthmen swarming around the station, pushing into their tunnels — and right there went their secret."

And he and the captain silently inspected the hole across the pond where the tremendous space-ship had lain buried under the spine-scrub and rusty black creeper.

"And once that space-ship was laid bare," Root continued, "there'd be a hullabaloo from here to Fomalhaut. A tremendous mass like that? We'd have to know everything — their space-drive, their history, everything about them. If what they wanted was privacy that would be a thing of the past. If they were a colony from another star they had to protect their secrets the same way we protect ours."

Barbara was standing by the ruins of the station, poking at the tangle with a stick. She turned and Root saw that she held his pipe. It was charred and battered but still recognizable. She slowly handed it to him. "Well?" said Root.

She answered in a quiet withdrawn voice: "Now that I'm leaving I think I'll miss Dicantropus." She turned to him, "Jim..."

"What?"

"I'd stay on another year if you'd like."

"No," said Root. "I don't like it here myself."

She said, still in the low tone: "Then — you don't forgive me for being foolish..."

Root raised his eyebrows. "Certainly I do. I never blamed you in the first place. You're human. Indisputably human."

"Then — why are you acting — like Moses?"

Root shrugged.

"Whether you believe me or not," she said with an averted gaze, "I never —"

He interrupted with a gesture. "What does it matter? Suppose you did — you had plenty of reason to. I wouldn't hold it against you."

"You would — in your heart."

Root said nothing.

"I wanted to hurt you. I was slowly going crazy — and you didn't seem to care one way or another. Told — him I wasn't — your property."

Root smiled his sad smile. "I'm human too."

He made a casual gesture toward the hole where the Dicantrop spaceship had lain. "If you still want diamonds go down that hole with a bucket. There's diamonds big as grapefruit. It's an old volcanic neck, it's the grand-daddy of all diamond mines. I've got a claim staked out around it; we'll be using diamonds for billiard balls as soon as we get some machinery out here."

They turned slowly back to the *Method*.

"Three's quite a crowd on Dicantropus," said Root thoughtfully. "On Earth, where there's three billion, we can have a little privacy."

Abercrombie Station

I

The doorkeeper was a big hard-looking man with an unwholesome horse-face, a skin like corroded zinc. Two girls spoke to him, asking arch questions.

Jean saw him grunt noncommittally. "Just stick around; I can't give out no dope."

He motioned to the girl sitting beside Jean, a blonde girl, very smartly turned out. She rose to her feet; the doorkeeper slid back the door. The blonde girl walked swiftly through into the inner room; the door closed behind her. She moved tentatively forward, stopped short. A man sat quietly on an old-fashioned leather couch, watching through half-closed eyes.

Nothing frightening here, was her initial impression. He was young—twenty-four or twenty-five. Mediocre, she thought, neither tall nor short, stocky nor lean. His hair was nondescript, his features without distinction, his clothes unobtrusive and neutral.

He shifted his position, opened his eyes a flicker. The blonde girl felt a quick pang. Perhaps she had been mistaken.

"How old are you?"

"I'm—twenty."

"Take off your clothes."

She stared, hands tight and white-knuckled on her purse. Intuition came suddenly; she drew a quick shallow breath. *Obey him once, give in once, he'll be your master as long as you live.*

"No... NO, I won't."

She turned quickly, reached for the door-slide. He said unemotionally, "You're too old anyway."

The door jerked aside; she walked quickly through the outer room, looking neither right nor left.

A hand touched her arm. She stopped, looked down into a face that was jet, pale rose, ivory. A young face with an expression of vitality and intelligence: black eyes, short black hair, a beautiful clear skin, mouth without make-up.

Jean asked, "What goes on? What kind of job is it?"

The blonde girl said in a tight voice, "I don't know. I didn't stay to find out. It's nothing nice." She turned, went through the outer door.

Jean sank back into the chair, pursed her lips speculatively. A minute passed. Another girl, nostrils flared wide, came from the inner room, crossed to the door, looking neither right nor left.

Jean smiled faintly. She had a wide mouth, expansive and flexible. Her teeth were small, white, very sharp.

The doorkeeper motioned to her. She jumped to her feet, entered the inner room.

The quiet man was smoking. A silvery plume rose past his face, melted into the air over his head. Jean thought, *there's something strange in his complete immobility. He's too tight, too compressed.*

She put her hands behind her back and waited, watching carefully.

"How old are you?"

This was a question she usually found wise to evade. She tilted her head sidewise, smiling, a mannerism which gave her a wild and reckless look. "How old do you think I am?"

"Sixteen or seventeen."

"That's close enough."

He nodded. "Close enough. What's your name?"

"Jean Parlier."

"Who do you live with?"

"No one. I live alone."

"Father? Mother?"

"Dead."

"Grandparents? Guardian?"

"I'm alone."

He nodded. "Any trouble with the law on that account?"

She considered him warily. "No."

He moved his head enough to send a kink running up the feather of smoke. "Take off your clothes."

"Why?"

"It's a quick way to check your qualifications."

"Well — yes. In a way I guess it is... Physical or moral?"

He made no reply, sat looking at her impassively, the gray skein of smoke rising past his face.

She shrugged, put her hands to her sides, to her neck, to her waist, to her back, to her legs, and stood without clothes.

He put the cigarette to his mouth, puffed, sat up, stubbed it out, rose to his feet, walked slowly forward.

He's trying to scare me, she thought, and smiled quietly to herself. He could try.

He stopped two feet away, stood looking down into her eyes. "You really want a million dollars?"

"That's why I'm here."

"You took the advertisement in the literal sense of the words?"

"Is there any other way?"

"You might have construed the language as — metaphor, hyperbole."

She grinned, showing her sharp white teeth. "I don't know what those words mean. Anyway I'm here. If the advertisement was only intended for you to look at me naked, I'll leave."

His expression did not change. Peculiar, thought Jean, how his body moved, his head turned, but his eyes always seemed fixed. He said as if he had not heard her, "Not too many girls have applied."

"That doesn't concern me. I want a million dollars. What is it? Blackmail? Impersonation?"

He passed over her question. "What would you do with a million if you had it?"

"I don't know... I'll worry about that when I get it. Have you checked my qualifications? I'm cold."

He turned quickly, strode to the couch, seated himself. She slipped into her clothes, came over to the couch, took a tentative seat facing him.

He said dryly, "You fill the qualifications almost too well!"

"How so?"

"It's unimportant."

Jean tilted her head, laughed. She looked like a healthy, very pretty high-school girl who might be the better for more sunshine. "Tell me what I'm to do to earn a million dollars."

"You're to marry a wealthy young man, who suffers from — let us call it, an incurable disease. When he dies, his property will be yours. You will sell his property to me for a million dollars."

"Evidently he's worth more than a million dollars."

He was conscious of the questions she did not ask. "There's somewhere near a billion involved."

"What kind of disease does he have? I might catch it myself."

"I'll take care of the disease end. You won't catch it if you keep your nose clean."

"Oh — oh, I see — tell me more about him. Is he handsome? Big? Strong? I might feel sorry if he died."

"He's eighteen years old. His main interest is collecting." Sardonically: "He likes zoology too. He's an eminent zoologist. His name is Earl Abercrombie. He owns —" he gestured up "— Abercrombie Station."

Jean stared, then laughed feebly. "That's a hard way to make a million dollars... Earl Abercrombie..."

"Squeamish?"

"Not when I'm awake. But I do have nightmares."

"Make up your mind."

She looked modestly to where she had folded her hands in her lap. "A million isn't a very large cut out of a billion."

He surveyed her with something like approval. "No. It isn't."

She rose to her feet, slim as a dancer. "All you do is sign a check. I have to marry him, get in bed with him."

"They don't use beds on Abercrombie Station."

"Since he lives on Abercrombie, he might not be interested in me."

"Earl is different," said the quiet man. "Earl likes gravity girls."

"You must realize that once he dies, you'd be forced to accept whatever I chose to give you. Or the property might be put in charge of a trustee."

"Not necessarily. The Abercrombie Civil Regulation allows property to be controlled by anyone sixteen or over. Earl is eighteen. He exercises complete control over the station, subject to a few unimportant restrictions. I'll take care of that end." He went to the door, slid it open. "Hammond."

The man with the long face came wordlessly to the door.

"I've got her. Send the others home."

He closed the door, turned to Jean. "I want you to have dinner with me."

"I'm not dressed for dinner."

"I'll send up the couturier. Try to be ready in an hour."

He left the room. The door closed. Jean stretched, threw back her head, opened her mouth in a soundless exultant laugh. She raised her arms over her head, took a step forward, turned a supple cart-wheel across the rug, bounced to her feet beside the window.

She knelt, rested her head on her hands, looked across Metropolis. Dusk had come. The great gray-golden sky filled three-quarters of her vision. A thousand feet below was the wan gray, lavender and black crumble of surface buildings, the pallid roadways streaming with golden motes. To the right, aircraft slid silently along force-guides to the mountain suburbs — tired normal people bound to pleasant normal homes. What would they think if they knew that she, Jean Parlier, was watching? For instance, the man who drove that shiny Skyfarer with the pale green chevrets ... She built a picture of him: pudgy, forehead creased with lines of worry. He'd be hurrying home to his wife, who would listen tolerantly while he boasted or grumbled. Cattle-women, cow-women, thought Jean without rancor. What man could subdue her? Where was the man who was wild and hard and bright enough? ... Remembering her new job, she grimaced. Mrs. Earl Abercrombie. She looked up into the sky. The stars were not yet out and the lights of Abercrombie Station could not be seen.

A million dollars, think of it! "What will you do with a million dollars?" her new employer had asked her, and now that she returned to it, the idea was uncomfortable, like a lump in her throat.

How would she feel? How would she ... Her mind moved away from the subject, recoiled with the faintest trace of anger, as if it were a subject not to be touched upon. "Rats," said Jean. "Time to worry about it after I get it ... A million dollars. Not too large a cut out of a billion, actually. Two million would be better."

Her eyes followed a slim red airboat diving along a sharp curve into the parking area: a sparkling new Marshall Moon-chaser. Now there was something she wanted. It would be one of her first purchases.

The door slid open. Hammond the doorkeeper looked briefly in. Then the couturier entered, pushing his wheeled kit before him, a slender little blond man with rich topaz eyes. The door closed.

Jean turned away from the window. The couturier—André was the name stencilled on the enamel of the box—spoke for more light, walked around her, darting glances up and down her body.

"Yes," he muttered, pressing his lips in and out. "Ah, yes... Now what does the lady have in mind?"

"A dinner gown, I suppose."

He nodded. "Mr. Fotheringay mentioned formal evening wear."

So that was his name—Fotheringay.

André snapped up a screen. "Observe, if you will, a few of my effects; perhaps there is something to please you."

Models appeared on the screen, stepping forward, smiling, turning away.

Jean said, "Something like that."

André made a gesture of approval, snapped his fingers. "Mademoiselle has good taste. And now we shall see... if mademoiselle will let me help her..."

He deftly unzipped her garments, laid them on the couch.

"First—we refresh ourselves." He selected a tool from his kit, and holding her wrist between delicate thumb and forefinger, sprayed her arms with cool mist, then warm, perfumed air. Her skin tingled, fresh, invigorated.

André tapped his chin. "Now, the foundation."

She stood, eyes half-closed, while he bustled around her, striding off, making whispered comments, quick gestures with significance only to himself.

He sprayed her with gray-green web, touched and pulled as the strands set. He adjusted knurled knobs at the ends of a flexible tube, pressed it around her waist, swept it away and it trailed shining black-green silk. He artfully twisted and wound his tube. He put the frame back in the kit, pulled, twisted, pinched, while the silk set.

He sprayed her with wan white, quickly jumped forward, folded, shaped, pinched, pulled, bunched and the stuff fell in twisted bands from her shoulders and into a full rustling skirt.

"Now—gauntlets." He covered her arms and hands with warm black-green pulp which set into spangled velvet, adroitly cut with scissors to bare the back of her hand.

"Slippers." Black satin, webbed with emerald-green phosphorescence.

"Now—the ornaments." He hung a red bauble from her right ear, slipped a cabochon ruby on her right hand.

"Scent—a trace. The Levailleur, indeed." He flicked her with an odor suggestive of a Central Asia flower patch. "And mademoiselle is dressed. And may I say—" he bowed with a flourish "—most exquisitely beautiful."

He manipulated his cart, one side fell away. A mirror uncoiled upward.

Jean inspected herself. Vivid naiad. When she acquired that million dollars—two million would be better—she'd put André on her permanent payroll.

André was still muttering compliments. "—Elan supreme. She is magic. Most striking. Eyes will turn..."

The door slid back. Fotheringay came into the room. André bowed low, clasped his hands.

Fotheringay glanced at her. "You're ready. Good. Come along."

Jean thought, *we might as well get this straight right now.*

"Where?"

He frowned slightly, stood aside while André pushed his cart out.

Jean said, "I came here of my own free will. I walked into this room under my own power. Both times I knew where I was going. Now you say 'Come along.' First I want to know where. Then I'll decide whether or not I'll come."

"You don't want a million dollars very badly."

"Two million. I want it badly enough to waste an afternoon investigating... But—if I don't get it today, I'll get it tomorrow. Or next week. Somehow I'll get it; a long time ago I made my mind up. So?" She performed an airy curtsey.

His pupils contracted. He said in an even voice, "Very well. Two million. I am now taking you to dinner on the roof, where I will give you your instructions."

II

They drifted under the dome, in a greenish plastic bubble. Below them spread the commercial fantasy of an out-world landscape: gray sward; gnarled red and green trees casting dramatic black shadows; a pond of fluorescent green liquid; panels of exotic blossoms; beds of fungus.

The bubble drifted easily, apparently at random, now high under the near-invisible dome, now low under the foliage. Successive courses appeared from the center of the table, along with chilled wine and frosted punch.

It was wonderful and lavish, thought Jean. But why should Fotheringay spend his money on her? Perhaps he entertained romantic notions... She dallied with the idea, inspected him covertly... The idea lacked conviction. He seemed to be engaging in none of the usual gambits. He neither tried to fascinate her with his charm, nor swamp her with synthetic masculinity. Much as it irritated Jean to admit it, he appeared — indifferent.

Jean compressed her lips. The idea was disconcerting. She essayed a slight smile, a side glance up under lowered lashes.

"Save it," said Fotheringay. "You'll need it all when you get up to Abercrombie."

Jean returned to her dinner. After a minute she said calmly, "I was — curious."

"Now you know."

Jean thought to tease him, draw him out. "Know what?"

"Whatever it was you were curious about."

"Pooh. Men are mostly alike. They all have the same button. Push it, they all jump in the same direction."

Fotheringay frowned, glanced at her under narrowed eyes. "Maybe you aren't so precocious after all."

Jean became tense. In a curious indefinable way, the subject was very important, as if survival were linked with confidence in her own sophistication and flexibility. "What do you mean?"

"You make the assumption most pretty girls make," he said with a trace of scorn. "I thought you were smarter than that."

Jean frowned. There had been little abstract thinking in her background. "Well, I've never had it work out differently. Although I'm willing to admit there are exceptions... It's a kind of game. I've never lost. If I'm kidding myself, it hasn't made much difference so far."

Fotheringay relaxed. "You've been lucky."

Jean stretched out her arms, arched her body, smiled as if at a secret. "Call it luck."

"Luck won't work with Earl Abercrombie."

"You're the one who used the word luck. I think it's, well — ability."

"You'll have to use your brains too." He hesitated, then said, "Actually, Earl likes — odd things."

Jean sat looking at him, frowning.

He said coolly, "You're making up your mind how best to ask the question, 'What's odd about me?' "

Jean snapped, "I don't need you to tell me what's odd about me. I know what it is myself."

Fotheringay made no comment.

"I'm completely on my own," said Jean. "There's not a soul in all the human universe that I care two pins for. I do just exactly as I please." She watched him carefully. He nodded indifferently. Jean quelled her exasperation, leaned back in her chair, studied him as if he were in a glass case... A strange young man. Did he ever smile? She thought of the Capellan Fibrates who by popular superstition were able to fix themselves along a man's spinal column and control his intelligence. Fotheringay displayed a coldness strange enough to suggest such a possession... A Capellan could manipulate but one hand at a time. Fotheringay held a knife in one hand, a fork in the other and moved both hands together. So much for that.

He said quietly, "I watched your hands too."

Jean threw back her head and laughed — a healthy adolescent laugh. Fotheringay watched her without discernible expression.

She said, "Actually, you'd like to know about me, but you're too stiff-necked to ask."

"You were born at Angel City on Codiron," said Fotheringay. "Your mother abandoned you in a tavern, a gambler named Joe Parlier took care of you until you were ten, when you killed him and three other men and stowed away on the Gray Line Packet *Bucyrus.* You were taken to the Waif's Home at Paie on Bella's Pride. You ran away and the Superintendent was found dead... Shall I go on? There's five more years of it."

Jean sipped her wine, nowise abashed. "You've worked fast... But you've misrepresented. You said, 'There's five years more of it, shall I go on?' as if you were able to go on. You don't know anything about the next five years."

Fotheringay's face changed by not a flicker. He said as if she had not spoken, "Now listen carefully. This is what you'll have to look out for."

"Go ahead. I'm all ears." She leaned back in her chair. A clever technique, ignoring an unwelcome situation as if it never existed. Of course, to carry it off successfully, a certain temperament was required. A cold fish like Fotheringay managed very well.

"Tonight a man named Webbard meets us here. He is chief steward at Abercrombie Station. I happen to be able to influence certain of his actions. He will take you up with him to Abercrombie and install you as a servant in the Abercrombie private chambers."

Jean wrinkled her nose. "Servant? Why can't I go to Abercrombie as a paying guest?"

"It wouldn't be natural. A girl like you would go up to *Capricorn* or *Verge.* Earl Abercrombie is extremely suspicious. He'd be certain to fight shy of you. His mother, old Mrs. Clara, watches him pretty closely, and keeps drilling into his head the idea that all the Abercrombie girls are after his money. As a servant you will have opportunity to meet him in intimate circumstances. He rarely leaves his study; he's absorbed in his collecting."

"My word," murmured Jean. "What does he collect?"

"Everything you can think of," said Fotheringay, moving his lips upward in a quick grimace, almost a smile. "I understand from Webbard, however, that he is rather romantic, and has carried on a number of flirtations among the girls of the station."

Jean screwed up her mouth in fastidious scorn. Fotheringay watched her impassively.

"When do I — commence?"

"Webbard goes up on the supply barge tomorrow. You'll go with him."

A whisper of sound from the buzzer. Fotheringay touched the button. "Yes?"

"Mr. Webbard for you, sir."

Fotheringay directed the bubble down to the landing stage.

Webbard was waiting, the fattest man Jean had ever seen.

The plaque on the door read, Richard Mycroft, Attorney-at-Law. Somewhere far back down the years, someone had said in Jean's hearing that Richard Mycroft was a good attorney.

The receptionist was a dark woman about thirty-five, with a direct penetrating eye. "Do you have an appointment?"

"No," said Jean. "I'm in rather a hurry."

The receptionist hesitated a moment, then bent over the communicator. "A young lady — Miss Jean Parlier — to see you. New business."

"Very well."

The receptionist nodded to the door. "You can go in," she said shortly.

She doesn't like me, thought Jean. *Because I'm what she was and what she wants to be again.*

Mycroft was a square man with a pleasant face. Jean constructed a wary defense against him. If you liked someone and they knew it, they felt obligated to advise and interfere. She wanted no advice, no interference. She wanted two million dollars.

"Well, young lady," said Mycroft. "What can I do for you?"

He's treating me like a child, thought Jean. *Maybe I look like a child to him.* She said, "It's a matter of advice. I don't know much about fees. I can afford to pay you a hundred dollars. When you advise me a hundred dollars' worth, let me know and I'll go away."

"A hundred dollars buys a lot of advice," said Mycroft. "Advice is cheap."

"Not from a lawyer."

Mycroft became practical. "What are your troubles?"

"It's understood that this is all confidential?"

"Certainly." Mycroft's smile froze into a polite grimace.

"It's nothing illegal — so far as I'm concerned — but I don't want you passing out any quiet hints to — people that might be interested."

Mycroft straightened himself behind his desk. "A lawyer is expected to respect the confidence of his client."

"Okay... Well, it's like this." She told him of Fotheringay, of Abercrombie Station and Earl Abercrombie. She said that Earl Abercrombie was sick with an incurable disease. She made no mention of Fotheringay's convictions on that subject. It was a matter she herself kept carefully brushing out of her mind. Fotheringay had hired her. He told her what to do, told her that Earl Abercrombie was sick. That was good enough for her. If she had asked too many questions, found that things were too nasty even for her stomach, Fotheringay would have found another girl less inquisitive... She skirted the exact nature of Earl's disease. She didn't actually know, herself. She didn't want to know.

Mycroft listened attentively, saying nothing.

"What I want to know is," said Jean, "is the wife sure to inherit on Abercrombie? I don't want to go to a lot of trouble for nothing. And after all Earl is under twenty-one; I thought that in the event of his death it was best to — well, make sure of everything first."

For a moment Mycroft made no move, but sat regarding her quietly. Then he tamped tobacco into a pipe.

"Jean," he said, "I'll give you some advice. It's free. No strings on it."

"Don't bother," said Jean. "I don't want the kind of advice that's free. I want the kind I have to pay for."

Mycroft grimaced. "You're a remarkably wise child."

"I've had to be... Call me a child, if you wish."

"Just what will you do with a million dollars? Or two million, I understand it to be?"

Jean stared. Surely the answer was obvious... or was it? When she tried to find an answer, nothing surfaced.

"Well," she said vaguely, "I'd like an airboat, some nice clothes, and maybe..." In her mind's eye she suddenly saw herself surrounded by friends. Nice people, like Mr. Mycroft.

"If I were a psychologist and not a lawyer," said Mycroft, "I'd say you wanted your mother and father more than you wanted two million dollars."

Jean became very heated. "No, no! I don't want them at all. They're dead." As far as she was concerned they were dead. They had died for her when they left her on Joe Parlier's pool-table in the old Aztec Tavern.

Jean said indignantly, "Mr. Mycroft, I know you mean well, but tell me what I want to know."

"I'll tell you," said Mycroft, "because if I didn't, someone else would. Abercrombie property, if I'm not mistaken, is regulated by its own civil code... Let's see —" he twisted in his chair, pushed buttons on his desk.

On the screen appeared the index to the Central Law Library. Mycroft made further selections, narrowing down selectively. A few seconds later he had the information. "Property control begins at sixteen. Widow inherits at minimum fifty percent; the entire estate unless specifically stated otherwise in the will."

"Good," said Jean. She jumped to her feet. "That's what I wanted to make sure of."

Mycroft asked, "When do you leave?"

"This afternoon."

"I don't need to tell you that the idea behind the scheme is — not moral."

"Mr. Mycroft, you're a dear. But I don't have any morals."

He tilted his head, shrugged, puffed on his pipe. "Are you sure?"

"Well — yes." Jean considered a moment. "I suppose so. Do you want me to go into details?"

"No. I think what I meant to say was, are you sure you know what you want out of life?"

"Certainly. Lots of money."

Mycroft grinned. "That's really not a good answer. What will you buy with your money?"

Jean felt irrational anger rising in her throat. "Oh — lots of things." She rose to her feet. "Just what do I owe you, Mr. Mycroft?"

"Oh — ten dollars. Give it to Ruth."

"Thank you, Mr. Mycroft." She stalked out of his office.

As she marched down the corridor she was surprised to find that she was angry with herself as well as irritated with Mr. Mycroft... He had no right making people wonder about themselves. It wouldn't be so bad if she weren't wondering a little already.

But this was all nonsense. Two million dollars was two million dollars. When she was rich, she'd call on Mr. Mycroft and ask him if honestly he didn't think it was worth a few little lapses.

And today — up to Abercrombie Station. She suddenly became excited.

III

The pilot of the Abercrombie supply barge was emphatic. "No sir, I think you're making a mistake, nice little girl like you."

He was a chunky man in his thirties, hard-bitten and positive. Sparse blond hair crusted his scalp, deep lines gave his mouth a cynical slant. Webbard, the Abercrombie chief steward, was billeted astern, in the special handling locker. The usual webbings were inadequate to protect his corpulence; he floated chin-deep in a tankful of emulsion the same specific gravity as his body.

There was no passenger cabin and Jean had slipped into the seat beside the pilot. She wore a modest white frock, a white toque, a gray and black striped jacket.

The pilot had few good words for Abercrombie Station. "Now it's what I call a shame, taking a kid like you to serve the likes of them... Why don't they get one of their own kind? Surely both sides would be the happier."

Jean said innocently, "I'm going up for only just a little bit."

"So you think. It's catching. In a year you'll be like the rest of them. The air alone is enough to sicken a person, rich and sweet like olive oil. Me, I never set foot outside the barge unless I can't help it."

"Do you think I'll be — safe?" She raised her lashes, turned him her reckless sidelong look.

He licked his lips, moved in his seat. "Oh, you'll be safe enough," he muttered. "At least from them that's been there a while. You might have to duck a few just fresh from Earth... After they've lived on the station a bit their ideas change, and they wouldn't spit on the best part of an Earth girl."

"Hmmph." Jean compressed her lips. Earl Abercrombie had been born on the station.

"But I wasn't thinking so much of that," said the pilot. It was hard, he thought, talking straight sense to a kid so young and inexperienced. "I meant in that atmosphere you'll be apt to let yourself go. Pretty soon you'll look like the rest of 'em — never want to leave. Some aren't *able* to leave — couldn't stand it back on Earth if they wanted to."

"Oh — I don't think so. Not in my case."

"It's catching," said the pilot vehemently. "Look, kid, I know. I've ferried out to all the stations, I've seen 'em come and go. Each station has its own kind of weirdness, and you can't keep away from it." He chuckled self-consciously. "Maybe that's why I'm so batty myself... Now take Madeira Station. Gay. Frou-frou." He made a mincing motion with his fingers. "That's Madeira. You wouldn't know much about that... But take Balchester Aerie, take Merlin Dell, take the Starhome —"

"Surely, some are just pleasure resorts?"

The pilot grudgingly admitted that of the twenty-two resort satellites, fully half were as ordinary as Miami Beach. "But the others — oh, Moses!" He rolled his eyes back. "And Abercrombie is the worst."

There was silence in the cabin. Earth was a monstrous, green, blue, white and black ball over Jean's shoulder. The sun made a furious hole in the sky below. Ahead were the stars — and a set of blinking blue and red lights.

"Is that Abercrombie?"

"No, that's the Masonic Temple. Abercrombie is on out a ways..." He looked diffidently at her from the corner of his eyes. "Now — look! I don't want you to think I'm fresh. Or maybe I do. But if you're hard up for a job — why don't you come back to Earth with me? I got a pretty nice shack in Long Beach — nothing fancy — but it's on the beach, and it'll be better than working for a bunch of side-show freaks."

Jean said absently, "No thanks." The pilot pulled in his chin, pulled his elbows close against his body, glowered.

An hour passed. From behind came a rattle, and a small panel slid back. Webbard's pursy face showed through. The barge was coasting on free momentum, gravity was negated. "How much longer to the station?"

"It's just ahead. Half an hour, more or less, and we'll be fished up tight and right." Webbard grunted, withdrew.

Yellow and green lights winked ahead. "That's Abercrombie," said the pilot. He reached out to a handle. "Brace yourself." He pulled. Pale blue check-jets streamed out ahead.

From behind came a thump and an angry cursing. The pilot grinned. "Got him good." The jets roared a minute, died. "Every trip it's the same way. Now in a minute he'll stick his head through the panel and bawl me out."

The portal slid back. Webbard showed his furious face. "Why in thunder don't you warn me before you check? I just now took a blow that might have hurt me! You're not much of a pilot, risking injuries of that sort!"

The pilot said in a droll voice, "Sorry sir, sorry indeed. Won't happen again."

"It had better not! If it does, I'll make it my business to see that you're discharged."

The portal snapped shut. "Sometimes I get him better than others," said the pilot. "This was a good one, I could tell by the thump."

He shifted in his seat, put his arm around Jean's shoulders, pulled her against him. "Let's have a little kiss, before we fish home."

Jean leaned forward, reached out her arm. He saw her face coming toward him—bright wonderful face, onyx, pale rose, ivory, smiling hot with life... She reached past him, thrust the check valve. Four jets thrashed forward. The barge jerked. The pilot fell into the instrument panel, comical surprise written on his face.

From behind came a heavy resonant thump.

The pilot pulled himself back into his seat, knocked back the check valve. Blood oozed from his chin, forming a little red wen. Behind them the portal snapped open. Webbard's face, black with rage, looked through.

When he had finally finished, and the portal had closed, the pilot looked at Jean, who was sitting quietly in her seat, the corners of her mouth drawn up dreamily.

He said from deep in his throat, "If I had you alone, I'd beat you half to death."

Jean drew her knees up under her chin, clasped her arms around, looked silently ahead.

✳

Abercrombie Station had been built to the Fitch cylinder-design: a power and service core, a series of circular decks, a transparent sheath. To the original construction a number of modifications and annexes had been added. An outside deck circled the cylinder, sheet steel to hold the magnetic grapples of small boats, cargo binds, magnetic shoes, anything which was to be fixed in place for a greater or lesser time. At each end of the cylinder, tubes connected to dependent constructions. The first, a sphere, was the private residence of the Abercrombies. The second, a cylinder, rotated at sufficient speed to press the water it contained evenly over its inner surface to a depth of ten feet; this was the station swimming pool, a feature found on only three of the resort satellites.

The supply barge inched close to the deck, bumped. Four men attached constrictor tackle to rings in the hull, heaved the barge along to the supply port. The barge settled into its socket, grapples shot home, the ports sucked open.

Chief Steward Webbard was still smouldering, but now a display of anger was beneath his dignity. Disdaining magnetic shoes, he pulled himself to the entrance, motioned to Jean. "Bring your baggage."

Jean went to her neat little trunk, jerked it into the air, found herself floundering helpless in the middle of the cargo space. Webbard impatiently returned with magnetic clips for her shoes, and helped her float the trunk into the station.

She was breathing different, rich, air. The barge had smelled of ozone, grease, hemp sacking, but the station...Without consciously trying to identify the odor, Jean thought of waffles with butter and syrup mixed with talcum powder.

Webbard floated in front of her, an imposing spectacle. His fat no longer hung on him in folds; it ballooned out in an even perimeter. His face was smooth as a watermelon, and it seemed as if his features were incised, carved, rather than molded. He focused his eyes at a point above her dark head. "We had better come to an understanding, young lady."

"Certainly, Mr. Webbard."

"As a favor to my friend, Mr. Fotheringay, I have brought you here to work. Beyond this original and singular act, I am no longer responsible. I am not your sponsor. Mr. Fotheringay recommended you highly, so see that you give satisfaction. Your immediate superior will be Mrs. Blaiskell, and you must obey her implicitly. We have very strict rules here at Abercrombie — fair treatment and good pay — but you must earn it. Your work must speak for itself, and you can expect no special favors." He coughed. "Indeed, if I may say so, you are fortunate in finding employment here; usually we hire people more of our own sort, it makes for harmonious conditions."

Jean waited with demurely bowed head. Webbard spoke on further, detailing specific warnings, admonitions, injunctions.

Jean nodded dutifully. There was no point antagonizing pompous old Webbard. And Webbard thought that here was a respectful young lady, thin and very young and with a peculiar frenetic gleam in her eye, but sufficiently impressed by his importance... Good coloring too. Pleasant features. If she only could manage two hundred more pounds of flesh on her bones, she might have appealed to his grosser nature.

"This way then," said Webbard.

He floated ahead, and by some magnificent innate power continued to radiate the impression of inexorable dignity even while plunging head-first along the corridor.

Jean came more sedately, walking on her magnetic clips, pushing the trunk ahead as easily as if it had been a paper bag.

They reached the central core, and Webbard, after looking back over his bulging shoulders, launched himself up the shaft.

Panes in the wall of the core permitted a view of the various halls, lounges, refectories, salons. Jean stopped by a room decorated with red plush drapes and marble statuary. She stared, first in wonder, then in amusement.

Webbard called impatiently, "Come along now, miss, come along."

Jean pulled herself away from the pane. "I was watching the guests. They looked like —" she broke into a sudden giggle.

Webbard frowned, pursed his lips. Jean thought he was about to demand the grounds for her merriment, but evidently he felt it beneath his dignity. He called, "Come along now, I can spare you only a moment."

She turned one last glance into the hall, and now she laughed aloud.

Fat women, like bladder-fish in an aquarium tank. Fat women, round and tender as yellow peaches. Fat women, miraculously easy and agile in the absence of gravity. The occasion seemed to be an afternoon musicale. The hall was crowded and heavy with balls of pink flesh draped in blouses and pantaloons of white, pale blue and yellow.

The current Abercrombie fashion seemed designed to accent the round bodies. Flat bands like Sam Browne belts molded the breasts down and out, under the arms. The hair was parted down the middle, skinned smoothly back to a small roll at the nape of the neck. Flesh, bulbs of tender flesh, smooth shiny balloons. Tiny twitching features, dancing fingers and toes, eyes and lips roguishly painted. On Earth any one of these women would have sat immobile, a pile of sagging sweating tissue. At Abercrombie Station — the so-called 'Adipose Alley' — they moved with the ease of dandelion puffs, and their faces and bodies were smooth as butter-balls.

"Come, come, come!" barked Webbard. "There's no loitering at Abercrombie!"

Jean restrained the impulse to slide her trunk up the core against Webbard's rotund buttocks, a tempting target.

He waited for her at the far end of the corridor.

"Mr. Webbard," she asked thoughtfully, "how much does Earl Abercrombie weigh?"

Webbard tilted his head back, glared reprovingly down his nose. "Such intimacies, miss, are not considered polite conversation here."

Jean said, "I merely wondered if he were as — well, imposing as you are."

Webbard sniffed. "I couldn't answer you. Mr. Abercrombie is a person of great competence. His — presence is a matter you must learn not to discuss. It's not proper, not done."

"Thank you, Mr. Webbard," said Jean meekly.

Webbard said, "You'll catch on. You'll make a good girl yet. Now, through the tube, and I'll take you to Mrs. Blaiskell."

Mrs. Blaiskell was short and squat as a kumquat. Her hair was steel-gray, and skinned back modishly to the roll behind her neck. She wore tight black rompers, the uniform of the Abercrombie servants, so Jean was to learn.

Jean suspected that she made a poor impression on Mrs. Blaiskell.

She felt the snapping gray eyes search her from head to foot, and kept her own modestly down-cast.

Webbard explained that Jean was to be trained as a maid, and suggested that Mrs. Blaiskell use her in the Pleasaunce and the bedrooms.

Mrs. Blaiskell nodded. "Good idea. The young master is peculiar, as everyone knows, but he's been pestering the girls lately and interrupting their duties; wise to have one in there such as her — no offense, miss, I just mean it's the gravity that does it — who won't be so apt to catch his eye."

Webbard signed to her, and they floated off a little distance, conversing in low whispers.

Jean's wide mouth quivered at the corners. Old fools!

Five minutes passed. Jean began to fidget. Why didn't they do something? Take her somewhere. She suppressed her restlessness. Life! How good, how zestful! She wondered, *will I feel this same joy when I'm twenty? When I'm thirty, forty?* She drew back the corners of her mouth. *Of course I will. I'll never let myself change... But life must be used to its best. Every flicker of ardor and excitement must be wrung free and tasted.* She grinned. Here she floated, breathing the over-ripe air of Abercrombie Station. In a way it was adventure. It paid well — two million dollars, and only for seducing an eighteen-year-old boy. Seducing him, marrying him — what difference? Of course he was Earl Abercrombie, and if he were as imposing as Mr. Webbard... She considered Webbard's great body in wry speculation. Oh well, two million was two million. If things got too bad, the price might go up. Ten million, perhaps. Not too large a cut out of a billion.

Webbard departed without a word, twitching himself easily back down the core.

"Come," said Mrs. Blaiskell. "I'll show you your room. You can rest and tomorrow I'll take you around."

IV

Mrs. Blaiskell stood by while Jean fitted herself into black rompers, frankly critical. "Lord have mercy, but you mustn't pinch in the waist so! You're rachity and thin to starvation now, poor child; you mustn't point it up so! Perhaps we can find a few air-floats to fill you out; not that it's essential, Lord knows, since you're but a dust-maid; still it always improves a household to have a staff of pretty women, and young Earl, I will say this for him and all his oddness, he does appreciate a handsome woman... Now then, your bosom, we must do something there; why you're nearly flat! You see, there's no scope to allow a fine drape down under the arms, see?" She pointed to her own voluminous rolls of adipose. "Suppose we just roll up a bit of cushion and —"

"No," said Jean tremulously. Was it possible that they thought her so ugly? "I won't wear padding."

Mrs. Blaiskell sniffed. "It's your own self that's to benefit, my dear. I'm sure it's not me that's the wizened one."

Jean bent over her black slippers. "No, you're very sleek."

Mrs. Blaiskell nodded proudly. "I keep myself well shaped out, and all the better for it. It wasn't so when I was your age, miss, I'll tell you; I was on Earth then —"

"Oh, you weren't born here?"

"No, miss, I was one of the poor souls pressed and ridden by gravity, and I burned up my body with the effort of mere conveyance. No, I was born in Sydney, Australia, of decent kind folk, but they were too poor to buy me a place on Abercrombie. I was lucky enough to secure just such a position as you have, and that was while Mr. Justus and old Mrs. Eva, his mother — that's Earl's grandmother — was still with us. I've never been down to Earth since. I'll never set foot on the surface again."

"Don't you miss the festivals and great buildings and all the lovely countryside?"

"Pah!" Mrs. Blaiskell spat the word. "And be pressed into hideous folds and wrinkles? And ride in a cart, and be stared at and snickered at by the home people? Thin as sticks they are with their constant worry and fight against the pull of the soil! No, miss, we have our own sceneries and fetes; there's a pavane for tomorrow night, a Grand Masque Pantomime, a Pageant of Beautiful Women, all in the month ahead. And best, I'm among my own people, the round ones, and I've never a wrinkle on my face. I'm fine and full-blown, and I wouldn't trade with any of them below."

Jean shrugged. "If you're happy, that's all that matters." She looked at herself in the mirror with satisfaction. Even if fat Mrs. Blaiskell thought otherwise, the black rompers looked well on her, now that she'd fitted them snug to her hips and waist. Her legs — slender, round and shining ivory — were good, this she knew. Even if weird Mr. Webbard and odd Mrs. Blaiskell thought otherwise. Wait till she tried them on young Earl. He preferred gravity girls; Fotheringay had told her so. And yet — Webbard and Mrs. Blaiskell had hinted otherwise. Maybe he liked both kinds?...Jean smiled, a little tremulously. If Earl liked both kinds, then he would like almost anything that was warm, moved and breathed. And that certainly included herself.

If she asked Mrs. Blaiskell outright, she'd be startled and shocked. Good proper Mrs. Blaiskell. A motherly soul, not like the matrons in the various asylums and waifs' homes of her experience. Strapping big women those had been — practical and quick with their hands...But Mrs. Blaiskell was nice; she would never have deserted her child on a pool table. Mrs. Blaiskell would have struggled and starved herself to keep her child and raise her nicely...Jean idly speculated how it would seem with Mrs. Blaiskell for a mother. And Mr. Mycroft for a father. It gave her a queer prickly feeling, and also somehow called up from deep inside a dark dull resentment tinged with anger.

Jean moved uneasily, fretfully. Never mind the nonsense! *You're playing a lone hand. What would you want with relatives? What an ungodly nuisance!* She would never have been allowed this adventure up to Abercrombie Station...On the other hand, with relatives there would be many fewer problems on how to spend two million dollars.

Jean sighed. Her own mother wasn't kind and comfortable like Mrs. Blaiskell. She couldn't have been, and the whole matter became an academic question. Forget it, put it clean out of your mind.

Mrs. Blaiskell brought forward service shoes, worn to some extent by everyone at the station: slippers with magnetic coils in the soles. Wires led to a power bank at the belt. By adjusting a rheostat, any degree of magnetism could be achieved.

"When a person works, she needs a footing," Mrs. Blaiskell explained. "Of course there's not much to do, once you get on to it. Cleaning is easy, with our good filters; still there's sometimes a stir of dust and always a little film of oil that settles from the air."

Jean straightened up. "Okay Mrs. B, I'm ready. Where do we start?"

Mrs. Blaiskell raised her eyebrows at the familiarity, but was not seriously displeased. In the main, the girl seemed to be respectful, willing and intelligent. And — significantly — not the sort to create a disturbance with Mr. Earl.

Twitching a toe against a wall, she propelled herself down the corridor, halted by a white door, slid back the panel.

They entered the room as if from the ceiling. Jean felt an instant of vertigo, pushing herself head-first at what appeared to be a floor.

Mrs. Blaiskell deftly seized a chair, swung her body around, put her feet to the nominal floor. Jean joined her. They stood in a large round room, apparently a section across the building. Windows opened on space, stars shone in from all sides; the entire zodiac was visible with a sweep of the eyes.

Sunlight came up from below, shining on the ceiling, and off to one quarter hung the half moon, hard and sharp as a new coin. The room was rather too opulent for Jean's taste. She was conscious of an overwhelming surfeit of mustard-saffron carpet, white panelling with gold arabesques, a round table clamped to the floor, surrounded by chairs footed with magnetic casters. A crystal chandelier thrust rigidly down; rotund cherubs peered at intervals from the angle between wall and ceiling.

"The Pleasaunce," said Mrs. Blaiskell. "You'll clean in here every morning first thing." She described Jean's duties in detail.

"Next we go to —" she nudged Jean. "Here's old Mrs. Clara, Earl's mother. Bow your head, just as I do."

A woman dressed in rose-purple floated into the room. She wore an expression of absent-minded arrogance, as if in all the universe there were no doubt, uncertainty or equivocation. She was almost perfectly globular, as wide as she was tall. Her hair was silver-white, her face a bubble of smooth flesh, daubed apparently at random with rouge. She wore stones spread six inches down over her bulging bosom and shoulders.

Mrs. Blaiskell bowed her head unctuously. "Mrs. Clara, dear, allow me to introduce the new parlor maid; she's new up from Earth and very handy."

Mrs. Clara Abercrombie darted Jean a quick look. "Emaciated creature."

"Oh, she'll healthen up," cooed Mrs. Blaiskell. "Plenty of good food and hard work will do wonders for her; after all, she's only a child."

"Mmmph. Hardly. It's blood, Blaiskell, and well you know it."

"Well, yes of course, Mrs. Clara."

Mrs. Clara continued in a brassy voice, darting glances around the room. "Either it's good blood you have or vinegar. This girl here, she'll never be really comfortable, I can see it. It's not in her blood."

"No, ma'am, you're correct in what you say."

"It's not in Earl's blood either. He's the one I'm worried for. Hugo was the rich one, but his brother Lionel after him, poor dear Lionel, and —"

"What about Lionel?" said a husky voice. Jean twisted. This was Earl. "Who's heard from Lionel?"

"No one, my dear. He's gone, he'll never be back. I was but commenting that neither one of you ever reached your growth, showing all bone as you do."

Earl scowled past his mother, past Mrs. Blaiskell, and his gaze fell on Jean. "What's this? Another servant? We don't need her. Send her away. Always ideas for more expense."

"She's for your rooms, Earl, my dear," said his mother.

"Where's Jessy? What was wrong with Jessy?"

Mrs. Clara and Mrs. Blaiskell exchanged indulgent glances. Jean turned Earl a slow arch look. He blinked, then frowned. Jean dropped her eyes, traced a pattern on the rug with her toe, an operation which she knew sent interesting movements along her leg. Earning the two million dollars wouldn't be as irksome as she had feared. Because Earl was not at all fat. He was stocky, solid, with bull shoulders and a bull neck. He had a close crop of tight blond curls, a florid complexion, a big waxy nose, a ponderous jaw. His mouth was good, drooping sullenly at the moment.

He was something less than attractive, thought Jean. On Earth she would have ignored him, or if he persisted, stung him to fury with a series of insults. But she had been expecting far worse: a bulbous creature like Webbard, a human balloon... Of course there was no real reason for Earl to be fat; the children of fat people were as likely as not to be of normal size.

Mrs. Clara was instructing Mrs. Blaiskell for the day, Mrs. Blaiskell nodding precisely on each sixth word and ticking off points on her stubby little fingers.

Mrs. Clara finished, Mrs. Blaiskell nodded to Jean. "Come, miss, there's work to be done."

Earl called after them, "Mind now, no one in my study!"

Jean asked curiously, "Why doesn't he want anyone in his study?"

"That's where he keeps all his collections. He won't have a thing disturbed. Very strange sometimes, Earl. You'll just have to make allowances, and be on your good behavior. In some ways he's harder to serve than Mrs. Clara."

"Earl was born here?"

Mrs. Blaiskell nodded. "He's never been down to Earth. Says it's a place of crazy people, and the Lord knows, he's more than half right."

"Who are Hugo and Lionel?"

"They're the two oldest. Hugo is dead, Lord rest him, and Lionel is off on his travels. Then under Earl there's Harper and Dauphin and Millicent and Clarice. That's all Mrs. Clara's children, all very proud and portly. Earl is the skinny lad of the lot, and very lucky too, because when Hugo died, Lionel was off gadding and so Earl inherited... Now here's his suite, and what a mess."

As they worked Mrs. Blaiskell commented on various aspects of the room. "That bed now! Earl wasn't satisfied with sleeping under a saddleband like the rest of us, no! He wears pajamas of magnetized cloth, and that weights him against the cushion almost as if he lived on Earth... And this reading and studying, my word, there's nothing the lad won't think of! And his telescope! He'll sit in the cupola and focus on Earth by the hour."

"Maybe he'd like to visit Earth?"

Mrs. Blaiskell nodded. "I wouldn't be surprised if you was close on it there. The place has a horrid fascination for him. But he can't leave Abercrombie, you know."

"That's strange. Why not?"

Mrs. Blaiskell darted her a wise look. "Because then he forfeits his inheritance; that's in the original charter, that the owner must remain on the premises." She pointed to a gray door. "That there's his study. And now I'm going to give you a peep in, so you won't be tormented by curiosity and perhaps make trouble for yourself when I'm not around to keep an eye open... Now don't be excited by what you see; there's nothing to hurt you."

With the air of a priestess unveiling mystery, Mrs. Blaiskell fumbled a moment with the door-slide, manipulating it in a manner which Jean was not able to observe.

The door swung aside. Mrs. Blaiskell smirked as Jean jumped back in alarm.

"Now, now, now, don't be alarmed; I told you there was nothing to harm you. That's one of Master Earl's zoological specimens and rare trouble and expense he's gone to —"

Jean sighed deeply, and gave closer inspection to the horned black creature which stood on two legs just inside the door, poised and leaning as if ready to embrace the intruder in leathery black arms.

"That's the most scary part," said Mrs. Blaiskell in quiet satisfaction. "He's got his insects and bugs there —" she pointed "— his gems there, his old music disks there, his stamps there, his books along that cabinet. Nasty things, I'm ashamed of him. Don't let me know of you peeking in them nasty books that Mr. Earl gloats over."

"No, Mrs. Blaiskell," said Jean meekly. "I'm not interested in that kind of thing. If it's what I think it is."

Mrs. Blaiskell nodded emphatically. "It's what you think it is, and worse." She did not expand on the background of her familiarity with the library, and Jean thought it inappropriate to inquire.

Earl stood behind them. "Well?" he asked in a heavy sarcastic voice. "Getting an eyeful?" He kicked himself across the room, slammed shut the door.

Mrs. Blaiskell said in a conciliatory voice, "Now Mr. Earl, I was just showing the new girl what to avoid, what not to look at, and I didn't want her swounding of heart stoppage if innocent-like she happened to peek inside."

Earl grunted. "If she peeps inside while I'm there, she'll be 'swounding' from something more than heart stoppage."

"I'm a good cook too," said Jean. She turned away. "Come, Mrs.

Blaiskell, let's leave until Mr. Earl has recovered his temper. I won't have him hurting your feelings."

Mrs. Blaiskell stammered, "Now then! Surely there's no harm..." She stopped. Earl had gone into his study and slammed the door.

Mrs. Blaiskell's eyes glistened with thick tears. "Ah, my dear, I do so dislike harsh words..."

They worked in silence and finished the bedroom. At the door Mrs. Blaiskell said confidentially into Jean's ear, "Why do you think Earl is so gruff and grumpy?"

"I've no idea," breathed Jean. "None whatever."

"Well," said Mrs. Blaiskell warily, "it all boils down to this — his appearance. He's so self-conscious of his thinness that he's all eaten up inside. He can't bear to have anyone see him; he thinks they're sneering. I've heard him tell Mrs. Clara so. Of course they're not; they're just sorry. He eats like a horse, he takes gland-pellets, but still he's that spindly and all hard tense muscle." She inspected Jean thoughtfully. "I think we'll put you on the same kind of regimen, and see if we can't make a prettier woman out of you." Then she shook her head doubtfully, clicked her tongue. "It might not be in your blood, as Mrs. Clara says. I hardly can see that it's in your blood..."

V

There were tiny red ribbons on Jean's slippers, a red ribbon in her hair, a coquettish black beauty spot on her cheek. She had altered her rompers so that they clung unobtrusively to her waist and hips.

Before she left the room she examined herself in the mirror. *Maybe it's me that's out of step! How would I look with a couple hundred more pounds of grade? No. I suppose not. I'm the gamin type. I'll look like a wolverine when I'm sixty, but for the next forty years — watch out.*

She took herself along the corridor, past the Pleasaunce, the music rooms, the formal parlor, the refectory, up into the bedrooms. She stopped by Earl's door, flung it open, entered, pushing the electrostatic duster ahead of her.

The room was dark; the transpar walls were opaque under the action of the scrambling field.

Jean found the dial, turned up the light.

Earl was awake. He lay on his side, his yellow magnetic pajamas pressing him into the mattress. A pale blue quilt was pulled up to his shoulders, his arm lay across his face. Under the shadow of his arm his eye smouldered out at Jean.

He lay motionless, too outraged to move.

Jean put her hands on her hips, said in her clear young voice, "Get up, you sluggard! You'll get as fat as the rest of them lounging around till all hours..."

The silence was choked and ominous. Jean bent to peer under Earl's arm. "Are you alive?"

Without moving Earl said in a harsh low voice, "Exactly what do you think you're doing?"

"I'm about my regular duties. I've finished the Pleasaunce. Next comes your room."

His eyes went to a clock. "At seven o'clock in the morning?"

"Why not? The sooner I get done, the sooner I can get to my own business."

"Your own business be damned. Get out of here, before you get hurt."

"No, sir. I'm a self-determined individual. Once my work is done, there's nothing more important than self-expression."

"Get out!"

"I'm an artist, a painter. Or maybe I'll be a poet this year. Or a dancer. I'd make a wonderful ballerina. Watch." She essayed a pirouette, but the impulse took her up to the ceiling — not ungracefully, this she made sure.

She pushed herself back. "If I had magnetic slippers I could twirl an hour and a half. Grand jetés are easy..."

He raised himself on his elbow, blinking and glaring, as if on the verge of launching himself at her.

"You're either crazy — or so utterly impertinent as to amount to the same thing."

"Not at all," said Jean. "I'm very courteous. There might be a difference of opinion, but still it doesn't make you automatically right."

He slumped back on the bed. "Argue with old Webbard," he said thickly. "Now — for the last time — get out!"

"I'll go," said Jean, "but you'll be sorry."

"Sorry?" His voice had risen nearly an octave. "Why should I be sorry?"

"Suppose I took offense at your rudeness and told Mr. Webbard I wanted to quit?"

Earl said through tight lips, "I'm going to talk to Mr. Webbard today and maybe you'll be asked to quit... Miraculous!" he told himself bitterly. "Scarecrow maids breaking in at sunup..."

Jean stared in surprise. "Scarecrow! Me? On Earth I'm considered a very pretty girl. I can get away with things like this, disturbing people, because I'm pretty."

"This is Abercrombie Station," said Earl in a dry voice. "Thank God!"

"You're rather handsome yourself," said Jean tentatively.

Earl sat up, his face tinged with angry blood. "Get out of here!" he shouted. "You're discharged!"

"Pish," said Jean. "You wouldn't dare fire me."

"I wouldn't dare?" asked Earl in a dangerous voice. "Why wouldn't I dare?"

"Because I'm smarter than you are."

Earl made a husky sound in his throat. "And just what makes you think so?"

Jean laughed. "You'd be very nice, Earl, if you weren't so touchy."

"All right, we'll take that up first. Why am I so touchy?"

Jean shrugged. "I said you were nice-looking and you blew a skull-fuse." She blew an imaginary fluff from the back of her hand. "I call that touchiness."

Earl wore a grim smile that made Jean think of Fotheringay. Earl might be tough if pushed far enough. But not as tough as—well, say Ansel Clellan. Or Fiorenzo. Or Party MacClure. Or Fotheringay. Or herself, for that matter.

He was staring at her, as if he were seeing her for the first time. This is what she wanted. "Why do you think you're smarter, then?"

"Oh, I don't know... Are you smart?"

His glance darted off to the doors leading to his study; a momentary quiver of satisfaction crossed his face. "Yes, I'm smart."

"Can you play chess?"

"Of course I play chess," he said belligerently. "I'm one of the best chess players alive."

"I could beat you with one hand." Jean had played chess four times in her life.

"I wish you had something I wanted," he said slowly. "I'd take it away from you."

Jean gave him an arch look. "Let's play for forfeits."

"No!"

"Ha!" She laughed, eyes sparkling.

He flushed. "Very well."

Jean picked up her duster. "Not now, though." She had accomplished more than she had hoped for. She looked ostentatiously over her shoulder. "I've got to work. If Mrs. Blaiskell finds me here she'll accuse you of seducing me."

He snorted with twisted lips. He looked like an angry blond boar, thought Jean. But two million dollars was two million dollars. And it wasn't as bad as if he'd been fat. The idea had been planted in his mind. "You be thinking of the forfeit," said Jean. "I've got to work."

She left the room, turning him a final glance over her shoulder which she hoped was cryptic.

The servants' quarters were in the main cylinder, the Abercrombie Station proper. Jean sat quietly in a corner of the mess-hall, watching and listening while the other servants had their elevenses: cocoa gobbed heavy with whipped cream, pastries, ice cream. The talk was high-pitched, edgy. Jean wondered at the myth that fat people were languid and easygoing.

From the corner of her eye she saw Mr. Webbard float into the room, his face tight and gray with anger.

She lowered her head over her cocoa, watching him from under her lashes.

Webbard looked directly at her; his lips sucked in and his bulbous cheeks quivered. For a moment it seemed that he would drift at her, attracted by the force of his anger alone; somehow he restrained himself. He looked around the room until he spied Mrs. Blaiskell. A flick of his fingers sent him to where she sat at the end table, held by magnets appropriately fastened to her rompers.

He bent over her, muttered in her ear. Jean could not hear his words, but she saw Mrs. Blaiskell's face change and her eyes go seeking around the room.

Mr. Webbard completed his dramatization and felt better. He wiped the palms of his hands along the ample area of his dark blue corduroy trousers, twisted with a quick wriggle of his shoulders, and sent himself to the door with a flick of his toe.

Marvellous, thought Jean, the majesty, the orbital massiveness of Webbard's passage through the air. The full moon-face, heavy-lidded, placid; the rosy cheeks, the chins and jowls puffed round and tumescent, glazed and oily, without blemish, mar or wrinkle; the hemisphere of the chest, then the bifurcate lower half, in the rich dark blue corduroy: the whole marvel coasting along with the inexorable momentum of an ore barge…

Jean became aware that Mrs. Blaiskell was motioning to her from the doorway, making cryptic little signals with her fat fingers.

Mrs. Blaiskell was waiting in the little vestibule she called her office, her face scene to shifting emotions. "Mr. Webbard has given me some serious information," she said in a voice intended to be stern.

Jean displayed alarm. "About me?"

Mrs. Blaiskell nodded decisively. "Mr. Earl complained of some very strange behavior this morning. At seven o'clock or earlier…"

Jean gasped. "Is it possible, that Earl has had the audacity to —"

"*Mr.* Earl," Mrs. Blaiskell corrected primly.

"Why, Mrs. Blaiskell, it was as much as my life was worth to get away from him!"

Mrs. Blaiskell blinked uneasily. "That's not precisely the way Mr. Webbard put it. He said you —"

"Does that sound reasonable? Is that likely, Mrs. B?"

"Well — no," Mrs. Blaiskell admitted, putting her hand to her chin, and tapping her teeth with a fingernail. "Certainly it seems odd, come to consider a little more closely." She looked at Jean. "But how is it that —"

"He called me into his room, and then —" Jean had never been able to cry, but she hid her face in her hands.

"There, now," said Mrs. Blaiskell. "I never believed Mr. Webbard anyway. Did he — did he —" she found herself unable to phrase the question.

Jean shook her head. "It wasn't for want of trying."

"Just goes to show," muttered Mrs. Blaiskell. "And I thought he'd grown out of that nonsense."

" 'Nonsense'?" The word had been invested with a certain overtone that set it out of context.

Mrs. Blaiskell was embarrassed. She shifted her eyes. "Earl has passed through several stages, and I'm not sure which has been the most troublesome... A year or two ago — two years, because this was while Hugo was still alive and the family was together — he saw so many Earth films that he began to admire Earth women, and it had us all worried. Thank Heaven, he's completely thrown off that unwholesomeness, but it's gone to make him all the more shy and self-conscious." She sighed. "If only one of the pretty girls of the station would love him for himself, for his brilliant mind... But no, they're all romantic and they're more taken by a rich round body and fine flesh, and poor gnarled Earl is sure that when one of them does smile his way she's after his money, and very likely true, so I say!" She looked at Jean speculatively. "It just occurred to me that Earl might be veering back to his old — well, strangeness. Not that you're not a nice well-meaning creature, because you are."

Well, well, thought Jean dispiritedly. Evidently she had achieved not so much this morning as she had hoped. But then, every campaign had its setbacks.

"In any event, Mr. Webbard has asked that I give you different duties, to keep you from Mr. Earl's sight, because he's evidently taken an antipathy to you... And after this morning I'm sure you'll not object."

"Of course not," said Jean absently. Earl, that bigoted, warped, wretch of a boy!

"For today, you'll just watch the Pleasaunce and service the periodicals and water the atrium plants. Tomorrow — well, we'll see."

Jean nodded, and turned to leave. "One more thing," said Mrs. Blaiskell in a hesitant voice. Jean paused. Mrs. Blaiskell could not seem to find the right words.

They came in a sudden surge, all strung together. "Be a little careful of yourself, especially when you're alone near Mr. Earl. This is Abercrombie Station, you know, and he's Earl Abercrombie, and the High Justice, and some very strange things happen..."

Jean said in a shocked whisper, "Physical violence, Mrs. Blaiskell?"

Mrs. Blaiskell stammered and blushed. "Yes, I suppose you'd call it that... Some very disgraceful things have come to light. Not nice, though I shouldn't be saying it to you, who's only been with us a day. But, be careful. I wouldn't want your soul on my conscience."

"I'll be careful," said Jean in a properly hushed voice.

Mrs. Blaiskell nodded her head, an indication that the interview was at an end.

Jean returned to the refectory. It was really very nice for Mrs. Blaiskell to worry about her. It was almost as if Mrs. Blaiskell were fond of her. Jean sneered automatically. That was too much to expect. Women always disliked her because their men were never safe when Jean was near. Not that Jean consciously flirted — at least, not always — but there was something about her that interested men, even the old ones. They paid lip-service to the idea that Jean was a child, but their eyes wandered up and down, the way a young man's eyes wandered.

But out here on Abercrombie Station it was different. Ruefully Jean admitted that no one was jealous of her, no one on the entire station. It was the other way around; she was regarded as an object for pity. But it was still nice of Mrs. Blaiskell to take her under her wing; it gave Jean a pleasant warm feeling. Maybe if and when she got hold of that two million dollars — and her thoughts went to Earl. The warm feeling drained from her mind.

Earl, hoity-toity Earl, was ruffled because she had disturbed his rest. So bristle-necked Earl thought she was gnarled and stunted! Jean pulled herself to the chair. Seating herself with a thump, she seized up her bulb of cocoa and sucked at the spout.

Earl! She pictured him: the sullen face, the kinky blond hair, the overripe mouth, the stocky body he so desperately yearned to fatten. This was the man she must inveigle into matrimony. On Earth, on almost any other planet in the human universe it would be child's play —

This was Abercrombie Station!

She sipped her cocoa, considering the problem. The odds that Earl would fall in love with her and come through with a legitimate proposal seemed slim. Could he be tricked into a position where in order to save face or reputation he would be forced to marry her? Probably not. At Abercrombie Station, she told herself, marriage with her represented almost the ultimate loss of face. Still, there were avenues to be explored. Suppose she beat Earl at chess, could she make marriage the forfeit? Hardly. Earl would be too sly and dishonorable to pay up. It was necessary to make him *want* to marry her, and that would entail making herself desirable in his eyes, which in turn made necessary a revision of Earl's whole outlook. To begin with, he'd have to feel that his own person was not entirely loathsome (although it was). Earl's morale must be built up to a point where he felt himself superior to the rest of Abercrombie Station, and where he would be proud to marry one of his own kind.

A possibility at the other pole: if Earl's self-respect were so utterly blasted and reduced, if he could be made to feel so despicable and impotent that he would be ashamed to show his face outside his room, he might marry her as the best bet in sight... And still another possibility: revenge. If Earl realized that the fat girls who flattered him were actually ridiculing him behind his back, he might marry her from sheer spite.

One last possibility. Duress. Marriage or death. She considered poisons and antidotes, diseases and cures, a straightforward gun in the ribs...

Jean angrily tossed the empty cocoa bulb into the waste hopper. Trickery, sex lure, flattery, browbeating, revenge, fear—which was the most farfetched? All were ridiculous.

She decided she needed more time, more information. Perhaps Earl had a weak spot she could work on. If they had a community of interests, she'd be much farther advanced. Examination of his study might give her a few hints.

A bell chimed, a number dropped on a call-board and a voice said, "Pleasaunce."

Mrs. Blaiskell appeared. "That's you, miss. Now go in, nice as you please, and ask Mrs. Clara what it is that's wanted, and then you can go off duty till three."

VI

Mrs. Clara Abercrombie, however, was not present. The Pleasaunce was occupied by twenty or thirty young folk, talking and arguing with rather giddy enthusiasm. The girls wore pastel satins, velvets, gauzes, tight around their rotund pink bodies, with frothing little ruffles and anklets, while the young men affected elegant dark grays and blues and tawny beiges, with military trim of white and scarlet.

Ranged along a wall were a dozen stage settings in miniature. Above, a ribbon of paper bore the words '*Pandora in Elis*. Libretto by A. Percy Stevanic, music by Colleen O'Casey'.

Jean looked around the room to see who had summoned her. Earl raised his finger peremptorily. Jean walked on her magnetic shoes to where he floated near one of the miniature stage sets. He turned to a mess of cocoa and whipped cream, clinging like a tumor to the side of the set — evidently a broken bulb.

"Clean up that spill," said Earl in a flinty voice.

Jean thought, *he half-wants to rub it in, half-wants to act as if he doesn't recognize me.* She nodded dutifully. "I'll get a container and a sponge."

When she returned, Earl was across the room, talking earnestly to a girl whose globular body was encased in a gown of brilliant rose velvet. She wore rose-buds over each ear and played with a ridiculous little white dog while she listened to Earl with a half-hearted affectation of interest.

Jean worked as slowly as possible, watching from the corners of her eyes. Snatches of conversation reached her: "Lapwill's done simply a marvellous job on the editing, but I don't see that he's given Myras the same scope —" "If the pageant grosses ten thousand dollars, Mrs. Clara says she'll put another ten thousand toward the construction fund. Think of it! a Little Theater all our own!" Excited and conspiratorial whispers ran through the Pleasaunce, "— and for the water scene why not have the chorus float across the sky as moons?"

Jean watched Earl. He hung on the fat girl's words, and spoke with a pathetic attempt at intimate comradeship and jocularity. The girl nodded politely, twisted up her features into a smile. Jean noticed her eyes followed a hearty youth whose physique bulged out his plum-colored breeches like wind bellying a spinnaker. Earl perceived the girl's inattention. Jean saw him falter momentarily, then work even harder at his badinage. The fat girl licked her lips, swung her ridiculous little dog on its leash, and glanced over to where the purple-trousered youth bellowed with laughter.

A sudden idea caused Jean to hasten her work. Earl no doubt would be occupied here until lunch time—two hours away. And Mrs. Blaiskell had relieved her from duty till three.

She took herself from the hall, disposed of the cleaning equipment, dove up the corridor to Earl's private chambers. At Mrs. Clara's suite she paused, listening at the door. Snores!

Another fifty feet to Earl's chambers. She looked quickly up and down the corridor, slid back the door and slipped cautiously inside.

The room was silent as Jean made a quick survey. Closet, dressing room to one side, sun-flooded bathroom to the other. Across the room was the tall gray door into the study. A sign hung upon the door, apparently freshly made:

PRIVATE. DANGER. DO NOT ENTER.

Jean paused to consider. What kind of danger? Earl might have set devious safeguards over his private chamber.

She examined the door-slide button. It was overhung by an apparently innocent guard—which might or might not control an alarm circuit. She pressed her belt-buckle against the shutter in such a way as to maintain an electrical circuit, then moved the guard aside, pressed the button with her fingernail—gingerly. She knew of buttons which darted out hypodermics when pressed.

There was no whisper of machinery. The door remained in place.

Jean blew fretfully between her teeth. No keyhole, no buttons to play a combination on... Mrs. Blaiskell had found no trouble. Jean tried to reconstruct her motions. She moved to the slide, set her head to where she could see the reflection of the light from the wall... There was a smudge on the gloss. She looked closely and a tell-tale glint indicated a photo-electric eye.

She put her finger on the eye, pressed the slide-button. The door slipped open. In spite of having been fore-warned, Jean recoiled from the horrid black shape which hung forward as if to grapple her.

She waited. After a moment the door fell gently back into place.

Jean returned to the outer corridor, stationed herself where she could duck into Mrs. Clara's apartments if a suspicious shape came looming up the corridor. Earl might not have contented himself with the protection of a secret electric lock.

Five minutes passed. Mrs. Clara's personal maid passed by, a globular little Chinese, eyes like two shiny black beetles, but no one else.

Jean pushed herself back to Earl's room, crossed to the study door. Once more she read the sign:

PRIVATE. DANGER. DO NOT ENTER.

She hesitated. "I'm sixteen years old. Going on seventeen. Too young to die. It's just like that odd creature to furnish his study with evil tricks." She shrugged off the notion. "What a person won't do for money."

She opened the door, slipped through.

The door closed behind her. Quickly she moved out from under the poised demon-shape and turned to examine Earl's sanctum. She looked right, left, up, down.

"There's a lot to see here," she muttered. "I hope Earl doesn't run out of sheep's-eyes for his fat girl, or decide he wants a particular newspaper clipping..."

She turned power into her slipper magnets, and wondered where to begin. The room was more like a warehouse or museum than a study, and gave the impression of wild confusion arranged, sorted, and filed by an extraordinary finicky mind.

After a fashion, it was a beautiful room, imbued with an atmosphere of erudition in its dark wood-tones. The far wall glowed molten with rich color—a rose window from the old Chartres cathedral, in full effulgence under the glare of free-space sunlight.

"Too bad Earl ran out of outside wall," said Jean. "A collection of stained glass windows runs into a lot of wall space, and one is hardly a collection... Perhaps there's another room..." For the study, large as it was, apparently occupied only half the space permitted by the dimensions of Earl's suite. "But — for the moment — I've got enough here to look at."

Racks, cases, files, walnut and leaded-glass cabinets surfaced the walls; glass-topped displays occupied the floor. To her left was a battery of tanks. In the first series swam eels, hundreds of eels: Earth eels, eels from the outer worlds. She opened a cabinet. Chinese coins hung on pegs, each documented with crabbed boyish handwriting.

She circled the room, marvelling at the profusion.

There were rock crystals from forty-two separate planets, all of which appeared identical to Jean's unpracticed eye.

There were papyrus scrolls, Mayan codices, medieval parchments illuminated with gold and Tyrian purple, Ogham runes on mouldering sheepskin, clay cylinders incised with cuneiform.

Intricate wood-carvings — fancy chains, cages within cages, amazing interlocking spheres, seven nested Brahmin temples.

Centimeter cubes containing samples of every known element. Thousands of postage stamps, mounted on leaves, swung out of a circular cabinet.

There were volumes of autographs of famous criminals, together with their photographs and Bertillon and Pevetsky measurements. From one corner came the rich aromas of perfumes — a thousand little flagons minutely described and coded, together with the index and code explanation, and these again had their origin on a multitude of worlds. There were specimens of fungus growths from all over the universe, and there were racks of miniature phonograph records, an inch across, micro-formed from the original pressings.

She found photographs of Earl's everyday life, together with his weight, height and girth measurement in crabbed handwriting, and each picture bore a colored star, a colored square, and either a red or blue disk. By this time Jean knew the flavor of Earl's personality. Near at hand there would be an index and explanation. She found it, near the camera which took the pictures. The disks referred to bodily functions; the stars, by a complicated system she could not quite comprehend, described Earl's morale, his frame of mind. The colored squares recorded his love life. Jean's mouth twisted in a wry grin. She wandered aimlessly on, fingering the physiographic globes of a hundred planets and examining maps and charts.

The cruder aspects of Earl's personality were represented in a collection of pornographic photographs, and near at hand an easel and canvas where Earl was composing a lewd study of his own. Jean pursed her mouth primly. The prospect of marrying Earl was becoming infinitely less enchanting.

She found an alcove filled with little chess-boards, each set up in a game. A numbered card and record of moves was attached to each board. Jean picked up the inevitable index book and glanced through. Earl played postcard chess with opponents all over the universe. She found his record of wins and losses. He was slightly but not markedly a winner. One man, William Angelo of Toronto, beat him consistently. Jean memorized the address, reflecting that if Earl ever took up her challenge to play chess, now she knew how to beat him. She would embroil Angelo in a game, and send Earl's moves to Angelo as her own and play Angelo's return moves against Earl. It would be somewhat circuitous and tedious, but fool-proof — almost.

She continued her tour of the study. Sea-shells, moths, dragon-flies, fossil trilobites, opals, torture implements, shrunken human heads. If the collection represented bona fide learning, thought Jean, it would have taxed the time and ability of any four Earth geniuses. But the hoard was essentially mindless and mechanical, nothing more than a boy's collection of college pennants or signs or match-box covers on a vaster scale.

One of the walls opened out into an ell, and here was communication via a freight hatch to outside space. Unopened boxes, crates, cases, bundles — apparently material as yet to be filed in Earl's rookery — filled the room. At the corner another grotesque and monumental creature hung poised, as if to clutch at her, and Jean felt strangely hesitant to wander within its reach. This one stood about eight feet tall. It wore the shaggy coat of a bear and vaguely resembled a gorilla, although the face was long and pointed, peering out from under the fur, like that of a French poodle.

Jean thought of Fotheringay's reference to Earl as an 'eminent zoologist'. She looked around the room. The stuffed animals, the tanks of eels, Earth tropical fish and Maniacan polywriggles were the only zoological specimens in sight. Hardly enough to qualify Earl as a zoologist. Of course, there was an annex to the room… She heard a sound. A click at the outer door.

Jean dove behind the stuffed animal, heart thudding in her throat. With exasperation she told herself, *He's an eighteen-year-old boy… If I can't face him down, out-argue, out-think, out-fight him, and come out on top generally, then it's time for me to start crocheting table-mats for a living.* Nevertheless, she remained hidden.

Earl stood quietly in the doorway. The door swung shut behind him. His face was flushed and damp, as if he had just recovered from anger or embarrassment. His delft-blue eyes gazed unseeingly down the roof, gradually came into focus.

He frowned, glanced suspiciously right and left, sniffed. Jean made herself small behind the shaggy fur. Could he smell her?

He coiled up his legs, kicked against the wall, dove directly toward her. Under the creature's arm she saw him approaching, bigger, bigger, bigger, arms at his sides, head turned up like a diver. He thumped against the hairy chest, put his feet to the ground, stood not six feet distant.

He was muttering under his breath. She heard him plainly. "Damnable insult… If she only *knew*! *Hah*!" He laughed a loud scornful bark. *"Hah!"*

Jean relaxed with a near-audible sigh. Earl had not seen her, and did not suspect her presence.

He whistled aimlessly between his teeth, indecisively. At last he walked to the wall, reached behind a bit of ornate fretwork. A panel swung aside, a flood of bright sunlight poured through the opening into the study.

Earl was whistling a tuneless cadence. He entered the room but did not shut the door. Jean darted from behind her hiding place, looked in, swept the room with her eyes. Possibly she gasped.

Earl was standing six feet away, reading from a list. He looked up suddenly, and Jean felt the brush of his eyes.

He did not move… Had he seen her?

For a moment he made no sound, no stir. Then he came to the door, stood staring up the study, and held this position for ten or fifteen seconds. From behind the stuffed gorilla-thing Jean saw his lips move, as if he were silently calculating.

She licked her lips, thinking of the inner room.

He went out into the alcove, among the unopened boxes and bales. He pulled up several, floated them toward the open door, and they drifted into the flood of sunshine. He pushed other bundles aside, found what he was seeking, and sent another bundle after the rest.

He pushed himself back to the door, where he stood suddenly tense, nose dilated, eyes keen, sharp. He sniffed the air. His eyes swung to the stuffed monster. He approached it slowly, arms hanging loose from his shoulders.

He looked behind, expelled his breath in a long drawn hiss, grunted. From within the annex Jean thought, *he can either smell me, or it's telepathy!* She had darted into the room while Earl was fumbling among the crates, and ducked under a wide divan. Flat on her stomach she watched Earl's inspection of the stuffed animal, and her skin tingled. *He smells me, he feels me, he senses me.*

Earl stood in the doorway, looking up and down the study. Then he carefully, slowly, closed the door, threw a bolt home, turned to face into the inner room.

For five minutes he busied himself with his crates, unbundling, arranging the contents, which seemed to be bottles of white powder, on shelves.

Jean pushed herself clear of the floor, up against the under side of the divan, and moved to a position where she could see without being seen. Now she understood why Fotheringay had spoken of Earl as an 'eminent zoologist'.

There was another word which would fit him better, an unfamiliar word which Jean could not immediately dredge out of her memory. Her vocabulary was no more extensive than any girl of her own age, but the word had made an impression.

Teratology. That was the word. Earl was a teratologist.

Like the objects in his other collections, the monsters were only such creatures as lent themselves to ready, almost haphazard collecting. They were displayed in glass cabinets. Panels at the back screened off the sunlight, and at absolute zero, the things would remain preserved indefinitely without taxidermy or embalming.

They were a motley, though monstrous group. There were true human monsters, macro- and micro-cephalics, hermaphrodites, creatures with multiple limbs and with none, creatures sprouting tissues like buds on a yeast cell, twisted hoop-men, faceless things, things green, blue and gray.

And then there were other specimens equally hideous, but possibly normal in their own environment: the miscellaneity of a hundred life-bearing planets.

To Jean's eyes, the ultimate travesty was a fat man, displayed in a place of prominence! Possibly he had gained the conspicuous position on his own merits. He was corpulent to a degree Jean had not considered possible. Beside him Webbard might show active and athletic. Take this creature to Earth, he would slump like a jelly-fish. Out here on Abercrombie he floated free, bloated and puffed like the throat of a singing frog! Jean looked at his face—looked again! Tight blond curls on his head...

Earl yawned, stretched. He proceeded to remove his clothes. Stark naked he stood in the middle of the room. He looked slowly, sleepily along the ranks of his collection.

He made a decision, moved languidly to one of the cubicles. He pulled a switch.

Jean heard a faint musical hum, a hissing, smelled heady ozone. A moment passed. She heard a sigh of air. The inner door of a glass cubicle opened. The creature within, moving feebly, drifted out into the room...

Jean pressed her lips tight together; after a moment looked away.

Marry Earl? She winced. *No, Mr. Fotheringay. You marry him yourself, you're as able as I am... Two million dollars?* She shuddered. Five million sounded better. For five million she might marry him. But that's as far as it would go. She'd put on her own ring, there'd be no kissing of the bride. She was Jean Parlier, no plaster saint. But enough was enough, and this was too much.

VII

Presently Earl left the room. Jean lay still, listened. No sound came from outside. She must be careful. Earl would surely kill her if he found her here. She waited five minutes. No sound, no motion reached her. Cautiously she edged herself out from under the divan.

The sunlight burnt her skin with a pleasant warmth, but she hardly felt it. Her skin seemed stained; the air seemed tainted and soiled her throat, her lungs. She wanted a bath… Five million dollars would buy lots of baths. Where was the index? Somewhere would be an index. There had to be an index… Yes. She found it, and quickly consulted the proper entry. It gave her much meat for thought.

There was also an entry describing the revitalizing mechanism. She glanced at it hurriedly, understanding little. Such things existed, she knew. Tremendous magnetic fields streamed through the protoplasm, gripping and binding tight each individual atom, and when the object was kept at absolute zero, energy expenditure dwindled to near-nothing. Switch off the clamping field, kick the particles back into motion with a penetrating vibration, and the creature returned to life.

She returned the index to its place, pushed herself to the door.

No sound came from outside. Earl might be writing or coding the events of the day on his phonogram… Well, so then? She was not helpless. She opened the door, pushed boldly through.

The study was empty!

She dove to the outer door, listened. A faint sound of running water reached her ears. Earl was in the shower. This would be a good time to leave.

She pressed the door-slide. The door snapped open. She stepped out into Earl's bedroom, pushed herself across to the outer door.

Earl came out of the bathroom, his stocky fresh-skinned torso damp with water.

He stood stock-still, then hastily draped a towel around his middle. His face suddenly went mottled red and pink. "What are you doing in here?"

Jean said sweetly, "I came to check on your linen, to see if you needed towels."

He made no answer, but stood watching her. He said harshly, "Where have you been this last hour?"

Jean made a flippant gesture. "Here, there. Were you looking for me?"

He took a stealthy step forward. "I've a good mind to —"

"To what?" Behind her she fumbled for the door-slide.

"To —"

The door opened.

"Wait," said Earl. He pushed himself forward.

Jean slipped out into the corridor, a foot ahead of Earl's hands.

"Come back in," said Earl, making a clutch for her.

From behind them Mrs. Blaiskell said in a horrified voice, "Well, I never! Mr. Earl!" She had appeared from Mrs. Clara's room.

Earl backed into his room hissing unvoiced curses. Jean looked in after him. "The next time you see me, you'll wish you'd played chess with me."

"Jean!" barked Mrs. Blaiskell.

Earl asked in a hard voice, "What do you mean?"

Jean had no idea what she meant. Her mind raced. Better keep her ideas to herself. "I'll tell you tomorrow morning." She laughed mischievously. "About six or six-thirty."

"Miss Jean!" cried Mrs. Blaiskell angrily. "Come away from that door this instant!"

Jean calmed herself in the servants' refectory with a pot of tea.

Webbard came in, fat, pompous, and fussy as a hedgehog. He spied Jean and his voice rose to a reedy oboe tone. "Miss, miss!"

Jean had a trick she knew to be effective, thrusting out her firm young chin, squinting, charging her voice with metal. "Are you looking for me?"

Webbard said, "Yes, I certainly am. Where on earth —"

"Well, I've been looking for you. Do you want to hear what I'm going to tell you in private or not?"

Webbard blinked. "Your tone of voice is impudent, miss. If you please —"

"Okay," said Jean. "Right here, then. First of all, I'm quitting. I'm going back to Earth. I'm going to see —"

Webbard held up his hand in alarm, looked around the refectory. Conversation along the tables had come to a halt. A dozen curious eyes were watching.

"I'll interview you in my office," said Webbard.

The door slid shut behind her. Webbard pressed his rotundity into a chair; magnetic strands in his trousers held him in place. "Now what is all this? I'll have you know there've been serious complaints."

Jean said disgustedly, "Tie a can to it, Webbard. Talk sense."

Webbard was thunderstruck. "You're an impudent minx!"

"Look. Do you want me to tell Earl how I landed the job?"

Webbard's face quivered. His mouth fell open; he blinked four or five times rapidly. "You wouldn't dare to —"

Jean said patiently, "Forget the master-slave routine for five minutes, Webbard. This is man-to-man talk."

"What do you want?"

"I've a few questions I want to ask you."

"Well?"

"Tell me about old Mr. Abercrombie, Mrs. Clara's husband."

"There's nothing to tell. Mr. Justus was a very distinguished gentleman."

"He and Mrs. Clara had how many children?"

"Seven."

"And the oldest inherits the station?"

"The oldest, always the oldest. Mr. Justus believed in firm organization. Of course the other children were guaranteed a home here at the station, those who wished to stay."

"And Hugo was the oldest. How long after Mr. Justus did he die?"

Webbard found the conversation distasteful. "This is all footling nonsense," he growled in a deep voice.

"How long?"

"Two years."

"And what happened to him?"

Webbard said briskly, "He had a stroke. Cardiac complaint. Now what's all this I hear about your quitting?"

"How long ago?"

"Ah — two years."

"And then Earl inherited?"

Webbard pursed his lips. "Mr. Lionel unfortunately was off the station, and Mr. Earl became legal master."

"Rather nice timing, from Earl's viewpoint."

Webbard puffed out his cheeks. "Now then, young lady, we've had enough of that! If—"

"Mr. Webbard, let's have an understanding once and for all. Either you answer my questions and stop this blustering or I'll ask someone else. And when I'm done, that someone else will be asking you questions too."

"You insolent little trash!" snarled Webbard.

Jean turned toward the door. Webbard grunted, thrashed himself forward. Jean gave her arm a shake; out of nowhere a blade of quivering glass appeared in her hand.

Webbard floundered in alarm, trying to halt his motion through the air. Jean put up her foot, pushed him in the belly, back toward his chair.

She said, "I want to see a picture of the entire family."

"I don't have any such pictures."

Jean shrugged. "I can go to any public library and dial the Who's-Who." She looked him over coolly, as she coiled her knife. Webbard shrank back in his chair. Perhaps he thought her a homicidal maniac. Well, she wasn't a maniac and she wasn't homicidal either, unless she was driven to it. She asked easily, "Is it a fact that Earl is worth a billion dollars?"

Webbard snorted. "A billion dollars? Ridiculous! The family owns nothing but the station and lives off the income. A hundred million dollars would build another twice as big and luxurious."

"Where did Fotheringay get that figure?" she asked wonderingly.

"I couldn't say," Webbard replied shortly.

"Where is Lionel now?"

Webbard pulled his lips in and out desperately. "He's—resting somewhere along the Riviera."

"Hm... You say you don't have any photographs?"

Webbard scratched his chin. "I believe that there's a shot of Lionel... Let me see... Yes, just a moment." He fumbled in his desk, pawed and peered, and at last came up with a snap-shot. "Mr. Lionel."

Jean examined the photograph with interest. "Well, well." The face in the photograph and the face of the fat man in Earl's zoological collection were the same. "Well, well." She looked up sharply. "And what's his address?"

"I'm sure I don't know," Webbard responded with some return of his mincing dignity.

"Quit dragging your feet, Webbard."

"Oh well — the Villa Passe-temps, Juan-les-Pins."

"I'll believe it when I see your address file. Where is it?"

Webbard began breathing hard. "Now see here, young lady, there's serious matters at stake!"

"Such as what?"

"Well —" Webbard lowered his voice, glanced conspiratorially at the walls of the room. "It's common knowledge at the station that Mr. Earl and Mr. Lionel are — well, not friendly. And there's a rumor — a rumor, mind you — that Mr. Earl has hired a well-known criminal to kill Mr. Lionel."

That would be Fotheringay, Jean surmised.

Webbard continued. "So you see, it's necessary that I exercise the utmost caution..."

Jean laughed. "Let's see that file."

Webbard finally indicated a card file. Jean said, "You know where it is; pull it out."

Webbard glumly sorted through the cards. "Here."

The address was: Hotel Atlantide, Apartment 3001, French Colony, Metropolis, Earth.

Jean memorized the address, then stood irresolutely, trying to think of further questions. Webbard smiled slowly. Jean ignored him, stood nibbling her fingertips. Times like this she felt the inadequacy of her youth. When it came to action — fighting, laughing, spying, playing games, making love — she felt complete assurance. But the sorting out of possibilities and deciding which were probable and which irrational was when she felt less than sure. Such as now... Old Webbard, the fat blob, had calmed himself and was gloating. Well, let him enjoy himself... She had to get to Earth. She had to see Lionel Abercrombie. Possibly Fotheringay had been hired to kill him, possibly not. Possibly

Fotheringay knew where to find him, possibly not. Webbard knew Fotheringay; probably he had served as Earl's intermediary. Or possibly Webbard was performing some intricate evolutions of his own. It was plain that, now, her interests were joined with Lionel's, rather than Fotheringay's, because marrying Earl was clearly out of the question. Lionel must stay alive. If this meant double-crossing Fotheringay, too bad for Fotheringay. He could have told her more about Earl's 'zoological collection' before he sent her up to marry Earl... Of course, she told herself, Fotheringay would have no means of knowing the peculiar use Earl made of his specimens.

"Well?" asked Webbard with an unpleasant grin.

"When does the next ship leave for Earth?"

"The supply barge is heading back tonight."

"That's fine. If I can fight off the pilot. You can pay me now."

"Pay you? You've only done a day's work. You owe the station for transportation, your uniform, your meals —"

"Oh, never mind." Jean turned, pulled herself into the corridor, went to her room, packed her belongings.

Mrs. Blaiskell pushed her head through the door. "Oh, there you are..." She sniffed. "Mr. Earl has been inquiring for you. He wants to see you at once." It was plain that she disapproved.

"Sure," said Jean. "Right away."

Mrs. Blaiskell departed.

Jean pushed herself along the corridor to the loading deck. The barge pilot was assisting in the loading of some empty metal drums. He saw Jean and his face changed. "You again?"

"I'm going back to Earth with you. You were right. I don't like it here."

The pilot nodded sourly. "This time you ride in the storage. That way neither of us gets hurt... I couldn't promise a thing if you're up forward."

"Suits me," said Jean. "I'm going aboard."

When Jean reached the Hotel Atlantide in Metropolis she wore a black dress and black pumps which she felt made her look older and more sophisticated. Crossing the lobby she kept wary look-out for the house detective. Sometimes they nursed unkind suspicions toward unaccompanied young girls. It was best to avoid the police, keep them at a distance. When they found that she had no father, no mother, no guardian, their minds were apt to turn to some dreary government institution. On several occasions rather extreme measures to ensure her independence had been necessary.

But the Hotel Atlantide detective took no heed of the black-haired girl quietly crossing the lobby, if he saw her at all. The lift attendant observed that she seemed restless, as with either a great deal of pent enthusiasm or nervousness. A porter on the thirtieth floor noticed her searching for an apartment number and mentally labelled her a person unfamiliar with the hotel. A chambermaid watched her press the bell at Apartment 3001, saw the door open, saw the girl jerk back in surprise, then slowly enter the apartment. Strange, thought the chambermaid, and speculated mildly for a few moments. Then she went to recharge the foam dispensers in the public bathrooms, and the incident passed from her mind.

The apartment was spacious, elegant, expensive. Windows overlooked Central Gardens and the Morison Hall of Equity behind. The furnishings were the work of a professional decorator, harmonious and sterile; a few incidental objects around the room, however, hinted of a woman's presence. But Jean saw no woman. There was only herself and Fotheringay.

Fotheringay wore subdued gray flannels and dark necktie. In a crowd of twenty people he would vanish.

After an instant of surprise he stood back. "Come in."

Jean darted glances around the room, half-expecting a fat crumpled body. But possibly Lionel had not been at home, and Fotheringay was waiting.

"Well," he asked, "what brings you here?" He was watching her covertly. "Take a seat."

Jean sank into a chair, chewed at her lip. Fotheringay watched her cat-like. Walk carefully. She prodded her mind. What legitimate excuse did she have for visiting Lionel? Perhaps Fotheringay had expected her to double-cross him...Where was Hammond? Her neck tingled. Eyes were on her neck. She looked around quickly.

Someone in the hall tried to dodge out of sight. Not quickly enough.

Inside Jean's brain a film of ignorance broke to release a warm soothing flood of knowledge.

She smiled, her sharp white little teeth showing between her lips. It had been a fat woman whom she had seen in the hall, a very fat woman, rosy, flushed, quivering.

"What are you smiling at?" inquired Fotheringay.

She used his own technique. "Are you wondering who gave me your address?"

"Obviously Webbard."

Jean nodded. "Is the lady your wife?"

Fotheringay's chin raised a hair's-breadth. "Get to the point."

"Very well." She hitched herself forward. There was still a possibility that she was making a terrible mistake, but the risk must be taken. Questions would reveal her uncertainty, diminish her bargaining position. "How much money can you raise — right now? Cash."

"Ten or twenty thousand."

Her face must have showed disappointment.

"Not enough?"

"No. You sent me on a bum steer."

Fotheringay sat silently.

"Earl would no more make a pass at me than bite off his tongue. His taste in women is — like yours."

Fotheringay displayed no irritation. "But two years ago —"

"There's a reason for that." She raised her eyebrows ruefully. "Not a nice reason."

"Well, get on with it."

"He liked Earth girls because they were freaks. In his opinion, naturally. Earl likes freaks."

Fotheringay rubbed his chin, watching her with blank wide eyes. "I never thought of that."

"Your scheme might have worked out if Earl were half-way rightside up. But I just don't have what it takes."

Fotheringay smiled frostily. "You didn't come here to tell me that."

"No. I know how Lionel Abercrombie can get the station for himself… Of course your name is Fotheringay."

"If my name is Fotheringay, why did you come here looking for me?"

Jean laughed, a gay ringing laugh. "Why do you think I'm looking for you? I'm looking for Lionel Abercrombie. Fotheringay is no use to me unless I can marry Earl. I can't. I haven't got enough of that stuff. Now I'm looking for Lionel Abercrombie."

VIII

Fotheringay tapped a well-manicured finger on a well-flanneled knee, and said quietly, "I'm Lionel Abercrombie."

"How do I know you are?"

He tossed her a passport. She glanced at it, tossed it back.

"Okay. Now — you have twenty thousand. That's not enough. I want two million … If you haven't got it, you haven't got it. I'm not unreasonable. But I want to make sure I get it when you do have it … So — you'll write me a deed, a bill of sale, something legal that gives me your interest in Abercrombie Station. I'll agree to sell it back to you for two million dollars."

Fotheringay shook his head. "That kind of agreement is binding on me but not on you. You're a minor."

Jean said, "The sooner I get clear of Abercrombie the better. I'm not greedy. You can have your billion dollars. I merely want two million … Incidentally, how do you figure a billion? Webbard says the whole set-up is only worth a hundred million."

Lionel's mouth twisted in a wintry smile. "Webbard didn't include the holdings of the Abercrombie guests. Some very rich people are fat. The fatter they get, the less they like life on Earth."

"They could always move to another resort station."

Lionel shook his head. "It's not the same atmosphere. Abercrombie is Fatman's World. The one small spot in all the universe where a fat man is proud of his weight." There was a wistful overtone in his voice.

Jean said softly, "And you're lonesome for Abercrombie yourself."

Lionel smiled grimly. "Is that so strange?"

Jean shifted in her chair. "Now we'll go to a lawyer. I know a good one. Richard Mycroft. I want this deed drawn up without loopholes. Maybe I'll have to find myself a guardian, a trustee."

"You don't need a guardian."

Jean smiled complacently. "For a fact, I don't."

"You still haven't told me what this project consists of."

"I'll tell you when I have the deed. You don't lose a thing giving away property you don't own. And after you give it away, it's to my interest to help you get it."

Lionel rose to his feet. "It had better be good."

"It will be."

The fat woman came into the room. She was obviously an Earth girl, bewildered and delighted by Lionel's attentions. Looking at Jean her face became clouded with jealousy.

Out in the corridor Jean said wisely, "You get her up to Abercrombie, she'll be throwing you over for one of those fat rascals."

"Shut up!" said Lionel, in a voice like the whetting of a scythe.

The pilot of the supply barge said sullenly, "I don't know about this."

Lionel asked quietly, "You like your job?"

The pilot muttered churlishly, but made no further protest. Lionel buckled himself into the seat beside him. Jean, the horse-faced man named Hammond, two elderly men of professional aspect and uneasy manner settled themselves in the cargo hold.

The ship lifted free of the dock, pushed up above the atmosphere, lined out into Abercrombie's orbit.

The station floated ahead, glinting in the sunlight.

The barge landed on the cargo deck, the handlers tugged it into its socket, the port sighed open.

"Come on," said Lionel. "Make it fast. Let's get it over with." He tapped Jean's shoulder. "You're first."

She led the way up the main core. Fat guests floated down past them, light and round as soap-bubbles, their faces masks of surprise at the sight of so many bone-people.

Up the core, along the vinculum into the Abercrombie private sphere. They passed the Pleasaunce, where Jean caught a glimpse of Mrs. Clara, fat as a blutwurst, with the obsequious Webbard.

They passed Mrs. Blaiskell. "Why, Mr. Lionel!" she gasped. "Well, I never, I never!"

Lionel brushed past. Jean, looking over her shoulder into his face, felt a qualm. Something dark smouldered in his eyes. Triumph, malice, vindication, cruelty. Something not quite human. If nothing else, Jean was extremely human, and was wont to feel uneasy in the presence of out-world life… She felt uneasy now.

"Hurry," came Lionel's voice. "Hurry."

Past Mrs. Clara's chambers, to the door of Earl's bedroom. Jean pressed the button; the door slid open.

Earl stood before a mirror, tying a red and blue silk cravat around his bull-neck. He wore a suit of pearl-gray gabardine, cut very full and padded to make his body look round and soft. He saw Jean in the mirror, behind her the hard face of his brother Lionel. He whirled, lost his footing, drifted ineffectually into the air.

Lionel laughed. "Get him, Hammond. Bring him along."

Earl stormed and raved. He was the master here, everybody get out. He'd have them all jailed, killed. He'd kill them himself…

Hammond searched him for weapons, and the two professional-looking men stood uncomfortably in the background muttering to each other.

"Look here, Mr. Abercrombie," one of them said at last. "We can't be a party to violence…"

"Shut up," said Lionel. "You're here as witnesses, as medical men. You're being paid to look, that's all. If you don't like what you see, that's too bad." He motioned to Jean. "Get going."

Jean pushed herself to the study door. Earl called out sharply: "Get away from there, get away! That's private, that's my private study!"

Jean pressed her lips together. It was impossible to avoid feeling pity for poor gnarled Earl. But — she thought of his 'zoological collection'. Firmly she covered the electric eye, pressed the button. The door swung open, revealing the glory of the stained glass glowing with the fire of heaven.

Jean pushed herself to the furry two-legged creature. Here she waited.

Earl made some difficulty about coming through the door. Hammond manipulated his elbows; Earl belched up a hoarse screech, flung himself forward, panting like a winded chicken.

Lionel said, "Don't fool with Hammond, Earl. He likes hurting people."

The two witnesses muttered wrathfully. Lionel quelled them with a look.

Hammond seized Earl by the seat of the pants, raised him over his head, walked with magnetic shoes gripping the deck across the cluttered floor of the study, with Earl flailing and groping helplessly.

Jean fumbled in the fretwork over the panel into the annex. Earl screamed, "Keep your hands out of there! Oh, how you'll pay, how you'll pay for this, how you'll pay!" His voice hoarsened, he broke into sobs.

Hammond shook him, like a terrier shaking a rat.

Earl sobbed louder.

The sound grated on Jean's ears. She frowned, found the button, pushed. The panel flew open.

They all moved into the bright annex, Earl completely broken, sobbing and pleading.

"There it is," said Jean.

Lionel swung his gaze along the collection of monstrosities. The out-world things, the dragons, basilisks, griffins, the armored insects, the great-eyed serpents, the tangles of muscle, the coiled creatures of fang, brain, cartilage. And then there were the human creatures, no less grotesque. Lionel's eyes stopped at the fat man.

He looked at Earl, who had fallen numbly silent.

"Poor old Hugo," said Lionel. "You ought to be ashamed of yourself, Earl."

Earl made a sighing sound.

Lionel said, "But Hugo is dead... He's as dead as any of the other things. Right, Earl?" He looked at Jean. "Right?"

"I guess that's right," said Jean uneasily. She found no pleasure baiting Earl.

"Of course he's dead," panted Earl.

Jean went to the little key controlling the magnetic field.

Earl screamed, "You witch! You witch!"

Jean depressed the key. There was a musical hum, a hissing, a smell of ozone. A moment passed. There came a sigh of air. The cubicle opened with a sucking sound. Hugo drifted into the room.

He twitched his arms, gagged and retched, made a thin crying sound in his throat.

Lionel turned to his two witnesses. "Is this man alive?"

They muttered excitedly, "Yes, yes!"

Lionel turned to Hugo. "Tell them your name."

Hugo whispered feebly, pressed his elbows to his body, pulled up his atrophied little legs, tried to assume a foetal position.

Lionel asked the two men, "Is this man sane?"

They fidgeted. "That of course is hardly a matter we can determine off-hand." There was further mumbling about tests, cephalographs, reflexes.

Lionel waited a moment. Hugo was gurgling, crying like a baby. "Well — is he sane?"

The doctors said, "He's suffering from severe shock. The deep-freeze classically has the effect of disturbing the synapses —"

Lionel asked sardonically, "Is he in his right mind?"

"Well — no."

Lionel nodded. "In that case — you're looking at the new master of Abercrombie Station."

Earl protested, "You can't get away with that, Lionel! He's been insane a long time, and you've been off the station!"

Lionel grinned wolfishly. "Do you want to take the matter into Admiralty Court at Metropolis?"

Earl fell silent. Lionel looked at the doctors, who were whispering heatedly together.

"Talk to him," said Lionel. "Satisfy yourself whether he's in his right mind or not."

The doctors dutifully addressed Hugo, who made mewing sounds. They came to an uncomfortable but definite decision. "Clearly this man is not able to conduct his own affairs."

Earl pettishly wrenched himself from Hammond's grasp. "Let go of me."

"Better be careful," said Lionel. "I don't think Hammond likes you."

"I don't like Hammond," said Earl viciously. "I don't like anyone." His voice dropped in pitch. "I don't even like myself." He stood staring into the cubicle which Hugo had vacated.

Jean sensed a tide of recklessness rising in him. She opened her mouth to speak.

But Earl had already started.

Time stood still. Earl seemed to move with bewildering slowness, but the others stood as if frozen in jelly.

Time turned on for Jean. "I'm getting out of here!" she gasped, knowing what the half-crazed Earl was about to do.

Earl ran down the line of his monsters, magnetic shoes slapping on the deck. As he ran, he flipped switches. When he finished he stood at the far end of the room. Behind him things came to life.

Hammond gathered himself, plunged after Jean. A black arm apparently groping at random caught hold of his leg. There was a dull cracking sound. Hammond bawled out in terror.

Jean started through the door. She jerked back, shrieking. Facing her was the eight-foot gorilla-thing with the French-poodle face. Somewhere along the line Earl had thrown a switch relieving it from magnetic catalepsy. The black eyes shone, the mouth dripped, the hands clenched and unclenched. Jean shrank back.

There were horrible noises from behind. She heard Earl gasping in sudden fear. But she could not turn her eyes from the gorilla-thing. It drifted into the room. The black dog-eyes looked deep into Jean's. She could not move! A great black arm, groping mindlessly, fell past Jean's shoulder, touched the gorilla-thing.

There was screaming bedlam. Jean pressed herself against the wall. A green flapping creature, coiling and uncoiling, twisted out into the study, smashing racks, screens, displays, sending books, minerals, papers, mechanisms, cases and cabinets floating and crashing. The gorilla-thing came after, one of its arms twisted and loose. A rolling flurry of webbed feet, scales, muscular tail and a human body followed — Hammond and a griffin from a world aptly named 'Pest-hole'.

Jean darted through the door, thought to hide in the alcove. Outside, on the deck, was Earl's space-boat. She shoved herself across to the port.

Behind, frantically scrambling, came one of the doctors that Lionel had brought along for witnesses.

Jean called, "Over here, over here!"

The doctor threw himself into the space-boat.

Jean crouched by the port, ready to slam it at any approach of danger... She sighed. All her hopes, plans, future had exploded. Death, debacle, catastrophe were hers instead.

She turned to the doctor. "Where's your partner?"

"Dead! Oh Lord, oh Lord, what can we do?"

Jean turned her head to look at him, lips curling in disgust. Then she saw him in a new, flattering, light. A disinterested witness. He looked like money. He could testify that for at least thirty seconds Lionel had been master of Abercrombie Station. That thirty seconds was enough to transfer title to her. Whether Hugo were sane or not didn't matter because Hugo had died thirty seconds before the metal frog with the knife-edged scissor-bill had fixed on Lionel's throat.

Best to make sure. "Listen," said Jean. "This may be important. Suppose you were to testify in court. Who died first, Hugo or Lionel?"

The doctor sat quiet a moment. "Why, Hugo! I saw his neck broken while Lionel was still alive."

"Are you sure?"

"Oh yes." He tried to pull himself together. "We must do something."

"Okay," said Jean. "What shall we do?"

"I don't know."

From the study came a gurgling sound, and an instant later, a woman's scream. "God!" said Jean. "The things have gotten out into the inner bedroom... What they won't do to Abercrombie Station..." She lost control and retched against the hull of the boat.

A brown face like a poodle-dog's, spotted red with blood, peered around the corner at them. Stealthily it pulled itself closer.

Mesmerized, Jean saw that now its arm had been twisted entirely off. It darted forward. Jean fell back, slammed the port. A heavy body thudded against the metal.

They were closed in Earl's space-boat. The man had fainted. Jean said, "Don't die on me, fellow. You're worth money..."

Faintly through the metal came crashing and thumping. Then came the muffled *spatttt* of proton guns.

The guns sounded with monotonous regularity. *Spatttt... spattt... spattt... spattt... spattt...*

Then there was utter silence.

Jean inched open the port. The alcove was empty. Across her vision drifted the broken body of the gorilla-thing.

Jean ventured into the alcove, looked out into the study. Thirty feet distant stood Webbard, planted like a pirate captain on the bridge of his ship. His face was white and wadded; pinched lines ran from his nose around his nearly invisible mouth. He carried two big proton guns; the orifices of both were white-hot.

He saw Jean; his eyes took on a glitter. "You! It's you that's caused all this, your sneaking and spying!"

He jerked up his proton guns.

"No!" cried Jean, "Its not my fault!"

Lionel's voice came weakly. "Put down those guns, Webbard." Clutching his throat he pushed himself into the study. "That's the new owner," he croaked sardonically. "You wouldn't want to murder your boss, would you?"

Webbard blinked in astonishment. "Mr. Lionel!"

"Yes," said Lionel. "Home again… And there's quite a mess to clean up, Webbard…"

Jean looked at the bank book. The figures burnt into the plastic, spread almost all the way across the tape.

"$2,000,000.00."

Mycroft puffed on his pipe, looked out the window. "There's a matter you should be considering," he said. "That's the investment of your money. You won't be able to do it by yourself; other parties will insist on dealing with a responsible entity — that is to say, a trustee or a guardian."

"I don't know much about these things," said Jean. "I — rather assumed that you'd take care of them."

Mycroft reached over, tapped the dottle out of his pipe.

"Don't you want to?" asked Jean.

Mycroft said with a compressed distant smile. "Yes, I want to… I'll be glad to administer a two million dollar estate. In effect, I'll become your legal guardian, until you're of age. We'll have to get a court order of appointment. The effect of the order will be to take control of the money out of your hands; we can include in the articles, however, a clause guaranteeing you the full income — which I assume is what you want. It should come to — oh, say fifty thousand a year after taxes."

"That suits me," said Jean listlessly. "I'm not too interested in anything right now... There seems to be something of a let-down."

Mycroft nodded. "I can see how that's possible."

Jean said, "I have the money. I've always wanted it, now I have it. And now —" she held out her hands, raised her eyebrows. "It's just a number in a bank book... Tomorrow morning I'll get up and say to myself, 'What shall I do today? Shall I buy a house? Shall I order a thousand dollars worth of clothes? Shall I start out on a two year tour of Argo Navis?' And the answer will come out, 'No, the hell with it all.'"

"What you need," said Mycroft, "are some friends, nice girls your own age."

Jean's mouth moved in rather a sickly smile. "I'm afraid we wouldn't have much in common... It's probably a good idea, but — it wouldn't work out." She sat passively in the chair, her wide mouth drooping.

Mycroft noticed that in repose it was a sweet generous mouth.

She said in a low voice, "I can't get out of my head the idea that somewhere in the universe I must have a mother and a father..."

Mycroft rubbed his chin. "People who'd abandon a baby in a saloon aren't worth thinking about, Jean."

"I know," she said in a dismal voice. "Oh Mr. Mycroft, I'm so damn lonely..." Jean was crying, her head buried in her arms.

Mycroft irresolutely put his hand on her shoulder, patted awkwardly.

After a moment she said, "You'll think I'm an awful fool."

"No," said Mycroft gruffly. "I think nothing of the kind. I wish that I..." He could not put it into words.

She pulled herself together, rose to her feet. "Enough of this..." She turned his head up, kissed his chin. "You're really very nice, Mr. Mycroft... But I don't want sympathy. I hate it. I'm used to looking out for myself."

Mycroft returned to his seat, loaded his pipe to keep his fingers busy. Jean picked up her little hand-bag. "Right now I've got a date with a couturier named André. He's going to dress me to an inch of my life. And then I'm going to —" She broke off. "I'd better not tell you. You'd be alarmed and shocked."

He cleared his throat. "I expect I would."

She nodded brightly. "So long." Then left his office.

Mycroft cleared his throat again, hitched up his trousers, settled his jacket, returned to his work... Somehow it appeared dull, drab, gray. His head ached.

He said, "I feel like going out and getting drunk..."

Ten minutes passed. His door opened. Jean looked in.

"Hello, Mr. Mycroft."

"Hello, Jean."

"I changed my mind. I thought it would be nicer if I took you out to dinner, and then maybe we could go to a show... Would you like that?"

"Very much," said Mycroft.

Cholwell's Chickens

I

Mr. Mycroft ran a hand through his gray hair and said in a wry voice, "I make no pretense of understanding you."

In the big leather chair reserved for the relaxation of Mycroft's high-strung clients Jean fidgeted, stretched her fingers, examined the backs of her hands. "I don't even understand myself."

Through the window she watched a tomato-red Marshall Moon-chaser fleeting along the blue April sky. "Money hasn't affected me quite the way I expected... I've always wanted a little boat like that. I could buy a dozen if I liked, but —" she shook her head, eyes still out in the blue distance.

Mycroft recalled the first time he had seen her: wary and wild, characterized by a precocious feral quality, a recklessness that made ordinary women seem pastel and insipid. Mycroft smiled grimly. He could hardly say that she had become dull. She still had her elan, her fey charm. She was jet and ivory and pale rose; her mouth was wide and flexible, her little teeth were white and sharp; she carried herself with a swash-buckling fervor — but something was gone, and not necessarily for the worse.

"Nothing's like what I thought it would be," said Jean. "Clothes..." She looked down at her dark green slacks, her black pullover sweater. "These are good enough. Men..." Mycroft watched her attentively. "They're all the same, silly jackasses."

Mycroft made a small involuntary grimace, settled himself in his chair. At fifty he was three times her age.

"The lovers are bad," said Jean, "but I'm used to them, I've never lacked there. But the other ones, the financiers, the sharp-shooters — they upset me. Like spiders."

Mycroft made haste to explain. "It's inevitable. They're after anyone with wealth. Cranks — promoters — confidence men — they won't leave you alone. Refer them to me. As your guardian I can dispose of them quickly."

"When I was poor," said Jean mournfully, "I wanted so many things. And now —" she swung out her arms in a gesture of abandon "— I can buy and buy and buy. And I don't want anything. I can have anything I want, and it's almost as if I had it already... I'd rather like to make some more money... I guess what I've got is like the first taste of blood to a wolf."

Mycroft sat back in alarm. "My dear girl, that's the occupational disease of old men! Not for a —"

Jean said fretfully, "You act, Mr. Mycroft, as if I'm not human." This was true; Mycroft instinctively behaved toward Jean as he might toward a beautiful, alarming and unpredictable animal.

"It's not that I especially want more money... I suppose the fact is that I'm bored."

Worse and worse, thought Mycroft. Bored people got into mischief. Desperately he searched his mind. "Ah — there's always the theater. You could finance a production and perhaps you'd like to act in it yourself?"

"Pish," said Jean. "Bunch of fakers!"

"You might go to school?"

"It sounds very tiring, Mr. Mycroft."

"I suppose it would be..."

"I'm not the scholastic type. And there's something else on my mind. It's probably foolish and pointless, but I can't seem to get away from it. I'd like to know about my father and mother... I've always felt bitter toward them — but suppose I have been kidnaped or stolen? If that were the case, they'd be glad to see me."

Mycroft privately considered such a possibility unlikely. "Well, that's perfectly normal and natural. We'll put an investigator on the trail. As I recall, you were abandoned in a saloon on one of the outer worlds."

Jean's eyes had become hard and bright. "At Joe Parlier's Aztec Tavern. Angel City on Codiron."

"Codiron," said Mycroft. "Yes, I know that district very well. As I recall, it's not a large world nor very populous."

"If it's like it was when I left — which was seven years ago — it's backward and old-fashioned. But never mind the investigator. I'd like to look around myself."

Mycroft opened his mouth to cluck disapproval when the door slid back and Ruth, Mycroft's receptionist, looked in.

"Dr. Cholwell to see you." She glanced sharply sidewise at Jean.

"Cholwell?" grunted Mycroft. "I wonder what he wants."

"He said that you arranged to have lunch with him."

"Yes, that's right. Show him in."

With a final hard glance at Jean, Ruth left the room.

Jean said, "Ruth doesn't like me."

Mycroft moved in his chair, embarrassed. "Don't mind her. She's been with me close to twenty years … I suppose the sight of a pretty girl in my office disturbs her sense of fitness. Especially —" his ears colored "— one that I take such an interest in."

Jean smiled faintly. "Someday I'll let her find me sitting in your lap."

"No," said Mycroft, arranging the papers on his desk. "I don't think you'd better."

Cholwell came briskly into the room — a man Mycroft's age, lean, bright-eyed, elegant in a jerky bird-like manner. He had a sharp chin, a handsome ruff of silver-gray hair, a long sensitive nose. He was precisely dressed, and on his finger Jean glimpsed the golden orb insignia of the Space-Dwellers Association.

Jean looked away, aware that she did not like Cholwell.

Cholwell stared at Jean, patently amazed. His mouth fell open. He took a short step forward. "What are you doing here?" he asked harshly.

Jean looked at him with wonder. "I'm just talking to Mr. Mycroft … Does it matter?"

Cholwell closed his eyes, shook his head as if he were about to faint.

II

Cholwell sank into a chair. "Excuse me," he muttered. "I need a pill … It's my little trouble — souvenir of a chlorosis bout in the Mendassir sloebanks." He stole another look at Jean, then pulled his eyes away. His lips moved as if he were silently reciting verse.

Mycroft said tartly, "My ward, Miss Parlier. Dr. Cholwell."

Cholwell regained his composure. "I'm charmed to make your acquaintance." He turned to Mycroft. "You never mentioned such a lovely young obligation."

"Jean's a recent addition. The court appointed me to take care of her money." He said to Jean, "Cholwell hails from your corner of space, at least the last I knew." He turned back to Cholwell. "You're still out at the Rehabilitation Home?"

Cholwell tore his eyes away from Jean. "Not precisely. Yes and no. I live on the old premises, but the Home has been abandoned — oh, a long time."

"Why in heaven's name do you hang on then? As I recall, it's a God-forsaken bleak hole."

Cholwell complacently shook his head. "I don't find it so. The scenery is grand, monumental. And then — well, I have a little venture which keeps me busy."

"Venture?"

Cholwell looked out the window. "I'm, ah, raising chickens. Yes." He nodded. "Chickens." His gaze alternated between Jean and Mycroft. "Indeed, I can offer you opportunity for an excellent investment."

Mycroft grunted. Cholwell continued easily.

"No doubt you've heard tales of a hundred percent profit and thought them pretty wild. Well, naturally I can't go quite that far. To be utterly frank, I'm not sure just what will eventuate. Perhaps nothing. My operation is still experimental; I'm short of capital, you see."

Mycroft stuffed his pipe with tobacco. "You've come to the wrong place, Cholwell." He struck a match, puffed. "But — out of curiosity — just what is your operation?"

Cholwell wet his lips, gazed an instant at the ceiling. "Well, it's modest enough. I've evolved a strain of chickens which prospers remarkably. I want to erect a modern plant. With the proper backing I can deliver chickens around all the Orion Circuit at a price no domestic supplier can meet."

Jean said doubtfully, "I should think that Codiron would be too cold and windy for chickens."

Cholwell shook his head. "I'm in a warm spot under the Balmoral Mountains. One of the old Trotter sites."

"Oh."

"What I'm leading up to is this. I want to take you out on an inspection tour of the premises and you can see for yourself. There'll be no obligation, none whatever."

Mycroft leaned back, looked Cholwell coolly up and down. "Isn't this rather an impulsive offer?"

Jean said, "I've been thinking of going out to Angel City for a visit —"

Mycroft rattled papers on his desk. "It sounds good, Cholwell. I hope you make out. But I've tied Jean's funds up in conservative stuff. She finds her income completely adequate. As far as I'm concerned personally, I'm lucky to pay the rent. So —"

"Of course, of course," said Cholwell. "I'm too hasty, too enthusiastic. It runs away with me at times." He rubbed his chin with his fingers. "You're acquainted with Codiron, Miss Parlier?"

"I was born in Angel City."

Doctor Cholwell nodded. "Not far from my own holdings... When do you plan to make your visit? Perhaps I could..." His voice faded politely, as if he were proffering anything Jean could lay her mind to.

"I'm not sure when I'll be going out... In the near future."

Cholwell nodded. "Well, I'll hope to see you again, and perhaps show you around and explain the scope of my work, and then —"

Jean shook her head. "I'm not really interested in chickens — except in the eating line. And anyway Mr. Mycroft has been put in charge of my money. I'm a minor, I'm not supposed to be responsible. So charm Mr. Mycroft, don't waste it on me."

Cholwell took no offense. He nodded gravely. "Well, it's definitely a speculation, and I know Mycroft has to be careful." He looked at his watch. "What about lunch, Mycroft?"

"I'll meet you downstairs in ten minutes."

Cholwell rose to his feet. "Good." He bowed to Jean. "It's been a pleasure meeting you."

After he had departed, Mycroft sank back into his chair, puffed reflectively at his pipe. "Rather an odd chap, old Cholwell. There's a good brain under that fancy exterior, although you wouldn't expect it... It sounds as if he might have a good proposition with his chickens."

"Codiron's awfully windy and cold," said Jean doubtfully. "A planet like Emeraud or Beau Aire would be better." She considered the far worlds, and all the strange sights, colors, sounds, the mysterious ruins, the bizarre peoples, came rushing into her mind.

In sudden excitement she jumped to her feet. "Mr. Mycroft, I'm going to leave on the next packet."

"That's tonight."

Jean's face fell. "The next after, then."

Mycroft expressionlessly knocked the charge out of his pipe. "I know better than to interfere."

Jean patted his shoulder. "You're really a nice man, Mr. Mycroft. I wish I were as nice as you are."

Looking into the glowing face, Mycroft knew that there would be no more work for him this day.

"Now I've got to run," said Jean. "I'll go right down and book passage." She stretched. "Oh heavens, Mr. Mycroft, I feel better already!"

She left the office, gay and swift as the red Moon-chaser which she had watched across the sky.

Mycroft silently put away his papers, rose to his feet, bent over the communicator.

"Ruth, if there's anything urgent I'll be at the club this afternoon, probably in the steam room."

Ruth nodded indignantly to herself. "Little minx! Why won't she stay away, keep to herself? Poor old Mycroft..."

III

A community fading from life is a dismal place. The streets become barren of people; the air swims clear overhead with lifeless serenity; the general aspect is between gray and dirty brown. Buildings fall into disrepair: piers crumble, trusses sag, windows gape with holes like black starfish.

The poor sections are abandoned first. The streets become pocked and pitted and littered with bits of yellow paper. The more prosperous districts coast on the momentum of the past, but only a few very old and a few very young people are left, the old with their memories, the young with their wistful daydreams. In attics and storerooms, old gear falls apart, releasing odors of varnish and wood, musty cloth and dry paper.

All during Jean's childhood, Angel City had been succumbing to moribundity and decay. Nearby three old volcanic necks, El Primo, El Panatela, El Tiempo, loomed clumsily on the silver Codiron sky. At one time the rotting shale at their bases had glittered with long hexagonal crystals. These possessed the singular property of converting sound into quick colored flashes of light. In the early times miners went forth at night to fire off guns, and stand watching the swift sparkle responding in a wave down the distance.

With the mines prosperity came to Angel City. Fortunes were founded, ripened, spent. Houses were built, a spaceport established with adequate warehouses, and Angel City became a typical back-planet settlement — like thousands of others in many respects, but still one to itself, with the unique flavor that made it Angel City. The sun Mintaka Sub-30 was a tiny disk of dazzling blue-white, the sky showed the color of black pearl. Earth vegetation refused the Codiron soil, and instead of geraniums, zinnia, pansies, petunias, growing around the white houses, there were mogadors, pilgrim vine with fluttering bumble-bee fruits, yeasty banks with great masses of bear-fungus.

Then one by one, like a clan of old men dying, the mines gave out and closed — quietly, apologetically, and Angel City started on its route to dissolution. The miners left town, the easy-money emporiums closed their doors, paint began peeling from the back-street houses.

But now a wild variable entered the picture: Lake Arkansas.

It spread from Angel City out to the horizon, rusty-green and smooth as a table-top, crusted with two feet of algae, brittle and tough enough to support considerable weight. Idle men looked across the flatness, and thought of wheat: North Africa, the Great Plains, the Ukraine. Botanists were called in from Earth and not only evolved strains of wheat to thrive on Codiron's mineral balance, to resist Codiron's soil viruses, but also corn, cane, citrus, melons and garden truck.

The course of Angel City's development altered. And when the wheezing taxi-boat lifted from the space-port and slanted down over Tobacco Butte, Jean was immeasurably surprised. Where she had remembered raffishness and grime she found a neat farming community, clean and apparently prosperous.

The pilot turned in his seat. "Where will I take you, miss?"

"To the hotel. Is it still Polton's Inn?"

The pilot nodded. "There's Polton's and then there's a new place downtown, the Soone House, sort of posh and expensive."

"Take me to Polton's," said Jean. It was no part of her plan to be conspicuous.

The pilot turned her an appraising glance. "You've been here before, seems like."

Jean bit her lip in annoyance. She wanted to be known as a stranger; she did not care to be associated with four dead men of seven years ago. "My father worked in the mines and he's told me about Angel City."

In all probability she was safe from recognition. Four deaths in the Angel City of seven years ago would have caused a week's sensation and then passed out of mind, to be blended with a hundred other killings. No one would think to connect Miss Alice Young, as she had decided to call herself, with the ragged wide-eyed creature that had been Jean Parlier at the age of ten. However — it was just as well to play safe. "Yes, I'll go to Polton's," said Jean.

Polton's Inn was a long ramshackle shed-roof building on a little rise overlooking the town, with a wide verandah and the front overgrown with blue pilgrim vine. In the first days of Angel City it had served as a bunk-house for miners; then as conditions became settled, Polton had added a few refinements and set himself up as innkeeper. In Jean's recollection he was a bent crabbed old man whose eyes seemed always to search the ground. He had never married and did all his own work, scorning even a scullery boy.

The pilot dropped the boat to the packed soil in front of Polton's office, turned to help, but Jean had already jumped like a cat to the ground. She ran up on the verandah, forgetting her determination to act the sedate young lady.

Polton was standing on a corner of the verandah, even more bent and crabbed than Jean had remembered.

"Well," he said in a rasping ugly voice, "you're back again. You've got your nerve with you."

Jean stared at him, drained of feeling. She opened her mouth to speak, but found no words.

"You pick up your grip," said Polton, "and get on out of here. I'm running a hotel, not a madhouse. Maybe that new place downtown will put up with your hijinks. Me, I'm once bitten, then I'm shy twice."

It came to Jean that he couldn't possibly remember her from seven years back; he must be confusing her with a more recent guest. She noticed that his cheeks, near the outside corner of each eye, bulged with the tiny artificial reservoirs for aqueous humor; by contracting his cheek muscles he could pump fluid into his eyeball, thus correcting for far-sightedness. The fact seemed to indicate that his sight was not the best. Jean said with an air of sweet reason, "Mr. Polton, you're mistaking me for someone else."

"Oh no I'm not," snapped Polton, raising his lip in wolfish looseness. "I got your name on the register if you want to look. Miss Sunny Mathison you call yourself, and your fingerprints too — they show who you are."

"It wasn't me!" cried Jean. "My name is Alice Young!"

Polton made a scornful sound. "I've just spent four hundred dollars to put pumps into my old eyes. I can see like a telescope. Do you think I'm making a mistake? I don't... Now clear off the premises. I don't want your kind around here." He stood there glowering at her, until she turned away.

Jean shrugged, stepped forlornly back into the cab.

The pilot said sympathetically, "Old Polton's half-cracked, that's well-known. And the Soone House is a lot better place anyhow..."

"Okay," said Jean, "let's try the Soone House."

The cab coasted down from the height. Before them spread first the town, then Lake Arkansas, an unfamiliar checker of yellow, dark green, light green, brown and black, and finally, rising from the horizon, the steel backdrop of the sky. The blue-hot spark of Mintaka Sub-30 hung at high noon, glittered in the cab's plastic canopy and into the corner of Jean's eye.

She traced out the familiar patterns of the town: Central Square, with the concrete dance pavilion, the blue-painted courthouse and jail, with Paradise Alley ducking furtively behind. And that angular brown façade almost out at the edge of town — that was Joe Parlier's old Aztec Tavern.

IV

The cab settled to a plat at the rear of the new Soone House, and the pilot carried Jean's modest luggage to the side entrance. The hotel was obviously new, and made superficial pretensions to luxury, achieving only a rather ridiculous straddle between metropolitan style and the hard fact of its location in a small back-planet town. There was a fine floor of local moss agate and hand-padded mosaic-rugs from one of the cheap-labor planets, a dozen Earth palms in celadon pots. But there was no lift to the second and third floors and the porter's shoes were noticeably scuffed.

The lobby was empty except for the clerk and a man who stood talking with apparent urgency. Jean stopped short in the doorway. The man was lean and bird-like, wore his clothes with something of the same elegance that the hotel wore its mosaic rugs and Earth palms. Cholwell.

Jean calculated. It was evident that he had come out on a faster ship than hers, possibly the mail express. While she hesitated, Cholwell turned, looked at her, looked once again. His mouth snapped shut, his eyebrows met in a stiff angry bar. He took three strides forward and Jean ducked back, thinking he meant to strike her.

Cholwell said in a furious voice, "I've been looking all over town for you!"

Jean's curiosity was greater than her alarm and anger. "Well — here I am. What of it?"

Cholwell looked past her, out into the street, breathing hard controlled breaths. "You came alone?"

Jean said with narrowed eyes, "What business is it of yours?"

Cholwell blinked and his mouth set in an ugly spiteful line.

"When I get you back at the compound I'll show you what business it is of mine!"

Jean said icily, "Just what in the world are you talking about?"

"What's your name?" Cholwell cried furiously. "Let me see your—" he snatched her arm, turned over her hand, looked at the underside of her wrist.

He stared in unbelief, looked into her face, stared back at her wrist.

Jean pulled away. "Are you crazy? Life among the chickens seems to have rattled you!"

"Chickens?" He frowned. "Chickens?" His face went void of expression. "Oh... Of course. How stupid. You're Miss Jean Parlier, and you're visiting Angel City... I didn't expect you for another week—the next packet."

"Who did you think I was?" she asked resentfully.

Cholwell cleared his throat. Anger had given way to solicitous courtesy with startling swiftness. "It's a combination of poor vision and poor lighting. I have a niece close to your age and for a moment—" he paused delicately.

Jean glanced at her wrist. "How is it that you're not acquainted with her name?"

Cholwell said easily, "It's a little joke we have between us." He laughed self-consciously. "One of those foolish family jokes, you know."

"I wonder if it was your niece that got me slung out of old Polton's place."

Cholwell became rigid. "What did Polton say?"

"He insisted that he was running a hotel, not a madhouse. He said he wouldn't put up with any more of my 'hijinks'."

Cholwell's fingers fluttered up and down his coat. "Old Polton, I'm afraid, is more than a little contentious." A new expression came to his face, eager gallantry. "Now that you're here on Codiron, I can't wait to show you my establishment. You and—my niece will surely become fast friends."

"I'm not so sure. We're too much alike, if old Polton is hitting at all close to the truth."

Cholwell made a sound of protestation in his throat.

Jean asked, "Just what is your niece's name, Mr. Cholwell?"

Cholwell hesitated. "It's Martha. And I'm sure Polton was exaggerating. Martha is quiet and gentle." He nodded emphatically. "I can depend on Martha."

Jean shrugged. And now Cholwell appeared to be lost in thought. He moved his elbows restlessly in and out from his body, nodded his head. At last he appeared to reach a decision. "I must be on my way, Miss Parlier. But I'll look you up on my next visit into Angel City." He bowed, departed.

Jean turned to the clerk. "I want a room... Does Mr. Cholwell come to town very often?"

"No-o-o," said the clerk hesitantly. "Not as often as he might."

"And his niece?"

"We see even less of her. In fact," the clerk coughed, "you might say we seldom see her."

Jean looked at him sharply. "Have you ever seen her?"

The clerk coughed again. "Well—actually no... Myself, I think Mr. Cholwell would be wiser to move into town, perhaps take a nice suite here at the hotel."

"Why so?"

"Well—Cornwall Valley is very wild, up under the Balmoral Mountains, very wild and primitive, now that they've abandoned the old Rehabilitation Home. No one near him for miles, in case of emergency..."

"Odd place for a chicken ranch," suggested Jean.

The clerk shrugged, as if to emphasize that it was not his place to gossip about patrons of the hotel. "Did you wish to register?"

V

Jean changed from her gray travel gabardines into quiet dark blue and wandered along Main Street. There was a new spirit in the air, but under a few cosmetic applications of glass and stainless metal, Angel City was almost as she remembered it. Faces passed that she seemed to recognize from the old days, and one or two of these faces regarded her curiously—inconclusive in itself; she was accustomed to the feel of eyes.

At the old city courthouse and jail, a building of solid blue-painted stone-foam from the early days, she turned to the right down Paradise Alley. A small constriction formed in her throat; this was the scene of her ragged and miserable youth...

"Pish," said Jean. "Enough of this sentimentality. Although I suppose it's for a sentimental reason that I'm here in the first place. Why bother with a father and mother otherwise?" She considered herself in the light of a sentimentalist, with detached amusement, then returned to the eventual discovery of her parents. "It's likely I'll stir up trouble. If they're poor they'll expect me to support them..." She smiled, and her little teeth gleamed. "They'll expect quite a while." It occurred to her that perhaps malice was at the bottom of her mission: she pictured herself confronting a sullen man and woman, and flaunting her prosperity. "You dropped two million dollars when you dropped me on Joe Parlier's pool table."

But more likely than not, her parents, together or on their separate ways, had vanished off among the illimitable dark vistas of the human universe; then it became a problem of following a seventeen-year-old trail among the stars and planets...Joe Parlier might have told her of her parentage; more than once he had hinted of his knowledge. But Joe Parlier was dead, seven years dead, and Jean felt no slightest pang of regret. Sober he had been surly and heavy-handed; drunk, he was lascivious, wild and dangerous.

When she was nine he had started to handle her; soon she learned to hide under the saloon whenever she saw him drink. Once he had tried to follow her, crawling on his stomach. With an old chair leg she beat at his sweating face, jabbed at his eyes, until mad with rage he backed out to find his gun. She had scurried to another hiding place, and returned to her garret because there was no other place for her to go.

Next morning he had slouched up to her, his face still scratched and bruised. She had a knife and stood her ground, pale, set, desperate. But he kept his distance, railing, taunting. "Sure you're a little devil and sure I'm the only pa you got—but I know more'n I let on. And anytime there comes a showdown I know where to go. I can bring it home too, and then it'll go hard on someone."

But she had killed Joe Parlier with his own gun, Joe and three of his drunken cronies, before he had ever told what he knew.

Down Paradise Alley she walked, and there it was ahead of her, Joe Parlier's saloon, the old Aztec Tavern, and changed by not a line or a board. The paint was duller and the swinging doors more battered, but even out in the street the smell of tobacco, beer, wine and spirits brought back hard and clear the first ten years of her life. She raised her eyes, up to the window under the gable—her private little outlook, down into the street and across to Dion Mulroney's second-hand store.

Joe Parlier was dead, but he had spoken of proof and tapped his old brown wallet with heavy significance. Perhaps his effects had not been destroyed, and here would be her first goal.

She slipped demurely into the saloon.

There were a few minor changes, but in general the tavern was as she remembered it. The bar ran down the room to the left; behind were six large color transparencies set into the wall like stained glass windows. Each depicted a nude woman in an artistic pose against a background intended to represent outworld scenery. A crudely painted legend above read, 'Beauty Among the Planets'.

Tables occupied the right side of the room; above on a shelf were dusty photographs of space-ships and models of the four Gray Line packets serving Codiron: the *Bucyrus*, the *Orestes*, the *Prometheus* and the *Icarus*. At the back were the two dilapidated pool tables, a line of mechanical game machines, a vendor of dry stimulants and narcotics, and a juke-box.

Jean anxiously scanned the faces along the bar, but recognized none of the old-time habitués. She slid up on a seat near the door.

The bartender wiped his hands on his towel, elevated his jaw, strode toward her. He was a striking young man with dark brown skin and crisp wheat-blond hair. He evidently thought well of his aquiline profile and emphasized his muscular torso by the tight fit of his shirt. Vain, silly, single-minded, thought Jean; no doubt fancied himself as a lady-killer with his magnificent dark skin and bright hair.

He swaggered to a stop before her, looked her over with heavy-lidded eyes. Along the bar, faces turned, the hum of conversation halted.

The young bartender said, "What'll it be?"

"Just plain lemon fizz."

He leaned confidentially closer. "I'll let you in on a little secret. Better take orange."

"Why?" Jean asked breathlessly.

"We don't have no lemon." And he slapped the towel into his hand.

"Okay." Jean nodded. "Orange."

Ten minutes later he had made a date. His name was Gem Morales, he lived at Hot-shot Carlson's, and he worked day shift at the Aztec.

Jean said that she had lost her way; she had been trying to find her uncle, but somehow had missed him.

"Oh," said Gem Morales, who had been wondering.

Jean rose to leave, and put a dime on the counter. Gem flipped it into the cash-drawer. "Eight o'clock, don't forget."

Jean forced a bright smile. Normally she liked handsome young men. She admired hard young bodies, the feel of muscular hands, breezy masculine egos. But Gem Morales jarred her. He was cocksure, flip and brassy, without the redeeming qualities of intelligence and humor.

VI

He arrived to keep his date a studious twenty minutes late, and swaggered across the lobby to where she sat reading a magazine. He wore an extreme suit of fawn plion, with copper piping; Jean was in modest dark blue and white.

He took her to a smart little air-boat four or five years old, and she saw with a twinge of wry amusement that it was a Marshall Moonchaser of the model she herself coveted. Darn it, back on Earth, first thing she'd do would be to buy herself a shiny new air-boat.

"Jump in, honey. We fly high, fly low, we got half a planet to cover, and there's only fourteen hours to Codiron night."

The boat growled up with a lunge that pressed Jean back into the foam, then levelled off and flew through the iron-colored night. Directly above hung Codiron's lone satellite, small bright Sadiron. Below were the black buttes, the desolate mountains, the tundras wadded over with olive-drab bear-fungus. Once they skimmed over a dreary little settlement, marked by a line of yellow lights; a few minutes later a faint glow in the south indicated the location of Delta, Codiron's largest city.

"Gem," said Jean, "is your home here in Angel City?"

He snorted with indignation. "Me? Here? Gad! I should say not. I'm from Brackstell on Alnitak Five."

"How come you're out here then?"

He jerked his shoulders flippantly. "Got into a little trouble. Guy figured I wasn't as tough as I said I was. He was wrong, I was right."

"Oh."

He slipped his arm around her. She said, "Gem, I need help."

"Sure, anything you say. But later. Let's talk about us."

"No, Gem, I'm serious."

He made a cautious inquiry. "How do you mean, help? What can I do?"

She wove him a tale with overtones of the illicit strong enough to arouse his interest. She had discovered, so she said, that the old owner of the Aztec, Joe Parlier, had owned bonds which he considered valueless. Actually they were worth a great deal, and were supposed to be somewhere among his effects. She wanted an opportunity to look for them.

Gem's pleasure was disturbed by the thought that Jean's presence was not the direct result of his appearance and personality. Half-sullenly he jerked the Moon-chaser down toward a high mountain-top spangled with blue, green and red lights.

"Skylark Haven," he said. "Pretty nice place — for Codiron, that is. The live ones come here from all over the planet."

Skylark Haven indeed appeared gay and popular. A hexagonal pylon reared fifty feet into the air, shimmering with waves of color, a representation of the sound-light crystals by which Codiron was known. The shifting colors reflected garishly from the hulls, domes and canopies of air-boats parked beside the building.

Gem seized Jean's arm, strode across the outside terrace, holding his aquiline profile pridefully out-thrust. Jean trotted along beside, half-amused, half-exasperated.

They entered the building through an arch in a great wall of bear-fungus, smelling pleasantly pungent. A man in black ushered them into a little circular booth with a flourish. As they seated themselves the booth moved slowly off, circling and twisting with silken smoothness on a long eccentric circuit of the room.

A waitress in translucent black slid up on power-skates. "Old-fashioned," said Gem. "Lemon fizz," said Jean.

Gem raised his eyebrows. "Gad! Take a drink! That's what you're here for!"

"I don't like to drink."

"Pah!" said Gem scornfully.

Jean shrugged. Plainly Gem considered her something of a blue-stocking... If she liked him better, it would have been fun letting him discover otherwise. But he was not only arrogant, he was callow to boot.

An attendant came offering power-skates for rent. Gem looked at Jean challengingly. She shook her head. "I'm too clumsy. I fall all over myself."

"It's easy," said Gem. "Look at those two —" he pointed to a couple dancing with easy effortless sweeps and circles. "You'll catch on. It's easy. Just turn your toe where you want to go, press a little and you're there. The harder you press, the faster you move. To stop, you press on your heel."

Jean shook her head. "I'd rather just sit here and talk."

"About those bonds?"

She nodded. "If you help me, I'll cut you in for a third."

He pursed his lips, narrowed his eyes. Jean realized that he was considering the feasibility of three thirds rather than one.

"Joe Parlier loaded up on lots of junk," said Jean carelessly. "Some of the bonds were stolen, and whoever presented them would have a lot of explaining to do. I know which are valuable and safe."

"Mmmph." Gem drank his Old-fashioned.

Jean said, "I don't know who owns the Aztec now; for all I know all Joe's things might have been burnt up."

"I can set you right there," said Gem thoughtfully. "The attic's full of old junk, and Godfrey says it's all left over Parlier. He's been going to clean it out but never gets around to it."

Jean drank her lemon fizz to hide her excitement. "What time does the place open?"

"Ten o'clock. I open up. I'm the day man."

"Tomorrow," said Jean, "I'll be there at nine."

"We'll be there together," said Gem. He leaned forward, took her hands meaningfully. "You're too pretty to be let out of my sight for —" There was a skirl and scrape of skates. A harsh voice cried, "You get your hands off my girl!" And a tough round face glared into the booth. Jean noticed a mop of black curls, a wide stocky frame.

Gem stared an instant, overcome by surprise and rage. He jumped to his feet. "Don't you tell me what to do, you —"

The black-haired youth had turned to Jean with a bitter expression. "As far as I'm concerned, Jade, you can go to hell."

He turned, stalked off.

Gem sat still as a statue. Jean saw a curious change come over his features. He had forgotten her completely, he was looking after the black-haired youth. His mouth broke into a humorless grin, but his eyelids, rather than drooping, lifted up, and his eyes took on a vitreous glaze. Slowly he rose to his feet.

Jean said in a matter-of-fact voice, "Don't be a child. Sit down and behave yourself."

He paid her no heed. Jean drew back a little. Gem was dangerous. "Sit down," she said sharply.

Gem's grin became a grimace. He vaulted the railing of the booth, quietly, stealthily, went after the black-haired youth.

Jean sat impatiently, tipping her glass back and forth across the table. Let them fight...Young bulls, young boars...She hoped the black-haired boy would wipe up the ground with Gem. Of course he had originally started the trouble. What did he mean, calling her Jade? She'd never seen him before. Could the ubiquitous Martha Cholwell be blamed? She seemed to precede Jean everywhere. Jean glanced around the floor with new interest.

Fifteen minutes passed before Gem returned to the table. The madness had left his face. He was bruised, torn and dirty, but clearly he had been the victor. Jean saw it in his swagger, in the tilt of his handsome dark brown head...Foolish young animal, thought Jean without emotion.

He swung his legs back into the booth, rather stiffly, Jean noted. "Fixed that guy for a while," he said in a pleasant voice. Jean's vocabulary was not particularly extensive, and the word 'catharsis' was not familiar to her. She thought to herself, "He's taken out his meanness on that black-haired boy and he feels better. He'll probably be halfway decent for a while."

And indeed Gem was quiet and almost self-effacing the remainder of the evening. At midnight he suggested leaving.

Jean made no protest. There had been no further sign of the black-haired youth or of anyone she could identify as Cholwell's niece.

In the air-boat he pulled her to him and kissed her passionately. Jean resisted a moment, then relaxed. Why not? she thought. It was easier than fighting him off. Though in a way she hated contributing further to his self-esteem...

VII

Sunrise on Codiron was accompanied by a phenomenon unique in the entire universe: a curtain of blue-white light dropping down the western skyline like an eyelid. It was as if a plug under the horizon had been pulled to let the darkness gush swiftly away, leaving behind the ice-color of Codiron day. The effect was ascribed to a fluorescent component of the air which became activated by Mintaka Sub-30's actinic light, and the sharp line of separation was explained by reference to the minute size of Mintaka Sub-30's disk — nearly a point source of light.

Jean slipped quietly from her room in time to witness the occurrence. Main Street was long and empty, steeped in blue gloom. Wind swept up the street, cut into her face. She licked her lips hungrily, and wondered where breakfast could be found. At one time a slatternly coffee-house down Paradise Alley served late-hour drunks, gamblers and surfeited patrons of the town's two brothels; perhaps the place was still in operation.

Jean shivered in the wind sweeping down from Codiron's desolate rocks, pulled the dark blue jacket close around her neck. Under her clothes she felt sticky, but so early there was not hot water for a bath — one of the petty economies by which the Soone House had achieved flashy trim for the street front. Superficial glitter, inner deficiency, like certain human beings, and the picture of Gem Morales came to her mind. Her mouth curled in a wintry smile. Arrogant opinionated creature. He had swaggered away from Soone House very satisfied with himself... She dismissed him from her mind. He was an atom in a vast universe; let him enjoy himself, so long as he forwarded her own goals.

She shivered. It was really very cold and very early to be undertaking such a business. The attic would reek of damp tobacco smoke, beer and whiskey fumes. Accumulated dirt and dust would be clammy under her fingers, but she could not expect her quest to be a round of pleasure. And it would be less complex to sort out Joe Parlier's old belongings before Gem Morales arrived on the scene.

She made the familiar turn past the courthouse into Paradise Alley, and saw ahead the yellow glow of the New York Café. She slipped in, took a seat at the counter next to a wheezing farm laborer still stupid from his revelry of the previous night. Quietly she drank coffee and ate toast, watching herself in the mirror behind the counter — a very pretty girl with heavy black hair cut short, a skin like a pane of ivory with golden light behind, a wide pale-rose mouth in a delicate jaw structure, black eyes that might be wide with excitement or long and narrow and veiled with heavy lashes... I'll be pretty a long time, thought Jean, if I don't let myself go stale. It's the look of vitality — aliveness — that does so much for me. I hope it's not just because I'm seventeen: adolescent, so to speak. It's more than that.

She finished her coffee, slipped back into Paradise Alley. Behind her, blue-white morning light shone down Main Street; corners and protuberances caught the glow and shone as with St. Elmo's Fire.

Ahead, dingy and dark, rose the front of Joe Parlier's old Aztec Tavern, the earliest home of her memory.

She slipped around to the back, entered by a well-remembered way: up to the roof of the little storage shed, where a yank at a panel of apparently solid louvres provided an opening. Then through, writhing and panting, to land breathless and scraped on a narrow stairs to the garret.

She listened. No sound.

Without hesitation she ran up the stairs, pulled open the dingy frame door.

She paused in the doorway, and memories flooded up to choke her throat and fill her with pity for the dark-eyed little wretch that had once slept here.

She blinked, and then set emotion to one side. She looked around the garret. Light seeped through the dirty window to show her a pile of dusty boxes, all that remained of leering Joe Parlier.

As she had feared it was dusty, damp and clammy, and smelled of the bar below.

In the first box she found bills, receipts, cancelled checks. The second held a photograph album, which she laid aside, and a number of sound tapes. The third box contained — she raised her head alertly. A stealthy creak in the floor. Jean sighed, turned her head.

Gem Morales stood looking through the door. He was half-smiling, lips drawn back over his teeth — a thoroughly unpleasant expression.

"Thought I'd find you here," he said softly.

"I thought I'd find you here," said Jean.

He took a step into the room. "You thieving little —"

Jean saw that his expression was passing through the sequence of the night before. She tensed herself. In another minute...

She said, "Gem."

"Yes?"

"Are you afraid to die?"

He made no answer, but stood watching like a cat.

She said, "If you're not very careful — you're going to die."

He stepped forward easily.

"Don't come any closer."

His body loomed above her; he bent slightly, reaching forward.

"Two more steps, Gem..."

She showed him what she held in her hand, a little metal box no larger than a match-case. From a tiny hole in its side a sliver of a dart would plunge six inches into a human body, and the little thread of mitrox would explode.

Gem stopped short. "You wouldn't dare. You wouldn't dare to kill me!" His mental powers were insufficient to envision a universe without Gem Morales. With a supple motion of his shoulders he lunged forward.

The dart whispered across the air, ruffled his shirt front. She heard the internal thump, saw the outward heave of his chest, felt the quiver in the floor when his body struck.

She grimaced, slowly tucked the dart-box back in her sleeve. She turned back to the boxes. Perhaps she should not have led Gem on with the tale of hidden wealth; it wasn't really fair to dangle temptation before one so vain and so weak.

She sighed, opened the third box. It contained calendars, as did the fourth. Joe Parlier had saved calendars, marking off day after day with red crayon and each year laying the record of used-up time to rest. Jean had seen him scribble in the spaces; possibly it had been memoranda. At the time she had been unable to read.

She leafed back seventeen years, searched along the chain of days. January, February, March — a scribble in faded black ink caught her eye: 'Tell Mollie, for the last time, to call for her damned brat.'

Mollie.

Mollie was her mother's name. And who was Mollie? Joe's mistress? Was it possible that Joe himself had been her father?

She considered, decided in the negative. Too many times Joe had vilified the fate that made him her keeper. And she remembered when Joe had the horrors after a terrible bellowing drunk. She had dropped a pan to the floor; the clang had jangled the discordant skein of his nerves.

Joe had cried out in a voice like a cornet; he cursed her presence, her eyes, her teeth, the very air she breathed. He told her in a reckless wild voice that he'd as soon kill her as look at her, that he only kept her until she grew old enough to sell. It settled the question. If she had been a part of him, he would have coddled her, given her his best; she would have been a vicarious new start in life for him.

Joe was not her father.

But who was Mollie?

She picked up the photograph album — froze to silence. Footsteps in the street outside. They stopped. She heard the outside door rattle, a voice call out something she could not understand. There was a rattle, then footsteps dying away. Then there was silence.

Jean seated herself on a box and opened the album.

VIII

The first pictures dated from Joe Parlier's childhood. There were a dozen shots of a stilt-house on Venus, evidently along the Brandy Coast. A sallow little boy in tattered pink shorts that she recognized as Joe stood beside a buxom hard-faced woman. A few pages later Joe had become a young man, posing beside an old Duraflite air-wagon. Behind were sagging brown and white tassel-trees; the locale was still Venus. On the next page was a single picture, a pretty girl with rather an empty expression. Scrawled in green ink were the words: 'Too bad, Joe'.

The scene changed to Earth: there were pictures of a bar, a restaurant, a large tableau with Joe placid and pompous among a dozen men and women, apparently his employees.

There were only a few more pictures in the album; evidently Joe's enthusiasm for pictures declined with his fortunes. Of these two were professional photographs of a brass-blonde woman, apparently an entertainer, smiling hugely. The inscription read, 'To a Good Guy, Wirlie'.

There was one more photograph. It showed the Aztec Tavern of twenty years before, so Jean judged by Joe's appearance. He stood in the doorway flanked on one side by two bartenders in short sleeves, a porter, a man Jean recognized as a gambler; on the other side by four bold-looking women in provocative poses. The legend read: 'Joe and the Gang'. Under each figure was a name: 'Wirlie, May, Tata, Mollie, Joe, Steve, Butch, Carl, Hopham'.

Mollie! With a dry mouth Jean scrutinized the face. Her mother? A big beefy woman with a truculent look. Her features were small, kneaded, doughy: a face like a jar full of pig's-feet.

Mollie. Mollie what? If her profession were what it seemed, the chance that she still lived in the neighborhood was small.

Jean petulantly went back to the calendar, turned back the months… Two years before the date of her birth she found a notation, 'Collect bail refund on Mollie and May'.

There was nothing more. Jean sat a moment pondering. If this revolting Mollie were her mother, who might her father be? Jean sniffed. It was doubtful if Mollie herself knew.

With a conscious effort Jean returned to the lard-colored face, the little pig eyes. It hurt. So this is Mother. Her eyes suddenly flooded with tears, her mouth twitched. She went on looking, as if it were some kind of penance. What in her arrogance had she expected? A Pontemma baronet and his lady, living in a white marble castle?…"I wish I hadn't been so nosy," said Jean mournfully. She sighed. "Maybe I have a distinguished father."

The idea amused her. "He must have been very, very drunk."

She detached the photograph, tucked it in her pocket, rose uncertainly to her feet. Time to go.

She repacked the boxes, stood looking indecisively at Gem's body. It wasn't nice leaving him here in the garret… Nothing about Gem was very nice. He might lay here weeks, months. She felt a small queasiness in her stomach which she repressed angrily. "Be sensible, you fool."

Better wipe up fingerprints… There was a rattle, a pounding at the front door, a hoarse voice called, "Gem! … Gem!"

Jean ran to the door. Time to go. Someone must have seen Gem enter.

She slipped down the stairs, wiggled out the louvre opening to the shed roof, carefully pushed the louvres home. She slid to the ground, ducked over a sagging fence into Aloha Place.

Ten minutes later she was back in her room at the Soone House, throwing off her clothes for a shower.

The sleek and lazy clerk in the courthouse grumbled when Jean modestly approached him with her request.

"Oh please," said Jean, smiling half-sidelong, an old ruse. It invested her with wistful appeal, magic daring, an unthinkable unimaginable proffer.

The clerk licked his wine-colored old lips. "Oh… Very well. Little girl like you should be home with your mother. Well?" he asked sharply. "What are you laughing at?"

Jean did not think it wise to mention that her mother was the topic of her inquiry.

Together they pored over the records, sliding tape after tape through the screen.

"That year we was busy as bees," grumbled the clerk. "But we ought to find that name if—well, now, here's a Mollie. Mollie Salomon. That the one? Arrested for vagrancy and narcotic addiction on January 12, remanded to the Rehabilitation Home February 1. Bail posted by Joe Parlier, man used to run the saloon down Paradise Alley."

"That's her," said Jean excitedly. "When was she discharged?"

The clerk shook his head. "We wouldn't have no record of that. Must have been when her addiction was cleared up, a year or two."

Jean calculated, chewing her lip with little sharp teeth, frowning. That would put Mollie back in circulation something before the date of her own birthday.

The clerk watched like an old gray cat, but made no comment.

Jean asked hesitantly, "I don't suppose this—Mollie Salomon lives around here now?"

The clerk showed signs of uneasiness, twitching a decorative tassel on his lapel. "Well, young lady, it's hardly the kind of place you'd be apt to care about..."

"What's the address?"

The clerk raised his head, met her glance. Quietly he said, "It's out on Meridian Road, past El Panatela. The Ten-Mile House."

Meridian Road led into the uplands, winding around the three volcanic necks which ruled the Angel City skyline, dipping like a hummingbird into each of the old mines, lining out into Plaghank Valley. Ten miles along the road was six miles by air, and in minutes after rising from Soone House, the cab set Jean down by a ramshackle old building.

Wherever men worked and produced and made money in hard and hostile back-country, Ten-Mile Houses appeared. When towns were built, when civilization brought comfort and moderation, the Ten-Mile Houses became quiet backwaters, drowsing through the years in a mellow amber gloom. The rooms became dusty and footfalls sounded loud where once only silence would have been noticed.

When Jean marched briskly up the stone-foam steps the downstairs saloon was empty. The bar extended along the back wall with the mirror behind overhung with a hundred souvenirs of the old days: choice sound-light crystals, fossils of Trotters and other extinct Codiron life-forms, drills, a tableau of six miner's hats, each painted with a name.

A voice rasped suspiciously, "What you want, girl?"

She turned, saw a hawk-nosed old man sitting in a corner. His eyes were blue and sharp; with his ruff of white hair he reminded her of an old white parakeet disturbed from its sleep.

"I'm looking for Mollie," said Jean. "Mollie Salomon."

"Nobody here by that name; what do you want her for?"

"I want to talk."

The old man's jaws moved up and down as if he were chewing something very hot. "What about?"

"If she wants you to know — she'll tell you herself."

The old man's chin wrinkled. "Pretty pert, ain't you?"

Soft footsteps sounded behind Jean; a woman in a drab evening gown entered the room, stood looking at Jean with an obvious expression of hunger and envy.

The old man barked, "Where's Mollie?"

The woman pointed at Jean. "Is she coming to work? Because I won't put up with it. I'll make trouble; the minute a young tart like that sets her —"

"I just want to talk to Mollie."

"She's upstairs... Cleaning the carpet." She turned to the old man. "Paisley did it again. If you'd keep that old drunk outa here, I'd thank you kindly for it."

"Money is money."

IX

Gingerly Jean started to climb the stairs, but a large female figure blocked the passage.

She was carrying a bucket and a brush. As she came into the light, Jean recognized the woman in Joe Parlier's photograph, modified by twenty years of ill health, bad temper, a hundred pounds of sour flesh.

"Mollie?" ventured Jean. "Are you Mollie Salomon?"

"That's me. What about it?"

"I'd like to talk to you. In private."

Mollie looked her over briefly, darted a bitter glance into the saloon where the old man and the woman sat listening with undisguised interest. "All right, come on out here."

She pushed open a rickety door, waddled out on a side porch overlooking a sad little garden of rattle-bush, pilgrim vine, rusty fungus. She sank into a wicker chair that squeaked under her weight.

"What's the story?"

Jean's imaginings had never quite envisioned a meeting like this. What was there to say? Looking into the pudgy white face, conscious of her sour woman-reek, the words came haltingly to her mouth... Sudden anger flared inside Jean.

"Seventeen years ago you left a baby with Joe Parlier in Angel City. I want to know who the father was."

Mollie Salomon's face changed by not a twitch. After a moment she said in a low harsh voice, "I've often wondered how that baby turned out..."

Jean asked in sudden hope, "It wasn't your own baby?"

Mollie laughed bitterly. "Don't run away with yourself. It was my brat, no doubt of that, no doubt at all... How did you find out?"

"Joe left a kind of diary... Who was the father? Was it Joe?"

The woman drew herself up into a ludicrous exposition of dignity. "Joe Parlier? Humph, I should say not."

"Who then?"

Mollie inspected Jean through crafty eyes. "You look like you're doing well in the world."

Jean nodded. "I knew it would come to this. How much?"

Mollie's price was surprisingly modest—perhaps the gauge of importance she put on the matter. "Oh ten, twenty dollars, just to pay for my time."

Jean would have given her a hundred, a thousand. "Here."

"Thank you," said Mollie Salomon with prim gentility. "Now I'll tell you what I know of the affair, which to my way of thinking is one of the queerest things I've ever heard of."

Jean said impatiently, "Never mind that, who is my father?"

Mollie said, "Nobody."

"Nobody?"

"Nobody."

Jean was silent a moment. Then: "There must have been someone."

Mollie said with dignity, "There's no one that should know better than me, and I'll tell you that for sure."

"Maybe you were drunk?" suggested Jean hopefully.

Mollie inspected her critically. "Pretty wise for a little snip your age... Ah well, deary me, I wasn't far behind you, and I was more'n cute... Look at me now, you'd never guess it, me that's been doin' slops at Ten-Mile House for over twelve years..."

"Who is my father?"

"Nobody."

"That's impossible!"

Mollie shook her head. "That's the way it happened. And how do I know? Because I was out in the Rehabilitation Home, and I'd been out there two years. Then I look down one day, I say, 'Mollie, you're getting big.' And then I say, 'Must be gas.' And the next day I say, 'Mollie, if it wasn't that this damn jail is run like a goldfish tank, with eyes on you every last minute, and you know for a fact that you haven't seen a man except old Cholwell and the Director' —"

"Cholwell!"

"Old Doc Cholwell was the medic, a cold fish… Lord on high, what a cold fish. Anyway I said to myself —"

"It couldn't be that Cholwell got to you?"

Mollie snorted. "Old Cholwell? More likely pin it on Archangel Gabriel. That old —" she broke into obscene muttering. "To this day I'd like to catch that cod-faced sissy-panty, him that wouldn't let me go when my time was up! Claimed I had disease, said I had to wait it out! Nothing doing. I made my own way out. I rode the truck in, and not a thing was there to do about it, because my time was up, and I was detained out of legal order. And then — I go to the doctor, old Doc Walsh, and he says, 'Mollie, the only trouble with you is that you're just pregnant as hell.' And the next thing you know, there's the brat, and me without a crust or cooky, and needing my freedom, so I just carry her out to my good friend Joe, and a rare fuss he made too…"

"How about the Director?"

"What about him?"

"Could he have —"

Mollie snorted incredulously. "Not old Fussy Richard. He never even showed his face around. Besides he was fooling around some young snip in the office."

There was the sound of humming airfoils. Jean jumped to the ground, craned her neck at the departing air-boat. "Now what in Heaven's name… I told him to wait. How will I get back to Angel City?"

"Well well," said a reedy precise voice from within the saloon. "Well well, this is indeed a quaint old relic."

Mollie Salomon heaved herself to her feet. "That voice!" Her face was tinged with an unhealthy pink. "That voice, I'd never miss it, it's old Cholwell."

Jean followed her into the saloon.

"Now, you pickle-faced little freak, what brings you out here? Do you know that I've swore long and time again that if ever I caught you off your nasty Home, I'd pour slops on you, and do you know that's just what I'm going to do...Just wait for my bucket..." Mollie turned and panted away down the corridor.

Jean said, "Did you send my cab away, Mr. Cholwell?"

Cholwell bowed. "Yes, Miss Parlier. I've been wanting to show you my chicken ranch, and I thought that today you might accept my invitation."

"And suppose I didn't, then how do I get back to Angel City?"

Cholwell made an elegant gesture. "Naturally I will take you anywhere you wish to go."

"And suppose I don't want to ride with you?"

Cholwell looked pained. "In that case, of course, I'm guilty of a grave imposition, and can only offer you my apologies."

Mollie Salomon came running into the room with a bucket, puffing and sobbing with anger. Cholwell backed out into the open with considerable agility, sacrificing none of his dignity.

Mollie ran out on the porch. Cholwell retreated further across the yard. Mollie chased him a few steps, then dashed the contents of the bucket in his direction. Cholwell dodged clear of the mess by twenty feet. Mollie shook her fist. "And don't set foot in Ten-Mile again, or there'll be worse for you, far worse, you nasty little swine." And she added further scurrility.

A squat dough-faced woman scuttling after fastidious Cholwell with a bucketful of slops was too much for Jean. She broke into delighted laughter. At the same time her eyes smarted with tears. Her father and her mother. In spite of Mollie's angry protests Cholwell owned to a daughter who resembled her, Martha, Sunny, Jade, whatever her name.

With not a glance for Jean, Mollie disappeared triumphantly into the saloon. Cholwell approached, mopping his forehead angrily. "For two cents I'd put a charge against her, and have her committed..."

"Are you my father, Mr. Cholwell?" asked Jean.

Cholwell turned a bright searching glance upon her. "Whyever do you ask that, Miss Parlier? It's a very curious question."

"Mollie is my mother. She says she became pregnant while you were the only man nearby."

Cholwell shook his head decidedly. "No, Miss Parlier. Morality to one side, I assure you that I am still a man of fastidious taste and discernment."

Jean admitted to herself that a passionate combination of Cholwell and Mollie was hard to conceive. "Who then is my father?"

X

Cholwell raised his eyebrows as if in apprehension of a painful duty he felt called on to perform. "It appears that — excuse me, I will be blunt; I feel that, young as you are, you are a realist — it appears that your mother's relations with men were such as to make responsibility indefinite."

"But she was at the Rehabilitation Home; she says she never saw any other man but you."

Cholwell shook his head doubtfully. "Perhaps you'd like to visit the old Home? It's almost adjacent to my own —"

Jean snapped, "Once and for all, I'm not interested in your damn chickens. I want to go back to Angel City."

Cholwell bowed his head in defeat. "Angel City it is, and I apologize for my presumption."

Jean said shortly, "Where's your boat?"

"This way, around the bear-pad." He led around the white slab of fungus.

The air-boat was old and stately. The words *Codiron Rehabilitation Home* had been painted over, but the outlines were still legible.

Cholwell slid back the door. Jean hesitated, glanced thoughtfully back toward the Ten-Mile House.

"Something you've forgotten?" asked Cholwell courteously.

"No… I guess not."

Cholwell waited patiently. Jean said angrily, "It's just this, Mr. Cholwell. I'm young and there's a lot I don't know, but —"

"Yes?"

"I've got an awful quick temper. So — let's get started. To Angel City."

"To Angel City," said Cholwell thoughtfully.

Jean jumped into the boat. Cholwell closed the door, circled the boat; then, as if struck by a sudden notion, slid back the access panel to the motor box.

Jean watched warily. He seemed to be making a minor adjustment.

The air was bad inside the cab, smelling of varnish and stale ozone. She heard the ventilation system turn on: evidently the object of Cholwell's ministrations. The air became cool and fresh. Very fresh. Smelling of pine needles and hay. Jean breathed deeply. Her nose and lungs tingled... She frowned. Odd. She decided to — but Cholwell had finished, was coming around the side of the boat. He approached the door, looked in.

Jean could see his face only from the corner of her eye. She was not certain of his expression. She fancied that he nodded, smiled.

He did not immediately climb into the boat, but stood looking off across the valley toward the three volcanic necks, black stumps on the dingy sky.

The smell of pine needles and hay permeated Jean's head, her body. She was faintly indignant...Cholwell at last opened the door, held it wide. The wind up Plaghank Valley swept through the boat, bringing in the familiar efflorescence of dust and hot rock.

Cholwell cautiously tested the air, finally climbed in, closed the door. The air-boat quivered; Ten-Mile House became a dilapidated miniature below. They flew north. Angel City was to the south.

Jean remonstrated, in the form of heavy breathing. Cholwell smiled complacently. "In the old days we sometimes transported obstreperous patients; very troublesome until we installed the pacifier tank and connected it to the air ducts."

Jean breathed hard.

Cholwell said indulgently, "In two hours you'll be as good as new." He began humming a song, an old-fashioned sentimental ballad.

They rode over a ridge, swung in blustering wind currents, settled into a valley. A great black escarpment rose opposite. Bright blue sunlight shone along the face, reflecting from vertical ridges as if they were fringes of foil.

The boat shuddered and vibrated along the valley lower than the great black cliff. Presently a cluster of pink buildings appeared, nestled against the rock.

"Can you see our destination, there ahead?" Cholwell asked solicitously. "It will be your home for a little while — but don't let me alarm you. There will be compensations." He hummed quietly for a moment. "And your money will be put to a good cause." He darted a glance into her face. "You are skeptical? You dislike the idea? But, I insist, there will be compensations, for you become one of my — little chickens." The idea amused him. "One of my little flock ... But I will be discreet; I don't wish to alarm you ..."

The boat settled toward the sprawling cluster of pink buildings. "One of the old Trotter sites," said Cholwell in a reverent voice. "Ancient past human imagination, and a perfect sun-trap. You see, I told you no more than the truth. I must confess that the plant is neglected, sadly neglected, these days, with only myself and a small staff to tend the flock ... Now that we are to be affluent, perhaps we will make some changes." He scanned the group of buildings with flared nostrils. "Hideous. The worst of the century, the Rococo Revival. And pink stucco over the sound old stone-foam ... But money can mend where wishing and hoping fails." He clicked his tongue. "Perhaps we will move to one of the tropical planets; this Codiron land is bleak and stern, and the blackwater frost begins to worry my old bones." He laughed. "I ramble on ... If I become a bore, you must interrupt ... And here we are. Home."

Bright pink walls rose up past Jean's vision. She felt a jar.

The door opened; she glimpsed Cholwell's face and the grinning yellow countenance of a spare muscular woman.

Hands helped her to the ground, hands went over her person. Her dart-box, her coiled glass-knife were taken from her; she heard Cholwell clucking in satisfaction.

Hands half-led, half-carried her into the gloom of a building.

They traversed an echoing hall lit through a row of high narrow panes. Cholwell stopped beside a heavy door, turned and his face came into the range of Jean's vision.

"When my little flock becomes restless, they must be penned securely... But trust wins trust, and—" his voice was lost in the rattle of the door-skids.

Jean moved forward. Face after face appeared in the channel of her vision. Startled face after startled face. As if she were looking in a succession of mirrors. Her own face looking back at her, again and again.

She felt softness beneath her, and now saw nothing but the ceiling. She heard Cholwell's voice. "This is your long-lost sister, returned to us at last. I think there'll be good news for us all shortly."

Something hot and very painful touched her wrist. She lay looking at the ceiling, breathing hard. The pain presently subsided to an ache.

Her eyelids sank shut.

Jean studied the girls covertly under her eyelids. There were six of them—slender dark-haired girls with impatient intelligent faces. They wore their hair longer than hers, and perhaps they were softer and prettier to a trifling degree. But essentially they were her. Not merely like her. They were her.

They wore a costume like a uniform—white knee-length breeches, a loose yellow blouse, black coolie sandals. Their faces suggested that they were bored and sullen, if not angry.

Jean sat up on the couch, yawned, yawned, yawned, as if she would never get enough. Her perceptions sharpened; memory returned to her.

The girls were sitting in a half-hostile circle. To understand them, Jean told herself, just put myself in their places.

"Well," said Jean, "don't just sit there."

The girls moved a trifle, each shifting her position as if by a common impulse.

"My name is Jean." She rose to her feet, stretched, smoothed back her hair. She looked around the room. A dormitory in the old Rehabilitation Home. "A hell of a rat's nest. I wonder if old Cholwell's listening?"

"Listening?"

"Does he have the place wired for sound? Can he—" she noted the lack of comprehension. "Wait. I'll take a look. Sometimes the mikes are easy to spot, sometimes not."

The pick-up button would be close to the door or close to the window, to allow the entry of wires. A radio pickup would be conspicuous in this barren room.

She found the button where she expected to find it, over the door, with hair wires leading through the crack. She snapped it loose, displayed it to the other girls. "There. Old Cholwell could hear every word we said."

One of the girls took the thing gingerly. "So that's how he always finds out what's going on ... How did you know it was here?"

Jean shrugged. "They're common enough ... How come we're all locked up? Are we prisoners?"

"I don't know about you. We're being punished. When Cholwell went away to Earth, some of us rode the supply boat into Angel City ... We don't get the chance very often. Cholwell was furious. He says we'll spoil everything."

"What's everything?"

She made a vague gesture. "In a little while we'll all be rich, according to Cholwell. We'll live in a fine house, we can do anything we want. First, he's got to get the money. It's been like that ever since I can remember."

"Cherry's gone after the money," said another girl.

Jean blinked. "There's another?"

"There were seven of us. You make eight. Cherry left this morning for Angel City. She's supposed to get money; I think she's taking the next packet to Earth."

"Oh," said Jean. Was it possible ... Could it be ... She thought she saw the scope of Cholwell's plan. She said, "Let me see your hand."

The girl held out her hand indifferently. Jean compared it with her own, squinted closely. "Look, it's the same."

"Of course it's the same."

"Why of course?"

The girl inspected Jean with a puzzled half-contemptuous expression. "Don't you know?"

Jean shook her head. "I never knew till—well, there were rumors and talk around Angel City—but until I saw you I thought I was the only one of me there was. All of a sudden there's six others."

"Seven others."

"Seven others. I'm really—well, astonished. Thunderstruck. But it hasn't sunk in yet."

"Cholwell says we should be grateful to him. But—none of us like him. He won't let us do anything."

XI

Jean looked around the six faces. They lacked some quality which she had. Fire? Willfulness? Jean tried to fathom the difference between herself and the others. They seemed as bright and as willful as she was herself. But they had not acquired the habit of thinking for themselves. There were too many of them subjected to the same stimuli, thinking the same thoughts. There was no leadership among them. She asked, "Aren't you curious about me? You don't seem to care one way or the other."

"Oh." The girl shrugged. "It'll all come out."

"Yes," said Jean. "No doubt... I don't like it here."

"We don't either."

"Why don't you leave? Run away?"

All the girls laughed. "Run where? Across two hundred miles of mountains and rock? And afterward, then what? We've no money to get away from Codiron."

Jean sniffed contemptuously. "A good-looking girl can always get money."

They looked genuinely interested. "How?"

"Oh—there's ways. I guess you've never traveled very much."

"No. We see a few films and watch the television and read books."

"Cholwell picks out all the books?"

"Yes."

"The old Svengali..."

"Who's he?"

"Somebody like Cholwell, only just about—no, exactly, one eighth as ambitious... How did it all start?"

The girl nearest her shrugged. Where the blouse had slipped back on her wrist there was a tattoo mark. Jean leaned forward, read, 'Felice'. Aroused by a sudden memory she looked at her own wrist. Tattooed into the ivory skin was 'Jean'.

Now she was really angry. "Tagging us like cattle!"

None of the others shared her indignation. "He says he has to tell us apart."

"Damned old scoundrel... In some way, somehow..." Her voice trailed away. Then: "How is it that we're all the same?"

Felice was watching her with bright calculating eyes. "You'll have to ask Cholwell. He's never told us."

"But your mothers? Who are your mothers?"

Felice wrinkled her nose. "Let's not talk of nastiness."

The girl next to her said with a trace of malice, "You saw old Svenska, the woman that helped you in? That's Felice's mother."

"Oooh!" said Felice. "I told you never to remind me! And don't forget your own mother, the woman that died with only half a face..."

Jean gritted her teeth, walked up and down the room. "I want to get out of this damn jail... I've been in jails and homes and camps and orphan asylums before; I've always got out. Somehow." She looked suspiciously around the six faces. "Maybe you're all stringing in with Cholwell. I'm not."

"We're not either. But there's nothing we can do."

"Have you ever thought of killing him?" Jean asked sarcastically. "That's easy enough. Stick him once with a good knife, and he'll change his mind the next time he wants to lock people up... I'll stick him if I get a chance..."

There was silence around the room.

Jean continued, "Do you know whose money Cherry is going after? No? Well, it's mine. I've got lots of it. And as soon as Cholwell knew it, he began scheming how to get it. Now he thinks he'll send Cherry to my trustee. He's told her what to do, how to pry at Mycroft. Mycroft won't know the difference. Because she's not only like me. She is me. Even our fingerprints, our handprints."

"Of course."

Jean cried out angrily, "The trouble with you is that you've never had to work or fight; you've sat around like pets. Chickens, Cholwell calls you. And now all your guts are gone. You put up with this—this..." Words failed her. She made a furious gesture around the room.

"You don't fight. You let him treat you like babies. Somehow he got us away from our mothers, somehow he treated us, molded us so that we're all the same, somehow—"

A dry cutting voice said, "Very interesting, Jean... May I have a few minutes with you please?"

There was a rustle of movement, apprehension. Cholwell stood in the doorway. Jean glared over her shoulder, marched out into the corridor.

Cholwell conducted her with grave courtesy to a cheerful room furnished as an office, taking a seat behind a modern electric desk. Jean remained standing, watching him defiantly.

Cholwell picked up a pencil, held it suspended between two fingers. He chose his words carefully.

"It becomes clear that you constitute a special problem."

Jean stamped her feet. "I don't care about your problems, I want to get back to Angel City. If you think you can keep me here very long, you're crazy!"

Cholwell inspected the pencil with every evidence of interest. "It's a very peculiar situation, Jean. Let me explain it, and you'll see the need for cooperation. If we all work together—you, me and the other girls—we can all be rich and independent."

"I'm rich already. And I'm independent already."

Cholwell smiled gently. "But you don't want to share your wealth with your sisters?"

"I don't want to share my wealth with old Polton, with you, with the cab driver, with the captain of the *Bucyrus*... Why should I want to share it with them?" She shook her head furiously. "No, sir, I want to get out of here, right now. And you'd better see to it, or you'll run into so darn much trouble—"

"In regard to money," said Cholwell smoothly, "out here we share and share alike."

Jean sneered. "You had it figured out from the first time you saw me in Mr. Mycroft's office. You thought you'd get me out here and send in one of your girls to collect. But you've got Mr. Mycroft wrong. He won't be hurried or rushed. Your girl Cherry won't get very much from him."

"She'll get enough. If nothing else we'll have the income on two million dollars. Somewhere around fifty thousand dollars a year. What more do we want?"

Jean's eyes were flooding with tears of anger. "Why do you risk keeping me alive? Sooner or later I'll get away, I'll get loose, and I won't care who gets hurt…"

"My dear girl," Cholwell chided gently. "You're overwrought. And there's so much of the background that you're not aware of; it's like the part of an iceberg that's below the water. Let me tell you a little story. Sit down, my dear, sit down."

"Don't 'my dear' me, you old—"

"Tut tut." He put away his pencil, leaned back. "Twenty years ago I was Resident Physician here at the Rehabilitation Home. Then of course it was still in full operation." He looked at her sharply. "All of this must remain confidential, do you understand?"

Jean started to laugh wildly, then a remark of monumental sarcasm came to her tongue. But she restrained herself. If old Cholwell were so eaten up with vanity, if the need for an intelligent ear were so extreme that he must use her, so much the better.

She made a non-committal sound. Cholwell watched her with veiled eyes, chuckled as if he were following the precise chain of her thoughts.

"No matter, no matter," said Cholwell. "But you must never forget that you owe me a great deal. Humanity owes me a great deal." He sat cherishing the thought, rolling the overtones along his mental palate. "Yes, a great deal. You girls, especially. Seven of you—it might be said—owe me your actual existences. I took one and I made eight."

Jean waited.

"Seventeen years ago," said Cholwell dreamily, "the director of the Home entered into an indiscreet liaison with a young social worker. The next day, fearing scandal if pregnancy developed, the director consulted me, and I agreed to examine the young woman. I did so and by a very clever bit of filtration I was able to isolate the fertilized egg. It was an opportunity for which I had been waiting. I nourished the egg. It divided—the first step on its march to a complete human being. Very carefully I separated the two cells. Each of these divided again, and again I separated the doublets. Once more the cells separated; once more I—"

Jean breathed a deep sigh. "Then Mollie isn't my mother after all. It's almost worth it…"

XII

The doctor reproved Jean with a look. "Don't anticipate…Where I had a single individual, I had eight. Eight identities. I let these develop normally, although I suppose I could have continued the process almost indefinitely… After a few days, when the cells had become well established, I brought eight healthy women prisoners into the dispensary. I drugged them with a hypnotic, and after priming them with suitable hormones, I planted a zygote in the womb of each."

Cholwell settled comfortably in his chair, laughed. "Eight pregnancies, and never have I seen women so amazed. One of these women, Mollie Salomon, was granted a remission and left the Home before the birth of her child. My child, I suppose I should say. She actually had very little to do with it. By a series of mishaps I lost her and this eighth child." He shook his head regretfully. "It left an unpleasant gap in the experiment — but after all, I had my seven… And then, seventeen years later, in Metropolis on Earth, I wander into an office and there — you! I knew that Destiny moved with me."

Jean licked her lips. "If Mollie isn't my real mother — who is?"

Cholwell made a brusque motion. "A matter of no importance. It's best that the direct correspondence be forgotten."

Jean said casually, "What is your goal? You've proved the thing can be done; why do you keep the poor girls hidden out here on Codiron?"

Cholwell winked roguishly. "The experiment is not quite at an end, my dear."

"No?"

"No. The first phase was brilliantly successful; now we will duplicate the process. And this time I will broadcast my own seed. I want eight great sons. Eight fine Cholwell boys."

Jean said in a small voice, "That's silly."

Cholwell winked and blinked. "Not at all. It's one of humanity's most compelling urges, the desire for offspring."

"People usually work it out differently… And it won't work."

"Won't work? Why on earth not?"

"You don't have access to foster-mothers as you had before. There's no —" She stopped short, almost bit her tongue.

"Obviously, I need search no farther than my own door. Eight healthy young girls, in the springtime flush of life."

"And the mother?"

"Any one of my eight. Dorothy, Jade, Bernice, Felice, Sunny, Cherry, Martha — and Jean. Any one of you."

Jean moved restlessly. "I don't want to be pregnant. Normally or any other way."

Cholwell shook his head indulgently. "It admittedly represents a hardship."

"Well," said Jean. "Whatever you're planning — don't include me. Because I'm not going to do it, I don't care what you say."

Cholwell lowered his head, and a faint pink flush rose in his cheeks. "My dear young woman —"

"Don't 'my dear young woman' me."

The telescreen buzzer sounded. Cholwell sighed, touched the button.

Jean's face shone from the screen, frightened and desperate. Behind was an official-looking room, two attentive men in uniform.

Cherry, no doubt, thought Jean.

At the sight of Cholwell's face, Cherry cried out in a quick rush, "— got me into this thing, Dr. Cholwell; you get me out of it!"

Cholwell blinked stupidly.

Cherry's narrow vivid face glowed with anger and indignation. "Do something! Say something!"

"But — what about?" demanded Cholwell.

"They've arrested me! They say I killed a man!"

"Ah," said Jean with a faint smile.

Cholwell jerked forward. "Just what is all this?"

"It's crazy!" cried Cherry. "I didn't do it! I didn't even know him — but they won't let me go!"

Behind her one of the policemen said in a gruff voice, "You're wasting your time and ours, sister. We've got you so tight you'll never get out."

"Dr. Cholwell — they say they can execute me, kill me for something I didn't do!"

Cholwell said in a guarded voice, "They can't prove it was you if it wasn't."

"Then why don't they let me go?"

Cholwell rubbed his chin. "When did the murder occur?"

"I think it was this morning."

"It's all nonsense," said Cholwell in relief. "You were out here this morning. I can vouch for that."

Behind the girl one of the policemen laughed hoarsely. Cherry cried, "But they say my fingerprints were on him! The sheriff says there's absolutely no doubt!"

"Ridiculous!" Cholwell burst out in a furious high-pitched voice.

One of the policemen leaned forward. "It's a clear-cut case, Cholwell. Otherwise your girl wouldn't be talking with you so free and easy. Me, I've never seen a cleaner case, and I'll bet a hundred dollars on the verdict."

"They'll kill me," wept Cherry. "That's all they talk about!"

"Barbarous!" Cholwell stormed. "Damned savages! And they boast about civilization here on Codiron!"

"We're civilized enough to catch our murderers," observed the sheriff equably. "And also fix it so they murder only once."

"Have you ever heard of de-aberration?" Cholwell asked in a biting voice.

The sheriff shrugged. "No use singing that song, Cholwell. This is still honest country. When we catch a murderer, we put him where he won't bother nobody. None of this fol-de-rol and fancy hospitals for us; we're plain folk."

Cholwell said carefully, "Why are you trying to pin it on — this girl?"

"There's eye-witnesses," said the sheriff complacently. "Two people identify her positively as entering the place where this Gem Morales was killed. There's half a dozen others that saw her in Paradise Alley at about the right time. Absolute identification, no question about it; she ate breakfast in the New York Café. And to tie on the clincher, there's her fingerprints all over the scene of the murder... I tell you, Cholwell, it's a case!"

Cherry cried desperately, "Dr. Cholwell, what shall I do? They won't let me — I just can't make them believe —"

Cholwell's face was a white mask. He said in a taut voice, "I'll call you back in a little while."

He turned off the contact. The screen died on the contorted face.

Jean sighed tremulously. Witnessing the scene had been more frightening than if she had been directly involved; it was watching herself in terror and unable to move a muscle to help: a nightmare where the feet refuse to move.

Cholwell was thinking, watching her from eyes which suddenly seemed detestably reptilian. He said, enunciating with faint sibilance, "You killed this man. You devil's imp."

Jean's wide flexible mouth spread into a smile. "What if I did?"

"You've ruined my plans!"

Jean shrugged. "You brought me out here. You sent her into Angel City to catch the packet — to go after my money. She was supposed to be me. That's what you wanted. Fine. Excellent." She laughed, a silver tinkle. "It's really funny, Cholwell."

A new thought struck Cholwell. He sank back into his chair. "It's not funny… It's terrible. It breaks up the octet. If she's found guilty and killed by those barbarians in Angel City, the circle is broken, this time irrevocably."

"Oh," said Jean brightly. "You're worried about Cherry's death because it — ruins the symmetry of your little circle?"

"You don't understand," Cholwell said in a waspish voice. "This has been my goal for so long… I had it, then phwish —" he jerked his hand, raised his eyebrows despairingly "— out of my reach."

"It's none of my business," Jean mused, "except that she's so much me. It makes me feel funny to see her scared. I don't care a cent for you."

Cholwell frowned dangerously.

Jean continued. "But — it should be easy to get her loose."

"Only by turning you in," Cholwell gloomed. "And that would bring publicity to bear on all of us, and we can't stand that just yet. I wouldn't be able to carry through…"

Jean looked at him as if she were seeing him for the first time. "You're actually serious about that?"

"Serious? Of course I'm serious." He glared angrily. "I don't understand what you're getting at."

"If I were really hard-hearted," said Jean, "I'd sit back and have a good laugh. It's so terribly funny. And cruel... I guess I'm not as mean and tough as I think I am. Or maybe it's because she's — me." She felt the glare of Cholwell's eyes. "Don't get me wrong. I don't plan to run into town, bare my bosom and say 'I did it'. But there's a very simple way to get her off."

"So?" — In a silky voice.

"I don't know much about law, except to keep the hell away from it. But suppose all of us trooped into court. What could they do? They couldn't arrest all of us. They couldn't pin it on Cherry. There's eight of us, all alike, even our fingerprints alike. They'd be sad. Their only case is identification and fingerprints; they think that points to one person. If there are seven others the evidence fits equally well, they can't do anything but throw up their hands, say please, whoever did it, don't do it again, and tell us to go home."

XIII

Cholwell's face was a mask carved in yellow wax. He said slowly, "What you say is perfectly true... But it's impossible." His voice rose into a snarl. "I told you we can't stand publicity. If we carried out a stunt like that, we'd be known across all space. Angel City would be overrun with journalists, busy-bodies, investigators. The great scheme would be — out of the question."

"By 'great scheme'," asked Jean politely, "you mean the project of making us all mothers?"

"Of course. Naturally. The great scheme."

"Even if it means sacrificing Cherry? Her life?"

Cholwell looked pained. "You express it in unpleasant terms. I don't like it in the slightest degree. It means seven instead of eight... But sometimes we are forced to be brave and bear up under setbacks. This is one of those times."

Jean looked at him with glowing eyes. "Cholwell," she whispered. She was unable to continue. Finally she said, "Sooner or later —"

The closet door banged open.

A harsh voice said, "Well, I've heard all I can stand. More'n enough."

Out from the closet marched Mollie Salomon, and behind her the tall yellow-faced woman Svenska.

Magic, a miracle, was Jean's first startled supposition; how else to explain two big women in a broom closet? Cholwell sat like an elegantly dressed statue, his face a brown study. Jean relaxed her breath. Conceivably they had squeezed themselves close; the air, she thought wryly, must have been rich and thick.

Mollie took three swift steps forward, put her hands on her hips, thrust her round white face forward. "You nasty thing, now I know what went on..."

Cholwell rose to his feet, backed away, quick and yellow as a tortoise-shell cat. "You've no right here, you'd better get out!"

Everything happened at once — a myriad bedlam jangle of sound, emotion, contorted faces. Farcical, grotesque, terrible — Jean sat back, unknowing whether to laugh madly or run.

Svenska cried in a voice guttural with passion, "You ruined me, you pig —"

"Rare puzzlement," snarled Mollie, "and all the time it was your fooling and fiddling!"

"— I beat my head, I cry, I think my husband is right, I am no good, I am —"

Cholwell held up his hands. "Ladies, ladies —"

"I'll 'ladies' you." Mollie snatched a broom from the closet, began whacking Cholwell with the flat of it. He seized hold, tried to tear it away; he and Mollie capered and wrestled across the floor. Svenska stepped in, flung long sinewy arms around his neck, squatted; Cholwell stumbled over backwards. They both sprawled to the floor. Mollie plied the broom.

Cholwell gained his feet, rushed to the desk, came up with Jean's dart-box. His hair fell lank, his mouth hung open, and he panted heavily. Deliberately he raised the box. Jean slid down in her seat, kicked out at his arm. The dart exploded in the door-frame with a dry clacking sound.

Svenska flung herself on him, Mollie hit his arm with the broom. The dart-box fell to the floor; Jean picked it up.

Mollie threatened him with her broom. "You should be ashamed of yourself for what you did!"

Svenska reached out, gave his shoulder a shake. He stood limp, unresisting.

"What you gonna do about it?" Svenska cried.

"Do about what?"

"My husband."

"I've never even seen him."

"No. You never seen him," she mimicked in elaborate scorn. "No. But me—he comes, he looks at me. Big; seven, eight months, that's me. He calls me no good woman, and so—he goes. Off to Puskolith, and I never get no more husband. That's eighteen year."

Jean said mischievously, "You should make Cholwell marry you."

Svenska considered Cholwell a minute, came to a decision. "Pah, little shrimp like him is no good."

Mollie said, "And he was just getting set to try out his nasty tricks again; I knew he was up to no good soon as I saw him." She turned a look at Jean. "Whether you're my girl or not, I didn't want no nasty Cholwell fooling with you, I knew that was what he was countin' on, so I got ol' Pop to run me up in his float, and it's a good thing too, I see now; I come just in time."

"Yes," said Jean. "I'm glad you came." She released a deep breath. "I'm glad you came."

Cholwell was gathering his wits, arranging his dignity around him like a tattered garment. He seated himself at his desk, moved some papers back and forth with trembling fingers. "You've—you've got no right intruding in here," he said in feeble indignation.

Mollie made a contemptuous blowing sound. "I go where I please, and don't give me no lip, or I'll use this broom on you again, which I got half a mind to anyway, thinking of how you kept me out here after my time, and all for your nasty experiments."

Cholwell turned venomously on Svenska. "You let her in, and I've kept you here and given you a good home all these years—"

"Yah! And working my fingers to the bone, keeping you and them girls up; it's been no bed of roses... And now we do different. You work for me now."

"You're a crazy woman," snapped Cholwell. "Now get out — both of you, before I call the police." He reached out to the telescreen.

"Here now!" barked Mollie. "Careful there, Cholwell!" She flourished the broom. "Now I'll tell you what I want; you've brought misery on me, and I want damages. Yes, sir," she nodded placidly, "damages. And if I don't get them, I'm gonna take 'em out of your hide with this broom."

"Ridiculous," said Cholwell weakly.

"I'll show you what's ridiculous. I want my rights."

Jean said archly, "I think this old place would make a good chicken ranch. Cholwell thinks so too. You could put chickens in here and Cholwell could work for you...Cholwell told me there'd be money in it."

Svenska looked at Mollie skeptically. Mollie said to Cholwell, "Is that right? What she said?"

Cholwell moved uneasily in his seat. "Too cold and windy for chickens."

"Pah," said Svenska. "Nice and warm. Right in the sun pocket."

"That's what Cholwell told me," said Jean.

Cholwell turned a passionate face at her. "Shut up! You've brought me the devil's own luck."

Jean rose to her feet. "If I can run that old air-wagon, I'm leaving." She nodded to Mollie. "Thanks for coming out after me. I wish you luck with your chicken-ranch idea."

She stepped out into the corridor, leaving heavy silence behind her.

She hesitated a moment, then turned down the corridor toward the library. She felt light, energetic, and ran most of the way. At the doorway she hesitated again.

"Oh hell," said Jean. "After all — they're me."

She flung open the door.

Six girls turned, looked at her curiously. "Well? What did old Cholwell want?"

Jean looked around from face to face with the smile that showed her sharp little teeth.

"Old Cholwell is going into the chicken business with Svenska." She laughed. "Silly old rooster."

There was silence in the room, a kind of breathlessness.

"Now," said Jean, "we're all leaving. First thing is Cherry. She's in trouble. She let Cholwell make a cat's-paw out of her, now she's in trouble. That's a good lesson. Never be somebody's cat's-paw against your sister. But we won't be vindictive. We'll all march into the courthouse." She laughed. "It'll be fun ... After that — we'll go back to Earth. I've got lots of money. I had to work like hell for it — but I guess there's no reason for me to be a pig." She looked around the circle of faces. It was like seeing herself in a multiple mirror. "After all — we're really the same person. It's a strange feeling ..."

XIV

Mycroft's secretary and receptionist looked up with a sudden tightening of the mouth. "Hello, Ruth," said Jean. "Is Mr. Mycroft in?"

Ruth said in a cool voice, "We'd prefer that you call in ahead for an appointment. It gives us a better chance to organize and arrange our work." She shot Jean a look under her eyelids ... Undeniably vital and pretty. But why did Mycroft go to pieces every time he looked at her?

Jean said, "We just arrived in town this morning. On the *Great Winter Star*. We haven't had time to call in."

"We?" asked Ruth.

Jean nodded. "There's eight of us." She giggled. "We'll send old Mycroft to his grave early." She looked back into the corridor. "Come on in, group."

Ruth slumped back into her chair. Jean smiled sympathetically, crossed the room, opened the door into Mycroft's office. "Hello, Mr. Mycroft."

"Jean!" said Mycroft. "You're back ... Did you —" his voice faltered. "Which one is Jean? I don't seem to be able to —"

"I'm Jean," she said cheerfully. "You'll get used to us. If there's ever any confusion, look at our wrists. We're all stencilled."

"But —"

"They're my sisters. You're guardian to octuplets."

"I'm — astounded," breathed Mycroft, "to put it mildly ... It's miraculous ... Am I to understand that you found your parents?"

"Well—yes and no. Mostly no. To tell you the truth, it more or less slipped my mind in the excitement."

Mycroft looked from face to face. "Are you sure it isn't a trick? Mirrors?"

"No mirrors," Jean assured him. "We're all flesh and blood, very troublesome."

"But the resemblance!"

Jean sighed. "It's a long story. I'm afraid your old friend Cholwell doesn't appear in a very favorable light."

Mycroft smiled faintly. "I'm under no illusions about Cholwell. He was resident physician out at the Codiron Women's Home when I was director. I know him very well, but I wouldn't call him a friend... What's the matter?"

Jean said tremulously, "You were director at the Rehabilitation Home?"

"Yes. What of it?"

"Just a minute. Let me think."

A moment later: "And Ruth has been with you a long time... How long?"

"Almost twenty years... Why?"

"Was she on Codiron?"

"Yes... What's this all about?" Mycroft's voice became sharper. "What's the mystery?"

Jean said, "No mystery. No mystery at all." She turned, looked around the room into the faces of her sisters. All eight burst into laughter.

In the reception room Ruth bent savagely over her work. Poor Mycroft.

THE MITR

A ROCKY HEADLAND made a lee for the bay and the wide empty beach. The water barely rose and fell. A high overcast grayed the sky, stilled the air. The bay shone with a dull luster, like old pewter.

Dunes bordered the beach, breaking into a nearby forest of pitchy black-green cypress. The forest was holding its own, matting down the drifts with whiskery roots.

Among the dunes were ruins: glass walls ground milky by salt breeze and sand. In the center of these walls a human being had brought grass and ribbon-weed for her bed. Her name was Mitr, or so the beetles called her. For want of any other, she had taken the word for a name.

The name, the grass bed, a length of brown cloth stolen from the beetles were her only possessions. Possibly her belongings might be said to include a mouldering heap of bones which lay a hundred yards back in the forest. They interested her strongly, and she vaguely remembered a connection with herself. In the old days when her arms and legs had been short and round she had not marked the rather grotesque correspondence of form. Now she had lengthened and the resemblance was plain. Eyeholes like her eyes, a mouth like her own, teeth, jaw, skull, shoulders, ribs, legs, feet. From time to time she would wander back into the forest and stand wondering, though of late she had not been regular in her visits.

Today was dreary and gray. She felt bored, uneasy, and after some thought decided that she was hungry. Wandering out on the dunes she listlessly ate a number of grass-pods. Perhaps she was not hungry after all.

She walked down to the beach, stood looking out across the bay.

A damp wind flapped the brown cloth, rumpled her hair. Perhaps it would rain. She looked anxiously at the sky. Rain made her wet and miserable. She could always take shelter among the rocks of the headland but — sometimes it was better to be wet.

She wandered down along the beach, caught and ate a small shellfish. There was little satisfaction in the salty flesh. Apparently she was not hungry. She picked up a sharp stick and drew a straight line in the damp sand — fifty feet — a hundred feet long. She stopped, looked back over her work with pleasure. She walked back, drawing another line parallel to the first, a hand's-breadth distant. Very interesting effect. Fired by sudden enthusiasm she drew more lines up and down the beach until she had created an extensive grate of parallel lines.

She looked over her work with satisfaction. Making such marks on the smooth sand was pleasant and interesting. Some other time she would do it again, and perhaps use curving lines or cross-hatching. But enough for now. She dropped the stick. The feeling of hunger that was not hunger came over her again. She caught a sand-locust but threw it away without eating it.

She began to run at full speed along the beach. This was better, the flash of her legs below her, the air clean in her lungs. Panting, she came to a halt, flung herself down in the sand.

Presently she caught her breath, sat up. She wanted to run some more, but felt a trifle languid. She grimaced, jerked uneasily. Maybe she should visit the beetles over the headland; perhaps the old gray creature called Ti-Sri-Ti would speak to her.

Tentatively she rose to her feet and started back along the beach. The plan gave her no real pleasure. Ti-Sri-Ti had little of interest to say. He answered no questions, but recited interminable data concerned with the colony: how many grubs would be allowed to mature, how many pounds of spider-eggs had been taken to storage, the condition of his mandibles, antennae, eyes...

She hesitated, but after a moment went on. Better Ti-Sri-Ti than no one, better the sound of a voice than the monotonous crash of gray surf. And perhaps he might say something interesting; on occasions his conversation went far afield and then Mitr listened with absorption: "The mountains are ruled by wild lizards and beyond are the Mercaloid

Mechanvikis, who live under the ground with only fuming chimneys and slag-runs to tell of activity below. The beetles live along the shore and of the Mitr only one remains by old Glass City, the last of the Mitr."

She had not quite understood, since the flux and stream of time, the concepts of before and after, meant nothing to her. The universe was static; day followed day, not in a series, but as a duplication.

Ti-Sri-Ti had droned on: "Beyond the mountains is endless desert, then endless ice, then endless waste, then a land of seething fire, then the great water and once more the land of life, the rule and domain of the beetles, where every solstice a new acre of leaf mulch is chewed and laid…" And then there had been an hour dealing with beetle fungiculture.

Mitr wandered along the beach. She passed the beautiful grate she had scratched in the damask sand, passed her glass walls, climbed the first shelves of black rock. She stopped, listened. A sound?

She hesitated, then went on. There was a rush of many feet. A long brown and black beetle sprang upon her, pressed her against the rocks. She fought feebly, but the fore-feet pinned her shoulders, arched her back. The beetle pressed his proboscis to her neck, punctured her skin. She stood limp, staring into his red eyes while he drank.

He finished, released her. The wound closed of itself, smarted and ached. The beetle climbed up over the rocks.

Mitr sat for an hour regaining her strength. The thought of listening to Ti-Sri-Ti now gave her no pleasure.

She wandered listlessly back along the beach, ate a few bits of seaweed and a small fish which had been trapped in a tide-pool.

She walked to the water's edge and stared out past the headland to the horizon. She wanted to cry out, to yell; something of the same urge which had driven her to run so swiftly along the beach. She raised her voice, called, a long musical note. The damp mild breeze seemed to muffle the sound. She turned away discouraged.

She wandered down the shore to the little stream of fresh water. Here she drank and ate some of the blackberries that grew in rank thickets.

She jerked upright, raised her head. A vast high sound filled the sky, seemed part of all the air. She stood rigid, then craned her neck, searching the overcast, legs half-bent for flight.

A long black sky-fish dropped into view, snorting puffs of fire. Terrified, she backed into the blackberry bushes. The brambles tore her legs, brought her to awareness. She dodged into the forest, crouched under a leaning cypress trunk.

The sky-fish dropped with astounding rapidity, lowered to the beach, settled with a quiet final belch and sigh. Mitr watched in frozen fascination. Never had she known of such a thing, never would she walk the beach again without watching the heavens.

The sky-fish opened. She saw the glint of metal, glass. From the interior jumped three creatures. Her head moved forward in wonder. They were something like herself, but large, red, burly. Strange, frightening things. They made a great deal of noise, talking in hoarse rough voices. One of them saw the glass walls, and for a space they examined the ruins with great interest.

The brown and black beetle which had drank her blood chose this moment to scuttle down the rocks to the beach. One of the newcomers set up a loud halloo and the beetle, bewildered and resentful, ran back up toward the rocks. The stranger held a shiny thing in his hand. It spat a lance of fire and the beetle burst into a thousand incandescent pieces. The three cried out in loud voices, laughing; Mitr shrank back under the tree trunk, making herself as small as possible.

One of the strangers noticed the place on the beach where she had drawn her grating. He called his companions and they looked with every display of attention, studying her footprints with extreme interest. One of them made a comment which caused the others to break into loud laughter. Then they all turned and searched up and down the beach.

They were seeking her, thought Mitr. She crouched so far under the trunk that the bark bruised her flesh.

Presently their interest waned and they went back to the sky-fish. One of them brought forth a long black tube which he took down to the edge of the surf and threw far out into the leaden water. The tube stiffened, pulsed, made sucking sounds. The sky-fish was thirsty and was drinking through his proboscis, thought Mitr.

The three strangers now walked along the beach toward the fresh-water stream. Mitr watched their approach with apprehension. Were they following her tracks? Her hands were sweating, her skin tingled.

They stopped at the water's edge, drank, only a few paces away. Mitr could see them plainly. They had bright copper hair and little hair-wisps around their mouths. They wore shining red carapaces around their chests, gray cloth on their legs, metal foot-wrappings. They were much like herself— but somehow different. Bigger, harder, more energetic. They were cruel, too; they had burnt the brown and black beetle. Mitr watched them fascinatedly. Where was their home? Were there others like them, like her, in the sky?

She shifted her position; the foliage crackled. Tingles of excitement and fear ran along her back. Had they heard? She peered out, ready to flee. No, they were walking back down the beach toward the sky-fish.

Mitr jumped up from under the tree-trunk, stood watching from behind the foliage. Plainly they cared little that another like themselves lived nearby. She became angry. Now she wanted to chide them, and order them off her beach.

She held back. It would be foolish to show herself. They might easily throw a lance of flame to burn her as they had the beetle. In any event they were rough and brutal. Strange creatures.

She stole through the forest, flitting from trunk to trunk, falling flat when necessary until she had approached the sky-fish as closely as shelter allowed.

The strangers were standing close around the base of the monster and showed no further disposition to explore.

The tube into the bay grew limp. They pulled it back into the sky-fish. Did that mean that they were about to leave? Good. They had no right on her beach. They had committed an outrage, landing so arrogantly, and killing one of her beetles. She almost stepped forward to upbraid them; then remembered how rough and hard and cruel they were, and held back with a tingling skin.

Stand quietly. Presently they will go, and you will be left in possession of your beach.

She moved restlessly. Rough red brutes. Don't move or they will see you. And then? She shivered.

They were making preparations for leaving. A lump came into her throat. They had seen her tracks and had never bothered to search. They could have found her so easily, she had hid herself almost in plain sight. And now she was closer than ever. If she moved forward only a step, then they would see her.

Skin tingling, she moved a trifle out from behind the tree-trunk. Just a little bit. Then she jumped back, heart thudding.

Had they seen her? With a sudden fluttering access of fright she hoped not. What would they do?

She looked cautiously around the trunk. One of the strangers was staring in a puzzled manner, as if he might have glimpsed movement. Even now he didn't see her. He looked straight into her eyes.

She heard him call out, then she was fleeing through the forest. He charged after her, and after him came the other two, battering down the undergrowth.

They left her, bruised and bleeding, in a bed of ferns, and marched back through the forest toward the beach, laughing and talking in their rough hoarse voices.

She lay quiet for a while. Their voices grew faint. She rose to her feet, staggered, limped after them.

A great glare lit the sky. Through the trees she saw the sky-fish thunder up — higher, higher, higher. It vanished through the overcast. There was silence along the beach, only the endless mutter of the surf.

She walked down to the water's edge, where the tide was coming in. The overcast was graying with evening.

She looked for many minutes into the sky, listening. No sound. The damp wind blew in her face, ruffling her hair. She sighed, turned back toward the ruined glass walls with tears on her cheeks.

The tide was washing up over the grate of straight lines she had drawn so carefully in the sand. Another few minutes and it would be entirely gone.

The World Between

I

Aboard the exploration-cruiser *Blauelm* an ugly variety of psycho-neural ailments was developing. There was no profit in extending the expedition, already in space three months overlong; Explorator Bernisty ordered a return to Blue Star. But there was no rise of spirits, no lift of morale; the damage had been done. Reacting from hypertension, the keen-tuned technicians fell into glum apathy, and sat staring like andromorphs. They ate little, they spoke less. Bernisty attempted various ruses: competition, subtle musics, pungent food, but without effect. Bernisty went further; at his orders the play-women locked themselves in their quarters, and sang erotic chants into the ship's address-system. These measures failing, Bernisty had a dilemma on his hands. At stake was the identity of his team, so craftily put together — such a meteorologist to work with such a chemist; such a botanist for such a virus analyst. To return to Blue Star thus demoralized — Bernisty shook his craggy head. There would be no further ventures in *Blauelm*.

"Then let's stay out longer," suggested Berel, his own favorite among the play-women.

Bernisty shook his head, thinking that Berel's usual intelligence had failed her. "We'd make bad matters worse."

"Then what will you do?"

Bernisty admitted he had no idea, and went away to think. Later in the day, he decided on a course of immense consequence; he swerved aside to make a survey of the Kay System. If anything would rouse the spirits of his men, this was it. There was danger to the detour, but none of great note; spice to the venture came from the fascination of the alien, the oddness of the Kay cities with their taboo against regular form, the bizarre Kay social system.

The star Kay glowed and waxed, and Bernisty saw that his scheme was succeeding. There was once more talk, animation, argument along the gray steel corridors.

The *Blauelm* slid above the Kay ecliptic; the various worlds fell astern, passing so close that the minute movement, the throb of the cities, the dynamic pulse of the workshops were plain in the viewplates. Kith and Kelmet — these two warted over with domes — Karnfray, Koblenz, Kavanaf, then the central sun-star Kay; then Kool, too hot for life; then Kerrykirk, the capital world; then Konbald and Kinsle, the ammonia giants frozen and dead — and the Kay System was astern.

Now Bernisty waited on tenterhooks; would there be a relapse toward inanition, or would the intellectual impetus suffice for the remainder of the voyage? Blue Star lay ahead, another week's journey. Between lay a yellow star of no particular note … It was while passing the yellow star that the consequences of Bernisty's ruse revealed themselves.

"Planet!" sang out the cartographer.

This was a cry to arouse no excitement; during the last eight months it had sounded many times through the *Blauelm*. Always the planet had proved so hot as to melt iron; or so cold as to freeze gas; or so poisonous as to corrode skin; or so empty of air as to suck out a man's lungs. The call was no longer a stimulus.

"Atmosphere!" cried the cartographer. The meteorologist looked up in interest. "Mean temperature — twenty-four degrees!"

Bernisty came to look, and measured the gravity himself. "One and one-tenth normal …" He motioned to the navigator, who needed no more to compute for a landing.

Bernisty stood watching the disk of the planet in the viewplate. "There must be something wrong with it. Either the Kay or ourselves must have checked a hundred times; it's directly between us."

"No record of the planet, Bernisty," reported the librarian, burrowing eagerly among his tapes and pivots. "No record of exploration; no record of anything."

"Surely it's known the star exists?" demanded Bernisty with a hint of sarcasm.

"Oh, indeed — we call it Maraplexa, the Kay call it Melliflo. But there is no mention of either system exploring or developing."

"Atmosphere," called the meteorologist, "methane, carbon dioxide, ammonia, water vapor. Unbreathable, but Type 6-D — potential."

"No chlorophyll, haemaphyll, blusk, or petradine absorption," muttered the botanist, an eye to the spectrograph. "In short — no native vegetation."

"Let me understand all this," said Bernisty. "Temperature, gravity, pressure okay?"

"Okay."

"No corrosive gas?"

"None."

"No native life?"

"No sign."

"And no record of exploration, claim or development?"

"None."

"Then," said Bernisty triumphantly, "we're moving in." To the radioman: "Issue notice of intent. Broadcast to all quarters, the Archive Station. From this hour, Maraplexa is a Blue Star development!"

The *Blauelm* slowed, and swung down to land. Bernisty sat watching with Berel the play-girl.

"Why — why — *why!*" Blandwick the navigator argued with the cartographer. "Why have not the Kay started development?"

"The same reason, evidently, that we haven't; we look too far afield."

"We comb the fringes of the galaxy," said Berel with a sly side-glance at Bernisty. "We sift the globular clusters."

"And here," said Bernisty, ruefully, "a near-neighbor to our own star — a world that merely needs an atmosphere modification — a world we can mold into a garden!"

"But will the Kay allow?" Blandwick put forth.

"What may they do?"

"This will come hard to them."

"So much the worse for the Kay!"

"They will claim a prior right."

"There are no records to demonstrate."

"And then —"

Bernisty interrupted. "Blandwick, go croak your calamity to the play-girls. With the men at work, they will be bored and so will listen to your woe."

"I know the Kay," maintained Blandwick. "They will never submit to what they will consider a humiliation — a stride ahead by Blue Star."

"They have no choice; they must submit," declared Berel, with the laughing recklessness that originally had called her to Bernisty's eye.

"You are wrong," cried Blandwick excitedly, and Bernisty held up his hand for peace.

"We shall see, we shall see."

Presently, Bufco — the radioman — brought three messages. The first, from Blue Star Central, conveyed congratulations; the second, from the Archive Station, corroborated the discovery; the third, from Kerrykirk, was clearly a hasty improvisation. It declared that the Kay System had long regarded Maraplexa as neutral, a no-man's-land between the two Systems; that a Blue Star development would be unfavorably received.

Bernisty chuckled at each of the three messages, most of all at the last. "The ears of their explorators are scorching; they need new lands even more desperately than we do, what with their fecund breeding."

"Like farrowing pigs, rather than true men," sniffed Berel.

"They're true men if legend can be believed. We're said to be all stock of the same planet — all from the same lone world."

"The legend is pretty, but — where is this world — this old Earth of the fable?"

Bernisty shrugged. "I hold no brief for the myth; and now — here is our world below us."

"What will you name it?"

Bernisty considered. "In due course we'll find a name. Perhaps 'New Earth', to honor our primeval home."

The unsophisticated eye might have found New Earth harsh, bleak, savage. The windy atmosphere roared across plains and mountains;

sunlight glared on deserts and seas of white alkali. Bernisty, however, saw the world as a diamond in the rough — the classic example of a world right for modification. The radiation was right; the gravity was right; the atmosphere held no halogens or corrosive fractions; the soil was free of alien life, and alien proteins, which poisoned even more effectively than the halogens.

Sauntering out on the windy surface, he discussed all this with Berel. "Of such ground are gardens built," indicating a plain of loess which spread away from the base of the ship. "And of such hills —" he pointed to the range of hills behind "— do rivers come."

"When aerial water exists to form rain," remarked Berel.

"A detail, a detail; could we call ourselves ecologists and be deterred by so small a matter?"

"I am a play-girl, no ecologist —"

"Except in the largest possible sense."

"— I can not consider a thousand billion tons of water a detail."

Bernisty laughed. "We go by easy stages. First the carbon dioxide is sucked down and reduced; for this reason we sowed standard 6-D Basic vetch along the loess today."

"But how will it breathe? Don't plants need oxygen?"

"Look."

From the *Blauelm*, a cloud of brown-green smoke erupted, rose in a greasy plume to be carried off downwind. "Spores of symbiotic lichens: Type Z forms oxygen-pods on the vetch. Type RS is non-photosynthetic — it combines methane with oxygen to make water, which the vetch uses for its growth. The three plants are the standard primary unit for worlds like this one."

Berel looked around the dusty horizon. "I suppose it will develop as you predict — and I will never cease to marvel."

"In three weeks the plain will be green; in six weeks the sporing and seeding will be in full swing; in six months the entire planet will be forty feet deep in vegetation; and, in a year we'll start establishing the ultimate ecology of the planet."

"If the Kay allow."

"The Kay can not prevent; the planet is ours."

Berel inspected the burly shoulders, the hard profile. "You speak with masculine positivity, where everything depends and stipulates from the traditions of the Archive Station. I have no such certainty; my universe is more dubious."

"You are intuitive, I am rational."

"Reason," mused Berel, "tells you the Kay will abide by the Archive laws; my intuition tells me they will not."

"But what can they do? Attack us? Drive us off?"

"Who knows?"

Bernisty snorted. "They'll never dare."

"How long do we wait here?"

"Only to verify the germination of the vetch, then back to Blue Star."

"And then?"

"And then — we return to develop the full scale ecology."

II

On the thirteenth day, Bartenbrock, the botanist, trudged back from a day on the windy loess to announce the first shoots of vegetation. He showed samples to Bernisty — small pale sprigs with varnished leaves at the tip.

Bernisty critically examined the stem. Fastened like tiny galls were sacs in two colors — pale green and white. He pointed these out to Berel. "The green pods store oxygen, the white collect water."

"So," said Berel, "already New Earth begins to shift its atmosphere."

"Before your life runs out, you will see Blue Star cities along that plain."

"Somehow, my Bernisty, I doubt that."

The head-set sounded. "X. Bernisty; Radioman Bufco here. Three ships circling the planet; they refuse to acknowledge signals."

Bernisty cast the sprig of vetch to the ground. "That'll be the Kay."

Berel looked after him. "Where are the Blue Star cities now?"

Bernisty hastening away made no answer. Berel came after, followed to the control room of the *Blauelm,* where Bernisty tuned the view-plate. "Where are they?" she asked.

"They're around the planet just now — scouting."

"What kind of ships are they?"

"Patrol-attack vessels. Kay design. Here they come now."

Three dark shapes showed on the screen. Bernisty snapped to Bufco, "Send out the Universal Greeting Code."

"Yes Bernisty."

Bernisty watched, while Bufco spoke in the archaic Universal language.

The ships paused, swerved, settled.

"It looks," said Berel softly, "as if they are landing."

"Yes."

"They are armed; they can destroy us."

"They can — but they'll never dare."

"I don't think you quite understand the Kay psyche."

"Do you?" snapped Bernisty.

She nodded. "Before I entered my girl-hood, I studied; now that I near its end, I plan to continue."

"You are more productive as a girl; while you study and cram your pretty head, I must find a new companion for my cruising."

She nodded at the settling black ships. "If there is to be more cruising for any of us."

Bufco leaned over his instrument as a voice spoke from the mesh. Bernisty listened to syllables he could not understand, though the peremptory tones told their own story.

"What's he say?"

"He demands that we vacate this planet; he says it is claimed by the Kay."

"Tell him to vacate himself; tell him he's crazy... No, better: tell him to communicate with Archive Station."

Bufco spoke in the archaic tongue; the response crackled forth.

"He is landing. He sounds pretty firm."

"Let him land; let him be firm! Our claim is guaranteed by the Archive Station!" But Bernisty nevertheless pulled on his head-dome, and went outside to watch the Kay ships settle upon the loess, and he winced at the energy singeing the tender young vetch he had planted.

There was movement at his back; it was Berel. "What do you do here?" he asked brusquely. "This is no place for play-girls."

"I come now as a student."

Bernisty laughed shortly; the concept of Berel as a serious worker seemed somehow ridiculous.

"You laugh," said Berel. "Very well, let me talk to the Kay."

"You!"

"I know both Kay and Universal."

Bernisty glared, then shrugged. "You may interpret."

The ports of the black ships opened; eight Kay men came forward. This was the first time Bernisty had ever met one of the alien system face-to-face, and at first sight he found them fully as bizarre as he had expected. They were tall spare men, on the whole. They wore flowing black cloaks; the hair had been shorn smooth from their heads, and their scalps were decorated with heavy layers of scarlet and black enamel.

"No doubt," whispered Berel, "they find us just as unique."

Bernisty made no answer, having never before considered himself unique.

The eight men halted, twenty feet distant, stared at Bernisty with curious, cold, unfriendly eyes. Bernisty noted that all were armed.

Berel spoke; the dark eyes swung to her in surprise. The foremost responded.

"What's he say?" demanded Bernisty.

Berel grinned. "They want to know if I, a woman, lead the expedition."

Bernisty quivered and flushed. "You tell them that I, Explorator Bernisty, am in full command."

Berel spoke, at rather greater length than seemed necessary to convey his message. The Kay answered.

"Well?"

"He says we'll have to go; that he bears authorization from Kerrykirk to clear the planet, by force if necessary."

Bernisty sized up the man. "Get his name," he said, to win a moment or two.

Berel spoke, received a cool reply.

"He's some kind of a commodore," she told Bernisty. "I can't quite get it clear. His name is Kallish or Kallis…"

"Well, ask Kallish if he's planning to start a war. Ask him which side the Archive Station will stand behind."

Berel translated. Kallish responded at length.

Berel told Bernisty, "He maintains that we are on Kay ground, that Kay colonizers explored this world, but never recorded the exploration. He claims that if war comes it is our responsibility."

"He wants to bluff us," muttered Bernisty from the corner of his mouth. "Well, two can play that game." He drew his needle-beam, scratched a smoking line in the dust two paces in front of Kallish.

Kallish reacted sharply, jerking his hand to his own weapon; the others in his party did likewise.

Bernisty said from the side of his mouth, "Tell 'em to leave — take off back to Kerrykirk, if they don't want the beam along their legs..."

Berel translated, trying to keep the nervousness out of her voice. For answer, Kallish snapped on his own beam, burned a flaring orange mark in front of Bernisty.

Berel shakily translated his message. "He says for us to leave."

Bernisty slowly burned another line into the dust, closer to the black-shod feet. "He's asking for it."

Berel said in a worried voice, "Bernisty, you underestimate the Kay! They're rock-hard — stubborn —"

"And they underestimate Bernisty!"

There was quick staccato talk among the Kay; then Kallish, moving with a jerky flamboyance, snapped down another flickering trench almost at Bernisty's toes.

Bernisty swayed a trifle, then setting his teeth, leaned forward.

"This is a dangerous game," cried Berel.

Bernisty aimed, spattered hot dust over Kallish's sandals. Kallish stepped back; the Kay behind him roared. Kallish, his face a saturnine grinning mask, slowly started burning a line that would cut across Bernisty's ankles. Bernisty could move back — or Kallish could curve aside his beam...

Berel sighed. The beam spat straight, Bernisty stood rock-still. The beam cut the ground, cut over Bernisty's feet, cut on.

Bernisty stood still grinning. He raised his needle-beam.

Kallish turned on his heel, strode away, the black cape flapping in the ammoniacal wind.

Bernisty stood watching; a taut shape, frozen between triumph, pain and fury. Berel waited, not daring to speak. A minute passed. The

Kay ships rose up from the dusty soil of New Earth, and the energy burnt down more shoots of the tender young vetch…

Berel turned to Bernisty: he was stumbling; his face was drawn and ghastly. She caught him under the armpits. From the *Blauelm* came Blandwick and a medic. They placed Bernisty in a litter, and conveyed him to the sick-ward.

As the medic cut cloths and leather away from the charred bones, Bernisty croaked to Berel, "I won today. They're not done… But today—I won!"

"It cost you your feet!"

"I can grow new feet—" Bernisty gasped and sweated as the medic touched a live nerve "—I can't grow a new planet…"

Contrary to Bernisty's expectations, the Kay made no further landing on New Earth. Indeed, the days passed with deceptive calm. The sun rose, glared a while over the ocher, yellow and gray landscape, sank in a western puddle of greens and reds. The winds slowed; a peculiar calm fell over the loess plain. The medic, by judicious hormones, grafts and calcium transplants, set Bernisty's feet to growing again. Temporarily he hobbled around in special shoes, staying close to the *Blauelm*.

Six days after the Kay had come and gone, the *Beaudry* arrived from Blue Star. It brought a complete ecological laboratory, with stocks of seeds, spores, eggs, sperm; spawn, bulbs, grafts; frozen fingerlings, copepods, experimental cells and embryos; grubs, larvae, pupae; amoebae, bacteria, viruses; as well as nutritive cultures and solutions. There were also tools for manipulating or mutating established species; even a supply of raw nuclein, unpatterned tissue, clear protoplasm from which simple forms of life could be designed and constructed. It was now Bernisty's option either to return to Blue Star with the *Blauelm*, or remain to direct the development of New Earth. Without conscious thought he made his choice; he elected to stay. Almost two-thirds of his technical crew made the same choice. And the day after the arrival of the *Beaudry*, the *Blauelm* took off for Blue Star.

This day was notable in several respects. It signalized the complete changeover in Bernisty's life; from Explorator, pure and simple, to the more highly-specialized Master Ecologist, with the corresponding rise in prestige. It was on this day that New Earth took on the semblance of a habitable world, rather than a barren mass of rock and gas to be molded. The vetch over the loess plain had grown to a mottled green-brown sea, beaded and wadded with lichen pods. Already it was coming to its first seed. The lichens had already spored three or four times. There was yet no detectable change in the New Earth atmosphere; it was still CO_2, methane, ammonia, with traces of water vapor and inert gases, but the effect of the vetch was geometrically progressive, and as yet the total amount of vegetation was small compared to what it would be.

The third event of importance upon this day was the appearance of Kathryn.

She came down in a small space-boat, and landed with a roughness that indicated either lack of skill or great physical weakness. Bernisty watched the boat's arrival from the dorsal promenade of the *Beaudry*, with Berel standing at his elbow.

"A Kay boat," said Berel huskily.

Bernisty looked at her in quick surprise. "Why do you say that? It might be a boat from Alvan or Canopus — or the Graemer System, or a Dannic vessel from Copenhag."

"No. It is Kay."

"How do you know?"

Out of the boat stumbled the form of a young woman. Even at this distance it could be seen she was very beautiful — something in the confidence of movement, the easy grace... She wore a head-dome, but little else. Bernisty felt Berel stiffening. Jealousy? She felt none when he amused himself with other play-girls; did she sense here a deeper threat?

Berel said in a throaty voice, "She's a spy — a Kay spy. Send her away!" Bernisty was pulling on his own dome; a few minutes later, he walked across the dusty plain to meet the young woman, who was pushing her way slowly against the wind.

Bernisty paused, sized her up. She was slight, more delicate in build than most of the Blue Star women; she had a thick cap of black elf-locks; pale skin with the luminous look of old vellum; wide dark eyes.

Bernisty felt a peculiar lump rising in his throat; a feeling of awe and protectiveness such as Berel nor any other woman had ever aroused.

Berel was behind him. Berel was antagonistic; both Bernisty and the strange woman felt it.

Berel said, "She's a spy — clearly! Send her away!"

Bernisty said, "Ask her what she wants."

The woman said, "I speak your Blue Star language, Bernisty; you can ask me yourself."

"Very well. Who are you? What do you do here?"

"My name is Kathryn —"

"She is a Kay!" said Berel.

"— I am a criminal. I escaped my punishment, and fled in this direction."

"Come," said Bernisty. "I would examine you more closely."

In the *Beaudry* wardroom, crowded with interested watchers, she told her story. She claimed to be the daughter of a Kirkassian freeholder —

"What is that?" asked Berel in a skeptical voice.

Kathryn responded mildly. "A few of the Kirkassians still keep their strongholds in the Keviot Mountains — a tribe descended from ancient brigands."

"So you are the daughter of a brigand?"

"I am more; I am a criminal in my own right," replied Kathryn mildly.

Bernisty could contain his curiosity no more. "What did you do, girl; what did you do?"

"I committed the act of —" here she used a Kay word which Bernisty was unable to understand. Berel's knitted brows indicated that she likewise was puzzled. "After that," went on Kathryn, "I upset a brazier of incense on the head of a priest. Had I felt remorse, I would have remained to be punished; since I did not I fled here in the space-boat."

"Incredible!" said Berel in disgust.

Bernisty sat watching in amusement. "Apparently, girl, you are believed to be a Kay spy. What do you say to that?"

"If I were or if I were not — in either case I would deny it."

"You deny it then?"

Kathryn's face creased; she broke out into a laugh of sheer delight. "No. I admit it. I am a Kay spy."

"I knew it, I knew it —"

"Hush, woman," said Bernisty. He turned to Kathryn, his brow creased in puzzlement. "You admit you are a spy?"

"Do you believe me?"

"By the Bulls of Bashan — I hardly know what I believe!"

"She's a clever trickster — cunning!" stormed Berel. "She's pulling her artful silk around your eyes."

"Quiet!" roared Bernisty. "Give me some credit for normal perceptiveness!" He turned to Kathryn. "Only a madwoman would admit to being a spy."

"Perhaps I am a madwoman," she said with grave simplicity.

Bernisty threw up his hands. "Very well, what is the difference? There are no secrets here in the first place. If you wish to spy, do so — as overtly or as stealthily as you please, whichever suits you. If you merely seek refuge, that is yours too, for you are on Blue Star soil."

"My thanks to you, Bernisty."

III

Bernisty flew out with Broderick, the cartographer, mapping, photographing, exploring and generally inspecting New Earth. The landscape was everywhere similar — a bleak scarred surface like the inside of a burned out kiln. Everywhere loess plains of wind-spread dust abutted harsh crags.

Broderick nudged Bernisty. "Observe."

Bernisty, following the gesture, saw three faintly-marked but unmistakable squares on the desert below — vast areas of crumbled stone, strewed over by wind-driven sand.

"Those are either the most gigantic crystals the universe has ever known," said Bernisty, "or — we are not the first intelligent race to set foot on this planet."

"Shall we land?"

Bernisty surveyed the squares through his telescope. "There is little to see… Leave it for the archaeologists; I'll call some out from Blue Star."

Returning toward the *Beaudry*, Bernisty suddenly called, "Stop!"

They set down the survey-boat; Bernisty alighted, and with vast satisfaction inspected a patch of green-brown vegetation: Basic 6-D vetch, podded over with the symbiotic lichens which fed it oxygen and water.

"Another six weeks," said Bernisty, "the world will froth with this stuff."

Broderick peered closely at a leaf. "What is that red blotch?"

"Red blotch?" Bernisty peered, frowned. "It looks like a rust, a fungus."

"Is that good?"

"No — of course not! It's — bad! ... I can't quite understand it. This planet was sterile when we arrived."

"Spores drop in from space," suggested Broderick.

Bernisty nodded. "And space-boats likewise. Come, let's get back to the *Beaudry*. You have the position of this spot?"

"To the centimeter."

"Never mind. I'll kill this colony." And Bernisty seared the ground clean of the patch of vetch he had been so proud of. They returned to the *Beaudry* in silence, flying in over the plain which now grew thick with mottled foliage. Alighting from the boat, Bernisty ran not to the *Beaudry* but to the nearest shrub, and inspected the leaves. "None here ... None here — nor here ..."

"Bernisty!"

Bernisty looked around. Baron the botanist approached, his face stern. Bernisty's heart sank. "Yes?"

"There has been inexcusable negligence."

"Rust?"

"Rust. It's destroying the vetch."

Bernisty swung on his heel. "You've got a sample?"

"We're already working out a counter-agent in the lab."

"Good ..."

But the rust was a hardy growth; finding an agency to destroy the rust and still leave the vetch and the lichens unharmed proved a task of enormous difficulty. Sample after sample of virus, germ, blot, wort and fungus failed to satisfy the conditions and were destroyed in the furnace. Meanwhile, the color of the vetch changed from brown-green to red-green to iodine-color; and the proud growth began to slump and rot.

Bernisty walked sleeplessly, exhorting, cursing his technicians. "You call yourselves ecologists? A simple affair of separating a rust from the vetch — you fail, you flounder! Here — give me that culture!" And Bernisty seized the culture-dish from Baron, himself red-eyed and irritable.

The desired agent was at last found in a culture of slime-molds; and another two days passed before the pure strain was isolated and set out in a culture. Now the vetch was rotting, and the lichens lay scattered like autumn leaves.

Aboard the *Beaudry* there was feverish activity. Cauldrons full of culture crowded the laboratory, the corridors; trays of spores dried in the saloon, in the engine-room, in the library.

Here Bernisty once more became aware of Kathryn, when he found her scraping dry spores into distribution boxes. He paused to watch her; he felt the shift of her attention from the task to himself, but he was too tired to speak. He merely nodded, turned and returned to the laboratory.

The slime-molds were broadcast, but clearly it was too late. "Very well," said Bernisty, "we broadcast another setting of seed — Basic 6-D vetch. This time we know our danger and we already have the means to protect ourselves."

The new vetch grew; much of the old vetch revived. The slime-mold, when it found no more rust, perished — except for one or two mutant varieties which attacked the lichen. For a time, it appeared as if these spores would prove as dangerous as the rust; but the *Beaudry* catalogue listed a virus selectively attacking slime-molds; this was broadcast, and the molds disappeared.

Bernisty was yet disgruntled. At an assembly of the entire crew he said, "Instead of three agencies — the vetch and the two lichens — there is now extant six, counting the rust, the slime-mold, the virus. The more life — the harder to control. I emphasize most strongly the need for care and absolute antisepsis."

In spite of the precautions, rust appeared again — this time a black variety. But Bernisty was ready; inside of two days, he disseminated counter-agent. The rust disappeared; the vetch flourished. Everywhere, now, across the planet lay the brown-green carpet. In spots it rioted forty feet thick, climbing and wrestling, stalk against stalk, leaf lapping leaf. It climbed up the granite crags; it hung festooned over precipices. And each day, countless tons of CO_2 became oxygen, methane became water and more CO_2

Bernisty watched the atmospheric-analyses closely; and one day the percentage of oxygen in the air rose from the 'imperceptible' to the 'minute trace' category. On this day, he ordered a general holiday and banquet. It was Blue Star formal custom for men and women to eat separately, the sight of open mouths being deemed as immodest as the act of elimination. The occasion however was one of high comradeship and festivity, and Bernisty, who was neither modest nor sensitive, ordered the custom ignored; so it was in an atmosphere of gay abandon that the banquet began.

As the banquet progressed, as the ichors and alcohols took effect, the hilarity and abandon became more pronounced. At Bernisty's side sat Berel, and though she had shared his couch during the feverish weeks previously she had felt that his attentions were completely impersonal; that she was no more than a play-girl. When she noticed his eyes almost of themselves on Kathryn's wine-flushed face, she felt emotions inside her that almost brought tears to her eyes.

"This must not be," she muttered to herself. "In a few months I am play-girl no more; I am student. I mate whom I choose; I do not choose this bushy egotistical brute, this philandering Bernisty!"

In Bernisty's mind there were strange stirrings too. "Berel is pleasant and kind," he thought. "But Kathryn! The flair! The spirit!" And feeling her eyes on him he thrilled like a schoolboy.

Broderick the cartographer, his head spinning and fuzzy, at this moment seized Kathryn's shoulders and drew her back to kiss her. She pulled aside, cast a whimsical glance at Bernisty. It was enough. Bernisty was by her side; he lifted her, carried her back to his chair, still hobbling on his burnt feet. Her perfume intoxicated him as much as the wine; he hardly noticed Berel's furious face.

This must not be, thought Berel desperately. And now inspiration came to her. "Bernisty! Bernisty!" She tugged at his arm.

Bernisty turned his head. "Yes?"

"The rusts — I know how they appeared on the vetch!"

"They drifted down as spores — from space."

"They drifted down in Kathryn's space-boat! She's not a spy — she's a saboteur!" Even in her fury Berel had to admire the limpid innocence of Kathryn's face. "She's a Kay agent — an enemy."

"Oh, bah," muttered Bernisty, sheepishly. "This is woman-talk."

"Woman-talk, is it?" screamed Berel. "What do you think is happening now, while you feast and fondle? —" she pointed a finger on which the metal foil flower blossom quivered "— that — that *besom*!"

"Why — I don't understand you," said Bernisty, looking in puzzlement from girl to girl.

"While you sit lording it, the Kay spread blight and ruin!"

"Eh? What's this?" Bernisty continued to look from Berel to Kathryn, feeling suddenly clumsy and rather foolish. Kathryn moved on his lap. Her voice was easy, but now her body was stiff. "If you believe so, check on your radars and viewscopes."

Bernisty relaxed. "Oh — nonsense."

"No, no no!" shrilled Berel. "She tries to seduce your reason!"

Bernisty growled to Bufco, "Check the radar." Then he, too, rose to his feet. "I'll come with you."

"Surely you don't *believe* —" began Kathryn.

"I believe nothing till I see the radar tapes."

Bufco flung switches, focussed his viewer. A small pip of light appeared. "A ship!"

"Coming or going?"

"Right now it's going!"

"Where are the tapes?"

Bufco reeled out the records. Bernisty bent over them, his eyebrows bristling. "Humph."

Bufco looked at him questioningly.

"This is very strange."

"How so?"

"The ship had only just arrived — almost at once it turned aside, fled out away from New Earth."

Bufco studied the tapes. "This occurred precisely four minutes and thirty seconds ago."

"Precisely when we left the saloon."

"Do you think —"

"I don't know what to think."

"It's almost as if they received a message — a warning…"

"But how? From where?" Bernisty hesitated. "The natural object of suspicion," he said slowly, "is Kathryn."

Bufco looked up with a curious glint in his eyes. "What will you do with her?"

"I didn't say she was guilty; I remarked that she was the logical object of suspicion…" He pushed the tape magazine back under the scanner. "Let's go see what's been done…What new mischief…"

No mischief was apparent. The skies were clear and yellowish-green; the vetch grew well.

Bernisty returned inside the *Beaudry*, gave certain instructions to Blandwick, who took off in the survey-boat and returned an hour later with a small silk bag held carefully. "I don't know what they are," said Blandwick.

"They're bound to be bad." Bernisty took the small silk bag to the laboratory and watched while the two botanists, the two mycologists, the four entomologists studied the contents of the bag.

The entomologists identified the material. "These are eggs of some small insect — from the gene-count and diffraction-pattern one or another of the mites."

Bernisty nodded. He looked sourly at the waiting men. "Need I tell you what to do?"

"No."

Bernisty returned to his private office and presently sent for Berel. He asked, without preliminary, "How did you know a Kay ship was in the sky?"

Berel stood staring defiantly down at him. "I did not know; I guessed."

Bernisty studied her for a moment. "Yes — you spoke of your intuitive abilities."

"This was not intuition," said Berel scornfully. "This was plain common sense."

"I don't follow you."

"It's perfectly clear. A Kay woman-spy appears. The ecology went bad right away; red rust and black rust. You beat the rust, you celebrate; you're keyed to a sense of relief. What better time to start a new plague?"

Bernisty nodded slowly. "What better time, indeed..."

"Incidentally—what kind of plague is it going to be?"

"Plant-lice—mites. I think we can beat it before it gets started."

"Then what?"

"I don't know..."

"It looks as if the Kay can't scare us off; they mean to work us to death."

"That's what it looks like."

"Can they do it?"

"I don't see how we can stop them from trying. It's easy to breed pests; hard to kill them."

Banta, the head entomologist, came in with a glass tube. "Here's some of them—hatched."

"Already?"

"We hurried it up a little."

"Can they live in this atmosphere? There's not much oxygen—lots of ammonia."

"They thrive on it; it's what they're breathing now."

Bernisty ruefully inspected the bottle. "And that's our good vetch they're eating, too."

Berel looked over his shoulder. "What can we do about them?"

Banta looked properly dubious. "The natural enemies are certain parasites, viruses, dragonflies, and a kind of small armored gnat that breeds very quickly, and which I think we'd do best to concentrate on. In fact we're already engaging in large-scale selective breeding, trying to find a strain to live in this atmosphere."

"Good work, Banta." Bernisty rose to his feet.

"Where are you going?" asked Berel.

"Out to check on the vetch."

"I'll come with you."

Out on the plain, Bernisty seemed intent not so much on the vetch as on the sky.

"What are you looking for?" Berel asked.

Bernisty pointed. "See that wisp up there?"

"A cloud?"

"Just a bit of frost — a few sprinkles of ice crystals... But it's a start! Our first rainstorm — that'll be an event!"

"Provided the methane and oxygen don't explode — and send us all to kingdom come!"

"Yes, yes," muttered Bernisty. "We'll have to set out some new methanophiles."

"And how will you get rid of all this ammonia?"

"There's a marsh-plant from Salsiberry that under proper conditions performs the equation: $12NH_3+9O_2 = 18H_2O+6N_2$."

"Rather a waste of time for it, I should say," remarked Berel. "What does it gain?"

"A freak, only a freak. What do we gain by laughing? Another freak."

"A pleasant uselessness."

Bernisty was examining the vetch. "There, here. Look. Under this leaf." He displayed the mites; slow yellow aphid-creatures.

"When will your gnats be ready?"

"Banta is letting half his stock free; maybe they'll feed faster on their own than in the laboratory."

"Does — does Kathryn know about the gnats?"

"You're still gunning for her, eh?"

"I think she's a spy."

Bernisty said mildly, "I can't think of a way that either one of you could have communicated with that Kay ship."

"Either one of us!"

"Someone warned him away. Kathryn is the logical suspect; but you knew he was there."

Berel swung on her heel, stalked back to the *Beaudry*.

IV

The gnats were countering the mites, apparently; the population of both first increased, then dwindled. After which the vetch grew taller and stronger. There was now oxygen in the air, and the botanists broadcast a dozen new species — broad-leaves, producers of oxygen;

nitrogen-fixers, absorbing the ammonia; the methanophiles from the young methane-rich worlds, combining oxygen with methane, and growing in magnificent white towers like carved ivory.

Bernisty's feet were whole again, a size larger than his old ones, and he was forced to discard his worn and comfortable boots for a new pair cut from stiff blue leather.

Kathryn was playfully helping him cram his feet into the hard vacancies. Casually, Bernisty said, "It's been bothering me, Kathryn: tell me, how did you call to the Kay?"

She started, gave him an instant piteous wide-eyed stare, like a trapped rabbit, then she laughed. "The same way you do—with my mouth."

"When?"

"Oh, every day about this time."

"I'd be glad to watch you."

"Very well." She looked up at the window, spoke in the ringing Kay tongue.

"What did you say?" asked Bernisty politely.

"I said that the mites were a failure; that there was good morale here aboard the *Beaudry*; that you were a great leader, a wonderful man."

"But you recommended no further steps."

She smiled demurely. "I am no ecologist—neither constructive, nor destructive."

"Very well," said Bernisty, standing into his boots. "We shall see."

Next day the radar-tapes showed the presence of two ships; they had made fleeting visits—"long enough to dump their villainous cargo," so Bufco reported to Bernisty.

The cargo proved to be eggs of a ferocious blue wasp, which preyed on the gnats. The gnats perished; the mites prospered; the vetch began to wilt under the countless sucking tubes. To counter the wasp, Bernisty released a swarm of feathery blue flying-ribbons. The wasps bred inside a peculiar, small brown puff-ball fungus (the spores for which had been released with the wasp larvae). The flying-ribbons ate these puff-balls. With no shelter for their larvae, the wasps died; the gnats revived in numbers, gorging on mites till their thoraxes split.

The Kay assaulted on a grander scale. Three large ships passed by night, disgorging a witches-cauldron of reptiles, insects, arachnids, land-crabs, a dozen phyla without formal classification. The human resources of the *Beaudry* were inadequate to the challenge; they began to fail, from insect stings; another botanist took a pulsing white-blue gangrene from the prick of a poisonous thorn.

New Earth was no longer a mild region of vetch, lichen, and dusty wind; New Earth was a fantastic jungle. Insects stalked each other through the leafy wildernesses; there were local specializations and improbable adaptations. There were spiders and lizards the size of cats; scorpions which rang like bells when they walked; long-legged lobsters; poisonous butterflies; a species of giant moth which, finding the environment congenial, grew ever more gigantic.

Within the *Beaudry* there was everywhere a sense of defeat. Bernisty walked limping along the promenade, the limp more of an unconscious attitude than a physical necessity. The problem was too complex for a single brain, he thought — or for a single team of human brains. The various life-forms on the planet, each evolving, mutating, expanding into vacant niches, selecting the range of their eventual destinies — they made a pattern too haphazard for an electronic computer, for a team of computers.

Blandwick, the meteorologist, came along the promenade with his daily atmospheric-report. Bernisty derived a certain melancholy pleasure to find that while there had been no great increase in oxygen and water-vapor, neither had there been any decrease. "In fact," said Blandwick, "there's a tremendous amount of water tied up in all those bugs and parasites."

Bernisty shook his head. "Nothing appreciable... And they're eating away the vetch faster than we can kill 'em off. New varieties appear faster than we can find them."

Blandwick frowned. "The Kay are following no clear pattern."

"No, they're just dumping anything they hope might be destructive."

"Why don't we use the same technique? Instead of selective counter-action, we turn loose our entire biological program. Shotgun tactics."

Bernisty limped on a few paces. "Well, why not? The total effect might be beneficial... Certainly less destructive than what's going on out there now." He paused. "We deal in unpredictables of course — and this is contrary to my essential logic."

Blandwick sniffed. "None of our gains to date have been the predictable ones."

Bernisty grinned, after a momentary irritation, since Blandwick's remark was inaccurate; had Blandwick been driving home a truth, then there would have been cause for irritation.

"Very well, Blandwick," he said jovially. "We shoot the works. If it succeeds we'll name the first settlement Blandwick."

"Humph," said the pessimistic Blandwick, and Bernisty went to give the necessary orders.

Now every vat, tub, culture tank, incubator, tray and rack in the laboratory was full; as soon as the contents achieved even a measure of acclimatization to the still nitrogenous atmosphere, they were discharged: pods, plants, molds, bacteria, crawling things, insects, annelids, crustaceans, land ganoids, even a few elementary mammals — life-forms from well over three dozen different worlds. Where New Earth had previously been a battleground, now it was a madhouse.

One variety of palms achieved instant success; inside of two months they towered everywhere over the landscape. Between them hung veils of a peculiar air-floating web, subsisting on flying things. Under the branches, the brambles, there was much killing; much breeding; much eating; growing; fighting; fluttering; dying. Aboard the *Beaudry*, Bernisty was well-pleased and once more jovial.

He clapped Blandwick on the back. "Not only do we call the city after you, we prefix your name to an entire system of philosophy, the Blandwick method."

Blandwick was unmoved by the tribute. "Regardless of the success of 'the Blandwick method', as you call it, the Kay still have a word to say."

"What can they do?" argued Bernisty. "They can liberate creatures no more unique or ravenous than those we ourselves have loosed. Anything the Kay send to New Earth now, is in the nature of anti-climax."

Blandwick smiled sourly. "Do you think they'll give up quite so easily?"

Bernisty became uneasy, and went off in search of Berel. "Well, playgirl," he demanded, "what does your intuition tell you now?"

"It tells me," she snapped, "that whenever you are the most optimistic, the Kay are on the verge of their most devastating attacks."

Bernisty put on a facetious front. "And when will these attacks take place?"

"Ask the spy-woman; she communicates secrets freely to anyone."

"Very well," said Bernisty. "Find her, if you please, and send her to me."

Kathryn appeared. "Yes, Bernisty?"

"I am curious," said Bernisty, "as to what you communicate to the Kay."

Kathryn said, "I tell them that Bernisty is defeating them, that he has countered their worst threats."

"And what do they tell you?"

"They tell me nothing."

"And what do you recommend?"

"I recommend that they either win at a massive single stroke, or give up."

"How do you tell them this?"

Kathryn laughed, showing her pretty white teeth. "I talk to them just as now I talk to you."

"And when do you think they will strike?"

"I don't know… It seems that certainly they are long overdue. Would you not think so?"

"Yes," admitted Bernisty, and turned his head to find Bufco the radioman approaching.

"Kay ships," said Bufco. "A round dozen — mountainous barrels! They made one circuit — departed!"

"Well," said Bernisty, "this is it." He turned upon Kathryn the level look of cold speculation, and she returned the expression of smiling demureness which both of them had come to find familiar.

V

In three days every living thing on New Earth was dead. Not merely dead, but dissolved into a viscous gray syrup which sank into the plain, trickled like sputum down the crags, evaporated into the wind. The effect was miraculous. Where the jungle had thronged the plain — now only plain existed, and already the wind was blowing up dust-devils.

There was one exception to the universal dissolution — the monstrous moths, which by some unknown method, or chemical make-up, had managed to survive. Across the wind they soared; frail fluttering shapes, seeking their former sustenance and finding nothing now but desert.

Aboard the *Beaudry* there was bewilderment; then dejection; then dull rage which could find no overt outlet, until at last Bernisty fell into a sleep.

He awoke with a sense of vague uneasiness, of trouble: the collapse of the New Earth ecology? No. Something deeper, more immediate. He jumped into his clothes, hastened to the saloon. It was nearly full, and gave off a sense of grim malice.

Kathryn sat pale, tense in a chair; behind her stood Banta with a garrote. He was clearly preparing to strangle her, with the rest of the crew as collaborators.

Bernisty stepped across the saloon, broke Banta's jaw and broke the fingers of his clenched fist. Kathryn sat looking up silently.

"Well, you miserable renegades," Bernisty began; but looking around the wardroom, he found no sheepishness, only growing anger, defiance. "What goes on here?" roared Bernisty.

"She is a traitor," said Berel; "we execute her."

"How can she be a traitor? She never promised us faith!"

"She is certainly a spy!"

Bernisty laughed. "She has never dissembled the fact that she communicates with the Kay. How can she then be a spy?"

No one made reply, there was uneasy shifting of eyes.

Bernisty kicked Banta, who was rising to his feet. "Get away, you cur... I'll have no murderers, no lynchers in my crew!"

Berel cried, "She betrayed us!"

"How could she betray us? She never asked us to give her trust. Quite the reverse; she came to us frankly as a Kay; frankly she tells me she reports to the Kay."

"But how?" sneered Berel. "She claims to talk to them — to make you believe she jokes!"

Bernisty regarded Kathryn with a speculative glance. "If I read her character right, Kathryn tells no untruths. It is her single defense. If she says she talks to the Kay, so she does..." He turned to the medic. "Bring an infrascope."

The infrascope revealed strange black shadows inside Kathryn's body. A small button beside her larynx; two slim boxes flat against her diaphragm; wires running down under the skin of each leg.

"What is this?" gasped the medic.

"Internal radio," said Bufco. "The button takes her voice, the leg-wires are the antenna. What better equipment for a spy?"

"She is no spy, I tell you!" Bernisty bellowed. "The fault lies not with her—it lies with me! She *told* me! If I had asked her how her voice got to the Kay, she would have told me—candidly, frankly. I never asked her; I chose to regard the entire affair as a game! If you must garrote someone—garrote me! I am the betrayer—not she!"

Berel turned, walked from the wardroom, others followed. Bernisty turned to Kathryn. "Now—now what will you do? Your venture is a success."

"Yes," said Kathryn, "a success." She likewise left the wardroom. Bernisty followed curiously. She went to the outdoor locker, put on her head-dome, opened the double-lock, stepped out upon the dead plain.

Bernisty watched her from a window. Where would she walk to? Nowhere... She walked to death, like one walking into the surf and swimming straight out to sea. Overhead the giant moths fluttered, flickered down on the wind. Kathryn looked up; Bernisty saw her cringe. A moth flapped close; strove to seize her. She ducked; the wind caught the frail wings, and the moth wheeled away.

Bernisty chewed his lip; then laughed. "Devil take all; devil take the Kay; devil take all..." He jammed on his own head-dome.

Bufco caught his arm. "Bernisty, where do you go?"

"She is brave, she is steadfast; why should she die?"

"She is our enemy!"

"I prefer a brave enemy to cowardly friends." He ran from the ship, across the soft loess now crusted with dried slime.

The moths fluttered, plunged. One clung to Kathryn's shoulders with barbed legs; she struggled, beat with futile hands at the great soft shape.

Shadows fell over Bernisty; he saw the purple-red glinting of big eyes, the impersonal visage. He swung a fist, felt the chitin crunch. Sick pangs of pain reminded him that the hand had already been broken on Banta's jaw. With the moth flapping on the ground he ran off down the wind. Kathryn lay supine, a moth probing her with a tube ill-adapted to cutting plastics and cloth.

Bernisty called out encouragement; a shape swooped on his back, bore him to the ground. He rolled over, kicked; arose, jumped to his feet, tackled the moth on Kathryn, tore off the wings, snapped the head up.

He turned to fight the other swooping shapes but now from the ship came Bufco, with a needle-beam puncturing moths from the sky, and others behind him.

Bernisty carried Kathryn back to the ship. He took her to the surgery, laid her on the pallet. "Cut that radio out of her," he told the medic. "Make her normal, and then if she gets information to the Kay, they'll deserve it."

He found Berel in his quarters, lounging in garments of seductive diaphane. He swept her with an indifferent glance.

Conquering her perturbation she asked, "Well, what now, Bernisty?"

"We start again!"

"Again? When the Kay can sweep the world of life so easy?"

"This time we work differently."

"So?"

"Do you know the ecology of Kerrykirk, the Kay capital world?"

"No."

"In six months — you will find New Earth as close a duplicate as we are able."

"But that is foolhardy! What other pests will the Kay know so well as those of their own world?"

"Those are my own views."

Bernisty presently went to the surgery. The medic handed him the internal radio. Bernisty stared. "What are these — these little bulbs?"

"They are persuaders," said the medic. "They can be easily triggered to red-heat…"

Bernisty said abruptly, "Is she awake?"

"Yes."

Bernisty looked down into the pale face. "You have no more radio."

"I know."

"Will you spy any longer?"

"No. I give you my loyalty, my love."

Bernisty nodded, touched her face, turned, left the room, went to give his orders for a new planet.

Bernisty ordered stocks from Blue Star: Kerrykirk flora and fauna exclusively and set them out as conditions justified. Three months passed uneventfully. The plants of Kerrykirk throve; the air became rich; New Earth felt its first rains.

Kerrykirk trees and cycads sprouted, grew high, forced by growth hormones; the plains grew knee-deep with Kerrykirk grasses.

Then once again came the Kay ships; and now it was as if they played a sly game, conscious of power. The first infestations were only mild harassments.

Bernisty grinned, and released Kerrykirk amphibians into the new puddles. Now the Kay ships came at almost regular intervals, and each vessel brought pests more virulent or voracious; and the *Beaudry* technicians worked incessantly countering the successive invasions.

There was grumbling; Bernisty sent those who wished to go home to Blue Star. Berel departed; her time as a play-girl was finished. Bernisty felt a trace of guilt as she bade him dignified farewell. When he returned to his quarters and found Kathryn there, the guilt disappeared.

The Kay ships came; a new horde of hungry creatures came to devastate the land.

Some of the crew cried defeat. "Where will it end? It is incessant; let us give up this thankless task!"

Others spoke of war. "Is not New Earth already a battleground?"

Bernisty waved a careless hand. "Patience, patience; just one more month."

"Why one more month?"

"Do you not understand? The Kay ecologists are straining their laboratories breeding these pests!"

"Ah!"

One more month, one more Kay visitation, a new rain of violent life, eager to combat the life of New Earth.

"Now!" said Bernisty.

The *Beaudry* technicians collected the latest arrivals, the most effective of the previous cargoes; they were bred; the seeds, spores, eggs, prepared, carefully stored, packed.

One day a ship left New Earth and flew to Kerrykirk, the holds bulging with the most desperately violent enemies of Kerrykirk life that Kerrykirk scientists could find. The ship returned to New Earth with its hold empty. Not till six months later did news of the greatest plagues in history seep out past Kay censorship.

During this time there were no Kay visits to New Earth. "And if they are discreet," Bernisty told the serious man from Blue Star who had come to replace him, "they will never come again. They are too vulnerable to their own pests — so long as we maintain a Kerrykirk ecology."

"Protective coloration, you might say," remarked the new governor of New Earth with a thin-lipped smile.

"Yes, you might say so."

"And what do you do, Bernisty?"

Bernisty listened. A far-off hum came to their ears. "That," said Bernisty, "is the *Blauelm*, arriving from Blue Star. And it's mine for another flight, another exploration."

"You seek another New Earth?" And the thin-lipped smile became broader, with the unconscious superiority the settled man feels for the wanderer.

"Perhaps I'll even find Old Earth ... Hm ..." He kicked up a bit of red glass stamped with the letters STOP. "Curious bit, this ..."

When the Five Moons Rise

Seguilo could not have gone far; there was no place for him to go. Once Perrin had searched the lighthouse and the lonesome acre of rock, there were no other possibilities — only the sky and the ocean.

Seguilo was neither inside the lighthouse nor was he outside.

Perrin went out into the night, squinted up against the five moons. Seguilo was not to be seen on top of the lighthouse.

Seguilo had disappeared.

Perrin looked indecisively over the flowing brine of Maurnilam Var. Had Seguilo slipped on the damp rock and fallen into the sea, he certainly would have called out... The five moons blinked, dazzled, glinted along the surface; Seguilo might even now be floating unseen a hundred yards distant.

Perrin shouted across the dark water: "Seguilo!"

He turned, once more looked up the face of the lighthouse. Around the horizon whirled the twin shafts of red and white light, guiding the barges crossing from South Continent to Spacetown, warning them off Isel Rock.

Perrin walked quickly toward the lighthouse; Seguilo was no doubt asleep in his bunk or in the bathroom.

Perrin went to the top chamber, circled the lumenifer, climbed down the stairs. "Seguilo!"

No answer. The lighthouse returned a metallic vibrating echo.

Seguilo was not in his room, in the bathroom, in the commissary, or in the storeroom. Where else could a man go?

Perrin looked out the door. The five moons cast confusing shadows. He saw a gray blot — "Seguilo!" He ran outside. "Where have you been?"

Seguilo straightened to his full height, a thin man with a wise doleful face. He turned his head; the wind blew his words past Perrin's ears.

Sudden enlightenment came to Perrin. "You must have been under the generator!" The only place he could have been.

Seguilo had come closer. "Yes... I was under the generator." He paused uncertainly by the door, stood looking up at the moons, which this evening had risen all bunched together. Puzzlement creased Perrin's forehead. Why should Seguilo crawl under the generator? "Are you — well?"

"Yes. Perfectly well."

Perrin stepped closer and in the light of the five moons, Ista, Bista, Liad, Miad and Poidel, scrutinized Seguilo sharply. His eyes were dull and noncommittal; he seemed to carry himself stiffly. "Have you hurt yourself? Come over to the steps and sit down."

"Very well." Seguilo ambled across the rock, sat down on the steps.

"You're certain you're all right?"

"Certain."

After a moment Perrin said, "Just before you — went under the generator, you were about to tell me something you said was important."

Seguilo nodded slowly. "That's true."

"What was it?"

Seguilo stared dumbly up into the sky. There was nothing to be heard but the wash of the sea, hissing and rushing where the rock shelved under.

"Well?" asked Perrin finally. Seguilo hesitated.

"You said that when five moons rose together in the sky, it was not wise to believe anything."

"Ah," nodded Seguilo, "so I did."

"What did you mean?"

"I'm not sure."

"Why is not believing anything important?"

"I don't know."

Perrin rose abruptly to his feet. Seguilo normally was crisp, dryly emphatic. "Are you sure you're all right?"

"Right as rain."

That was more like Seguilo. "Maybe a drink of whiskey would fix you up."

"Sounds like a good idea."

Perrin knew where Seguilo kept his private store. "You sit here, I'll get you a shot."

"Yes, I'll sit here."

Perrin hurried inside the lighthouse, clambered the two flights of stairs to the commissary. Seguilo might remain seated or he might not; something in his posture, in the rapt gaze out to sea, suggested that he might not. Perrin found the bottle and a glass, ran back down the steps. Somehow he knew that Seguilo would be gone.

Seguilo was gone. He was not on the steps, nowhere on the windy acre of Isel Rock. It was impossible that he had passed Perrin on the stairs. He might have slipped into the engine room and crawled under the generator once more.

Perrin flung open the door, switched on the lights, stooped, peered under the housing. Nothing.

A greasy film of dust, uniform, unmarred, indicated that no one had ever been there.

Where was Seguilo?

Perrin went up to the top-most part of the lighthouse, carefully searched every nook and cranny down to the outside entrance. No Seguilo.

Perrin walked out on the rock. Bare and empty; no Seguilo.

Seguilo was gone. The dark water of Maurnilam Var sighed and flowed across the shelf.

Perrin opened his mouth to shout across the moon-dazzled swells, but somehow it did not seem right to shout. He went back to the lighthouse, seated himself before the radio transceiver.

Uncertainly he touched the dials; the instrument had been Seguilo's responsibility. Seguilo had built it himself, from parts salvaged from a pair of old instruments.

Perrin tentatively flipped a switch. The screen sputtered into light, the speaker hummed and buzzed. Perrin made hasty adjustments. The screen streaked with darts of blue light, a spatter of quick, red blots. Fuzzy, dim, a face looked forth from the screen. Perrin recognized a junior clerk in the Commission office at Spacetown. He spoke urgently. "This is Harold Perrin, at Isel Rock Lighthouse; send out a relief ship."

The face in the screen looked at him as through thick pebble-glass. A faint voice, overlaid by sputtering and crackling, said, "Adjust your tuning... I can't hear you..."

Perrin raised his voice. "Can you hear me now?"

The face in the screen wavered and faded.

Perrin yelled, "This is Isel Rock Lighthouse! Send out a relief ship! Do you hear? There's been an accident!"

"... signals not coming in. Make out a report, send..." the voice sputtered away.

Cursing furiously under his breath, Perrin twisted knobs, flipped switches. He pounded the set with his fist. The screen flashed bright orange, went dead.

Perrin ran behind, worked an anguished five minutes, to no avail. No light, no sound.

Perrin slowly rose to his feet. Through the window he glimpsed the five moons racing for the west. "When the five moons rise together," Seguilo had said, "it's not wise to believe anything." Seguilo was gone. He had been gone once before and come back; maybe he would come back again. Perrin grimaced, shuddered. It would be best now if Seguilo stayed away. He ran down to the outer door, barred and bolted it. Hard on Seguilo, if he came wandering back... Perrin leaned a moment with his back to the door, listening. Then he went to the generator room, looked under the generator. Nothing. He shut the door, climbed the steps.

Nothing in the commissary, the storeroom, the bathroom, the bedrooms. No one in the light-room. No one on the roof.

No one in the lighthouse but Perrin.

He returned to the commissary, brewed a pot of coffee, sat half an hour listening to the sigh of water across the shelf, then went to his bunk.

Passing Seguilo's room he looked in. The bunk was empty.

When at last he rose in the morning, his mouth was dry, his muscles like bundles of withes, his eyes hot from long staring up at the ceiling. He rinsed his face with cold water and, going to the window, searched the horizon. A curtain of dingy overcast hung halfway up the east; blue-green Magda shone through like an ancient coin covered with verdigris. Over the water oily skeins of blue-green light formed and joined and broke and melted... Out along the south horizon Perrin spied a pair of black barges riding the Trade Current to Spacetown. After a few moments they disappeared into the overcast.

Perrin threw the master switch; above him came the fluttering hum of the lumenifer slowing and dimming.

He descended the stairs, with stiff fingers unbolted the door, flung it wide. The wind blew past his ears, smelling of Maurnilam Var. The tide was low; Isel Rock rose out of the water like a saddle. He walked gingerly to the water's edge. Blue-green Magda broke clear of the overcast; the light struck under the water. Leaning precariously over the shelf, Perrin looked down, past shadows and ledges and grottos, down into the gloom... Movement of some kind; Perrin strained to see. His foot slipped, he almost fell.

Perrin returned to the lighthouse, worked a disconsolate three hours at the transceiver, finally deciding that some vital component had been destroyed.

He opened a lunch unit, pulled a chair to the window, sat gazing across the ocean. Eleven weeks to the relief ship. Isel Rock had been lonely enough with Seguilo.

Blue-green Magda sank in the west. A sulfur overcast drifted up to meet it. Sunset brought a few minutes of sad glory to the sky: jade-colored stain with violet streakings. Perrin started the twin shafts of red and white on their nocturnal sweep, went to stand by the window.

The tide was rising, the water surged over the shelf with a heavy sound. Up from the west floated a moon: Ista, Bista, Liad, Miad, or Poidel? A native would know at a glance. Up they came, one after the other, five balls blue as old ice.

"It's not wise to believe..." What had Seguilo meant? Perrin tried to think back. Seguilo had said, "It's not often, very rare, in fact, that the five moons bunch up—but when they do, then there're high tides." He had hesitated, glancing out at the shelf. "When the five moons rise together," said Seguilo, "it's not wise to believe anything."

Perrin had gazed at him with forehead creased in puzzlement.

Seguilo was an old hand, who knew the fables and lore, which he brought forth from time to time. Perrin had never known quite what to expect from Seguilo; he had the trait indispensable to a lighthouse-tender — taciturnity. The transceiver had been his hobby; in Perrin's ignorant hands, the instrument had destroyed itself. What the lighthouse needed, thought Perrin, was one of the new transceivers with self-contained power unit, master control, the new organic screen, soft and elastic, like a great eye... A sudden rain squall blanketed half the sky; the five moons hurtled toward the cloud bank. The tide surged high over the shelf, almost over a gray mass. Perrin eyed it with interest; what could it be?... About the size of a transceiver, about the same shape. Of course, it could not possibly *be* a transceiver; yet, what a wonderful thing if it were... He squinted, strained his eyes. There, surely, that was the milk-colored screen; those black spots were dials. He sprang to his feet, ran down the stairs, out the door, across the rock... It was irrational; why should a transceiver appear just when he wanted it, as if in answer to his prayer? Of course it might be part of a cargo lost overboard...

Sure enough, the mechanism was bolted to a raft of Manasco logs, and evidently had floated up on the shelf on the high tide.

Perrin, unable to credit his good fortune, crouched beside the gray case. Brand new, with red seals across the master switch.

It was too heavy to carry. Perrin tore off the seals, threw on the power: here was a set he understood. The screen glowed bright.

Perrin dialed to the Commission band. The interior of an office appeared and facing out was, not the officious subordinate, but Superintendent Raymond Flint himself. Nothing could be better.

"Superintendent," cried out Perrin, "this is Isel Rock Lighthouse, Harold Perrin speaking."

"Oh, yes," said Superintendent Flint. "How are you, Perrin? What's the trouble?"

"My partner, Andy Seguilo, disappeared — vanished into nowhere; I'm alone out here."

Superintendent Flint looked shocked. "Disappeared? What happened? Did he fall into the ocean?"

"I don't know. He just disappeared. It happened last night —"

"You should have called in before," said Flint reprovingly. "I would have sent out a rescue copter to search for him."

"I tried to call," Perrin explained, "but I couldn't get the regular transceiver to work. It burnt up on me...I thought I was marooned here."

Superintendent Flint raised his eyebrows in mild curiosity. "Just what are you using now?"

Perrin stammered, "It's a brand new instrument...floated up out of the sea. Probably was lost from a barge."

Flint nodded. "Those bargemen are a careless lot—don't seem to understand what good equipment costs...Well, you sit tight. I'll order a plane out in the morning with a relief crew. You'll be assigned to duty along the Floral Coast. How does that suit you?"

"Very well, sir," said Perrin. "Very well indeed. I can't think of anything I'd like better...Isel Rock is beginning to get on my nerves."

"When the five moons rise, it's not wise to believe anything," said Superintendent Flint in a sepulchral voice.

The screen went dead.

Perrin lifted his hand, slowly turned off the power. A drop of rain fell on his face. He glanced skyward. The squall was almost on him. He tugged at the transceiver, although well aware that it was too heavy to move. In the storeroom was a tarpaulin that would protect the transceiver until morning. The relief crew could help him move it inside.

He ran back to the lighthouse, found the tarpaulin, hurried back outside. Where was the transceiver?...Ah—there. He ran through the pelting drops, wrapped the tarpaulin around the box, lashed it into place, ran back to the lighthouse. He barred the door, and whistling, opened a canned dinner unit.

The rain spun and slashed at the lighthouse. The twin shafts of white and red swept wildly around the sky. Perrin climbed into his bunk, lay warm and drowsy...Seguilo's disappearance was a terrible thing; it would leave a scar on his mind. But it was over and done with. Put it behind him; look to the future. The Floral Coast...

In the morning the sky was bare and clean. Maurnilam Var spread mirror-quiet as far as the eye could reach. Isel Rock lay naked to the sunlight. Looking out the window, Perrin saw a rumpled heap—the tarpaulin, the lashings. The transceiver, the Manasco raft had disappeared utterly.

Perrin sat in the doorway. The sun climbed the sky. A dozen times he jumped to his feet, listening for the sound of engines. But no relief plane appeared.

The sun reached the zenith, verged westward. A barge drifted by, a mile from the rock. Perrin ran out on the shelf, shouting, waving his arms.

The lank, red bargemen sprawled on the cargo stared curiously, made no move. The barge dwindled into the east.

Perrin returned to the doorstep, sat with his head in his hands. Chills and fever ran along his skin. There would be no relief plane. On Isel Rock he would remain, day in, day out, for eleven weeks.

Listlessly he climbed the steps to the commissary. There was no lack of food, he would never starve. But could he bear the solitude, the uncertainty? Seguilo going, coming, going…The unsubstantial transceiver…Who was responsible for these cruel jokes? The five moons rising together—was there some connection?

He found an almanac, carried it to the table. At the top of each page five white circles on a black strip represented the moons. A week ago they strung out at random. Four days ago Liad, the slowest, and Poidel, the fastest, were thirty degrees apart, with Ista, Bista, and Miad between. Two nights ago the peripheries almost touched; last night they were even closer. Tonight Poidel would bulge slightly out in front of Ista, tomorrow night Liad would lag behind Bista…But between the five moons and Seguilo's disappearance—where was the connection?

Gloomily, Perrin ate his dinner. Magda settled into Maurnilam Var without display, a dull dusk settled over Isel Rock, water rose and sighed across the shelf.

Perrin turned on the light, barred the door. There would be no more hoping, no more wishing—no more believing. In eleven weeks the relief ship would convey him back to Spacetown; in the meantime he must make the best of the situation.

Through the window he saw the blue glow in the east, watched Poidel, Ista, Bista, Liad, and Miad climb the sky. The tide came with the moons. Maurnilam Var was still calm, and each moon laid a separate path of reflection along the water.

Perrin looked up into the sky, around the horizon. A beautiful, lonesome sight. With Seguilo he sometimes had felt lonely, but never isolation such as this. Eleven weeks of solitude... If he could select a companion... Perrin let his mind wander.

Into the moonlight a slim figure came walking, wearing tan breeches and a short-sleeved white sports shirt.

Perrin stared, unable to move. The figure walked up to the door, rapped. The muffled sound came up the staircase. "Hello, anybody home?" It was a clear girl's voice.

Perrin swung open the window, called hoarsely, "Go away!"

She moved back, turned up her face, and the moonlight fell upon her features. Perrin's voice died in his throat. He felt his heart beating wildly.

"Go away?" she said in a soft puzzled voice. "I've no place to go."

"Who are you?" he asked. His voice sounded strange to his own ears — desperate, hopeful. After all, she was possible — even though almost impossibly beautiful... She might have flown out from Spacetown. "How did you get here?"

She gestured at Maurnilam Var. "My plane went down about three miles out. I came over on the life raft."

Perrin looked along the water's edge. The outline of a life raft was barely visible.

The girl called up, "Are you going to let me in?"

Perrin stumbled downstairs. He halted at the door, one hand on the bolts, and the blood rushed in his ears.

An impatient tapping jarred his hand. "I'm freezing to death out here."

Perrin let the door swing back. She stood facing him, half-smiling. "You're a very cautious lighthouse-tender — or perhaps a woman-hater?"

Perrin searched her face, her eyes, the expression of her mouth. "Are you... real?"

She laughed, not at all offended. "Of course I'm real." She held out her hand. "Touch me." Perrin stared at her — the essence of night-flowers, soft silk, hot blood, sweetness, delightful fire. "Touch me," she repeated softly.

Perrin moved back uncertainly, and she came forward, into the lighthouse. "Can you call the shore?"

"No... my transceiver is out of order."

She turned him a quick firefly look. "When is your next relief boat?"

"Eleven weeks."

"Eleven weeks!" she sighed a soft shallow sigh.

Perrin moved back another half-step. "How did you know I was alone?"

She seemed confused. "I didn't know... Aren't lighthouse-keepers always alone?"

"No."

She came a step closer. "You don't seem pleased to see me. Are you... a hermit?"

"No," said Perrin in a husky voice. "Quite the reverse... But I can't quite get used to you. You're a miracle. Too good to be true. Just now I was wishing for someone... exactly like you. Exactly."

"And here I am."

Perrin moved uneasily. "What's your name?"

He knew what she would say before she spoke. "Sue."

"Sue what?" He tried to hold his mind vacant.

"Oh... just Sue. Isn't that enough?"

Perrin felt the skin of his face tighten. "Where is your home?"

She looked vaguely over her shoulder. Perrin held his mind blank, but the word came through.

"Hell."

Perrin's breath came hard and sharp.

"And what is Hell like?"

"It is... cold and dark."

Perrin stepped back. "Go away. Go away." His vision blurred; her face melted as if tears had come across his eyes.

"Where will I go?"

"Back where you came from."

"But —" forlornly "— there is nowhere but Maurnilam Var. And up here —" She stopped short, took a swift step forward, stood looking up into his face. He could feel the warmth of her body. "Are you afraid of me?"

Perrin wrenched his eyes from her face. "You're not real. You're something which takes the shape of my thoughts. Perhaps you killed Seguilo... I don't know what you are. But you're not real."

"Not real? Of course I'm real. Touch me. Feel my arm." Perrin backed away. She said passionately, "Here, a knife. If you are of a mind, cut me; you will see blood. Cut deeper... you will find bone."

"What would happen," said Perrin, "if I drove the knife into your heart?"

She said nothing, staring at him with big eyes.

"Why do you come here?" cried Perrin. She looked away, back toward the water.

"It's magic... darkness..." The words were a mumbled confusion; Perrin suddenly realized that the same words were in his own mind. Had she merely parrotted his thoughts during the entire conversation? "Then comes a slow pull," she said. "I drift, I crave the air, the moons bring me up... I do anything to hold my place in the air..."

"Speak your own words," said Perrin harshly. "I know you're not real — but where is Seguilo?"

"Seguilo?" She reached a hand behind her head, touched her hair, smiled sleepily at Perrin. Real or not, Perrin's pulse thudded in his ears. Real or not...

"I'm no dream," she said. "I'm real..." She came slowly toward Perrin, feeling his thoughts, face arch, ready.

Perrin said in a strangled gasp, "No, no. Go away. *Go away*!"

She stopped short, looked at him through eyes suddenly opaque. "Very well. I will go now —"

"Now! Forever!"

"— but perhaps you will call me back..."

She walked slowly through the door. Perrin ran to the window, watched the slim shape blur into the moonlight. She went to the edge of the shelf; here she paused. Perrin felt a sudden intolerable pang; what was he casting away? Real or not, she was what he wanted her to be; she was identical to reality... He leaned forward to call, "Come back... whatever you are..." He restrained himself. When he looked again she was gone... Why was she gone? Perrin pondered, looking across the moonlit sea. He had wanted her, but he no longer believed in her. He had believed in the shape called Seguilo; he had believed in the transceiver — and both had slavishly obeyed his expectations. So had the girl, and he had sent her away... Rightly, too, he told himself regretfully. Who knows what she might become when his back was turned...

When dawn finally came, it brought a new curtain of overcast. Blue-green Magda glimmered dull and sultry as a moldy orange. The water shone like oil... Movement in the west — a Panapa chieftain's private barge, walking across the horizon like a water-spider. Perrin vaulted the stairs to the light-room, swung the lumenifer full at the barge, dispatched an erratic series of flashes.

The barge moved on, jointed oars swinging rhythmically in and out of the water. A torn banner of fog drifted across the water. The barge became a dark, jerking shape, disappeared.

Perrin went to Seguilo's old transceiver, sat looking at it. He jumped to his feet, pulled the chassis out of the case, disassembled the entire circuit.

He saw scorched metal, wires fused into droplets, cracked ceramic. He pushed the tangle into a corner, went to stand by the window.

The sun was at the zenith, the sky was the color of green grapes. The sea heaved sluggishly, great amorphous swells rising and falling without apparent direction. Now was low tide; the shelf shouldered high up, the black rock showing naked and strange. The sea palpitated, up, down, up, down, sucking noisily at bits of sea-wrack.

Perrin descended the stairs. On his way down he looked in at the bathroom mirror, and his face stared back at him, pale, wide-eyed, cheeks hollow and lusterless. Perrin continued down the stairs, stepped out into the sunlight.

Carefully he walked out on the shelf, looked in a kind of fascination down over the edge. The heave of the swells distorted his vision; he could see little more than shadows and shifting fingers of light.

Step by step he wandered along the shelf. The sun leaned to the west. Perrin retreated up the rock.

At the lighthouse he seated himself in the doorway. Tonight the door remained barred. No inducement could persuade him to open up;

the most entrancing visions would beseech him in vain. His thoughts went to Seguilo. What had Seguilo believed; what being had he fabricated out of his morbid fancy with the power and malice to drag him away?... It seemed that every man was victim to his own imaginings. Isel Rock was not the place for a fanciful man when the five moons rose together.

Tonight he would bar the door, he would bed himself down and sleep, secure both in the barrier of welded metal and his own unconsciousness.

The sun sank in a bank of heavy vapor. North, east, south flushed with violet; the west glowed lime and dark green, dulling quickly through tones of brown. Perrin entered the lighthouse, bolted the door, set the twin shafts of red and white circling the horizon.

He opened a dinner unit, ate listlessly. Outside was dark night, emptiness to all the horizons. As the tide rose, the water hissed and moaned across the shelf.

Perrin lay in his bed, but sleep was far away. Through the window came an electric glow, then up rose the five moons, shining through a high overcast as if wrapped in blue gauze.

Perrin heaved fitfully. There was nothing to fear, he was safe in the lighthouse. No human hands could force the door; it would take the strength of a mastodon, the talons of a rock choundril, the ferocity of a Maldene land-shark...

He elbowed himself up on his bunk... A sound from outside? He peered through the window, heart in his mouth. A tall shape, indistinct. As he watched, it slouched toward the lighthouse — as he knew it would.

"No, no," cried Perrin softly. He flung himself into his bunk, covered his head in the blankets. "It's only what I think up myself, it's not real... Go away," he whispered fiercely. "Go away." He listened. It must be near the door now. It would be lifting a heavy arm, the talons would glint in the moonlight.

"No, no," cried Perrin. "There's nothing there..." He held up his head and listened.

A rattle, a rasp at the door. A thud as a great mass tested the lock.

"Go away!" screamed Perrin. "You're not real!"

The door groaned, the bolts sagged.

Perrin stood at the head of the stairs, breathing heavily through his mouth. The door would slam back in another instant. He knew what he would see: a black shape tall and round as a pole, with eyes like coach-lamps. Perrin even knew the last sound his ears would hear — a terrible grinding discord…

The top bolt snapped, the door reeled. A huge black arm shoved inside. Perrin saw the talons gleam as the fingers reached for the bolt.

His eyes flickered around the lighthouse for a weapon…Only a wrench, a tableknife.

The bottom bolt shattered, the door twisted. Perrin stood staring, his mind congealed. A thought rose up from some hidden survival-node. Here, Perrin thought, was the single chance.

He ran back into his room. Behind him the door clattered, he heard heavy steps. He looked around the room. His shoe.

Thud! Up the stairs, and the lighthouse vibrated. Perrin's fancy explored the horrible, he knew what he would hear. And so came a voice — harsh, empty, but like another voice which had been sweet. "I told you I'd be back."

Thud — thud — up the stairs. Perrin took the shoe by the toe, swung, struck the side of his head.

Perrin recovered consciousness. He stumbled to the wall, supported himself. Presently he groped to his bunk, sat down.

Outside there was still dark night. Grunting, he looked out the window into the sky. The five moons hung far down in the west. Already Poidel ranged ahead, while Liad trailed behind.

Tomorrow night the five moons would rise apart.

Tomorrow night there would be no high tides, sucking and tremulous along the shelf.

Tomorrow night the moons would call up no yearning shapes from the streaming dark.

Eleven weeks to relief. Perrin gingerly felt the side of his head… Quite a respectable lump.

Meet Miss Universe

I

Hardeman Clydell turned toward his smart young assistant Tony LeGrand. "Your idea has a certain mad charm," he said. "But — can it add to what we've already got?"

"That's a good question," LeGrand said. He looked down across what they already had: the California Tri-Centennial Exposition, a concrete disk two miles wide, crusted with white towers, rust-red terraces, emerald gardens, sapphire pools, segmented by four great boulevards: North, East, South, West — 3.1416 square miles of grandeur and expense in the middle of the Mojave Desert.

A five-thousand-foot pylon, rearing from the Conclave of the Universe, held a tremendous magnesium parasol against the sting of the desert sun. Half-way up the pylon, a platform supported the administrative offices and an observation deck where Hardeman Clydell, the Exposition's General Director, and Tony LeGrand now stood.

"I believe," said LeGrand, frowning at the cigar Clydell had given him, "that anything can stand improvement, including the California Tri-Centennial Exposition."

Hardeman Clydell smiled indulgently. "Assuming all these beautiful women exist —"

"I'm sure they do."

"— how do you propose to lure them here across all that space, all those light years?"

LeGrand, glib, insouciant, handsome, considered himself an authority on female psychology. "In the first place, all beautiful women are vain."

"As well as all the rest of them."

LeGrand nodded. "Exactly. So we offer free passage on a deluxe packet and a grand prize for the winner. We won't have any trouble collecting contestants."

Clydell puffed on his cigar. He had enjoyed a good lunch; the construction, furbishing, decoration of the Exposition was proceeding on schedule; he was in the mood for easy conversation.

"It's a clever thought," said Clydell. "But —" He shrugged. "There are considerations past and beyond the mere existence of beautiful women."

"Oh, I agree one hundred per cent."

"Lots of the out-world folk don't like to travel. I believe the word is 'parochial'. And what do we use for prizes? There's a problem!"

LeGrand nodded thoughtfully. "It's got to be something spectacular." He was usually able to shift the ground under Clydell, maneuvering so that Clydell's objections *con* insensibly became arguments *pro*.

"'Spectacular' isn't enough," said Clydell. "We've also got to be practical. We offer a yacht. A girl from Deserta Delicta wins. She's never seen more than a mud-puddle. What does she do with the yacht?"

"Something we've got to consider."

Clydell went on. "Take a girl on Conexxa. Give her jewels and she'd laugh at you. She's thrown diamonds big as your fist at strange dogs."

"Maybe a Rolls Royce Aeronaut —"

"There again. Veidranus ride butterflies. Picture a Veidranu girl driving an Aeronaut through all those vines and flowers!"

LeGrand took a shallow puff at the cigar. "It's a challenge, Hardeman... What kind of prize would you suggest?"

"Something indefinite," said Clydell. "Give 'em whatever they want. Let the winner name it."

"Suppose she named the city of Los Angeles?" LeGrand said with a merry laugh.

"Anything within reason. Set a valuation of a hundred thousand dollars on it."

"By golly, Hardeman, I think you've come up with something!" Tony put down his cigar. "Of course there are problems..."

This was a key gambit. Hardeman Clydell's favorite aphorism was, "Every problem has its solution." To use the word 'problem' was to push one of Clydell's most reliable buttons.

"Hmmf. Nothing which couldn't be solved," said Clydell. "Every problem has its solution."

Tony approached the second phase of his plan; so startling and outré was the entirety that he had not dared to broach the whole thing at once.

"We'd be pretty limited, of course," he said. "There's only half a dozen worlds with humanoid life. Some of those are C's and D's — not really human at all. And we wouldn't want to fool with anything second-rate." He slapped his fist into his palm. "I've got it! Listen to this, Hardeman, it's a killer!"

"I'm listening," said Clydell noncommittally.

"Let's throw the contest wide open! Come one, come all! Every planet sends their most beautiful female!"

Clydell stared blankly. "What do you mean, 'every planet'? Every planet in the Solar System?"

"No!" cried LeGrand enthusiastically. "Every planet that's got an intelligent civilization. Let the whole galaxy in on it!"

Clydell smiled at the whimsy of his aide. "Okay. We get a Millamede and a Johnsonian, a Pentacynth or two, and maybe a Jangrill from Bluestar if we can find one. So horrible that even their own husbands won't look them in the face. And we set them up against, say, Althea Daybro, or Mercedes O'Donnell." Clydell spat over the railing, made a rasping noise in his throat. "I admit it makes a macabre spectacle — but where does 'beauty contest' come in?"

LeGrand nodded thoughtfully. "It's a problem that's got to be worked out. A problem…"

Clydell shook his head. "I'm not sold on this last angle. It lacks dignity."

"You're right," said Tony LeGrand. "We can't let this become a farce. Because it's not just an ordinary beauty contest — it's more important. An experiment in inter-world relations. Now if we got some very distinguished men for judges — yourself for instance — the Secretary General — Mathias Bradisnek — Herve Christom. Also judges from some of the other worlds. The Prime of Ursa Major. The Veidranu Prefect — what's his name? And the Baten Kaitos Grand Marshall…"

Clydell puffed his cigar. "Organizing it that way would make the judging impartial... But how in the world could I compare some cute little Earth girl with a Sadal Suud Isobrod? Or one of those Pleiades dragon-women? That's the rub of the whole matter."

"It's a stumbling block... A big problem. A big problem."

"Well," said Clydell. "Every problem has its solution. That's an axiom."

Tony said thoughtfully, "Suppose we judged each candidate by her own standards — by the ideals of her own people? That way the contest becomes perfectly fair."

Clydell puffed vigorously on his cigar. "Possible, possible."

"We do some research, get the ideal of every race. A set of specifications. Whoever most closely approaches the ideal specifications is winner. Miss Universe!"

Hardeman Clydell cleared his throat. "All this is very well, Tony... But you're neglecting one very important aspect. Financing."

"It's too bad," said Tony.

"What's too bad?"

"You and I being in the position we are. We're stuck by the ethics of the situation."

Clydell looked at him with a puzzled frown, opened his mouth to speak, but Tony hurried on.

"There's no way we could honorably stage this tremendous spectacle ourselves."

Clydell looked interested. "You think it would make money?"

Tony LeGrand smiled wryly. "How many people have seen as much as a Mars Arenasaur? Let alone a Pentacynth or a Sagittarius Helmet-head? And we'll have the beauty queens of the whole universe gathered here!"

"True," said Clydell. "Very true indeed."

"It'll be the biggest thing in the whole Exposition."

Clydell threw his cigar over the side. "It'll bear thinking about."

Which Tony LeGrand knew to be a form of qualified approval.

II

Hardeman Clydell, for reasons known best to himself, had never married. At this stage in his life he was portly, with a smooth pink face, fine white hair which he wore in dashing sideburns. An extremely wealthy man, he was serving as General Director at a salary of a dollar a year. He was an ardent sportsman; he owned his own space-boat; he enjoyed cooking and serving little dinners of viands imported from distant worlds. His cigars were rolled to order from a special black tobacco grown on the Andaman Islands, smoked over native campfires, cured with arrack, and aged between oak leaves.

He had met Tony LeGrand on the beach at Tannu Tuva, offered him a cigar. When Tony pronounced it the best he had ever smoked, Clydell knew that here was a man whose judgment he could trust absolutely. He hired Tony as his private assistant and troubleshooter.

Tony had made himself invaluable. Clydell found that some of his most ingenious ideas occurred during talks with Tony...The Galactic Beauty Contest for instance. From the germ of an idea — who had voiced it first, himself or Tony? — Clydell had organized a scheme that would make talk for years to come! With the grand design sketched in, Clydell allowed Tony to manage the morass of petty detail. When Tony ran into something he couldn't handle, he came to Clydell for advice. By and large he seemed to be doing a good workman-like job.

After considering the extensive list of worlds known to be inhabited by intelligent or quasi-intelligent races, Tony, with Clydell's counsel, eliminated all but thirty-three. The criteria which they applied were:

1. Is the race socially organized?
   (Races living without social structure, in a state of intense competition, or anarchy, might not comprehend the theory of the contest, and so might prove uncooperative, perhaps make trouble if they failed to win.)

2. Can we adequately communicate? Are interpreters available?
   (The Merak tribes used clairvoyance to read another individual's internal flagella. The Gongs of Fomalhaut transmitted information through the medium of complex odors, impregnated into wads of hair and spit. The air-swimming Carboids of Cepheus 9621 communicated by a system susceptible to no explanation whatever. None of these races were considered.)

3. Is the race's environment easily duplicable on Earth?
(The weirdly beautiful Pavos d'Oro lived at a temperature of 2,000°K. The complex molecules of the Sabik Betans exploded in pressures less than 30,000 Earth atmospheres. The viability of the Chastainian Grays depended on their fluid-gaseous helium blood-stream, a state which could be maintained only at or near 0°K.)

4. Is there an element of the race which reasonably can be spoken of as female?
(Styles of reproduction among the life forms of the universe admitted of the most extreme variation. The Giant Annelids of Mauvaise collapsed into two hundred segments, each of which might become an adult organism. Among the Grus Gammans not two but five different sexes participated in the procreative act. The humanoid Churo of Gondwana were mono-sexual.)

5. Is the race notoriously short-tempered, vicious or truculent? Are they able to check any habits or instincts which might prove offensive or dangerous to visitors at the Exposition?

When the five criteria had been applied to the life-forms which peopled the worlds of the galaxy, all were eliminated but thirty-three, eight of which were humanoid, classes A to D. (Class A comprised true men and close variants; anything less man-like than Class D was no longer really man-like.)

Hardeman Clydell made a quick check of Tony's research, pointing out a flaw here, a miscalculation there; adding a race or two, finding others unsuitable on one score or another. Tony argued over Clydell's decisions.

"These Soteranians — they're beautiful things! I've seen pictures! Great filmy wings!"

"Too ticklish taking care of them," Clydell said. "They breathe fluorine... Same way with those porcelain insects that live in a vacuum."

Tony shrugged. "Okay. But here —" he pointed to one of Clydell's additions "— Mel. I don't get it. In fact I've never heard of the place."

Clydell nodded placidly. "Interesting race. I read an article about them. Rigidly stratified; the males do the work and the females stay at home and preen. Should make a fine addition."

"What do they look like?"

Clydell clipped the end from one of his cigars. Tony tried to appear busy, but Clydell held out his cigar-case. "Here, Tony, have a smoke. You appreciate 'em; wouldn't waste them on anyone else."

"Thanks, Hardeman. About these Mels —"

"To tell you the truth, I don't remember much about them. They live in monstrous cities, they're said to be hospitable to a fault, extremely friendly all around. Just the sort we want. Good-sized creatures."

"Okay," said Tony. "Mel it is."

The final list numbered thirty-one races. It was at this point that Tony secured the ideal specifications. He sent coded space-wave messages to Earth representatives on each planet, describing his problem and requesting absolutely exact data on the local concept of female beauty.

When the information had been returned and filed, Tony prepared invitations, which were signed by Hardeman Clydell, and dispatched to each of the planets. The value of the prize had been hiked to a million dollars, both to entice contestants and to make more of a splash in the news organs of the world.

Twenty-three of the thirty-one worlds agreed to send representatives.

"Think of it!" marvelled Hardeman Clydell. "Twenty-three worlds confident enough in the beauty of their women to pit them against the class of the galaxy!"

And Tony LeGrand started grinding out publicity.

"The most beautiful creatures in the universe! Meet Miss Universe, at the California Tri-Centennial Exposition!"

III

The California Tri-Centennial Exposition opened at eight o'clock on the morning of Admission Day. During the first twenty-four hours well over a million men, women and children entered the grounds through turnstiles at the heads of the four great boulevards, or up from the underground tube terminals. Second day attendance was almost

900,000; the count on the third day was 800,000. After the first week, attendance levelled off at a steady half-million a day.

The Trans-Galactic Beauty Contest was scheduled for the month of February, when attendance might be expected to undergo a seasonal lull.

Twenty-three glass-walled cases, fifty-five feet long, thirty feet deep, twenty feet high, were being constructed under joint supervision of the Astro-physical Society of America and the World Bureau for Biological Research. Each case carefully duplicated home conditions of pressure, temperature, gravity, radiation and chemistry for one of the contestants. In most cases the adjustments were minor: the addition of a few per cent of sulphur dioxide to the atmosphere; the elimination of water vapor; regulation of the temperature.

The interior of each vivarium simulated a landscape on the contestant's home planet. Case #21 was a lake of quicksilver, broken by carborundum crags. The floor of Case #6 was crusted over with brown algae. A curtain of liverish Spiratophore hung at the back; a long igloo of dried moss humped up at the right.

Case #17 was upholstered with a brown shaggy fiber, like enormously magnified sponge. Hanging on hooks were massive toilet implements. This was the vivarium in which Miss Mel would display herself to the eyes of curious Earth people.

Case #20 was a jungle of the red, yellow, blue and green vegetation of Veidranu. Case #15 depicted the Martian desert, with the crystal curve of a dome-wall at the back. Case #9 simulated a street in Montparnasse: plane trees, a sidewalk café, kiosks plastered with posters. This last was Exposition headquarters for Miss Earth, Sancha Garay of Paris.

During the middle of January contestants began to arrive at Los Angeles space-port. Hardeman Clydell, a judge, decided to see none of the off-world beauties before the actual contest, and Tony LeGrand delivered official greetings in his name.

Back at the Exposition office, he reported to Clydell.

"There's one or two cute ones among the humanoids. The others may be beautiful in a technical sense — but not for me."

Clydell looked curiously at a bruise on Tony's face. "Did you get in a fight?"

"That's your friendly Miss Mel. She reached out to pat my cheek."

"Oh," said Clydell. "She's the big one, isn't she?"

"Big and rough. Miss Mel. Or better Miss Smell. Part elephant, part dragon, part gorilla, part lion. And affectionate? Already she's invited me home for a visit. I can stay as long as I want."

"No trifling with the ladies' affections," Clydell warned with a waggish shake of the finger, and a mocking smile.

"I wouldn't mind trifling with Miss Veidranu or Miss Alschain… " He handed Clydell a packet of blue-bound pamphlets.

"What am I supposed to do with these?" asked Clydell.

"Read them. It's information you'll need for the judging: a briefing on the background of each of the contestants, a description of her home planet, and most important, the standards on which she is to be judged."

"Well, well," said Clydell. "Let's see what we have here." He reached in his humidor for a cigar, pushed it across to Tony.

"Not now, Chief. I've just had lunch."

"That's when they're best!"

Tony slowly selected a cigar.

"Now," said Clydell, "to business." He glanced at a paper clipped to the cover of the first pamphlet.

"That's a master-list," said Tony. "We'll print 'em up in the bulk and give them away to the audience."

Clydell studied the sheet.

THE FIRST TRANS-GALACTIC BEAUTY CONTEST!

Quest for Miss Universe!

PRIZE FOR WINNER: HER HEART'S DESIRE.

Judging begins February 1st. Each contestant will be rated by the standards of beauty of her own world.

JUDGES:

1. Mr. Skde Shproske, Ambassador from Gamma Grus.
2. Mr. 92-14-63-55, Commercial Factor from Aspidiske (Iota Argus).
3. Mr. A-O-INH, Student from Persigian (Leo 4A563).

4. Mr. SSEET-TREET, Commercial Factor from Kaus Australis (Eta Sagittarii).
5. The Honorable Hardeman Clydell of Earth.

THE CONTESTANTS:

1. *Miss Conexxa* —

Tony LeGrand interrupted Hardeman Clydell's reading. "You will notice that I've made an informal note or two after each of the contestants. They're for your own information only — they won't be included on the public program."

Clydell nodded, took a luxuriant puff of his cigar, read on down the list.

1. *Miss Conexxa* (Beta Trianguli). Humanoid, Type A. Tall, rangy. Red hair in varnished spikes, copper skin, black lips and ears. Shins overgrown with glossy black fur, like cowboys' chaps. Attractive in a weird kind of way. Weight 150 lbs.

2. *Miss Alschain* (Beta Aquilae). Humanoid, Type B. Little, like a big-eyed elf. Eyebrows like tufts of green feathers. Thin pale hair like corn-silk. Insectivorous. Weight 80 lbs.

3. *Miss Chromosphoro* (Centauri 9518). Upper half like a big red fish, surrounded by eighteen jointed legs, the knees at eye-level. Weight 150 lbs.

4. *Miss Shaula* (Lambda Scorpii). Inverted tub. Mottled brown and gray. Shiny. A hundred little sucker-legs underneath. Eye in center like a periscope. Weight 200 lbs.

5. *Miss TIX* (Tau Draconis). Humanoid D. Jackstraw type. 9 feet tall, spindly. Big head, no chin. Faceted eyes. Cockroach-color. Suckers at tips of fingers (16 fingers). Weight 90 lbs.

6. *Miss Aries 44R951*. A big dry tumbleweed, with a hundred jellyfish tangled in it. Weight 40 lbs.

7. *Miss Vindemiatrix* (Eta Virginis). Translucent eel with dorsal spines and four hands around mouth. Brain in long spinal band, phosphoresces visibly during thought processes. Weight 60 lbs 3 ounces.

8. *Miss Achernar* (Alpha Eridani). Armadillo with wasp head. Green scales. Highly telepathic. Be careful what you think around this one. Weight 150 lbs.

9. *Miss Earth*. Sancha Garay of Paris. Need I describe her? Humanoid A. Weight 115 lbs.

10. *Miss Theta Piscium*. 40 starfish strung on a seven-foot length of bamboo. She rolls, walks upright, or jumps. Weight 30 lbs.

11. Miss Arneb (Alpha Leporis). A globe of blue jelly. Inside are 7 balls of yellow light floating around 3 balls of red light. Weight: ?

12. *Miss Jheripur* (Omega Crucis). Humanoid C. Four feet high, three feet wide, yellow as butter. No hair. Weight 250 lbs. Quite an armful.

13. *Miss Delta Corvi*. The name fits. She looks like a crow. Tall, no beak, black skin, no feathers except crest running down neck. Weight 200 lbs.

14. *Miss Alphard* (Alpha Draconis). Like a metal lobster, without claws, antennae. Low to the ground. Said to be fast on feet; also rather touchy. Don't joke with this one. Weight: ? Maybe 500 lbs. Maybe more.

15. *Miss Mars*. Lorraine Jorgensen, of Polar Colony. Blonde, big blue eyes. Very nice. Weight 124 lbs.

16. *Miss Claverops*. Humanoid C. Amphibious, sleek like a seal. Greenish-brown. Hands and feet like a frog. Weight 180 lbs.

17. *Miss Mel*. A monster. Eighteen feet long, color of raw oysters. Six big arms. Makes constant noise like a loud laugh. Head something like a gorilla, thorax like queen termite.

Weight — I don't dare guess. Be careful of this one. She likes to pet you. I'm black and blue from her love-taps. Smells like slaughter-house. There's something she seems to want, but I can't make out what it is.

18. *Miss Sadal Suud* (Beta Aquarii). Mandrake. Body like green-white carrot. Red foliage sprouting from head. Sadal Suud means Luckiest of the Lucky. Will she win? Weight 150 lbs.

19. *Miss Persigian* (Auriga 225-G). Bright blue lizard. Pretty color. Said to sting like a nettle on contact. Weight 100 lbs.

20. *Miss Veidranu* (Psi Hercules). Humanoid B. Fragile thing. Covered with moth-dust. Pink, green, blue film for hair, running down her back. Nice figure. Pretty. Weight 100 lbs.

21. *Miss Gomeisa* (Beta Canis Minor). A ten-foot pontoon with an iron sail. Lives in an ocean of mercury. Charged electrically. Care! Don't touch! Weight: ? Heavy.

22. *Miss Procyon* (Alpha Canis Minor). Forty feet of Manila hawser.

23. *Miss Grglash* (Eta Cassiopeiae). Humanoid D. Woman-like form misleading. Basic chemistry siliconic. Skull is a furnace, flames shoot out of holes in scalp. Looks like beautiful orange hair. She's hot. Don't touch! Weight 180 lbs.

Hardeman Clydell laid down the paper. "Good job. Thumb-nail sketch of each contestant." He picked out one of the blue-bound pamphlets at random. "Miss Aries 44R951." He looked back at the master-list. " 'A big tumbleweed with a hundred jellyfish tangled in it.' Let's see…'She lives on the surface of shallow lakes crusted over with algae. Males construct igloos of peat-moss on shore.' Mmmm…'Perform complicated dances on sacred lakes…' Mm hm…Mm hm…Here's what I'm looking for. The specifications."

"You'll find 'em definite," said Tony. "To the hundredth of an inch."

"They look rather technical," said Clydell. " 'Diameter measured from agrix to therulta' —" He looked up at Tony. "What in heaven's name is an agrix? And a therulta? Should I know?"

"They're explained in the appendix. There's a diagram of the creature's physiology. The agrix and therulta, as I recall, are terminal kinks of one of the veruli. A veruli, naturally, is a fiber."

"I see, I see," muttered Clydell. "Well, well. 'Diameter measured from agrix to therulta: 42.571 centimeters. From clavon to gadel —' I suppose these terms are also explained?"

"Oh yes. Definitely."

Clydell puffed his cigar. " '38.092 centimeters. Ganglionic orgotes' —"

"They're the jellyfish things."

"— 'should number 43.' What are all these figures?" He pointed.

Tony came around the desk, looked down at the pamphlet. "Oh, those. They're the indexes of hardness, viscosity, temperature and color of the orgotes — which, by the way, should give off no perceptible odor."

"Am I expected to smell these orgotes — all forty-three of them?"

"I suppose so — to do a fair job."

Hardeman Clydell's face became stubborn and sulky. "I don't mind examining thighs and measuring bosoms — but this fooling with agrices and smelling of orgotes — I just don't have the time." Thoughtfully he contemplated Tony LeGrand, who quickly leaned forward, found another pamphlet.

"Now this Miss Veidranu. I've seen her. She's cute as a bug's ear. Golly, some of the things you've got to measure on her!"

But Hardeman Clydell was not to be diverted. "Tony, I trust your judgment as I do my own."

"Oh, I wouldn't say that!"

"Yes," said Clydell firmly. "We will let my name stand on the list of judges — but you'll do the judging."

"But Hardeman — I don't think I'm up to it!"

"Of course you are," said Clydell bluffly. "You're acquainted with these creatures. You've studied them."

"Yes, but —"

"You make your measurements, come to a fair verdict. I'll look it over and then at the right time, I'll be the figure-head."

Tony grimaced. "It's mainly that Miss Mel. If only she'd keep her big hands off me. Frankly, Chief —" He looked at his cigar, gently tapped the ash in a pottery dish, looked up; Clydell was gazing at him with a mildly questioning glance.

"Very well," muttered Tony. "I suppose this is the kind of thing I'm being paid for."

Hardeman Clydell nodded. "Exactly."

IV

Tony paid a visit to Hotel Mira Vista, in Los Angeles, where Miss Zzpii Koyae, from the fourteenth of Alschain's planetary throng, occupied a suite. Miss Koyae was lovely by the standards of anybody's world. Hardly five feet tall, she was light as a puff of smoke, charming and saucy as a kitten in tall grass. Her skin was pastel green, the tuft of hair over her delicate face was pale as moonlight. She wore scarlet slippers, a smock of blue gauze, and a green chrysanthemum-like bangle in her ear.

She looked like a fairy from one of the ancient fables: not quite human. She greeted Tony with a burst of eager chatter, and when she learned that Tony was to judge the contest she became even more vivacious. She knew a few words of English, and taking both Tony's hands in hers, she expressed her pleasure at his visit.

"And after the contest — then you must come see me! On Plais, by the star you call Alschain. Ah, it is a lovely planet! You will be my guest, you will live with me in my little house by River Chthis. Of course I will win, and I will buy a million yards of rich black silk, and then you will find what gratitude means to one of my race!"

Tony laughed. "You're sweet, you little rascal!" He put his arm around her shoulders, which pulsed like the breast of a bird. He kissed the tip of her nose, and would have proceeded further, but she held him off. "No, no, my Tony! After the contest!"

Miss Sancha Garay had taken an apartment at the Desert Inn on the slopes of Mount Whitney. The call-button sounded and a maid answered the summons. She recognized the face in the reception plate, and spoke to Miss Garay over the intercom. "It's that young man from the Exposition. The one that wanted all the information."

"Peste!" said Sancha. "How tiresome. Must I see him?" She gave the pillow by her feet a petulant kick. "Very well. Allow him in the room for two minutes. No more. Be firm. Take no excuse."

Tony came into the room. "Hello, Miss Garay." He looked around. "Completely comfortable, I hope?"

"Yes. Very." Sancha scowled out across Death Valley, jumped up to her knees, turned her back on Tony, put her chin on her hands.

"It's a nuisance," said Tony. "As if I don't have enough work, now I'm one of the judges at the beauty contest."

With one movement Sancha Garay had whirled, jumped to her feet, and was facing him, her lovely face radiant. "Toneee! How wonderful! And to think that we're such friends!"

"It is nice, isn't it?" said Tony.

"Mmm," said Sancha, "you're so sweet, Tony, coming to see me like this — So sweet. Give me a little kiss —"

The maid entered the room. "I'm sorry, Miss Garay. The dress-fitter is here. She won't wait. You have got to come at once."

"Rats," said Tony. "Very well. I guess I better go."

"Grand diable du sacré feu!" said Sancha Garay under her breath.

"You're so strong," said Miss Fradesut Consici, of Veidranu, in her husky-sweet voice. "On my planet the men are effete. After the contest I will stay on Earth, where men are strong! The money I win — perhaps you help me spend it? Eh, Tony?"

"I'd sure like to help," said Tony. "Ah, but you're so soft, fragile…" He put his hands on her arm, stroked the skin which glowed with subtle moth-wing colors, began to draw her toward him. She fluttered like one of the butterflies she was accustomed to ride through the Veidranu swamps.

"No, no! Love is not for now! You would not wish the gloss to leave my skin? I must be beautiful! Afterwards — then you will see!"

"Afterwards," grumbled Tony. "Always afterwards!"

"Tony!" sighed the Veidranu girl, "you frown, you sulk. It is not because of me?"

Tony sighed. "No. Not altogether. I've got to go see that blasted Mel monster, arrange to have her brought down to the Exposition. She's so big I'll need two air-freighters instead of one…"

✷

He paused outside of the vivarium in which Miss Magdalipe, of Mel, made her residence, and the interpreter, an officious little Breiduscan, humanoid, thin as a willow whistle, with a voice like a cricket, spied him.

"Ah, Mr. LeGrand, at last you have come. Miss Magdalipe is anxious; she is waiting to see you."

"Just a minute," growled Tony. At last he found a use for Hardeman Clydell's cigars: the smoke tended to over-power the Mel atmosphere.

The cigar was alight. Tony coughed, spat. "Okay," he said grimly. "I'm ready."

The interpreter preceded him into the vivarium. Magdalipe was crouching with her great thorax toward the door. At the first shrill sounds of the interpreter's speech, she lurched around, and seeing Tony, roared in pleasure. She patted him, squeezed. Tony's ribs creaked; his feet left the ground. The great maw bellowed a foot from his ear.

Behind Tony the interpreter translated. "Miss Magdalipe is glad to see you. She likes you. She says if she wins the contest, she will invite you to her palace on Mel. She says she is very fond of you; you will enjoy yourself."

"Not bloody likely," thought Tony. He puffed vigorously on his cigar, blew smoke in her face. If one of Clydell's special cigars failed to daunt her, nothing could. She gurgled in pleasure, reached out to pat him again, but missing his back, cuffed the side of his face. And Tony's head rang like a bell.

V

On the night of January 31, twenty-three air-freighters grappled twenty-three enormous glass cases in various parts of California, lifted them high, conveyed them across the Mojave Desert to the glinting metal mushroom crouching on the pale sand. On the morning of February 1, visitors to the Tri-Centennial Exposition found the Conclave of the Universe ringed by twenty-three show-cases displaying the beauty of the universe.

On February 1, paid admission to the Exposition exceeded a million and a half. Judging commenced at four o'clock in the afternoon. Each judge was required to inspect each of the contestants separately, measure her every dimension, analyze her color, determine her viscosity, elasticity, density, area, temperature, refractive index, conductivity; then he must compare all these results with the previously ascertained racial ideal.

It was slow work. But there was no hurry. Each day the turnstiles clicked a million times or more. By February 14 all expenses incident to the beauty contest had been liquidated; it was pure gravy until February 28.

The public as a whole saw no reason to delay the final decision. The consensus made Sancha Garay winner, Lorraine Jorgensen of Mars runner-up, followed closely by Miss Zzpii Koyae of Alschain, Miss Fradesut Consici of Veidranu and Miss Arednillia of Beta Trianguli, the Type A humanoid with the spiky red hair and the black fur on her legs.

One of the more sensational news organs pulled a switch and conducted an Ugliness Contest, announcing its results February 15.

> We have conducted this Ugliness Contest on a basis as fair as the five judges are conducting their Beauty Contest. Our standards are those of physical reaction. We have asked ourselves, which of these twenty-three lovelies nauseate us most completely? On these bases, Miss Earth, Miss Mars, Miss Veidranu, Miss Beta Trianguli and Miss Alschain fail miserably. None of them nauseate us. Otherwise it's a close race.
>
> We make the following judgments:
>
> Most frightening and hideous face. #17, #8.
> Most disgusting color. #17, #5.
> Most violent odor. #17.
> Most unbelievable. #21, #23, #5.
> Least desired opponent in catch-as-catch-can match. #17.
> Least dainty. #17.
> Consensus and winner. #17, Miss Magdalipe of Mel.

The public agreed. It was the conclusion to which roughly twenty million of them had already arrived. So, on February 28, it came as a tremendous surprise when the judges unanimously named Contestant

#17, Miss Magdalipe of Mel, winner of the contest, and crowned her Miss Universe, Queen of Interstellar Beauty.

The joint statement, subsequently published in the press, sounded a defensive note.

"There is no possibility of doubt or question. The decision of the judges has been based on most careful measurements and is final. By the rules of the contest and by unanimous agreement of the judges, Miss Magdalipe of Mel, having most closely approximated the ideal standards of her world, is hereby declared Miss Universe, Queen of Interstellar Beauty.

"Tomorrow, March 1, at four o'clock, Miss Universe will name her Heart's Desire, and if it lies within the power of the officials of the California Tri-Centennial Exposition, her desire will be satisfied."

VI

Tony LeGrand called on Miss Sancha Garay. "Look, kid," he said, "you don't know how I worked for you. Gave you every possible break..."

She sidled up to him with the prancing gait of a colt. "You filthy name of a blue dog!" She hissed, "Go and never return! I spit at you!"

Miss Zzpii Koyae of Alschain was less vehement. "In my country there is no fighting, no enemies. Everyone is friendly... And why? Because when we have enemies we do — *this*!" And she slapped a ribbon across his cheek. It vibrated with small black dots, which jumped to Tony's skin and scurried down inside his clothes. Presently they began to bite.

A doctor managed to remove most of the virulent creatures from Tony's flesh, and prescribed a soothing ointment. Tony made no attempt to contact either Miss Veidranu or Miss Beta Trianguli, both of whose races on occasion practiced human sacrifice.

It was nearly time for the Grand Award, the presenting of Heart's Desire. Tony returned to the Exposition, rode the elevator up to the administration office.

Clydell greeted him cordially. "Well, Tony, everything went off beautifully. Good work all around... Better arrange to have those vivaria freighted out of here tonight. All except Miss Universe, I suppose...

Miss Universe." Clydell wrinkled up his pink face. "There couldn't possibly have been a slip-up?"

"No… She just melted into those specifications."

"All I can say is the men on her planet don't show any kind of taste… Well, it's quarter to four. Let's go down, find what she wants. We'll get it for her, ship her home."

Descending to the Conclave of the Universe, they mounted the presentation platform which had been erected in front of Case #17. It was festooned with flowers, metal ribbons, and gala insignia. Places were ready for each of the five judges, none of whom were yet on the scene. Reporters and TV photographers were busy with Miss Universe. They were inclined to be facetious, joking and laughing among themselves, hinting of improper relations between Miss Magdalipe and her pipe-stem interpreter.

"Tell us, Miss Universe, how does it feel to be the most beautiful female in the universe?"

"Just like always," she bellowed. "No different."

"You get lots of attention on Mel? Lots of boy friends?"

"Oh, yes. Very many."

"The men must be pretty rugged, eh?"

"No. Weaklings, pipsqueaks. They do the work."

"Were you surprised when you won?"

"No surprise."

"You expected to win?"

"Of course. There is no way I could lose."

"Exactly why is that?" he asked.

Both Miss Universe and the interpreter seemed surprised by the question; they conversed back and forth — contrabass and piccolo. Finally Miss Magdalipe made a statement and the pipe-stem Breiduscan translated.

"The letter comes in from Earth asking measurements of most beautiful woman. They measure me. I permit nothing else. I am most beautiful woman. In fact I am only woman. I lay eggs for whole planet."

There was great excitement, amusement. The reporters spotted Clydell and Tony, and demanded a statement. "Has Miss Mel won the contest fairly? Any chance of disqualification?"

Hardeman Clydell flushed angrily, looked at Tony. "What's the truth of all this, Tony?"

"To the best of my knowledge and belief," said Tony, "Miss Universe has fulfilled all the conditions of winning the contest. The fact that she is the only woman on the planet constitutes a mere technicality."

Clydell recovered his poise. "That is my position exactly. Now, if you gentlemen will be so good, we are about to find out what that lady wants for her prize. Her Heart's Desire."

The reporters made way. Clydell and Tony approached the vivarium. Clydell tipped his hat to Miss Universe, who, on the other side of the glass, thumped her tremendous thorax upon the floor. Clydell looked around the presentation platform. "Where are the other judges?"

A messenger girl in blue slacks approached, whispered to Clydell. He cleared his throat, addressed the reporters and the TV cameras. "The other judges have given us as much of their time as they were able; and in the name of the Exposition I want to make known my gratitude to them. It is my duty to ask of Miss Universe her Heart's Desire; and if it lies within my capabilities, to provide it for her."

He turned, approached the vivarium. "Miss Universe, it now becomes my privilege to ascertain your Heart's Desire."

The interpreter piped across his message. Miss Universe growled and grumbled a statement in return. The interpreter faced back to Clydell. The reporters poised their recorders; the TV cameras brought the scene to a hundred million eyes.

"She says she wants only one thing. That's him." The interpreter pointed at Tony.

Tony's knees went limp. "She wants me?"

"She says you must come to live with her at her palace on Mel. She says she likes you very much."

Tony laughed nervously. "I can't leave Earth ... It's impossible!" Tony looked around the circle of faces. Clydell was solemn; the reporters were shaking their heads. The TV cameras scrutinized his face with impersonal glass eyes.

Why couldn't they wink?

The interpreter continued, "She says you come to spend at least a month with her."

Clydell said, "That's not unreasonable, Tony. A month soon passes."

The reporters agreed. "Sounds fair enough."

The interpreter remarked, "A year on Mel equals fourteen Earth-years."

Tony cried, "That makes a month more than an Earth-year!"

"Each year," said the interpreter, "is divided into four months."

"Cripes!" yelped Tony. "That's two and a half years!"

A reporter asked, "What's the basis for this beautiful friendship? Interests in common? Attraction of the minds? Romance of the souls?"

"Don't be asinine!" snarled Tony.

The interpreter said, "Miss Magdalipe likes the way he smells. He smells very good. She likes to pet him."

"Just a minute," said Tony. "I've got to check something. I want to talk to her alone." He moved forward as he spoke, brushing past Clydell and jostling him slightly, then as quickly apologizing. "Sorry, old man. That was awkward of me."

Tony entered the vivarium with the interpreter; Miss Universe thumped him cordially.

"Look here," said Tony. "You like the way I smell?"

Miss Universe croaked assent.

He stepped closer to her. "Smell me now. Do you notice a change?"

Miss Universe backed away, her massive thorax vibrating as if in startled affirmation.

"Well look here," Tony said. "You see that man with the pink face, in the light brown suit? He still smells the way I did. It was just temporary with me. With him it's permanent."

Clydell rapped the glass jovially. "What's going on in there?"

Tony and the interpreter came out. Miss Universe lumbered to the door of the vivarium.

The interpreter beckoned to Clydell. "Miss Universe wants to smell you."

"Sure," said Clydell breezily. "First I apply the old equalizer — so I don't smell Miss Mel." He sucked on his cigar, and letting a fine plume of smoke escape through his nostrils, approached Miss Universe. She rumbled and banged Clydell on the back.

The interpreter said, "Miss Universe said the wrong thing. She don't want Tony. She wants *you*."

Tony nodded thoughtfully. "I thought she had made a mistake."

"I don't understand this!" cried Clydell.

"Looks like you're in for a trip to Mel," said one of the reporters.

"It's only a month, old man," said Tony.

"You and your fancy ideas!" said Clydell savagely.

"I'll keep the office going, Hardeman."

Miss Universe's clumsy arm circled Clydell's waist. The interpreter said, "She is ready to go."

"But I'm not ready," cried Clydell. "I'm not even packed, I need clothes, my shaving equipment!"

"It's not cold on Mel. Especially inside the hive. You don't need clothes."

"My affairs, my business!"

"She says she wants to go now. Immediately—this minute."

Tony smiled, remembering how badly he had been tempted to light the cigar he'd borrowed from Clydell only a moment before. If he had not jostled Clydell and returned the noxious weed to that inveterate smoker's pocket where would he be now? In Clydell's shoes, undoubtedly.

Tony's smile broadened. A fast thinker and a deviously subtle one was he! He'd even remembered Clydell's odd way with cigars. Clydell carried four or five, usually in his vest pocket, but just before lighting one he had a peculiar habit of transferring the weed to his loose, easily accessible jacket pocket, a vantage point or midway stop, so to speak, from whence he could the more readily pop it into his mouth.

On her home planet Miss Universe quite possibly reveled in the rich bouquet of decaying vegetable matter in lieu of champagne. Surely only decaying vegetation on an alien world could smell quite as rank as one of Clydell's cigars. Or possibly Miss Universe had even more decadent tastes, from a Terrestrial point of view, and feasted on—

Tony shuddered. Well, he might as well think it. Protein detritus—nitrogenous organic compounds yielding amino acids, in a state of advanced decay. *Dried death.*

Tony moved up close to the cage, the grin once more on his face. "Good-bye, old man!" he shouted. "Have a pleasant trip!"

The Insufferable Red-headed Daughter of Commander Tynnott, O.T.E.

I

A CERTAIN ANGUS BARR, officer's steward aboard the spaceship *Danaan Warrior,* had taken his pay and gone forth into that district of the city Hant known as Jillyville in search of entertainment. There, according to information received by the police, he fell into the company of one Bodred Histledine, a well-known bravo of the North River district. The two had entertained themselves briefly at the Epidrome, where Angus Barr won two hundred dollars at a gambling machine. They then sauntered along the Parade to the Black Opal Café, where they drank lime beer and tried to pick up a pair of women tourists without success. Continuing north along the Parade, they crossed the River Louthe by the Boncastle Bridge and rode the clanking old escalator up Semaphore Hill to Hongo's Blue Lamp Tavern and Angus Barr was seen no more.

The disappearance of Angus Barr was reported to the police by the chief steward of the *Danaan Warrior*. Acting on a tip, Detectives Clachey and Delmar located Bo Histledine, whom they knew well, and took him to Central Authority for examination.

Mind-search produced no clear evidence. According to Bo's memory, he had spent an innocent evening in front of his term*. Unluckily

* From the acronym TERM: Total Experience Reproduction Mechanism.

for Bo, his memory also included fragmentary recollections of the Epidrome, the Parade and the Black Opal Café. The female tourists not only described the missing Angus Barr, but also positively identified Bo.

Delmar nodded with grim satisfaction and turned to Bo. "What do you say to that?"

Bo hunched down in the chair, his face a mask of belligerent obstinacy. "I told you already. I know nothing about this case. Those backwads* got me mixed with somebody else. Do you think I'd work on a pair like that? Look at her!" Bo jerked his head toward the closer of the angry women. "Face like a plateful of boiled pig's feet. She's not wearing a sweater; that's the hair on her arms. And her cross-eyed mother —"

"I'm not her mother! We're not related!"

"— she's no better; she walks with her legs bent, as if she's sneaking up on somebody."

Delmar chuckled; Clachey nodded gravely. "I see. And how do you know the way she walks? They were sitting down when we brought you in. Your bad mouth has brought you trouble."

Delmar said, "That's all, ladies. Thank you for your help."

"It's been a pleasure. I hope he gets sent out to Windy River." She referred to a penal colony on the far planet Resurge.

"It might well be," said Delmar. The tourists departed. Clachey said to Bo: "Well then, what about it? What did you do to Barr?"

"Never heard of him."

"You had your memory blanked," said Delmar. "It won't do you any good. Windy River, get ready."

"You haven't got a thing on me," said Bo. "Maybe I was drunk and don't remember too well, but that doesn't mean I scragged Barr."

Clachey and Delmar, who recognized the limitations of their case as well as Bo, vainly sought more direct evidence. In the end Bo was arraigned on the charge of memory-blanking without a permit: not a trivial offense when committed by a person with an active criminal record. The magistrate fined Bo a thousand dollars and placed him upon stringent probation. Bo resented both provisions to the depths

---

* Backwad: Slang of the period: an ill-favored or otherwise repulsive woman. Etymology uncertain.

of his passionate soul, and he detested the probation officer, Inspector Guy Dalby, at sight.

For his part, Inspector Dalby, an ex-spacefarer, liked nothing about Bo: neither his dense blond-bronze curls, his sullenly handsome features — marred perhaps by a chin a trifle too heavy and a mouth a trifle too rich and full — nor his exquisitely modish garments, nor the devious style of Bo's life. Dalby suspected that for every offense upon Bo's record, a dozen existed which had never come to official attention. As a spaceman he took an objective attitude toward wrong-doing, and held Bo to the letter of his probationary requirements. He subjected Bo's weekly budget to the most skeptical scrutiny. "What is this figure — one hundred dollars — repayment of old debt?"

"Exactly that," said Bo, sitting rigid on the edge of the chair.

"Who paid you this money?"

"A man named Henry Smith: a gambling debt."

"Bring him in here. I'll want to check this."

Bo ran a hand through his cap of golden curls. "I don't know where he is. I happened to meet him on the street. He paid me my money and went his way."

"That's your total income of the week?"

"That's it."

Guy Dalby smiled grimly and flicked a sheet of paper with his fingertips. "This is a statement from a certain Polinasia Glianthe, occupation: prostitute. 'Last week I paid Big Bo Histledine one hundred and seventy-five dollars, otherwise he said he would cut my ears.' "

Bo made a contemptuous sound. "Who are you going to believe? Me or some swayback old she-dog who never made a hundred and seventy-five the best week of her life?"

Dalby forbore a direct response. "Get yourself a job. You are required to support yourself in an acceptable manner. If you can't find work, I'll find it for you. There's plenty out on Jugurtha." He referred to that world abhorred by social delinquents for its rehabilitation farms.

Bo was impressed by Dalby's chilly succinctness. His last probation officer had been an urbanite, whose instinctive tactic was empathy. Bo found it a simple matter to explain his lapses. The probation officer in turn was cheered by Bo's ability to distinguish between right and wrong, at least verbally. Inspector Dalby, however, obviously cared not a twitch for the pain or travail which afflicted Bo's psyche. Cursing and seething, Bo took himself to the City Employment Office and was dispatched to the Orion Spaceyards as an apprentice metal-worker, at a wage he considered a bad joke. One way or another he'd outwit Dalby! In the meantime he found himself under the authority of a foreman equally unsympathetic: another ex-spaceman named Edmund Sarkane. Sarkane explained to Bo that to gain an hour's pay he must expend an hour's exertion, which Bo found a novel concept. Sarkane could not be serious! He attempted to circumvent Sarkane's precepts by a variety of methods, but Sarkane had dealt with a thousand apprentices and Bo had known only a single Sarkane. Whenever Bo thought to relax in the shadows, or ignore a troublesome detail, Sarkane's voice rasped upon his ears, and Bo began to wonder if after all he must accept the unacceptable. The work, after all, was not in itself irksome; and Sarkane's contempt was almost a challenge to Bo to prove himself superior in every aspect, even the craft of metal-working, to Sarkane himself. At times to his own surprise and displeasure he found himself working diligently.

The spaceyards themselves he found remarkable. His eye, like that of most urbanites, was sensitive; he noted the somber concord of color: black structures, ocher soil, grey concrete, reds, blues and olive greens of signs and symbols, all animated by electric glitters, fires and steams, the constant motion of stern-faced workmen. The hulls loomed upon the sky; for these Bo felt a curious emotion: half-awe, half-antipathy; they symbolized the far worlds which Bo, as an urbanite, had no slightest intention of visiting, not even as a tourist. Why probe these far regions? He knew the look, odor and feel of these worlds through the agency of his term; he had seen nothing which wasn't done better here in Hant.

If one had money. Money! A word resonant with magic. From where he worked with his buffing machine he could see south to Cloudhaven, floating serene and golden in the light of afternoon. Here was where he would live, so he promised himself, and muttered slow oaths of longing as he looked. Money was what he needed.

The rasp of Sarkane's voice intruded upon his daydreams. "Put a No. Five head on your machine and bring it over to the aerie bays. Look sharp; there's a hurry-up job we've got to get out today." He made what Bo considered an unnecessarily brusque gesture.

Bo slung the machine over his shoulder and followed Sarkane, walking perforce with the bent loose-kneed stride of a workman carrying a load. He knew the look of his gait; introversion and constant self-evaluation are integral adjuncts to the urbanite's mental machinery; he felt humiliation and fury: he, Bo Histledine, Big Bo the Boodlesnatch, hunching along like a common workman! He longed to shout at Sarkane, something like: "Hey! Slow down, you old gutreek; do you think I'm a camel? Here, carry the damn machine yourself, or put it in your ear!" Bo only muttered the remarks, and loped to catch up with Sarkane: through the clangor of the cold-belling shop, across the pulsion-pod storage yard with the great hulls massive overhead; over the gantry ways to a cluster of three platforms at the southern edge of the yard. On one of the platforms rested a glass-domed construction which Bo recognized for an aerie: the honorary residence of a commander in the Order of the Terrestrial Empire, and reserved for the use of such folk alone.

Sarkane motioned to Bo, and indicated the underside of the peripheral flange. "Polish that metal clean, get all that scurf and oxide off, so the crystallizer can lay on a clean coat. They'll be arriving at any time and we want it right for them."

"Who is 'them'?"

"A party from Rampold: an O.T.E. and his family. Get cracking now, we don't have much time."

Sarkane moved away. Bo considered the aerie. Rampold? Bo thought he had heard the place mentioned: a far half-savage world where men strove against an elemental environment and hostile indigenes to create new zones of habitability. Why didn't they stay out there if they liked it so much? But they always came swanking back to Earth with their titles and prerogatives, and here he was, Bo Histledine, polishing metal for them.

Bo jumped up to the deck and went to peer into the interior. He saw a pleasant but hardly lavish living room with white walls, a scarlet and blue rug, an open fireplace. In the center of the room a number of cases had been stacked. Bo read the name stenciled on the sides: Commander M.R. Tynnott, S.E.S.—the S.E.S. for *Space Exploration Service.*

Sarkane's voice vibrated against his back. "Hey! Histledine! Get down from there! What do you think you're up to?"

"Just looking," said Bo. "Keep your shirt on." He jumped to the ground. "Nothing much to see anyway. They don't even have a TV let alone a term. Still, I'd take one if they gave it to me."

"There's no obstacle in your way." Sarkane's tone was edged with caustic humor. "Just go work out back of beyond for twenty or thirty years; they'll give you an aerie."

"Bo Histledine isn't about to start out there."

"I expect not. Buff down that flange now, and make a clean job of it."

While Bo applied his machine, Sarkane wandered here and there, inspecting the repairs which had been made on the aerie's underbody, waiting for the crystallizer crew and keeping an eye on Bo.

The work was tiresome; Bo was forced to stand in a cramped position, holding the machine above him. His zeal, never too keen, began to flag. Whenever Sarkane was out of sight, Bo straightened up and relaxed. Commander Tynnott and his family could wait another hour or two, or two or three days, so far as Bo was concerned. Starlanders were much too haughty and self-satisfied for Bo's taste. They acted as if the simple process of flying space made them somehow superior to the folk who chose to stay home in the cities.

During one of his rest periods he watched a cab glide down to a halt nearby. A girl alighted and walked toward the aerie. Bo stared in fascination. This was a girl of a sort he had never seen before: a girl considerably younger than himself, perfectly formed, slender but lithe and supple, a creature precious beyond value. She approached with an easy jaunty stride, as if already in her short life she had walked far and wide, across hill and dale, forest trails and mountain ridges: wherever she chose to go. Her polished copper hair hung loose, just past her jaw-line; she was either ignorant or heedless of the intricate coiffures currently fashionable in Hant. Her clothes were equally simple: a blue-gray frock, white sandals, no ornaments whatever. She halted beside the aerie and Bo was able to study her face. Her eyes were dark blue and deep as lakes; her cheeks were flat; her mouth was wide and through some charming mannerism seemed a trifle wry and crooked. Her skin was a clear pale tan; her features could not have been more exquisitely formed. She spoke to Bo without actually looking at him. "I wonder where I get aboard."

Instantly gallant, Bo stepped forward. "Here; let me give you a leg up." To touch her, to caress (even for an instant) one of those supple young legs would be a fine pleasure indeed. The girl seemed not to hear him; she jumped easily up to the rail and swung herself over.

Sarkane came forward. He made a brusque gesture toward Bo, then turned to the girl. "I expect you're one of the owners. Tynnott I think is the name?"

"My father is Commander Tynnott. I thought he'd already be here with my mother. I suppose they'll be along soon." The girl's voice was as easy and light-hearted as her appearance, and she addressed gray old Ed Sarkane as if they had been friends for years. "You're no urbanite; where did you get your cast?" She referred to the indefinable aspect by which starlanders and spacemen were able to identify their own kind.

"Here, there and everywhere," said Sarkane. "Most of my time I worked for Slade out in the Zumberwalts."

The girl looked at him with admiration. "Then you must have known Vode Skerry and Ribolt Troil, and all the others."

"Yes, Miss, well indeed."

"And now you're living in Hant!" The girl spoke in a marvelling voice. Bo's lips twitched. What, he wondered, was so wrong about living in Hant?

"Not for long," said Sarkane. "Next year I'm going out to Tinctala. My son farms a station out there."

The girl nodded in comprehension. She turned to inspect the aerie. "This is all so exciting; I've never lived in such splendor before."

Sarkane smiled indulgently. "It's not all that splendid, Miss, or I should say not compared to the way the rich folk live up there." He gestured toward Cloudhaven. "Still, they'd trade for aeries anytime, or so I'm told."

"There's not all that many aeries then?"

"Two thousand is all there'll ever be; that's the law. Otherwise they'd be hanging in the sky thick as jellyfish. Every cheap-jack and politician and plutocrat around the world would want his aerie. No Miss, they're reserved to the O.T.E. and that's how it should be. Are you to be here long?"

"Not too long; my father has business with the Agency, and I'll undertake a bit of research while I'm here."

"Ah, you'll be a student at the Academy? It's an interesting place, the last word on everything, or so they say."

"I'm sure it is. I plan to visit the Hall of History tomorrow, as a matter of fact." She pointed toward a descending cab. "Here they are at last."

Bo, who had worked to within casual earshot, wielded his machine until Sarkane went off to confer with the Tynnotts. He buffed along the flange to where the girl stood leaning on the rail; raising his eyes he glimpsed a pair of smooth slender brown legs, a glint of thigh. She was only peripherally aware of his existence. Bo straightened up and put on that expression of mesmeric masculinity which had served him so well in the past. But the girl, rather than heeding him, went down the deck a few steps. "I'm already here," she called, "but I don't know how to get in."

Bo quivered with wrath. So the girl wouldn't look at him! So she thought him a stupid laborer! Couldn't she tell he was Bo Histledine, the notorious Big Boo, known up and down the North Shore, from Dipshaw Heights to Swarling Park?

He moved along the rail. Halting beside the girl he contrived to drop his adjustment wrench on her foot. She yelped in pain and surprise. "Sorry," said Bo. He could not restrain a grin. "Did it hurt?"

"Not very much." She looked down at the black smear of grease on her white sandal, then she turned and joined her parents who were entering the aerie.

She said in a puzzled voice: "Do you know, I believe that workman purposely dropped his tool on my foot."

Tynnott said after a moment: "He probably wanted to attract your attention."

"I wish he'd thought of some other way... It still hurts."

Two hours later, with the sun low in the west, Tynnott took the aerie aloft. The spaceyards dwindled below; the black buildings, the skeletal spaceships, the ramps, docks and gantries, became miniatures. The Louthe lay across the panorama in lank mustard-silver sweeps, with a hundred bridges straddling. Dipshaw Heights rose to the west with white structures stepping up and down the slope; beyond and away to the north spread residential suburbs among a scatter of parks and greenways. In the east stood the decaying towers of the Old City; in the south, golden among a tumble of cumulus clouds, Cloudhaven floated like a wonderful fairy castle.

The aerie drifted full in the light of sunset. The Tynnotts, Merwyn, Jade and Alice, leaned on the railing looking down upon the city.

"Now you've seen old Hant," said Merwyn Tynnott, "or at least the scope of it. What do you think?"

"It's a wild confusion," said Alice. "At least it seems that way. So many incongruous elements: Cloudhaven, the Old City, the working class slums..."

"Not to mention Jillyville, which is just below us," said Jade, "and College Station, and the Alien Quarter."

"And Dipshaw Heights, and Goshen, and River Meadow, and Elmhurst, and Juba Valley."

"Exactly," said Alice. "I wouldn't even try to generalize."

"Wise girl!" said Merwyn Tynnott. "In any event, generalization is a job for the subconscious, which has a very capable integrating apparatus."

Alice found the idea interesting. "How do you distinguish between generalization and emotion?"

"I never bother."

Alice laughed at her father's whimsy. "I use my subconscious whenever I can, but I don't trust it. For instance, my subconscious insists that a workman carefully dropped his wrench on my foot. My common sense doesn't believe it."

"Your common sense isn't common enough," said Merwyn Tynnott. "It's perfectly simple. He fell in love and wanted to let you know."

Alice, half-amused, half-embarrassed, shook her head. "Ridiculous! I'd only just jumped aboard the boat!"

"Some people make up their minds in a hurry. As a matter of fact, you were unusually cordial with Waldo Walberg last night."

"Not really," said Alice airily. "Waldo of course is a pleasant person, but certainly neither of us has the slightest romantic inclination. In the first place, I couldn't spare the time, and secondly I doubt if we have anything in common."

"You're right, of course," said Jade. "We're only teasing you because you're so pretty and turn so many heads and then pretend not to notice."

"I suppose I could make myself horrid," mused Alice. "There's always the trick Shikabay taught me."

"Which trick? He's taught you so many."

"His new trick is rather disgusting, but he insists that it works every time."

"I wonder how he knows," said Jade with a sniff. "Wretched old charlatan! And lewd to boot."

"In this connection," said Merwyn Tynnott, "I want to warn you: be careful around this old city. The people here are urbanites. The city festers with subjectivity."

"I'll be careful, although I'm sure I can take care of myself. If I couldn't, Shikabay would feel very humiliated... I'll get it." She went in to answer the telephone. Waldo's face looked forth from the screen: a handsome face, with an aquiline profile, the eyes stern, the nose straight, the droop of the mouth indicating sensitivity, or charm, or self-indulgence, or impatience, or all, or none, depending upon who made the appraisal and under what circumstances. In accordance with the current mode, Waldo's hair had been shorn to a stubble, then enameled glossy black, and carefully carved into a set of rakish curves, cusps, and angles. His teeth were enameled black; he wore silver lip-enamel and his ears were small flat tabs, with a golden bauble dangling from his right ear. To a person schooled in urban subtleties, Waldo's costume indicated upper-class lineage and his mannerisms were those of Cloudhaven alone.

"Hello Waldo," said Alice. "I'll call Father."

"No, no, wait! It's you I want."

"Oh? For what?"

Waldo licked his lips and peered into the screen. "I was right."

"How so?"

"You're the most exciting, entrancing, exhilarating person in, on, above or below the city Hant."

"How ridiculous," said Alice. "I'm just me."

"You're fresh as a flower, an orange marigold dancing in the wind."

"Please be serious, Waldo. I assume you called about that book *Cities of the Past*."

"No. I'm calling about cities of the present, namely Hant. Since you'll be here so short a time, why don't we look the old place over?"

"That's just what we're doing," said Alice. "We can see all the way south to Elmhurst, north to Birdville, east to the Old Town, west to the sunset."

Waldo peered into the screen. Flippancy? Ponderous humor? Sheer stupidity? Utter naïveté? Waldo could not decide. He said politely: "I meant that we should look in on one of the current presentations, something that you might not see out on Rampold. For instance, a concert? an exhibition? a percept?...What's that you're doing?"

"I'm noting down an idea before I forget it."

Waldo raised his expressive eyebrows. "Then afterwards we could take a bite of supper somewhere and get acquainted. I know an especially picturesque place, the Old Lair, which I think you might enjoy."

"Waldo, I really don't want to leave the aerie; it's so peaceful up here, and we're having such a nice talk."

"You and your parents?" Waldo was amazed.

"There's no one else here."

"But you'll be in Hant such a very short time!"

"I know...Well, perhaps I should make the most of my time. I can enjoy myself later."

Waldo's voice became thick. "But I want you to enjoy yourself tonight!"

"Oh, very well. But let's not stay out late. I'm visiting the Academy tomorrow morning."

"We'll let circumstances decide. I'll be across in about an hour. Will that give you time to do your primping?"

"Come sooner, if you like. I'll be ready in ten minutes."

II

Waldo arrived half an hour later to find Alice waiting for him. She wore a simple gown of dull dark green stuff; a fillet of flat jade pebbles bound with gold wire confined her hair. She inspected Waldo with curiosity, and for a fact Waldo's habiliments were remarkable both for elegance and intricacy. His trousers, of a light material patterned in black, brown and maroon, bagged artfully at the hips, gripped the calves, and hung carelessly awry over the slippers of black- and red-enameled metal. Waldo's blouse was a confection of orange, gray and black; above this he wore a tight-waisted black jacket, pinched at the elbow, flaring at the sleeve, and a splendid cravat of silk, which shimmered with the colors of an oil-film on water. "What an interesting costume!" Alice exclaimed. "I suppose each detail has its own symbological value."

"If so, I'm not aware of it," said Waldo. "Good evening, Commander."

"Good evening, Waldo. And where are you bound tonight?"

"It depends upon Alice. There's a concert at the Contemporanea: the music of Vaakstras, highly interesting."

"Vaakstras?" Alice reflected. "I've never heard of him. Of course that means nothing."

Waldo laughed indulgently. "A cult of dissident musicians emigrated to the coast of Greenland. They raised their children without music of any sort, without so much as knowledge of the word 'music'. At adolescence they gave the children a set of instruments and required that they express themselves, and in effect create a musical fabric based upon their innate emotive patterns. The music which resulted is indeed challenging. Listen." From his pocket he brought a small black case. A window glowed to reveal an index; Waldo set dials. "Here's a sample of Vaakstras; it's not obvious music."

Alice listened to the sounds from the music-player. "I've heard better cat fights."

Waldo laughed. "It's demanding music, and certainly requires empathy from the participant. He must search his own file of patterns, rummaging and discarding until he finds the set at the very bottom of the pile, and these should synthesize within his mind the wild emotions of the Vaakstras children."

"Let's not bother tonight," said Alice. "I'd never be sure that I'd uncovered the proper patterns and I might feel all the wrong emotions, and anyway I'm not all that interested in feeling someone else's emotions; I've got enough of my own."

"We'll find something you'll like, no fear of that." Waldo bowed politely to Merwyn and Jade, and conducted Alice into the cab. They slanted down toward the city.

Waldo looked sidewise at Alice. He declared, "Tonight you're an enchanted princess from a fairy tale. How do you do it?"

"I don't know," said Alice. "I didn't try anything special. Where are we going?"

"Well, there's an exhibition of Latushenko's spirit crystals, which he grows in new graves; or we could go to the Arnaud Intrinsicalia, where there's a very clever performance, which I've already seen three times; I know you'd enjoy it. Operators are prosthetically coupled to puppets, who perform the most adventurous and outrageous acts. There's a performance of *Salammbô* on tonight, with *The Secret Powder-puff,* which is rather naughty, if you like such things."

Alice smiled and shook her head. "I happened upon the mammoth atrachids of Didion Swamp in a state of oestrus, and since then I've lost all interest in voyeurism."

Waldo was taken aback. He blinked and adjusted his cravat. "Well — there's always the Perceptory — but you're not wired and you'd miss a great deal. There's an exhibit at the Hypersense: John Shibe's *Posturings.* Or we might luck into a couple seats at the Conservatory; tonight they're doing Oxtot's *Generation of Fundamental Pain,* with five music machines."

"I'm not really all that interested in music," said Alice. "I just don't care to sit still that long, wondering why someone saw fit to perform this or that particular set of notes."

"My word," said Waldo in astonishment. "Isn't there any music on Rampold?"

"There's music enough, I suppose. People sing or whistle when the mood strikes them. Out on the stations there's always someone with a banjo."

"That's not quite what I mean," said Waldo. "Music, and in fact, art in general, is the process of consciously communicating an emotional judgment or point of view in terms of abstract symbology. I don't believe whistling a jig fits this definition."

"I'm sure you're right," said Alice. "I know it's never occurred to me when I'm whistling. When I was very little we had a school teacher from Earth — an elderly lady who was dreadfully afraid of everything. She tried to teach us subjectivity; she played us plaque after plaque of music without effect; all of us enjoyed our own emotions more than someone else's."

"What a little barbarian you are, for a fact!"

Alice only laughed. "Poor old Miss Burch! She was so upset with us! The only name I remember is Bargle, or Bangle, or something like that, who always ended his pieces with a great deal of pounding and fanfares."

" 'Bargle'? 'Bangle'? Was it possibly Baraungelo?"

"Why yes, I'm sure that's the name! How clever of you!"

Waldo laughed ruefully. "One of the greatest composers of the last century. Well — you don't want to go to concerts or exhibitions, or to the Perceptory," said Waldo plaintively. "What are you doing? Making more notes?"

"I have a bad memory," said Alice. "When an idea arrives, I've got to record it."

"Oh," said Waldo flatly. "Well — what do you suggest we do?"

Alice tried to soothe Waldo's feelings. "I'm a very impatient person. I just don't care for subjectivizing, or vicarious experience... Oh my, I've done it again, and made it even worse. I'm sorry."

Waldo was dazed by the whirl of ideas. "Sorry for what?"

"Perhaps you didn't notice, which is just as well."

"Oh come now. It couldn't have been all that bad. Tell me!"

"It's not important," said Alice. "Where do spacemen go for amusement?"

Waldo responded in a measured voice. "They drink in saloons, or escort fancy ladies to the High Style Restaurant, or prowl Jillyville, or gamble in the Epidrome."

"What is Jillyville?"

"It's the old market plaza, and I suppose it's sometimes amusing. The Alien Quarter is just down Light-year Road; the jeeks and wampoons and tinkos all have shops along the Parade. There are little bistros and drunken spacemen, mystics, charlatans and inverts, gunkers and gunk peddlers and all sorts of furtive desperate people. It's more than a trifle vulgar."

"Jillyville might be interesting," said Alice. "At least it's alive. Let's go there."

What an odd girl! thought Waldo. Beautiful to melt a man's mind, a daughter of Commander Merwyn Tynnott, O.T.E., a member of the galactic nobility with a status far superior to his own; yet how provincial, how incredibly self-assured for her age, which could hardly be more than seventeen or eighteen! She seemed at times almost patronizing, as if he were the culturally impoverished starlander and she the clever sophisticate! Well then, thought Waldo, let's divert matters into a more amusing channel. He leaned close, put his hand to her cheek and sought to kiss her, which would re-establish his initiative. Alice ducked back and Waldo was thwarted. She asked in astonishment, "Why did you do that?"

"The usual reasons," said Waldo in a muffled voice. "They're quite well known. Haven't you ever been kissed before?"

"I'm sorry if I hurt your feelings, Waldo. But let's just be casual friends."

Waldo said largely: "Why should we limit ourselves in any way? There's scope for whatever relationship we want! Let's start over. Pretend now that we've just met, but already we've become interested in one another!"

"The last person I want to deceive is myself," said Alice. She hesitated. "I hardly know how to advise you."

Waldo looked at Alice with a slack jaw. "As to what?"

"Subjectivity."

"I'm afraid I don't understand you."

Alice nodded. "It's like talking to a fish about being wet...Let's speak of something else. The lights of the city are really magnificent. Old Earth is certainly picturesque! Is that the Epidrome down there?"

Looking askance at the charming features, Waldo responded in a somewhat metallic voice. "That's Meridian Circle, at the end of the Parade, where the cults and debating societies meet. See that bar of white luciflux? That marks the Parade. The luminous green circle is the Epidrome. See those colored lights across the Parade? That's the Alien Quarter. The jeeks like blue lights, the tinkos insist on yellow, the wampoons won't have any lights at all, which accounts for that rather strange effect."

The cab landed; Waldo gallantly assisted Alice from the craft. "We're at the head of the Parade; that's all Jillyville ahead of us...What's that you're carrying?"

"My camera. I want to record some of those beautiful costumes, and yours too."

"Costume?" Waldo looked down at his garments. "Barbarians wear costumes. These are just clothes."

"Well, they're very interesting in any event...What a remarkable assortment of people!"

"Yes," said Waldo glumly. "You'll see everybody and everything along the Parade. Don't walk too closely behind the jeeks. They have a rather noxious defensive mechanism right above their tail horn. If you see a man with a red hat, he's a bonze of the External Magma. Don't look at him or he'll want an 'enlightenment fee' for divining his thoughts. Those three men yonder are spacemen — drunk, of course. Down at the end of the Parade is Spaceman's Rest: a jail reserved for over-exuberant spacemen. Out yonder is the Baund, the most garish section of Jillyville: saloons, bordellos, shampoo parlors, cult studios, curio shops, mind-readers, evangelists and prophets, gunk-peddlers — all in the Baund."

"What a picturesque place!"

"Yes indeed. Here's the Black Opal Café, and there's a table; let's sit and watch for a bit."

For a period they sat and sipped drinks: Waldo a clear cold Hyperion Elixir, Alice a goblet of the popular Tanglefoot Punch. They watched the passersby: tourists from the backlands, spacemen, the young folk of Hant. Ladies of the night sauntered past with an eye for the spacemen, their wrist-chains jingling with socket adapters. They dressed in the most modish extremes, hair piled high and sprinkled with sparkling lights. Some varnished their skins, others wore cheek-plates plumed with jaunty feathers. Their ears were uniformly clipped into elf-horns; their shoulder finials rose in grotesque spikes. Waldo suggested that Alice take their picture, and she did so. "But I'm really more interested in representative pictures of representative folk, such as yourself and that fine young couple yonder. Aren't they picturesque? My word, what are those creatures?"

"Those are jeeks," said Waldo. "From Caph III. There's quite a colony here. Notice the organ above the dorsal horn? It ejects body-tar, which smells like nothing on Earth... Look yonder, those tall whitish creatures. They're wampoons from Argo Navis. About five hundred live in an old brick warehouse. They don't walk out too often. I don't see any tinkos, and the spangs won't appear until just before dawn."

A tall man stumbled against the railing and thrust a hairy face over their table. "Can you spare a dollar or two, your lordships? We're poor backlanders looking for work, and hungry so that we can hardly walk."

"Why not try gunk," suggested Waldo, "and take your mind off your troubles."

"Gunk is not free either, but if you'll oblige with some coins, I'll make myself merry and gay."

"Try that white building across the Parade. They'll fix you up."

The gunker roared an obscenity. He looked at Alice. "Somewhere, my lovely darling, we've met. Out there somewhere, in some lovely land of glory; I'll never forget your face. For old times' sake, a dollar or two!"

Alice found a five dollar bill. The gunker, chuckling in mad glee, seized it and shambled away.

"Money wasted," said Waldo. "He'll buy gunk, some cheap new episode."

"I suppose so... Why isn't wiring illegal?"

Waldo shook his head. "The perceptories would go out of business. And never discount the power of love."

"Love?"

"Lovers wire themselves with special sockets, so that they can plug into one another. You don't do this on Rampold?"

"Oh no indeed."

"Aha. You're shocked."

"Not really. I'm not even surprised. Just think, you could even make love by telephone or television, or even by a recording; all you need is the right kind of wiring."

"It's been done. In fact, the gunk producers have gone far beyond: brain-wiring plus a percept equals gunk."

"Oh. That's what gunk is. I thought it was a hallucinatory drug."

"It's controlled hallucination. The more you turn up the voltage, the more vivid it becomes. To the gunker life is gray; the colors come back when he dials up the gunk. Real life is a dismal interlude between the sumptuous experiences of gunk... Oh, it's seductive!"

"Have you tried it?"

Waldo shrugged. "It's illegal — but most everybody tries it. Are you interested?"

Alice shook her head. "In the first place I'm not wired. In the second place — but no matter." She became busy with her notes.

Waldo asked, "What are you writing about now? Gunk?"

"Just an idea or two."

"Such as?"

"You probably wouldn't be interested."

"Oh but I would! I'd be interested in all your notes."

"You might not understand them."

"Try me."

Alice shrugged and read: " 'Urbanites as explorers of inner space: i.e. — subjectivity. The captains: psychologists. The pioneers: abstractionists. The creed: perceptiveness, control of ideas. The fuglemen: critics. The paragons: the 'well-read man', the 'educated listener', the 'perceptive spectator'.

" 'Precursive to gunk: theater-attendance, percepts, music, books: all urbanite cult-objects.

" 'Abstraction: the work of urbanity. Vicarious experience: the life-flow of urbanity. Subjectivity: the urban mind-flow.' "

She looked at Waldo. "These are only a few rough notes. Do you want to hear any more?"

Waldo sat with a grim expression. "Do you really believe all that?"

" 'Belief' is not quite the right word." Alice reflected a moment. "I've simply arranged a set of facts into a pattern. For an urbanite the implications go very far — in fact very far indeed. But let's talk of something else. Have you ever visited Nicobar?"

"No," said Waldo, looking off across the Baund.

"I've heard that the Sunken Temple is very interesting. I'd like to try to decipher the glyphs."

"Indeed?" Waldo lifted his eyebrows. "Are you acquainted with Ancient Gondwanese?"

"Of course not! But glyphs usually have a symbolic derivation. Don't stare at those lights, Waldo; they'll put you to sleep."

"What?" Waldo sat up in his chair. "Nothing of the sort. They're just the lights of a carousel."

"I know, but passing behind those pillars they fluctuate at about ten cycles a second, or so I'd estimate."

"And what of that?"

"The lights send impulses to your brain which create electrical waves. At that particular frequency, if the waves are strong enough or continue long enough, you'll very likely become dazed. Most people do."

Waldo gave a skeptical grunt. "Where did you learn that?"

"It's common knowledge — at least among neurologists."

"I'm no neurologist. Are you?"

"No. But our odd-jobs man on Rampold is, or at least claims to be. He's also a magician, bear wrestler, cryptologist, boat-builder, herbalist, and half a dozen other wonderful things. Mother considers him bizarre, but I admire him tremendously, because he is competent. He's taught me all kinds of useful skills." Alice picked a pink flower from a potted plant beside the table. She placed it on the table, and put her hands down flat, covering the flower. "Which hand is it under?"

Waldo somewhat condescendingly pointed to her left hand. Alice lifted her right hand to reveal a red flower.

"Aha," said Waldo. "You picked two flowers! Lift your other hand."

Alice lifted her left hand. On the table glittered the gold ornament which had hung at Waldo's ear. Waldo blinked, felt his ear, then stared at Alice. "How did you get hold of that?"

"I took it while you were watching the lights. But where is the pink flower?" She looked up grinning like an imp. "Do you see it?"

"No."

"Touch your nose."

Waldo blinked once more and touched his nose. "There's no flower there."

Alice laughed in great merriment. "Of course not. What did you expect?" She sipped from her goblet of punch, and Waldo, somewhat annoyed, leaned back with his own glass of punch, to find within the pink flower. "Very clever." He rose stiffly to his feet. "Shall we continue?"

"As soon as I photograph the picturesque couple at the table yonder. They seem to know you. At least they've been watching us."

"I've never seen them before in my life," said Waldo. "Are you ready? Let's go on."

They continued along the Parade.

"There's a really big jeek," said Alice. "What's that it's carrying?"

"Probably garbage for its soup. Don't stand too close behind it… Well, we're behind it anyway. Just don't jostle it, or—"

An arm reached in from the side and dealt the jeek's tail horn a vigorous blow. Alice ducked aside; the spurt of body tar missed her and struck Waldo on the neck and chest.

III

After his day's work Bo Histledine rode a slideway to the transit tube, and was whisked northwest to Fulchock, where he inhabited a small apartment in an ancient concrete warren. Waiting for him was Hernanda Degasto Confurias whom he had only recently wooed and won. Bo stood in the doorway looking at her. She was perfectly turned out, he thought; no one was more sensitive to the latest subtleties of fashion; no one surpassed her at adapting them to herself, so that she and the style were indistinguishable; with every change of clothes she assumed a corresponding temperament. A toque or cylinder of transparent film clasped the top of her head and contained a froth of black curls, artfully mingled with bubbles of pale green glass. Her ears were concave shells three inches high, rounded on top, with emerald plugs. Her skin was marmoreal; her lips were enameled black; her eyes and eyebrows, both black, could not be improved upon and remained in their natural condition. Hernanda was a tall girl. Her breasts had been artificially reduced to little rounded hummocks; her torso was a rather gaunt cylinder over which she had drawn a tube of coarse white cloth, which compressed her haunches. On her shoulders stood small bronze ornaments, like urns or finials, into each of which she had placed a dram of her personal scent. On her hands she wore greaves of black metal clustered with green jewels. Under her right armpit was a socket and the bottom terminal was decorated with a pink heart on which were inscribed the initials *B H.*

Hernanda stood proud and silent before Bo's inspection, knowing herself perfect. Bo gave her no word of greeting; she said nothing to him. He strode into his inner room, bathed, and changed into a black and white diapered blouse, loose lime-green pantaloons, the legs long over his heels and tucked into sandals to expose his long white toes. He tied a purple and blue kerchief at a rakish angle to his head, and hung a string of black pearls from his right ear. When he returned to the living room Hernanda apparently had not moved. Silent as an obelisk she waited beside the far wall. Bo stood brooding. Hernanda was just right in every aspect. He was a lucky man to own the private plug to her socket. And yet... And yet what? Bo angrily thrust aside the thought.

"I want to go to the Old Lair," said Hernanda.

"Do you have money?"

"Not enough."

"I'm short as well. We'll go down to Fotzy's."

They left the apartment and carefully adjusted the alarms; only last week gunkers had broken in and stolen Bo's expensive term.

At Fotzy's they pressed buttons to order the dishes of their choice: hot gobbets of paste in spice-sauce, a salad of nutrient crisps on a bed of natural lettuce from the hydroponic gardens of Old Town. After a moment or two Bo said: "The spaceyards are no good. I'm going to get out."

"Oh? Why?"

"A man stands watching me. Unless I work like a kaffir he harangues me. It's simply not comfortable."

"Poor old Bo."

"But for that flashing probation I'd tie him in a knot and kite off. I was built for beauty, not toil."

"You know Suanna? Her brother has gone off into space."

"It's like jumping into nothing. He can have all he wants."

"If I got money I'd like to take an excursion. Give me a thousand dollars, Bo."

"You give me a thousand dollars. I'll go on the excursion."

"But you said you wouldn't go!"

"I don't know what I want to do."

Hernanda accepted the rejoinder in silence. They left the restaurant and walked out upon Shermond Boulevard. South beyond Old Town, Cloudhaven rode among the sunset clouds; in the halcyon light it seemed as if it might have been, or should have been, the culminating glory of human endeavour; but everyone knew differently.

"I'd rather have an aerie," muttered Bo.

One of Hernanda's few faults was a tendency to enunciate the obvious with the air of one transmitting a startling new truth. "You're not licensed for an aerie. They only give them to O.T.E.'s."

"That's all tripe. They should go to whoever can pay for them."

"You still wouldn't have one."

"I'd get the money, never fear."

"Remember your probation."

"They'll never fix on me again."

Hernanda thought her private thoughts. She wanted Bo to take a cottage in Galberg, and work in the artificial flavor factory. Tonight the prospect seemed as flimsy as smoke. "Where are we going?"

"I thought we'd look into Hongo's for the news."

"I don't like Hongo's all that much."

Bo said nothing. If Hernanda did not like Hongo's she could go somewhere else. And only as recently as yesterday she had seemed such a prize!

They rode the slideway to the Prospect Escalator and up to Dipshaw Knob. Hongo's Blue Lamp Tavern commanded a fine view of the River Louthe, the spaceyards and most of West Hant, and was old beyond record or calculation. The woodwork was stained black, the brick floors were worn with the uneven passage of footsteps; the ceiling was lost in the dark blur of time. Tall windows looked across the far vistas of Hant, and on a rainy day Hongo's was a tranquil haven from which to contemplate the city.

Hongo's reputation was not altogether savory; curious events had occurred on the premises or shortly after patrons had departed. The Blue Lamp was known as a place where one must keep his wits about him, but the reputation incurred no loss of patronage; indeed the suffusion of vice and danger attracted folk from all Hant, as well as backland tourists and spacemen.

Bo led Hernanda to his usual booth, and found there a pair of his cronies: Raulf Dido and Paul Amhurst. Bo and Hernanda seated themselves without words of greeting, according to the tenets of current custom.

Bo presently said: "The spaceyard keeps me off punition, but this aside, it's just too bad."

"You're earning an honest wage," said Raulf Dido.

"Hah! Bah! Bo Histledine, a sixteen-dollar-a-day apprentice? You give me fits!"

"Talk to Paul. He's on to something good."

"It's a beautiful new line of gunk," said Paul Amhurst. "It's produced in Aquitaine and it's as good as the best." He displayed a selection of stills; the views were vivid and provocative. "Ow-wow," said Bo. "That's good stuff. I'll take some of that myself."

Hernanda made a restless movement and pouted; it was bad manners to talk of gunk in front of one's lady friend, inasmuch as gunk inevitably included erotic and hyper-erotic episodes.

"Somebody will get the Hant distributorship," said Paul, "and I'm hoping it's me. If so I'll need help: you and Raulf, maybe a few more if we have to bust into Julio's territory."

"Hmm," said Bo. "What about the Old Man?"

"I put through an application a week ago. He hasn't bounced it back. I saw Jantry yesterday and he gave me an up-sign. So it looks good."

"Genine won't fix it with Julio."

"No. We'd have to gut it through by ourselves. It might get warm."

"And wet," said Paul referring to the bodies sometimes found floating in the Louthe.

"That flashing probation," spat Bo. "I've got to worry about that. In fact, look over there! My personal vermin, Clachey and Delmar. Hide that gunk! They're coming by."

The two detectives halted beside the table; they looked down with mercury-colored eyes, back and forth between Bo, Raulf and Paul. "A fine lot of thugs," said Clachey. "What deviltry are you working up now?"

"We're planning a birthday party for our mothers," said Raulf. "Would you care to come?"

Delmar scrutinized Bo. "Your probation, as I recall, depends on avoiding bad company. Yet here you sit with a pair of gunk merchants."

Bo returned a stony gaze. "They've never mentioned such things to me. In fact we're all planning to enter the Police Academy."

Clachey reached to the seat between Bo and Paul and came up with the stills. "Now what have we here? Could it be gunk?"

"It looks like some photographs," said Raulf. "They were on the seat when we arrived."

"Indeed," said Clachey. "So you think you're going to import Aquitanian gunk? Do you have any tablets on you?"

"Of course not," said Raulf. "What do you take us for? Criminals?"

"Empty your pockets," said Delmar. "If there's gunk in the group, somebody's probation is in bad trouble."

Paul, Raulf and Bo wordlessly arranged the contents of their pockets on the table. One at a time they stood up while Delmar deftly patted them up and down. "Oh, what's this?" From Paul's waistband he extracted one of those devices known as stingers, capable of hurling needles of lethal or anaesthetic drugs across a room or a street and into a man's neck. Bo and Raulf were clean.

"Pay your respects to all," Clachey told Paul. "I believe that this is up and out, Amhurst."

"It might well be," Paul agreed dolefully.

A drunk lurched away from the bar and careened into the two detectives. "Can't a man drink in peace without you noses breathing down his neck?"

A waiter tugged at his arm and muttered a few words.

"So they're after gunkers!" stormed the drunk. "What of that? Up in Cloudhaven there's fancy gunk-parlors; why don't the noses go raid up there? It's always the poor scroffs what get the knocks."

The waiter managed to lead him away.

Bo said, "For a fact, how come you don't raid Cloudhaven?"

"We got our hands full with the scroffs, like the man said," replied Delmar, without heat.

Clachey amplified the remark. "They pay; they have the money. The scroffs don't have the money. They loot to get it. They're the problem, them and you merchants."

Delmar said to Bo: "This is a final notification, which will be inserted into your record. I warn you that you have been observed in the company of known criminals. If this occurs again, it's up and out."

"Thank you for your concern," said Bo in a heavy voice. He rose to his feet and jerked his hand at Hernanda. "Come along. We can't even take a drink in a respectable tavern without persecution."

Delmar and Clachey led away the despondent Paul Amhurst.

"Just as well," said Raulf. "He's too erratic."

Bo grunted. "I'm going to have to lay low. Until I think of something."

Raulf made a sign of comprehension; Bo and Hernanda departed Hongo's. "Where now?" asked Hernanda.

"I don't know... I don't feel like much. There's nowhere to go." As if involuntarily he glanced up to the stars which burnt through the night-glare. Rampold? Where was Rampold?

Hernanda took Bo's arm and led him down the escalator to the Shermond slideway. "I haven't been over to Jillyville for a while. It's just across the bridge."

Bo grumbled automatically, but could think of nothing better.

They crossed River Louthe by the Vertes Avenue Bridge, and sauntered through the flower market which for centuries had created a zone of clotted color in the shadow of the Epidrome.

Hernanda wanted to wander through the Epidrome and perhaps risk a dollar or two at one of the games of chance. "So long as you use your own money," said Bo gracelessly. "I don't intend to throw gold down a rat-hole. Not at sixteen dollars a day on that buffing machine."

Hernanda became sulky and refused to enter the Epidrome, which suited Bo well enough. The two moodily walked up to the Parade. As they passed the Black Opal Café, Bo noticed Alice's copper-glinting hair. He stopped short, then led Hernanda to a table. "Let's have a drink."

"Here? It's the most expensive place along the Parade!"

"Money means nothing to Big Bo the Histle."

Hernanda shrugged, but made no objection.

Bo selected a table twenty feet from where Waldo sat with Alice. He punched buttons, deposited coins; a moment later a waitress brought out their refreshment: lime beer for Bo and frozen rum for Hernanda.

Alice saw them and raised her camera; in irritation Bo put his head down on his hand. Hernanda stared at Alice and the camera. Tourists everywhere, taking photographs.

"We should be flattered." Bo gave Waldo a baleful examination. "Toffs out slumming—him, anyway. She's off-world. A starlander."

Hernanda scrutinized each detail of Alice's gown, hair, face and her fillet of jade pebbles. "She's just a child and a bit tatty. She looks as if she'd never seen a stylist in her life."

"Probably hasn't."

Hernanda looked at him suspiciously sidelong. "Are you interested?"

"Not all so much. She looks happy. I wonder why. It's probably her first time to Hant; soon she'll be heading back into nowhere. What has she got to live for?"

"She's probably rolling in money. I could have it too if I were willing to put up with her kind of life."

Bo chuckled. "It's remarkable, for a fact. Well, she's harmless, or so I suppose."

"Certainly nothing much to look at. All young eagerness and dancing around the maypole. Hair like a straw pile... Bo!"

"What?"

"You're not listening to me."

"My mind is roving the star lanes."

Waldo and Alice rose from their table and left the café. Bo's lewd conjectures caused him to suck in his breath. "Come along."

Hernanda sulkily swung her head away, and remained in her seat. Bo paid her no heed. Speechless with indignation she watched him go.

Waldo and Alice halted to avoid a jeek. Bo reached from the side and gave the jeek's tail horn a hard slap. The jeek voided upon Waldo. Alice glanced at Bo in consternation, then turned to Waldo. "It's that man there who did it!"

"Where? Which man?" croaked Waldo.

Suddenly alive to the danger of apprehension and police charges, Bo slid away through the crowd. Reeking and smarting, Waldo pursued him. Bo ran across the Parade, off into one of the rancid little alleys of the Alien Quarter. Wild with rage, Waldo followed.

Bo ran across the plaza where a dozen or more jeeks stood at a chest-high bench ingesting salt-froth. Waldo halted, looking here and there;

Bo darted forth and thrust him into the group of jeeks; Waldo's impetus overturned the bench. Bo ran fleetly away, while the jeeks trampled Waldo, struck him with their secondary stubs, squirted him with tar.

Alice appeared with a pair of patrolmen, who flashed red lights at the jeeks and froze them into rigidity.

Waldo crept across the plaza on his hands and knees, and vomited the contents of his stomach.

"Poor Waldo," said Alice.

"Leave him to us, Miss," said the corporal. "Just a question or two, then I'll call down a cab. Who is this gentleman?"

Alice recited Waldo's name and address.

"And how did he get in this mess?"

Alice explained as best she could.

"Was this man in the green pants known to either of you?"

"I'm sure not. The whole affair seems so strange."

"Thank you, Miss. Come along, I'll call the cab."

"What of poor Waldo?"

"He'll be all right. We'll take him to the dispensary to be cleaned up. Tomorrow he'll be as good as new."

Alice hesitated. "I don't like to leave him, but I'd better be getting home; I've a great deal to do tomorrow."

IV

Bo gave no thought to Hernanda; he strode along the Parade in a strange savage mood, comprehensible to himself least of all. Why had he acted so? Not that he was sorry; to the contrary, he had hoped to soil the girl as well.

He returned to his Fulchock apartment, where he thought of Hernanda for the first time. She was nowhere in evidence, nor had he expected her, nor did he want her. What he craved was something unattainable, something indescribable.

He wanted the red-haired girl, and for the first time in his life he thought not in terms of sheer submission, but admiration and affection and a manner of living he could only sluggishly imagine.

He flung himself upon his couch and fell into a torpor.

*

Gray-blue light awoke Bo. He groaned, rolled over on his couch and sat up.

He went to look at himself in the mirror. The sullen heavy-jawed face under the tangle of blond ringlets provided him neither distress nor joy; Bo Histledine merely looked at Bo Histledine.

He showered, dressed, drank a mug of bitter mayhaw tea, and ruminated.

Why not? Bo rasped at himself. He was as good as anyone, and better than most. If not one way, then another — but own her, possess her he would. The aspirations of the night before were flimsy shadows; Bo was a practical man.

The spaceyards? The buffing machine? As remote as the winds of last summer.

Bo dressed with care in gray and white pantaloons, a loose dark blue shirt with a dark red cravat, a soft gray cap pulled low over his forehead. Examining himself in the mirror Bo found himself oddly pleased with his appearance. He looked, so he thought, less bulky and even somewhat younger: perhaps because he felt excited.

He removed the cravat and opened the collar of his shirt. The effect pleased him: he looked — so he thought — casual and easy, less heavy in the chin and jaw. What of the tight blond curls which clustered over his ears and gave his face — so he thought — a sullen, domineering look? Bo yanked the cap down over his forehead and left his apartment.

At a nearby studio, a hairdresser trimmed away clustering curls and rubbed brown toner into the hair remaining. Different, thought Bo. Better? Hard to say. But different.

He rode the tube south to Lake Werle in Elmhurst, then went by slideway to the Academy.

Bo now moved tentatively; never before had he visited the Academy. He passed under the Gate of the Universe and stood looking across the campus. Giant elms stood dreaming in the wan morning sunlight; beyond rose the halls of the various academic disciplines. Students streamed past him: young men and women from the backlands and the far worlds, a few from Cloudhaven and the patrician suburbs, others from the working-class areas to the north.

The business of the day was only just beginning. Bo asked a few questions and was directed to the central cab landing; here he leaned against a wall and composed himself for a possibly long wait.

An hour passed. Bo frowned through a discarded student journal, wondering why anyone considered such trivia worth the printing.

A cab dropped from the sky; Alice stepped to the ground. Bo dropped the journal and watched her, keen as a hawk. She wore a black jacket, a gray skirt, black stockings reaching up almost to her knees; at her waist hung her note-taking apparatus. For a moment she stood looking about her, alert and attentive, mouth curved in a half-smile.

Bo leaned forward, encompassing her with the hot force of his will. He scrutinized her inch by inch, memorizing each of her attributes. Body: supple, slender; delightful slim legs. Hair flowing and glowing like brushed copper. Face: calm, suffused with — what? gayety? merriment? optimism? The air around her quivered with the immediacy of her presence.

Bo resented her assurance. This was the whole point! She was smug! Arrogant! She thought herself better than ordinary folk because her father was a commander of the O.T.E.... Bo had to admit that this was not true. He would have preferred that it were. Her self-sufficiency was inherent. Bo envied her: a bubble of self-knowledge opened into his brain. He wanted to be like her: easy, calm, magnificent. The inner strength of the starlander was such that he never thought to measure himself against someone else. True! Alice was neither smug nor arrogant; to the contrary, she knew no vanity, nor even pride. She was herself; she knew herself to be intelligent, beautiful and good; nothing more was necessary.

Bo compressed his lips. She must concede him equality. She must know his strength, recognize his fierce virility.

Tragedy might be latent in the situation. If so, let it come! He was Bo Histledine, Big Boo the Blond Brute, who did as he pleased, who drove through life, reckless, feckless, giving way to no one.

Alice walked toward the halls of learning. Bo followed, twenty feet behind, admiring the jaunty motion of her body.

V

That morning, immediately after breakfast, Alice had telephoned Waldo at Cloudhaven. The Waldo who appeared on the screen was far different from that handsome, serene and gallant Waldo who had arrived by cab the previous evening to show her the city. This Waldo was pale, gaunt and grim, and met Alice's sympathetic inspection with a shifting darting gaze.

"No bones broken," he said in a muffled voice. "I'm lucky there. Once the jeeks start on a man they'll kill him, and they can't be punished because they're aliens."

"And this stuff they squirted on you: is it poisonous?"

Waldo made a guttural sound and directed one of his burning suspicious glances into the screen. "They scoured me and scrubbed me, and shaved all my hair. Still I smell it. The stuff apparently reacts with skin protein, and stays until a layer of skin wears off."

"Certainly a remarkable affair," mused Alice. "I wonder who would do a thing like that? And why?"

"I know who, at least. It was the fellow in green pantaloons at the table opposite. I've been meaning to ask you: didn't you photograph that couple?"

"Yes indeed I did! They seemed such a typical pair! I don't think you can identify the man; his head is turned away. But the woman is clear enough."

Waldo thrust his head forward with something of his old animation. "Good! Will you bring over the photograph? I'll show it to the police; they'll work up an identification fast enough. Somebody's going to suffer."

"I'll certainly send over the photograph," said Alice. "But I'm afraid that I don't have time to drop by. The Academy is on my schedule for today."

Waldo drew back, eyes glittering. "You won't learn much in one day. It usually takes a week just for orientation."

"I think I can find the information I want in just an hour or two; anyway, that's all the time I can spare."

"And may I ask the nature of this information?" Waldo's voice now had a definite edge. "Or is it a secret?"

"Of course not!" Alice laughed at the thought. "I'm mildly curious as to the formal methods of transmitting the urbanite ideology. Academicians are naturally a diverse lot, but in general they are confirmed urbanites: in fact, I suppose this is the basis upon which they attain their positions. After all, rabbits don't hire lions to teach their children."

"I don't follow you," said Waldo haughtily.

"It's perfectly simple. The Academy indoctrinates young rabbits in rabbitry, to pursue the metaphor, and I'm mildly curious as to the techniques."

"You'll be wasting your time," said Waldo. "I attend the Academy and I'm not aware of any 'rabbitry', as you put it."

"You would be more apt to notice its absence," said Alice. "Goodbye, Waldo. It was kind of you to show me Jillyville; I'm sorry the evening ended unpleasantly."

Waldo stared at the fresh young face, so careless and gay. "'Goodbye'?"

"I may not be seeing you again. We won't be in Hant all that long. But perhaps some day you'll come out to the starlands."

"Not bloody likely," Waldo muttered.

A curious affair, Alice reflected, as she rode the cab down to the Academy. The man in the green pantaloons probably mistook Waldo for someone else. Or he might have acted out of sheer perversity; such folk were probably not uncommon in the psychological stew of the great city Hant.

The cab discharged her on a plat at the center of the campus. She stood a moment admiring the prospect: the walks and slideways leading here and there across landscaped vistas, the white halls under great elms, the great Enoie Memorial Clock Tower, formed from a single quartz crystal four hundred and sixty feet high. Students passed in their picturesque garments, each a small lonely cosmos exquisitely sensitive to the psychic compulsions of his environment. Alice gave her head a wistful shake and went to an information placard where the component structures of the Academy were identified: the Halls of Physical Science, Biologics, Mathematics, Human History, Anthropology and Comparative Culture, Xenology, Cosmology, Human Ideas and Arts, a dozen others. She read an informational notice addressed to visitors:

> Each hall consists of a number of conduits, or thematic passages, equipped with efficient pedagogical devices. The conduits are interconnected, to provide a flexible passage through any particular discipline, in accordance with the needs of the individual. The student determines his special field of interest, and is issued a chart designating his route through the hall. He moves at a rate dictated by his assimilative ability; his comprehension is continuously verified; when the end is reached he has mastered his subject.

Alice proceeded to the Hall of History. Entering, she gazed in awe around the splendid lobby, which enforced upon the visitor an almost stupefying awareness of the human adventure. Under a six-inch floor of clear crystal spread a luminous map of the terrestrial surface, projected by some curious shifting means which minimized distortion. The dark-blue dome of the ceiling scintillated with constellations. Around the walls, somewhat above eye-level, ran a percept-continuum where marched a slow procession of men, women and children: straggling peasants; barbarians in costumes of feathers and leather; clansmen marching to a music of clarions and drums; heroes striding alone; prelates and sacerdotes; hetairae, flower-maidens and dancing girls; blank-faced folk in drab garments, from any of a dozen ages; Etruscans, Celts, Scythians, Zumbelites, Dagonites, Mennonites; posturing priests of Babylon, warriors of the Caucasus. At one side of the hall they appeared from a blur of fog; as they marched they turned an occasional glance out toward those who had come to visit the Hall of History; to the far side of the great room they faded into the blur and were gone.

Alice went to the information desk where she bought a catalogue. Listed first were the basic routes through the conduits, then more complicated routes to encompass the aspects of special studies. Alice settled upon the basic survey course: 'Human History: from the origin of man to the present'. She paid the three dollar fee for non-credit transit, received a chart indicating her route through the conduits. A young man in a dark shirt immediately behind her, so she chanced to notice, elected the same course: evidently a subject popular with the students.

Her route proved to be simple enough: a direct transit of Conduit 1, with whatever detours, turn-offs, loops into other conduits, which happened to arouse her interest.

The young man in the dark shirt went on ahead. When she entered the conduit she discovered him studying the display of human precursors. He glanced at Alice and politely moved aside so that she might inspect the diorama as well. "Rough-looking thugs!" he commented in a jocular voice. "All hairy and dirty."

"Yes, quite so." Alice moved along the diorama.

The young man kept pace with her. "Excuse me, but aren't you a starlander? From Engsten, or more likely Rampold?"

"Why yes! I'm from Rampold. How did you know?"

"Just a lucky guess. How do you like Hant?"

"It's interesting, certainly." Alice, rather primly erect, moved on along the display.

"Ugh," said Bo. "What's that they're eating?"

"Presumably some sort of natural food," said Alice.

"I guess you're right," said Bo. "They weren't too fussy in those days. Are you a student here?"

"No."

"Oh I see. Just sightseeing."

"Not exactly that either. I'm curious as to the local version of history."

"I thought history was history," said Bo.

Alice turned him a quick side-glance. "It's hard for the historian to maintain objectivity, especially for the urban historian."

"I didn't know there was all that much to it," said Bo. "I thought they just showed a lot of percepts and charts. Don't they do it the same way on Rampold?"

"We have nothing quite so elaborate."

"It all amounts to the same thing," said Bo generously. "What's done is dead and gone, but here they call it history and study it."

Alice gave a polite shrug and moved on. Bo understood that he had struck the wrong tone, which annoyed him. Oh why must he pussyfoot? Why must he appease? He said: "Of course I don't know all that much about the subject. That's why I'm here; I want to learn!"

The statement was uttered in a mincing over-delicate voice which

Alice found amusing, and hence worth some small exploration. "All very well, if you learn anything useful. In your case, I doubt if…" Alice let her voice trail off; why discourage the poor fellow? She asked: "I take it you're not a student either?"

"Well no. Not exactly."

"What do you do?"

"I — well, I work in the spaceyards."

"That's useful work," Alice said brightly. "And it's work you can be proud of. I hope you profit from your studies." She gave him a gracious nod and passed on down the conduit, to a percept detailing the daily activities of a mesolithic family. Bo looked after her with a frown. He had pictured the encounter going somewhat differently, with Alice standing wide-eyed and coy, enthralled by the magnetism of his personality. He had worried only that she might recognize him, for she had seen him on two previous occasions. His fears were groundless. Evidently she had paid no attention to him. Well, she'd make up for that. And her attitude now was far too casual; she treated him as if he were a small boy. He'd fix that, as well.

Bo followed her slowly along the conduit. He considered the percept, then sidled a step closer. In a bluff voice he said: "Sometimes we don't realize how lucky we are, and that's a fact."

" 'Lucky'?" Alice spoke in an abstracted voice. "Who? The people of Hant? Or the Cro-magnons?"

"Us, of course."

"Oh."

"You don't think so?" Bo spoke indulgently.

"Not altogether."

"Look at them! Living in caves. Dancing around a campfire. Eating a piece of dead bear. That doesn't look so good."

"Yes, their lives lacked delicacy." Alice continued along the conduit, moving briskly, and frowning just a trifle. She glanced into percepts depicting aspects of the proto-civilizations; she halted at a percept presenting in a time-compression sequence the development of Hialkh, the first city known to archaeologists. The annunciator commented: "At this particular instant in the human epic, civilization has begun. Behind: the long gray dawn ages. Ahead: the glories which culminate in Hant! Achievement then as now derives from the energies concentrated by the urban environment. But beware! look yonder across the Pontus! The cruel barbarians of the steppes, those expert wielders of sword and axe who time and time again have ravaged the cities!"

Bo's now familiar voice spoke: "The only ravagers nowadays are the tourists."

Alice made no comment, and continued along the conduit. She looked into the faces of Xerxes, Subotai, Napoleon, Shgulvarsko, Jensen, El Jarm. She saw battles, sieges, slaughters and routs. Cities developed from villages, grew great, collapsed into ruins, disappeared into flames. Bo enunciated his impressions and opinions, to which Alice made perfunctory acknowledgments. He was something of a nuisance, but she was too kind to snub him directly and hurt his feelings. Altogether she found him somewhat repulsive, a curious mixture of innocence and cynicism; of ponderous affability and sudden sinister silences. She wondered if he might not be a trifle deranged; odd for a person of his attributes to be studying the history of man! The percepts and displays, for all their splendor, began to bore her; there was simply too much to be encompassed at a casual inspection, and long ago she had learned what she wanted to know. She said to Bo: "I think I'll be leaving. I hope you profit by your studies; in fact I know you will if you apply yourself diligently. Goodbye."

"Wait," said Bo. "I've seen enough for today." He fell into step beside her. "What are you going to do now?"

Alice looked at him sidewise. "I'm going to find some lunch. I'm hungry. Why do you ask?"

"I'm hungry too. We're not all that different, you and I."

"Just because we're both hungry? That's not logical. Crows, vultures, rats, sharks, dogs: they all get hungry. I don't identify myself with any of these."

Bo frowned, examining the implications of the remark. They left the Hall of History and came out into the daylight. Bo asked gruffly: "You mean that you think I'm like a bird or a rat or a dog?"

"No, of course not!" Alice laughed at the quaint conceit. "I mean that we're people of different societies. I'm a starlander; you're an urbanite. Yours is a very old way of life, which is perhaps a bit — well, let's say, passive, or introverted."

Bo grunted. "If you say so. I never thought about it that way. Anyway just yonder is a branch of the Synthetique. Do you care to eat there? It's on me."

"No, I think not," said Alice. "I've seen those colored pastes and nutritious shreds of bark and they don't look very good. I think I'll go up home for lunch. So once again: goodbye. Have a good lunch."

"Wait!" cried Bo. "I've got a better idea! I know another place, an old tavern where spacemen and all kinds of people go. It's very old and famous: Hongo's Blue Lamp. It would be a shame if you didn't see it." He modulated his voice into that husky cajoling tone which had always dissolved female will-power like warm water on sugar. "Come along, I'll buy you a nice lunch and we'll get to know each other better."

Alice smiled politely and shook her head. "I think I'll be getting on. Thank you anyway."

Bo stood back, mouth compressed. He turned glumly away, raising a hand to his face. The gesture closed a circuit in Alice's memory-bank. Why, this was the man who had victimized Waldo! How very odd! What a strange coincidence that she should meet him at the Academy! Coincidence? The chances seemed remote. She asked, "What is your name?"

Bo spoke in a grumbling resentful voice. "Bo, short for Bodred. The last name is Histledine."

"Bodred Histledine. And you work at the spaceyards?"

Bo nodded. "What's your name?"

Alice seemed not to hear. "Perhaps I'll have lunch at this tavern after all — if you care to show me the way."

"It's not exactly a big expedition, with me running ahead like a guide," growled Bo. "I'll take you there as my guest."

"No, I wouldn't care for that," said Alice. "But I'll visit this tavern: yes. I think I'd like to talk with you."

VI

Waldo pushed the photograph across the desk to Inspector Vole, who examined it with care. "The man isn't identifiable, as you can see for yourself," said Vole. "The woman — I don't recognize her, but I'll put her through identification procedure and maybe something will show up." He departed the room. Waldo sat drumming his fingers. From time to time a faint waft of jeek body-tar odor reached his nostrils, causing him to wince and twist his head.

Inspector Vole returned with the photograph and a print-out bearing the likenesses of a dozen women. He pushed the sheet across the desk. "This is what the machine gave me. Do you recognize any of them?"

Waldo nodded. "This is the one." He touched a face on the sheet.

"I thought so too," said Vole. "Do you intend to place criminal charges?"

"Maybe. But not just yet. Who is she?"

"Her name is Hernanda Degasto Confurias. Her address is 214-19-64, Bagram. If you plan to confront this woman and her friend I advise you to go in company with a police officer."

"Thank you; I'll keep your advice in mind," said Waldo. He left the office.

Vole reflected a moment, then punched a set of buttons. He watched the display screen, which flashed a gratifying run of green lights: the name Hernanda Confurias was not unknown to the criminal files. Instead of a data read-out, the screen flickered to show the face of Vole's colleague Inspector Delmar.

"What have you got on Hernanda Confurias?" asked Delmar.

"Nothing of import," said Vole. "Last night on the Parade —" Vole described the occurrence. "A senseless matter, or so it seems offhand."

"Put through the photograph," said Delmar. Vole facsimilated across a copy of the photograph.

"I wouldn't swear to it," said Delmar, "but that looks to me like Big Bo Histledine."

Waldo found the apartment numbered 214-19-64, then went to a nearby park where he approached a pair of adolescent girls. "I need your help," said Waldo. "A certain lady friend is angry with me, and I don't think she'll answer the door if she sees my face in the robber's portrait, so I want one, or both, of you to press the door button for me." Waldo produced a five-dollar note. "I'll pay you, of course, for your trouble."

The girls looked at each other and giggled. "Why not? Where does she live?"

"Just yonder," said Waldo. "Come along." He gave the girls instructions and led them to the door, while he waited beyond the range of the sensor eye, which produced the 'robber portrait' on the screen within.

The girls pressed the button, and waited while the person within scrutinized their images.

"Who do you want?"

"Hernanda Degasto Confurias. We're from the charm school."

"Charm school?" The door opened; Hernanda looked forth. "Which charm school?"

Waldo stepped forward. "You girls come some other time. Hernanda, I want to speak with you."

She tried to close the door, but Waldo pushed through the opening. Hernanda ran across the room to the alarm button. "Get out of here! Or I'll press for the police!"

"I am the police," said Waldo.

"No, you're not! I know who you are."

"Who am I?"

"Never mind. Leave here at once!"

Waldo tossed the photograph to the table. "Look at that."

Hernanda gingerly examined the picture. "Well — what of it?"

"Who's the man?"

"What's it to you?"

"You say you know who I am."

Hernanda gave her head a half-fearful half-defiant jerk of assent. "He shouldn't have done it — but I'm not saying anything."

"You'll either tell me or the police."

"No! He'd cut my ears; he'd sell me to the gunkers."

"He won't get the chance. You can either tell me now in secret, or the police will take you in as his accomplice."

"In secret?"

"Yes. He won't know where I got his name."

"You swear this?"

"I do."

Hernanda came a timid step forward. She picked up the photograph, glanced at it, threw it contemptuously back down on the table. "Bodred Histledine. He lives in Fulchock: 663-20-99. He works in the spaceyards."

"Bodred Histledine." Waldo noted the name and address. "Why did he do what he did?"

Hernanda gave her head a meditative strike. "He's a strange man. Sometimes he's like a little boy, sad and sweet; then sometimes he's a beast of the jungle. Have you noticed his eyes? They're like the eyes of a tiger."

"That may be. But why did he victimize me?"

Hernanda's own eyes flashed. "Because of the girl you were with! He's a crazy man!"

Waldo gave a grunt of bitter amusement. He inspected Hernanda thoughtfully; in her turn she looked at him. A patrician for certain: one of those Cloudhaven types.

"He's always up at the Blue Lamp Tavern," said Hernanda. "That's his headquarters. He's on probation, you know. Just yesterday the detectives warned him." Hernanda, relaxing, had become limpid and charming; she came forward to the table.

Waldo looked her over without expression. "What did they warn him for?"

"Consorting with gunkers."

"I see. Anything else you care to tell me?"

"No." Hernanda now was almost arch. She came around the table. "You won't tell him that you saw me?"

"No, definitely not." Waldo once again caught a breath of that hateful odor. Rolling his eyes up and around, he turned and left the apartment.

VII

Entering the Blue Lamp Tavern Alice halted and peered through the gloom. For possibly the first time in her brash young life she felt the living presence of time. Upon that long black mahogany bar men of ten centuries had rested their elbows. The old wood exhaled vapors of the beer and spirits they had quaffed; their ghosts were almost palpable and their conversations hung in the gloom under the age-blackened ceiling. Alice surveyed the room, then crossed to a table under one of the tall windows which overlooked the many-textured expanse of Hant. Bo came at a rather foolish trot behind her, to pluck at her arm and urge her toward his usual booth. Alice paid him no heed, and seated herself placidly at the table she had chosen. Bo, drooping an eyelid and mouth, settled into the seat across from her. For a long moment he stared at her. Her features were fine and clean, but hardly extraordinary; how did she produce so much disturbance? Because she was insufferably confident, he told himself; because she enforced her own evaluation of herself upon those who admired her... He'd do more than admire her; she'd remember him to the last day of her life. Because he was Bo Histledine! Bo the Histle! Big Boo the Whangeroo! who accepted nothing but the best. So now: to work, to attract her interest, to dominate her with his own pride. He said: "You haven't told me your name."

Alice turned from the window and looked at Bo as if she had forgotten his presence. "My name? Miss Tynnott. My father is Commander Tynnott."

"What is your first name?" Bo asked patiently.

Alice ignored the question. Signaling the waiter, she ordered a sandwich and a mug of Tanglefoot. She looked around at the other patrons. "Who are these people? Workmen like yourself?"

"Some are workmen," said Bo in a measured voice. "Those two —" he nodded his head "— are off a sea-ship from the river docks. That tall thin man is from the backlands. But I'm more interested in you. What's your life like out on Rampold?"

"It's always different. My father's work takes him everywhere. We go out into the wilderness to plan canals and aquifers; sometimes we camp out for weeks. It's a very exciting life. We're about finished on Rampold; it's becoming quite settled, and we may move on to a new wild planet; in fact that's why we're here on Earth."

"Hmmf," said Bo. "Seems as if you'd want to stay in Hant and enjoy yourself a while; take in the percepts, meet people, buy new clothes, get your hair fixed in the latest style, things like that."

Alice grinned. "I don't need clothes. I like my hair as it is. As for percepts, I don't have either time or inclination for vicarious living.

Most urbanites, of course, don't have much choice; it's either vicarious experience or none."

Bo looked at her blankly. "I don't altogether understand you. Are you sure you know what you're talking about?"

"Of course. Passive, fearful, comfort-loving people tend to live in cities. They have no taste for real existence; they make do with second-hand second-best experience. When they realize this, as most do consciously or subconsciously, sometimes they become hectic and frantic."

"Bah," growled Bo. "I live in Hant; I'd live nowhere else. Second-best isn't good enough for me. I go after the best; I always get the best."

"The best what?"

Bo looked sharply at the girl. Was she mocking him? But no, above the sandwich her eyes were guileless.

"The best of whatever I want," said Bo.

"What you think you want is a shadow of what you really do want. Urbanites are dissatisfied people; they're all lonesome for the lost paradise, but they don't know where to find it. They search all the phases of subjectivity: they try drugs, music, percepts —"

"And gunk. Don't forget gunk!"

"Urban life is the ultimate human tragedy," said Alice. "People can't escape except through catastrophe. Wealth can't buy objectivity; the folk in Cloudhaven are the most subjective of any in Hant. You're lucky to work in the spaceyards; you have contact with something real."

Bo shook his head in wonder. "How old are you?"

"It's really not relevant."

"You certainly didn't figure all that stuff out by yourself. You're too young."

"I've learned from my father and mother. Still, the truth is obvious, if you dare to look at it."

Bo felt baffled and savage. "I'd say that maybe you're not all that experienced yourself. Have you ever had a lover?"

"Last night," said Alice, "someone put the question rather more delicately. He asked me if I'd ever been in love, and of course I didn't care to discuss the matter."

Bo drank deep from a tankard of lime beer. "And what do you think of me?"

Alice gave him a casual appraisal. "I'd say that you are an individual of considerable energy. If you directed and disciplined yourself you might someday become an important person: a foreman or even a superintendent."

Bo looked away. He picked up his tankard, drank and set it down with a carefully measured effort. He looked back at Alice. "What are you writing about?"

"Oh — I'm just jotting down ideas as they occur to me."

"In regard to what?"

"Oh — the folk of the city and their customs."

Bo sat glowering at her. "I suppose you've been studying me all morning. Am I one of the picturesque natives?"

Alice laughed. "I must be starting home."

"One moment," said Bo. "I see a man I want to talk to." He crossed to a booth from which Raulf Dido quietly observed comings and goings.

Bo spoke in a harsh clipped voice. "You notice who I'm sitting with?"

Raulf nodded impassively. "Very tasty, in an odd sort of way. What is she?"

"She's a starlander, and to talk to her you'd think she owns all Hant. I've never seen such conceit."

"She looks like she's dressed for a masquerade."

"That's the style out back of beyond. She's absolutely innocent, pure as the morning dew. I'll deliver. How much?"

"Nothing whatever. The heat's on. It's just too much of a hassle."

"Not if it's handled right."

"I'd have to ship her off to Nicobar or Mauritan. It wouldn't be worth the risk."

"Come now. Why not work up a quick sequence over in the studio like we did with that set of twins?"

Raulf gave his head a dubious shake. "There's no scenery; we don't have a script; we'd need a buck —"

"I'll be the buck. All we need is the studio. No story, no sets: just the situation. She's so arrogant, so haughty! She'll throw a first-class display! Outrage. Apprehension. Fury. The works! I'm itching to lay hands on her beautiful body."

"She'll turn you in. If she's around to do so."

"She'll be around. I want her to remember a long time. I'll have to wear a clown-mask; I can't risk having Clachey or Delmar look at the gunk and say 'Hey! there's Bo!' Here's how we can arrange it so we're both clear —"

Raulf inclined his head toward Alice. "You're too late. She's leaving."

"The wicked little wench, I told her to wait!"

"I guess she just remembered," said Raulf mildly. "Because suddenly now she's waiting."

Alice had seen enough of the Blue Lamp Tavern, more than enough of Hant; she wanted to be back up on the aerie, high in the clear blue air. But a man had entered the room, to take an unobtrusive seat to the side, and Alice peered in wonder. Surely it wasn't Waldo? But it was! though he wore a loose golden brown slouch-hat, bronze cheek-plates, a voluminous parasol cape of beetle-back green, all of which had the effect of disguising his appearance. Now why had Waldo come to the Blue Lamp Tavern? Alice curbed a mischievous impulse to cross the room and put the question directly. Bo and his friend had their heads together; they were obviously plotting an escapade of some sort, probably to the discredit of both. Alice glanced back to Waldo to find him staring at her with furtive astonishment. Alice found his emotion highly amusing, and she decided to wait another few minutes to learn what eventuated.

Two other men approached Waldo and joined him at his table. One of the two directed Waldo's attention to Bo with an almost imperceptible inclination of the head. Waldo darted a puzzled look across the room, then returned to his informant. He seemed to be saying: "But he's not blond! The photograph showed blond hair!" And his friend perhaps remarked: "Hair dye is cheap." To which Waldo gave a dubious nod.

Alice began to quiver with merriment. Waldo had been surprised to find her at the Blue Lamp Tavern, but in a moment Bo would come swaggering back across the room, and indeed Bo now rose to his feet. For a moment he stood looking off into nothing, with what Alice thought a rather unpleasant smirk on his face. His bulk, his meaty jaw, the round stare of his eyes, the flaring nostrils, suggested the portrayal of a Minoan man-bull she had noticed earlier in the day; the resemblance was fascinating.

Bo crossed the room to the table where Alice sat. Waldo leaned forward, jaw sagging in shock.

Bo seated himself. Alice was more than ever conscious of his new mood. The rather obsequious manner he had cultivated at the Academy was gone; now he seemed to exude a reek of bravado and power. Alice said, "I'm just about ready to go. Thank you for showing me the tavern here; it's really a quaint old place, and I'm glad to have seen it."

Bo sat looking at her, with rather more intimacy than she liked. He said in a husky voice: "My friend yonder is a police agent. He wants to show me a gunk studio they've just raided; perhaps you'd like to come along."

"What's a gunk studio?"

"A place where fanciful percepts are made. Sometimes they're erotic; sometimes they're wonderful experiences, and the person who wires into them becomes the person who takes part in the adventures. It's illegal, naturally; a gunk addict can't do much else but stay wired into gunk once he's had a taste of it."

Alice considered. "It sounds interesting, if one is in the mood for depravity. But I think I've had enough for today."

"Enough what?" asked Bo jocularly. "Depravity? You haven't seen anything yet."

"Still, I'll be leaving for home." Alice rose to her feet. "It was pleasant meeting you, and I hope you do well at the spaceyards."

Bo joined her. "I'll show you the cab pad. This way, out the back. It's just around the corner."

Alice somewhat dubiously went with Bo along a dim corridor, down concrete steps to an iron door, which opened into an alley. Alice paused, glanced sidewise at Bo who was standing rather closer than she liked. He lifted his hand and stroked her hair. Alice moved back with raised eyebrows. "And where is the cab pad?"

Bo grinned. "Just around the corner."

Keeping a wary eye on Bo, Alice marched off down the alley, with Bo a pace or two behind. She noticed a small van parked to the side. As she passed, footsteps pounded behind her; she swung around to see two men bearing Bo to the ground. Another man threw a blanket over her head, looped a strap around her knees; she was picked up and tossed into the van. The door closed and a moment later the van moved off.

Alice rolled over and made herself as comfortable as possible. She found no difficulty breathing and her first emotion was outrage. How dared anyone treat her with such disrespect! She began to speculate as to the purpose of the deed, and her probable prospects; she was not at all cheered.

Kicking and elbowing, she worked the blanket loose, and freed herself, but her situation was hardly improved. The interior of the van was dark and the doors were locked.

The van halted; the back door opened to reveal the interior of a concrete-walled room. Two men looked in at her; Alice was somewhat reassured by the hoods which concealed their faces, which would seem to indicate that they planned to spare her life, if nothing else.

She jumped out of the van and looked about her. "What's the reason for all this?"

"Come along; this way. You're going to be famous."

"Oh? In what way?"

"You're to be the star of an exciting new percept."

"I see. Is this what is called 'gunk'?"

"I've heard it called 'gunk'. I like to think of it as 'art'."

"I'm afraid you'll find me an uncooperative performer. The production will be a failure."

"Nothing in life is a sure thing. Still it's worth trying. Come along this way."

Alice went as she was directed, along a hall and into a large windowless room illuminated by panels in the ceiling and around the walls. From four angles and from above recording apparatus surveyed the room. A man in a white beret, a domino and cheek-plates stood waiting. He came to inspect Alice. "You don't seem concerned."

"I'm not, particularly."

Raulf Dido, the man in the white beret, was momentarily disconcerted. "Maybe you like the idea?"

"I wouldn't quite go that far."

"Are you wired?"

Alice smiled, as if at the naïve question of a child. "No."

"We'll want you to wear this induction device. It's not as accurate as the direct connection but better than nothing."

"Just what do you propose to do?" asked Alice.

"We plan to produce an erotic percept with emotional accompaniment. As you see, we have no exotic props, but we feel that your special personality will make the production interesting. Before you indulge in any tantrums or hysterics, we'll want to attach this induction device to your neck."

Alice looked at the adjuncts of the room: a couch, a chair, a case containing several objects which caused Alice to compress her lips in wry disgust. "You don't understand my 'special personality' as you put it. The percept will be very uninteresting. I wonder if you have a magazine or a newspaper I might read while you're trying to make your percept?"

"You won't be bored, never fear." This was the comment of another man who had entered the room: a man tall and strong, bulky about the shoulders, with a head shaved bald. A mask of gold foil clung to his face; he wore loose black pantaloons, a blouse checked red, white and black; he looked almost monumental in his strength. Alice instantly recognized Bo, and burst out laughing.

"What's so funny?" he growled.

"The whole affair is ridiculous. I really don't care to be a party to such a farce. After all I have my pride."

The man in the gold mask stood looking at her sullenly. "You'll find whether it's ridiculous or not." He spoke to the man in the domino. "Check my signals." He pushed a clip into the socket under his right arm.

"Signals fine. You're in good shape."

"Put on her induction; we'll get on with the business."

The man in the domino advanced; Alice gestured, took the induction-cell, waved her hands and the cell was gone. Bo and Raulf Dido stared in annoyance. "What did you do with it?" asked Bo in a hard voice.

"It's gone," said Alice. "Forever. Or maybe it's somewhere up here." She jumped up to the recorder platform and pushed over equipment. Cameras, recorders crashed to the floor, evoking cries of rage from Raulf and Bo. They ran to catch her, then stopped short at the sound of contention: calls and curses, the thud of blows. Into the room burst four men. Waldo stood to the side while his companions advanced upon

Raulf and Bo and commenced to beat them with leather truncheons. Raulf and Bo bellowed in rage and sought to defend themselves, with only small success, as the blows fell upon them from all sides.

Alice said, "Hello Waldo. What are you doing here?"

"I might ask you the same thing."

"Bodred brought me here in a van," said Alice. "He seemed to want my help in making percepts; I was about to go when you arrived."

"You were about to go?" Waldo laughed scornfully. He put his arm around Alice's waist and drew her toward him. She put her hands on his chest and held him away. "Now Waldo, control yourself. I don't need reassurance."

"Do you know what they were going to do?" asked Waldo in a thick voice.

"I wasn't particularly interested. Please, Waldo, don't be amorous. I'm sure women of your own race are adequate to your needs."

Waldo made a guttural sound. He called to his hirelings. "Hold off. Don't kill them. Bring that man over here."

The men pushed Bo across the room. Waldo held a small gun which he waved carelessly. "You were about to produce some gunk, evidently."

"What if we were?" Bo panted. "Is it any of your affair? Why did you come busting in on us?"

"Think back to last night."

"Oh. You were the geezer behind the jeek."

"Correct. Go on with your gunk." Waldo jerked his head toward Alice. "Take her. Use her. I don't want her."

Bo glanced uncertainly toward Raulf, still on the floor. He looked back to Waldo, glaring sidelong at Waldo's gun. "What then?"

"I'm not done with you, if that's what you're worried about. You've got a lot coming, and you're going to get it."

Alice spoke in a puzzled voice: "Waldo, are you suggesting that these nasty creatures continue with what they were doing?"

Waldo grinned. "Why not? A little humility might do you good."

"I see. Well, Waldo, I don't care to participate in anything so sordid. I'm surprised at you."

Waldo leaned forward. "I'll tell you exactly why I'm doing this. It's because your arrogance and your vanity absolutely rub me raw."

"Hear, hear!" croaked Bo. "You talk the way I feel."

Alice spoke in a soft voice, "Both you boys are mistaken. I'm not vain and arrogant. I'm merely superior." She could not control her mirth at the expressions on the faces of Waldo and Bo. "Perhaps I'm unkind. It's really not your fault; you're both rather pitiful victims of the city."

"A 'victim'? Hah!" cried Waldo. "I live in Cloudhaven!"

And almost in the same instant: "Me, Big Bo, a victim? Nobody fools with me!"

"Both of you, of course, understand this — subconsciously. The result is guilt and malice."

Waldo listened with a sardonic smile, Bo with a lowering sneer.

"Are you finished?" Waldo asked. "If so —"

"Wait! One moment," said Alice. "What of the cameras and the induction-cell?"

Raulf, limping and groaning, went to one of the cameras which Alice had not thrown to the floor. "This one will work. The cell is gone; I guess we'll have to dub in her track."

Bo looked around the room. "I don't know as I like all this company. Everybody's got to go. I can't concentrate."

"I'm not going," said Waldo. "You three wait in the hall. There'll be more work for you after a bit."

"Well, don't beat me any more," whined Raulf. "I didn't do anything."

"Quit sniveling!" Bo snarled. "Fire up that camera. This isn't quite like I planned, but if it's not good, we'll do a retake."

"Wait!" said Alice. "One thing more. Watch my hands. Are you watching?" She stood erect, and performed a set of apparently purposeless motions. She halted, held her palms toward Bo and Waldo, and each held a small mechanism. From the object in her right hand burst a gush of dazzling light, pulsating ten times per second; the mechanism in the left hand vented an almost solid tooth-chattering mass of sound: a throbbing scream in phase with the light: *erreek erreek erreek*! Waldo and Bo flinched and sagged back, their brain circuits overloaded and rendered numb. The gun dropped from Waldo's hand. Prepared for the event, Alice was less affected. She placed the beacon on the table, picked up the gun. Waldo, Bo and Raulf staggered and lurched, their brain-waves now surging at disorientation frequency.

Alice, her face taut with concentration, left the room. In the hall she sidled past Waldo's three hireling thugs, who stood indecisively, and so gained the street. From a nearby public telephone, she called the police, who dropped down from the sky two minutes later. Alice explained the circumstances; the police in short order brought forth a set of sullen captives.

Alice watched as they were loaded into the conveyance. "Goodbye Waldo. Goodbye Bo. At least you evaded your beating. I don't know what's going to happen to you, but I can't extend too much sympathy, because you've both been rascals."

Waldo asked sourly: "Do you make as much trouble as this wherever you go?"

Alice decided that the question had been asked for rhetorical effect and required no exact or accurate reply; she merely waved and watched as Waldo, Bo, Raulf Dido and the three thugs were wafted aloft and away.

Alice arrived back at the aerie halfway through the afternoon, to find that her father had completed his business. "I was hoping you'd get back early," said Merwyn Tynnott, "so that we could leave tonight. Did you have a good day?"

"It's been interesting," said Alice. "The teaching processes are spectacular and effective, but I wonder if by presenting events so categorically they might not stifle the students' imaginations?"

"Possible. Hard to say."

"Their point of view is urbanite, naturally. Still, the events speak for themselves and I suspect that the student of history falls into urbanite doctrine through social pressure."

"Very likely so. Social pressure is stronger than logic."

"I had lunch at the Blue Lamp Tavern, a spooky old place."

"Yes. I know it well. It's a back-eddy of ancient times, and also something of an underworld hangout. Dozens of spacemen have disappeared from the Blue Lamp."

"I had an adventure there myself; in fact, Waldo Walberg misbehaved rather badly and I believe he's now been taken away for penal processing."

"I'm sorry to hear that," said Merwyn Tynnott. "He'll miss Cloudhaven, especially if he's sent out to the starlands."

"It's a pity about poor Waldo, and Bodred as well. Bodred is the workman who flung his wrench upon my foot. You were quite right about his motives. I'm a trifle disillusioned, although I know I shouldn't be."

Merwyn Tynnott hugged his daughter and kissed the top of her head. "Don't worry another instant. We're off and away from Hant, and you never need come back."

"It's a strange wicked place," said Alice, "though I rather enjoyed Jillyville."

"Jillyville is always amusing."

They went into the dome; Commander Tynnott touched the controls, and the aerie drifted away to the southeast.

About the Author

Jack Vance was born in 1916 to a well-off California family that, as his childhood ended, fell upon hard times. As a young man he worked at a series of unsatisfying jobs before studying mining engineering, physics, journalism and English at the University of California Berkeley. Leaving school as America was going to war, he found a place as an ordinary seaman in the merchant marine. Later he worked as a rigger, surveyor, ceramicist, and carpenter before his steady production of sf, mystery novels, and short stories established him as a full-time writer.

His output over more than sixty years was prodigious and won him three Hugo Awards, a Nebula Award, a World Fantasy Award for lifetime achievement, as well as an Edgar from the Mystery Writers of America. The Science Fiction and Fantasy Writers of America named him a grandmaster and he was inducted into the Science Fiction Hall of Fame.

His works crossed genre boundaries, from dark fantasies (including the highly influential *Dying Earth* cycle of novels) to interstellar space operas, from heroic fantasy (the *Lyonesse* trilogy) to murder mysteries featuring a sheriff (the Joe Bain novels) in a rural California county. A Vance story often centered on a competent male protagonist thrust into a dangerous, evolving situation on a planet where adventure was his daily fare, or featured a young person setting out on a perilous odyssey over difficult terrain populated by entrenched, scheming enemies.

Late in his life, a world-spanning assemblage of Vance aficionados came together to return his works to their original form, restoring material cut by editors whose chief preoccupation was the page count of a pulp magazine. The result was the complete and authoritative *Vance Integral Edition* in 44 hardcover volumes. Spatterlight Press is now publishing the VIE texts as ebooks, and as print-on-demand paperbacks.

Colophon

This book was printed using Adobe Arno Pro as the primary text font, with NeutraFace used on the cover.

This title was created from the digital archive of the Vance Integral Edition, a series of 44 books produced under the aegis of the author by a worldwide group of his readers. The VIE project gratefully acknowledges the editorial guidance of Norma Vance, as well as the cooperation of the Department of Special Collections at Boston University, whose John Holbrook Vance collection has been an important source of textual evidence.

Special thanks to R.C. Lacovara, Patrick Dusoulier, Koen Vyverman, Paul Rhoads, Chuck King, Gregory Hansen, Suan Yong, and Josh Geller for their invaluable assistance preparing final versions of the source files.

Source: Mike Berro, Norma Vance, Digitize: Derek W. Benson, Richard Chandler, Joel Hedlund, Damien G. Jones, Chris Reid, Paul Rhoads, Thomas Rydbeck, John A. Schwab, Gan Uesli Starling, Per Sundfeldt, Koen Vyverman, Suan Hsi Yong; Format: Arjan Bokx, Ron Chernich, Patrick Dusoulier, Joel Hedlund, Steve Sherman, Suan Hsi Yong; Diff: Mark Adams, Christian J. Corley, Rob Gerrand, Damien G. Jones, David A. Kennedy, R.C. Lacovara, John A. Schwab, Steve Sherman, Mark Shoulder, Tim Stretton, Hans van der Veeke, Suan Hsi Yong; Diff-Merge: Lori Hanley; Tech Proof: Danny Beukers, Mark Bradford, Rob Friefeld, Rob Gerrand, Bob Moody, Errico Rescigno, Matt Westwood; Text Integrity: Derek W. Benson, Rob Friefeld, Rob Gerrand, R.C. Lacovara, Paul Rhoads, Jeffrey Ruszczyk, John A. Schwab, Steve Sherman, Tim Stretton, Suan Hsi Yong; Implement: Donna Adams, Derek W. Benson, Mike Dennison, Damien G. Jones, John McDonough, Chris Reid, Thomas Rydbeck, Hans van der Veeke; Security: Paul Rhoads; Compose: John A. Schwab; Comp Review: Andreas Björklind, Christian J. Corley, John A. D. Foley, Marcel van Genderen, Brian Gharst, Charles King, Bob Luckin, Robert Melson, Paul Rhoads, Robin L. Rouch; Update Verify: Top Changwatchai, John A. D. Foley, Rob Friefeld, Marcel van Genderen, Charles King, R.C. Lacovara, Bob Luckin, Paul Rhoads, Robin L. Rouch, John A. Schwab; RTF-Diff: Mark Bradford, Patrick Dusoulier, Charles King, Bill Schaub; Textport: Patrick Dusoulier, Charles King; Proofread: Enrique Alcatena, Neil Anderson, Erik Arendse, Mike Barrett, Michel Bazin, Brian Bieniowski, Arjan Bokx, Malcolm Bowers, Mark Bradford, Angus Campbell-Cann, Daniel Chang, Top Changwatchai, Deborah Cohen, Matthew Colburn, Robert Collins, Owen Davidson, Jurgen Devriese, Michael Duncan, Patrick Dusoulier, Andrew Edlin, Rob Friefeld, Marcel van Genderen, Rob Gerrand, Jasper Groen, Evert Jan de Groot, Lori Hanley, Joel Hedlund, Mark Henricks, Marc Herant, Brent Heustess, Patrick Hudson,

Jon Hunt, Peter Ikin, Damien G. Jones, Lucie Jones, Jurriaan Kalkman, Karl Kellar, David A. Kennedy, A.G. Kimlin, Charles King, John Kleeman, Rob Knight, Brian Koning, Stephane Leibovitsch, Thomas Lindgren, Bob Luckin, Chris McCormick, Lawrence McKay, Robert Melson, Bob Moody, Till Noever, Turlough O'Connor, Jim Pattison, Matt Picone, Quentin Rakestraw, David Reitsema, Errico Rescigno, Joel Riedesel, John Robinson, Axel Roschinski, Robin L. Rouch, Jeffrey Ruszczyk, Bill Schaub, Mike Schilling, Bill Sherman, Lyall Simmons, Michael J. Smith, Mark J. Straka, Anthony Thompson, Willem Timmer, Michael Turpin, Hans van der Veeke, Dirk Jan Verlinde, Russ Wilcox

Artwork (maps based on original drawings by Jack and Norma Vance):

Paul Rhoads, Christopher Wood

Book Composition and Typesetting: Joel Anderson

Art Direction and Cover Design: Howard Kistler

Proofing: Steve Sherman, Dave Worden

Jacket Blurb: Steve Sherman, John Vance

Management: John Vance, Koen Vyverman

Made in the USA
Middletown, DE
16 June 2020

97805014R00161